I dedicate this novel first and foremost to my parents, Arnaldo Sr. and Flora Lopez—two of the hardest working people I've ever known. And yet they found the time and love in their hearts to never falter in their love for me, their understanding and indulgence of me and my eccentricities, and never failed to support and encourage me. All that I am, all that I ever will be, I owe to them. Thanks mom. Thanks pop. Bendición.

I also dedicate this novel to my wife of 34 years, Cecelia. She put up with a lot and shared so many of my hopes and dreams for so many years. Thank you Cece, I couldn't have done it without you.

Chickenhawk
by Arnaldo Lopez Jr

ISBN 978-1-63393-006-3

This is a work of fiction. The characters are both actual and fictitious. With the exception of verified historical events and persons, all incidents, descriptions, dialogue and opinions expressed are the products of the author's imagination and are not to be construed as real.

Published by

Café con Leche
an imprint of Köehler Books

3 Griffin Hill Court
The Woodlands, TX 77382
281-465-0119
www.cafeconlechebooks.com

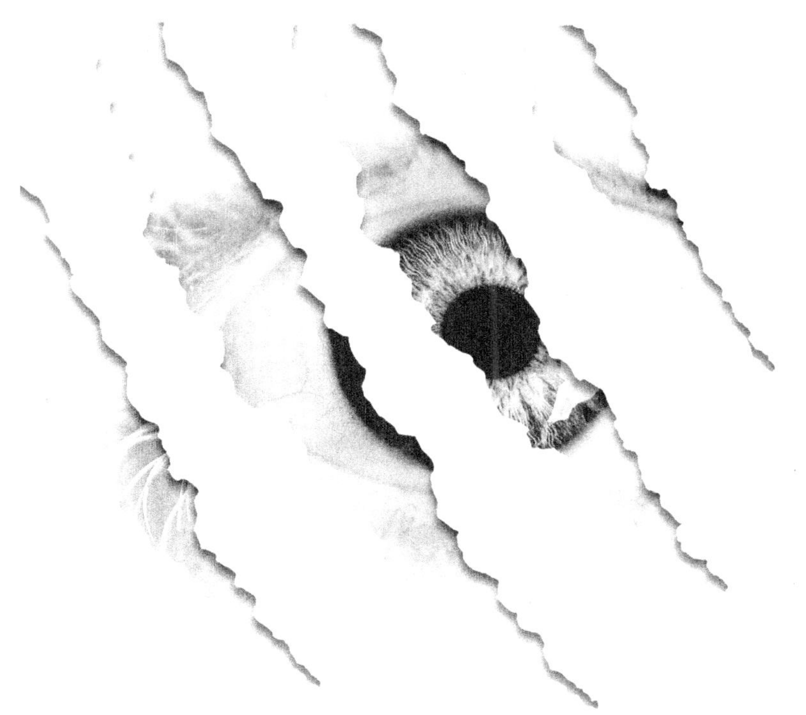

CHICKENHAWK

ARNALDO LOPEZ JR

HOUSTON

CHAPTER 1

ABE LOOKED AROUND the premises nervously. He didn't like spending so much time with a customer. Earlier on, he had nearly bolted out of there when a patrol car, siren hooting and warbling, slowly moved up the street. He watched quietly as the strobed reflection of the car's flashing lights alternately colored the facades of the surrounding buildings a vivid shade of red. Then white. Then red again. The colors bounced off the windows of the nearby skyscrapers in blinding explosions of refracted light, spilling like spent fluid along the naked girders around him, disappearing then reappearing further away as they receded.

Abe nodded in the direction of the lights. "Don't worry man," he said. "That's the last time they're gonna come around tonight."

The customer nodded in understanding. The police considered Abe and his fellow hustlers little more than pesky annoyances, lowlife perpetrators of victimless crimes who rarely even had the nerve to pick an occasional pocket. The well-heeled residents of this part of Midtown Manhattan, however, were not quite so forgiving. They convinced the local merchants to join them in demanding an increase in police surveillance in the area. Not long after that, cops from the nearby precinct were assigned to make at least three nightly trips up Lexington Avenue from Fifty-First to Sixty-Eighth Streets, rousting and occasionally even arresting the young male prostitutes who worked the strip and catered to the desires of the mostly suburban, married businessmen who comprised the bulk of their clientele; some of whom hailed from as far away as Connecticut.

Abe worked his hand feverishly, focusing on his customer's now flaccid penis with disdain. *Man, this is ridiculous,* he thought as he gave the penis a shake, scattering droplets of semen and saliva into the night. *If this guy's dick doesn't get hard again in another few seconds, I'm just gonna tell 'im to forget it. I mean, damn—I already sucked him off once!* Abe again studied the expensive looking material that framed the limp penis in his hand before returning it to his mouth, *This guy is gonna have to pay me something extra just for wasting my time,* he thought. *What made him think he could go twice anyway?*

He let the still soft penis slip out of his mouth. A viscous strand of saliva, glistening like spider's silk covered in morning dew, still connected Abe to his customer's stubborn member. Abe plucked the string of saliva and it collapsed into a fine mist. He sighed agitatedly and made as if to get up. His customer stopped him by placing a strong but gentle hand on his shoulder.

"No, don't get up," he said.

Abe's new denim pants creaked as he settled back down on his knees. The voice didn't sound threatening or even particularly demanding. His customer had a deep, rich baritone voice, the kind that made you think of overstuffed leather chairs, mahogany bookcases, and giant oak desks. Clearly it was the voice of a wealthy and powerful man. Abe wished he had been blessed with a voice like that. If he had been, Abe could have easily been an actor or a singer. Instead, he was just another homeboy giving blow jobs to rich guys from "The Island" at thirty bucks a pop. That was his reality.

"Keep doing what you're doing," that voice said. "It feels really good."

Abe dismissed the thoughts he was having moments before and shrugged. "I don't care how good it feels to you man," he said. He winced at how high and whiney his own voice sounded. "It's taking you too fuckin' long. I'm either gonna catch a cramp or the fuckin' cops are gonna bust us."

Abe flinched in surprise when his customer raised an immaculately manicured left hand. The gold ring on the third finger flashed cold fire as his hand settled on Abe's head. Long, thick fingers lost themselves in the thick mat of tousled black curls, then gently extricated themselves. The man stroked Abe's hair. It drove Abe crazy. He hated when they did that.

Finally, Abe felt the penis in his hand stiffen. "About fuckin' time," he muttered to himself.

"Ah yeah," the customer groaned with a contented sigh. "I knew you could get it up for me again, you little cocksucker, and I do mean that literally."

Abe didn't like anyone calling him names.

"You little spic bitch," the man with the rich voice continued softly. "You love sucking white cock, don't you?"

That was the last straw for Abe. He sprung to his feet. "Man, fuck this shit," he whispered harshly, his anger tempered by the prospect of being detected by the police. He'd had enough and couldn't stomach this asshole any longer.

The man with the great voice just stood there, a bemused expression on his face, and watched Abe's reaction and growing anger. His now fully erect penis pointed at Abe's chin like an obscene divining rod. He crossed his arms and thrust his hips forward in an exaggerated motion. His penis bounced up and down, and swung in circles as if held up by an invisible wire.

"Come on *Pancho,*" he said, making that great voice ugly now. "Or do you think I should save some for your *mamasita,* huh? I bet she's the one who taught you how to suck cock! Or maybe it was your *papasit*a? Is that it *Pancho*?

Abe charged at the man with a roar burning in his throat. His rage could no longer be contained, police or no police.

Then a sudden move that Abe did not see coming. It was a blur and before he had a chance to react, it was too late. Abe saw his customer pull a gun from under his jacket. So many thoughts ran through his mind at once. *It's huge. Black. A revolver. The barrel is impossibly long, it can't be real...*

Reality was a sledgehammer jolt of shock and pain as the gun's barrel was shoved into Abe's mouth—gouging lips and splintering teeth. Abe tried to pull his head back, but the other man gripped the back of his neck and kept feeding him the gun. He tried to scream but nearly gagged on his own blood. The only sound he managed to make was a gurgling cough.

"Ah, you like that, don't you?" It was the rich man's voice again. "Tell you what," he continued. "You're going to give my friend here," indicating the gun he was holding, "the *best* goddamn blow job of your miserable life." The man moved his face closer to Abe's, almost whispering in his ear. "Only this time," he said. "*You—better—hope—it—doesn't—cum!*"

Abe squeezed his watering eyes shut, tears searing twin rivulets of molten fear down his quivering face. He could feel the gun's barrel slide back and forth in his mouth, mimicking the act of fellatio. Ice-cold shards of pain shot through his body as the gun barrel rubbed against the newly exposed nerves of his shattered teeth.

"That's it now. Oh-h, you're doing a wonderful job. Good. Good."

More tears welled up in Abe's eyes and coursed down his cheeks. His mind was a hodgepodge of frantic thought.

This fuckin' guy's crazy! How can I get outta this? Who is this guy? Maybe I can snatch the gun away! Why me? What will mom and pop think when the cops tell them how I died? Oh shit! Oh shit! OH SHIT! Oh my God, I'm gonna fuckin' die!

Abe pressed his eyes shut and felt more hot tears run down his face where they mixed with the clear mucus that was now running freely from his nose.

Then, the in and out motion of the gun barrel stopped. It was the most frightening moment of Abe's young life. He literally wet his pants.

Abe waited. A heartbeat. Two. Three. He opened his eyes. The crazy man with the beautiful voice was staring at him. His eyes were terrible to look at. Empty.

"I'm cumming."

The man with the rich voice pulled the trigger on the big, old revolver. The tension of the pull. The sudden release of the hammer. The smell of burnt gunpowder. It was all familiar to him now, but he still jumped at the gun's loud report.

The slug pierced the boy's soft palette, drove neatly through his brain, and then flattened somewhat on impact with the inside of Abe's skull. It exited the back of Abe's head, compressed almost to the diameter of a nickel, and created a wound on its way out big enough for a man to put his fist through.

The boy fell back, his knees still bent, a spray of blood and brain tissue that had erupted from his now shattered head soiled the fence behind him.

The killer slowly lowered his still smoking gun. He turned and started to walk away, then stopped.

The trembling started in his knees and worked its way up to his shoulders and arms. Soon he shivered so violently his teeth chattered. Every hair on his body stood painfully on end. His eyes watered uncontrollably and distorted his vision. Then, just as suddenly as it started, the episode ended. A monstrous headache remained in its wake.

The killer whipped around, eyes wild, face shiny with sweat. Shakily, he aimed his gun in the direction of the youth he'd just murdered.

"You sonofabitch!" He yelled. "You gave me this shit! But if I have to die, you're going to die—all of you bastards are going to die! You hear me? Hear me?"

He thumbed back the hammer of the gun. The long, black barrel telegraphed the trembling in his hand. He stood that way for several seconds as light drizzle fell to earth and the rage melted from his eyes. He sniffed and lowered the gun, simultaneously easing the hammer back into place.

A brief coughing jag shook him then. It was a wet, roiling noise that bubbled up from the depths of his sickened lungs. He cleared his throat, hawked, and spat out a thick wad of greenish phlegm. Then, shoes crunching on broken glass and gravel, he left the construction site and the scene of the murder.

Eyes darting to and fro, he took pains not to be seen. He stayed in the shadows and mentally cursed the bright lights that almost seemed to increase in incandescence at his approach. He tucked the gun into his waistband and headed for the darkened subway entrance at 53rd Street.

This entrance to the subway used to be closed at night, and so was a popular meeting place for the young male prostitutes who plied their trade here. Now that the entrance was open around the clock, business had to be conducted a bit more discreetly, such as construction sites, under stairwells, the freight or delivery bays of some of the older buildings and department stores, and, of course, inside hastily parked cars.

The subway entrance remained the primary meeting place, however, where deals were made, prices quoted, and acts performed.

He walked down the subway steps and entered the station, the bright fluorescent lights hurt his eyes after the relative darkness of the night outside. He hunched down into his jacket, hands in pockets, and looked around furtively.

He walked quickly past the token booth and stole a glance in its direction, avoiding the bored glances of the workers inside, and continued walking toward the opposite stairway. He mounted the steps two at a time until he was back outside. By exiting through this stairway, he was now about a block away from where his victim's corpse lay growing cold and stiff on the ground.

A moment later there was the soft sound of a car door being closed, an engine turning over, and a car being driven away into the night. The sidewalk was deserted.

CHAPTER 2

BY THE TIME Detective Eddie Ramos walked onto the crime scene, Emergency Medical Services and the officers of the Crime Scene Unit were just finishing up. He walked toward a line of yellow barricade tape surrounded by a small group of gawking men in hard hats, stepping over the shallow puddles of rust colored water and mounds of dirt that dotted the area, and walked around a nearby mountain of gravel.

The hard-hatted construction workers parted as Ramos neared them. He ducked under the barricade tape, barely noticing that it had been hung upside down.

Ramos walked over to the ambulance crew first.

"Hey detective," called out a familiar voice. It belonged to Nancy "Nance" Collins, the EMS supervisor. She greeted Ramos with a knuckle-cracking handshake. He winced, flexing and rubbing his hand after he'd extricated it from the vise known as Nance Collins.

"Hey Nance," Ramos answered. "What's the word?" Ramos had known Nance almost as long as he'd been in the department—and that was a lifetime.

Nance was a big woman. At an even six feet in height, she was a good two inches taller than Ramos. From previous conversations he'd had with Nance, he knew that she weighed close to two hundred pounds. Ramos self-consciously sucked in his belly. Whereas lately it seemed that he was always dieting in an effort to keep his weight from straying too far over the two hundred mark, Nance's weight appeared to consist of solid muscle.

Nance (she preferred that to her actual name) was into weight lifting, bodybuilding, that kind of thing. That is, when she wasn't lifting corpses or near-corpses into the back of her ambulance.

Ramos had heard rumors about Nance being a lesbian, and he didn't doubt them or even particularly care—but in the department, if you listened long enough, every woman who wasn't at home cooking and raising kids, attending PTA meetings, or screwing a male cop, simply had to be a batting for the wrong team.

There were times when Ramos couldn't help but marvel at the narrow-minded views of his fellow cops, even the younger ones. But he knew that he was a long way from being "Mr. Open-minded and liberal" himself. Working in the department, you see too many things, do too many things, and talk to too many *types* of people. After a while you want to pull back and distance yourself from *them*. Before you realize it, everybody's a *them*. Unless you're a cop. And a male. Ramos was glad he happened to be both.

Nance noticed him nursing his hand and the left corner of her mouth edged up into a half-smile. "Uh-oh, sorry about that detective," she said. "I keep forgetting that you homicide cops aren't really as tough as everyone makes you out to be."

"Yeah, that's me Nance," Ramos growled. "A real marshmallow."

He liked Nance. He considered her more than just an acquaintance, but not quite a friend. She was already working for EMS when he joined the NYPD. He had met her just after he'd seen his first body. He was fresh out of the academy, full of bravado. Full of expectations. "Full of shit," was what he overheard one veteran cop remark to another behind his back.

The body belonged to a homeless man who'd hung himself in an abandoned warehouse near the docks on the west side. It was a hot, humid August afternoon, and the body had been hanging there for about a week. Generations of flies had already been at this poor guy, and the ants had found him too. A discoloration on a nearby wall was determined to be body fluids propelled there when the gases trapped inside the body finally burst through the skin.

Ramos had never seen or smelled anything so bad in his entire life. He tried to play the tough cop, joking with the other cops at the scene, hanging around waiting for the EMS crew to arrive and declare the body officially dead so they all could leave. Ramos remembered hoping the offensive stench wouldn't get into his brand new uniform.

"Holy shit! That fucking guy's dead! Dead! D. O. Fuckin' A!"

EMS had arrived and Nance was able to pronounce the person dead from a doorway more than fifty feet away. She and her partner came pushing an ambulance gurney with a large, vinyl zippered bag on top. A carry case of equipment rode along on top of the bag. Both EMTs held their noses.

The two technicians halted when they reached the body. The flies, fat with eggs, buzzed angrily at being disturbed. From the river outside came the cries of gulls and the long, low sigh of a ships horn.

Nance reached into the case and pulled out a large pair of shears. She looked around for confirmation. A detective nodded and waved his hand noncommittally.

"Cut 'em down," he said.

Nance nodded and walked around the suicide, kicking aside the old wooden milk crate he'd used to launch himself on his short trip through space.

"Aw-w-w, I hate this shit," Nance said eventually as she straightened her shoulders. "C'mon man." She motioned to her partner who by this time had backed away a considerable distance from the scene. Nance grew annoyed. "C'mon man," she repeated. "He's too high up off the ground. One of us is going to have to hold him while the other one cuts him down." She snipped at the air a few times with the shears to make her point. "And I've got *seniority*."

Her partner visibly turned several shades of gray before retching and fleeing from the warehouse through its open doorway. Motes of dust danced in his wake.

All of the cops laughed, including Ramos.

Nance's shoulders sagged. She knew she wasn't getting any

help from this bunch. She sighed, lifted her shears, and moved closer to the insect-ridden, decaying husk of what was once a human being.

"Probie, help her out."

All eyes turned to look at the uniformed officer who'd uttered those words. Sergeant Liszt was a grizzled veteran of both the NYPD and the Marine Corps. His gray hair was cropped into a severe buzz cut, and his blue eyes stared directly at Ramos.

"Go on rookie, hold that DOA while it gets cut down."

Ramos felt his face blanch. Those blue eyes bored into him like twin lasers.

"You're a cop, *right*?"

Ramos straightened his shoulders and slowly joined the EMS lady at the body. He faced her and noticed that, despite the strong lines of her face, she was really quite attractive. He also noticed how her breasts strained the buttons of her uniform shirt.

"Hi," Ramos mumbled. "How ya doin'?" The smell was much worse this close to the body and Ramos tried to keep the bile from rising to this throat.

"A lot better than this guy," she answered. The left corner of her mouth curled up into a half smile.

"My name's Eddie," Ramos said as he stuck out his hand. The EMS lady gripped his hand so hard the knuckles cracked.

"Okay officer, I'm Nance. Let's get this done."

She let go of his hand and turned again to face the corpse. Ramos turned too, albeit much more slowly. A slight bump or an almost nonexistent breeze started the dead man slowly twisting at the end of his rope made up of knotted up plastic bags and discarded neckties. Ramos pulled on his new leather gloves, his *cop* gloves, and edged closer to the body. He noticed that his fellow officers were now very quiet, studying him. Ramos shuffled around the corpse in much the same way Nance had done earlier, trying to find some vantage point, some area of better leverage, but in the end, there was only one thing he could do. He wrapped his arms around the dead man's rotting legs and lifted.

Ramos wound up pressing his face into the dead man's belly, his chin in what was left of its crotch, to better balance the dead body. His hat now sat askew on his head, trapped between the corpse and his ear. Finally, Nance cut him down.

Later, because of the smell, the other officers refused to let Ramos ride back to the precinct with them in a patrol car, so he hitched a ride with the corpse in the back of the EMS van.

"He shouldn't mind the smell so much," reasoned Ramos glumly.

That night, after numerous washings and failed home remedies, Ramos buried his brand new uniform and gloves.

After that day, whenever he and Nance ran into each other, she'd rib him about what happened. They'd even gone out for drinks together a few times, nothing intimate—just two people who worked odd hours in an odd city, too keyed up to just go home right away. She used to crack him up with stories about her job, or her life growing up with three brothers, all of them firefighters now. Yeah, he liked Nance. She was okay.

"Heard from the ME yet Nance?" Ramos ran a thick hand through his hair. He wished he'd worn a hat; the day was turning out to be a brisk one.

"Nah," Nance replied. "As soon as he gives me the high sign, we're going to bag 'im, drag 'im, and get out of here."

"Yeah, works for me," Ramos said. He stuck his hands into the pockets of his gray trench coat and looked into Nance's cynical blue eyes. They were a lot like his brown ones. The years and the things they'd seen had left their stamp on them. Lines at their corners were like the rings on a tree stump—they told on you. They could deepen into a cascade of fissures during a smile, or resemble coils of concertina wire during moments of anger or accusation.

"So what do you think, Nance?" Ramos asked quietly.

Nance's eyebrows went up, but otherwise her expression didn't change.

"Unofficially?"

"Of course, unofficially."

Nance leaned close to him, her lips brushing his ear. Her breath smelled faintly of licorice. "Looks real familiar detective," she said. "Real familiar. I'd say somebody's developed a real nasty habit." She stepped back and Ramos could see that she no longer smiled.

Ramos sighed, "Gotcha Nance." Then he turned, tossed her a wave, and walked away.

CHAPTER 3

THE OFFICERS FROM the CSU were just finishing up. The search for latent fingerprints was pretty much a bust due to the rain of the night before. The police photographer was scrolling through his camera for the crime scene photos he'd just taken, while the cop with the video camera was in the process of putting his equipment away.

"Hey guys," Ramos called them over with a quick nod of his head. "Do me a favor and get some pictures and video of the looky-loos. Try not to be too obvious about it."

Then Ramos nodded toward where the victim still lay on the muddy ground. "You guys get a picture of the blood spray on the fence by the victim?" Ramos fanned his hand in the general direction of the large plywood fence that separated the construction site from the rest of the world. The bottom half of the board directly behind the victim looked as if someone had sprayed it with an exceptionally ugly shade of reddish-brown paint.

The photographer nodded and loudly popped the bubble gum he was chewing. The videographer simply answered, "Sure."

"Anybody get me some pictures of any footprints? I notice the ground is muddy."

"No good detective," the photographer answered, popping his gum again. He was holding onto the camera with both hands, so he used his elbow to point toward the group of men still gawking from the far side of the barricade tape.

"By the time we got here, those construction workers had already trampled all over the place. There aren't any clear prints—can't tell when one starts and another ends. It's all just a big, muddy mess." He finished with a loud pop from his gum.

Ramos nodded, looked around and saw that it was true. He then carefully used the toe of his shoe to give one of the victim's legs a slight nudge. The ground was dry underneath.

"Okay, doesn't much matter anyhow," Ramos said. "Looks like it rained after the kid was already dead." The two CSU cops nodded, and the photographer snapped a picture. "All right," Ramos continued. "You guys know who the first officer on the scene was?"

The cop with the video cam answered. "I don't know 'im personally," he said. "But that's them over there by the tape, near the toilet."

Ramos turned his head and followed the line of barricade tape to where it ended, tied to the door handle of a portable toilet. A young officer in uniform stood next to it and scribbled furiously into his duty log.

"Okay, talk to you guys later." Ramos started to walk away, then stopped and turned. "Get those things done for me, okay?" Both CSU cops nodded, and Ramos made his way to the young cop near the toilet.

The cop was still writing in his log when Ramos approached and introduced himself.

"So, what's the word?" Ramos asked casually. He glanced at the officer's leather accoutrements, his belt, holster, etc.—they shone like black mirrors and barely had a crease in them. *The kid's a probie,* Ramos thought. *Looks to be about twenty-two, twenty-three, maybe.* Ramos took in the spiky blond hair that peaked out from under the young cop's hat, and at the spatter of freckles that dotted his cheeks and the bridge of his nose.

Kid looks like he just fell off a truck from Iowa, Ramos' thoughts continued. He frowned at the officer's narrow shoulders. *He'll get tired of being tossed around like a rag doll by mutts soon enough and bulk up,* Ramos mused. The cop in question flipped through several pages of his entry log, oblivious to Ramos' critical observations. Ramos looked away, examined his fingernails, and rocked back and forth on his heels as he tried not to be impatient. *What's taking so long?* Ramos thought. *What is the kid writing a fuckin' book?* Finally the officer found what he was looking for and started reciting from his notes. Ramos took out his own pen and pad, and took notes as the young cop spoke.

"At approximately 0500 hours, Mr. Nathaniel Gilman, construction foreman for E&E Construction Corp. arrived at the construction site located at the corner of East Five Three Street and Lexington Avenue. Upon his arrival, Mr. Gilman discovered an unidentified male youth, Hispanic, at the site. Mr. Gilman stated that at first he assumed this male youth was asleep whereupon he tapped the youth in the left side rib area with his foot in an effort to wake him up."

Ramos rolled his eyes—*kicked* the kid in the ribs was probably more like it.

"When he was unable to awaken the youth, Mr. Gilman tried to examine the body more closely, but was unable to ascertain the youth's condition due to the darkness of the hour. Thinking the youth may be in need of assistance, Mr. Gilman proceeded to try and find some sort of identification on him. Unable to find any identification, Mr. Gilman then walked to his trailer located approximately thirty yards from the youth's location and dialed nine one one. Mr. Gilman is unsure of which nine one one operator he spoke to, eight sixty-five or eight sixty-nine, but..."

Ramos pulled a mint from his pocket and popped it into his mouth. He stuck the empty cellophane back into his pocket. *This kid's putting me to sleep,* he thought. Ramos crushed the mint with his teeth, the crunching noise was extraordinarily loud in his head, and forced himself to listen.

"...At 0545 hours, Mr. Gilman returned to the youth's location and waited for police to arrive..."

Ramos looked up. Something didn't sound quite right to him. "Hold on a second, uh-h..." Ramos squinted at the officer's nameplate. "...Crawford."

The young cop stopped reading and looked at Ramos with a confused look on his face.

"You're tellin' me that this Gilmore guy..."

"Gilman, sir."

"Whatever. This guy finds the body at five in the morning, trashes the crime scene, practically *rolls* the victim like some bum in an alley, finally decides to make a call to nine one one, and then returns to the crime scene forty-five minutes after first finding the body?" Ramos shook his head in disbelief. "Doesn't that sound strange to you, Crawford? Doesn't that sound like bullshit to you?"

Officer Crawford nervously shifted his weight from one foot to the other. "I-I don't..." he began to say.

"Okay, okay, check this out," Ramos said. "Most people, when they find a body, are *scared*. I don't know for sure if it's the shock of actually seeing another human being dead, or maybe they think the killer might still be around, or maybe it's the sight of blood—whatever. All I know is most people are scared shitless when they find a dead body; they call the cops or an ambulance, or even the goddamn fire department right away. Most people don't go through a dead guy's pockets before calling the cops and then come back and keep the corpse company 'til we get there, and the ones who do are either cops themselves, or sickos gettin' their jollies, or maybe they're the *perp*."

Crawford stared at him.

"What time did he place that call to nine one one?"

The officer's brow furrowed as he flipped back and forth through the pages of his shiny new duty log. "Uh, um, I don't think, I mean, I'm not sure." he stammered.

"Okay, I can find that out later. Where's this Gilmore, I mean *Gilman*, now?"

Officer Crawford used his pen to point out a distant trailer standing on cinderblocks.

"Okay," Ramos said. "You sure he didn't leave?"

Crawford nodded.

"Are there any other witnesses?"

"Uh, no. Not that I know of."

Ramos eyed the head-sized "peepholes" cut into the plywood boards of the fence, spaced at intervals of about six feet apart. Could someone have seen something? That would be a helluva break.

"The rest of the construction crew started showing up about the same time Gilman says he returned to the crime scene," Crawford offered. "I heard the call over the radio, and I got here about five minutes later."

"And about what time was that?"

"Ten to six, uh, oh—five fifty hours, sir."

"Okay Crawford," Ramos said. "I'm going to talk to Gilman, see what he has to say."

"Yes sir."

"Cut it out with that sir shit; I work for a living."

"Uh, right."

"Where are you stationed?" Ramos asked.

"The one seven annex."

"Oh yeah," Ramos replied. "That's only a couple of blocks from here."

"Yes sir, uh, I mean detective. That's why I was able to get here so quick."

"Uh-huh, good work," Ramos said. "Listen, do me a favor. I'm going to go back to the body, if Gilman tries to leave that trailer before I get there, you sit on him, okay?"

"Yes detective," Crawford said.

Ramos nodded and walked back to where the corpse still lay on the ground.

The cops with the cameras were gone. Most of the construction workers were busily bringing the site to life. Except for a couple of uniformed cops and EMS workers, it was pretty much Ramos and the dead kid. Dead kid. *That's what he was,* Ramos thought. *Just a fuckin' kid who couldn't get a break. Just like the other two. Street kids with their own crazy twisted rules and morals, having sex with men for money. Now one of those men is killing them.*

Ramos looked into the dead boy's face. His dark hair clung to what was left of his head in loose whorls. His eyes, dark like his hair, were half-open; as if he were just awakening from a deep sleep.

Ramos popped another mint into his mouth. *Yeah*, he thought, *but this poor kid's never going to wake up again.* The kid's mouth was open into an almost perfect circle. A joke surfaced in his thoughts, unwelcome and unexpected...something about the fastest way to a promotion in the department being to drop to your knees and make an "O." Ramos squatted, knees protesting, and balanced himself on the balls of his feet. The boy's mouth was filled with a pinkish-brown mixture of congealed blood and brains. Ramos found himself feeling grateful that it was autumn in New York; if the weather had been any warmer this corpse would have been much riper.

The kid was dressed in the current style—an oversized shirt under an even bigger hooded sweatshirt and baggy jeans that lay halfway down his bony hips and pooled around his ankles in thick folds. Expensive sneakers covered his feet.

What was Gilman looking for? Ramos wondered.

"The hard part's gonna be getting back up Eddie."

Ramos sighed, shaking his head, and rested his forearms on his knees. "I can get up, no problem," he said. After a slight rocking motion, followed by a ratchet-like cracking sound that originated from his knees and a loud grunt, he did stand.

Ramos stuck out his hand. "Hey Tommy," he said.

The taller man with the sandy brown hair and very light blue eyes took Ramos' hand. Then suddenly he pulled Ramos toward him, simultaneously shaking his hand and slapping him repeatedly on the back.

"Whassup my Latin brother?" Tommy greeted him loudly. He pushed Ramos back at arm's length. "Damn man, are you gaining weight?"

Ramos self-consciously sucked in his belly. His partner, Tommy Cucitti, always teased him about his weight. He knew it made him feel uncomfortable, but Tommy considered it a form of tough love, a way to convince Ramos to cut down on the meals and snacks. Tommy was also a rascal, and Ramos suspected he actually enjoyed making him feel uncomfortable.

Tommy Cucitti was a strapping thirty-four-year-old jokester with a quick smile and a casual demeanor that sometimes bordered on insubordination. Yet, he was Ramos' partner and the youngest detective assigned to the Manhattan North Homicide division. He was a little over six feet tall, liked to brag about his 33-inch waist, and had been a cop for almost fifteen years; practically right out of high school. Ramos knew that some of the other detectives often found Tommy irritating, but he knew Tommy was a good cop, and that's all that mattered.

Tommy Cucitti walked around the dead youth, his thumb and forefinger holding his chin. Ramos watched him and shook his head—Tommy was wearing a pair of well-pressed black jeans, a plain white shirt, a bluish-gray wool blazer, black shoes, and a black leather trench coat. His mostly black tie was decorated with cartoon characters.

Jeans, Ramos thought. *Jeans aren't regulation attire for a homicide detective. Tommy must want the looey to cut him a new asshole.*

"Yep," Tommy said. He was standing near the dead boy's shoulder, his thumb and forefinger still cradled his chin. "I think we could definitely say that this here dead Latino homeboy wearing the rare Reeboks is numero tres on the fill 'em and kill 'em hit parade."

By fill 'em and kill 'em, Ramos knew that Tommy was referring to the killer's M.O. (so far) of probably having the victims perform fellatio on him before killing them. Traces of semen with a different DNA pattern than the victim's had been found in or near their mouths.

"One thing bothers me though," Tommy blurted out.

Ramos' antenna went up. "Yeah?"

Tommy shook himself and thrust his hands deep into his pant pockets. "How could the fuckin' perp have the goddamn nerve to pull his dick out in this cold-ass weather?"

Ramos stared at Tommy for a minute, pushed his own hands into his coat pockets, and headed to the trailer of construction foreman Nathaniel Gilman. Tommy followed.

CHAPTER 4

RAMOS KNOCKED ON the trailer's flimsy door. Tommy hummed a tune that Ramos was unfamiliar with.

"What's that?" he asked.

"What's what?"

Ramos rolled his eyes. "That tune, that song you were humming a minute ago."

"Oh. That's "Own It" by Rick Ross."

"Who?"

"Rick Ross."

"Rick Ross is the name of an actual person? I never heard of him"

Tommy started to explain, but realized it was probably hopeless and gave Ramos a wave of his hand. "Ah, forget it," he said.

Ramos shrugged and knocked on the trailer door more insistently. "So, you still listen to that rap shit?"

Tommy looked at him aghast. "Yo, man," he said. "First of all it ain't *shit*, and second of all, if you had an inkling of what it was I was humming then why did you ask?"

Ramos shrugged and suppressed a smile. Tommy took a lot of ribbing from his fellow detectives because of his love of rap music and, although Ramos never joined in with them on these occasions, he couldn't help teasing Tommy in private every now and then. Especially in light of all the jokes Tommy usually made at his expense.

Ramos shrugged again and pretended to pick at some lint on his coat. "Hey Tommy," he said. "I was just wondering if you still listened to that stuff, that's all. That music is mostly for kids anyway, isn't it?"

When Cucitti answered his voice was tinged with exasperation. He'd explained this so many times..."Yeah, I listen to Hip-Hop, Rap, Gangsta Rap, all 'a that. I enjoy, really *enjoy* getting into what's being said by the true soldiers, uh, warriors, of the streets. I'm talkin' ODB, Lil' Kim, Busta, Killer Cam, 50 Cent, Snoop, Eminem...You already know I cried when Biggie got capped!"

Ramos looked at him, his fist poised to knock on the door again.

Tommy continued. "The music is real Eddie. It's about people's struggles, people's lives, tryin' to get by with dignity. It's about respect. It's the music of the street..."

"The street?" Ramos' voice rose in mock disbelief. He and Tommy had debated this particular point several times in the past. "The street? Man, your white ass grew up in the sticks, out in Long fuckin' Island. The street? You probably didn't even see asphalt 'til you joined the force."

"What are you talkin' about, son?" Cucitti said. "We got asphalt in Long Island, and besides, I told you before, I'm not white, I'm Italian..." Tommy was about to continue when the door to the trailer finally opened.

Nathaniel Gilman was a gnome-like man in his fifties, a shock of unruly white hair danced in the autumn breeze. His sagging cheeks and hawk's beak of a nose were crisscrossed with a maze of broken capillaries. He glanced at the gold badges on the detective's coats and motioned them inside with a surly toss of his heavy head.

Inside, the trailer was almost as cold as it was outside. A small space heater cast its orange light and meager heat from a nearby corner. Tommy shut the door behind him with a slam and a rattle. They both quickly took in the dim, ramshackle environs of the crowded trailer. Only their eyes moved as they took notice of the precariously balanced piles of paper that seemed to be everywhere. A coffee machine and a hot plate shared a sagging folding table. The obligatory pin-ups of scantily dressed women decorated one wall and a large blueprint covered another. Two mugs sat on the rickety desk, one held pencils, pens, and markers, the other, coffee. A beige multi-line touch-tone phone (a blinking light indicated that someone was on hold) also shared the desk's limited space, as did a small desktop fax/copier, an obviously homemade in/out box, an outdated personal computer, several scattered files, some overstuffed binders, and an aluminum takeout plate that contained the congealed remains of a sausage and egg breakfast with hash browns and toast.

In front of the desk was a scarred wooden chair laden with more papers, a fist-sized rock acted as a paperweight. Behind the desk was a battered office chair on casters, a coat rack holding a heavy red and black plaid jacket, and a small, scratched up metal typewriter table on which rested an old IBM Selectric typewriter.

"I already talked with the cops," Gilman glared at them with a combination of anger and suspicion. His quick, wary eyes belied the heavy, hound dog look of the rest of his face.

"Yes sir," Ramos said. "And we appreciate that. We just want to confirm some of the information—you know, get your side of the story."

Tommy hid a smirk. He knew Ramos was putting on his "Public Servant" face as he tried to feel Gilman out.

Gilman's voice rose a notch higher. "*My* side of the story! *My* side of the story?" Gilman sat behind his desk, shuffling some papers as he did so. "You guys want *my* side of the story, go and get it from the cops I already talked to. I ain't got time for this bullshit."

The two detectives made no effort to leave. Gilman stood and wiped perspiration from his face with one hand while he leaned on the desk with the other. Tommy leaned toward Ramos.

"Freezin' in here and the little prick's sweatin' like he's in a sauna," he whispered.

Ramos nodded. Tommy took a few steps toward Gilman's desk. Gilman straightened up as if jerked back by an invisible string.

"Mr. Gilman. Nathaniel. Nat. Can I call you Nat?"

Gilman nodded, his jowls quivering.

"Look," Tommy began. "We understand where you're coming from, yo—but we just want to talk to you. We just need to find out what the deal is, know what I'm sayin'? Now, it would be a whole lot easier to do it here, unofficially. It would probably only take a few minutes. If you want though, we can head on to the precinct where I guarantee it will take *hours*." Tommy picked up the rock paperweight, examined it, and replaced it atop its pile of paper on the chair. "Not to mention," he continued. "That here it's just us, you know, on the down low. Man to man. Nobody else has to know what you told us. It's just our business what's said in here today, know what I'm sayin'? Once we go outside these walls Nat, whatever's said will become everybody's business. Whatever happens will be out of our hands."

The two detectives looked at Gilman, measured his mettle, and waited. Outside, the roar of a bulldozer's engine sounded distant and detached, like the foghorn on an unseen ship. The sound seemed to shrink and further isolate the trailer. All three of its current occupants experienced a mild feeling of claustrophobia.

Gilman's face shined with perspiration. His eyes searched the room with the intensity of a cornered animal. Suddenly he reached behind him. Ramos felt his gut tighten. He reached for his gun, a .38 revolver tucked into a pancake holster on the back of his belt. He knew instinctively that Tommy would be going for his own gun as well. The detective's movements were not lost on Gilman. His face blushed crimson, the tiny blood vessels on his nose and cheeks darkened to purple.

"Hey, what the hell's the matter with you guys? Wait! Wait!" Gilman's hand reappeared holding a stained handkerchief, which he immediately used to mop at his damp face.

The two detectives let out a collective breath, letting their hands drop slowly back to their sides.

"Shee-it!" Tommy hissed between clenched teeth. Ramos shook his head.

Gilman wadded up his handkerchief and threw it the width of the trailer. "This is great! This is just mother-fuckin' A-number-one!" He yelled. "First, I show up for work and I find that some little asshole picked my site to die in. Then I gotta talk to the cops about something I don't know nothin' about, then comes the fun part—I gotta call my boss who's now got a wild hair up his ass about the whole fuckin' thing. Then I gotta start dealin' with insurance companies, auditors, adjusters...and now the shit-flavored icing on the goddamn cake is almost getting blown away by two trigger happy cops 'cause I reached for my hankie!"

Gilman collapsed into his chair and, elbows on his desk, buried his face in his hands. Ramos and Tommy glanced at each other, neither one had moved since Gilman started his tirade.

"I gotta get the phone," Gilman said without looking up.

Ramos glanced at the telephone; there were no longer any blinking lights on the console. Gilman picked up the receiver, put it to his ear, grimaced, and then slammed it back into its cradle.

"Hung up," he said. He looked up at the two detectives. "You still here?"

"Nat," Tommy began as he sat on a corner of Gilman's desk. It groaned in protest under the added weight. "When you found the kid this morning, did you notice anyone else around—anyone? Maybe a homeless guy or a banker, maybe another Kid."

"Jesus!" Gilman exclaimed. "I already told all this stuff to the other cops..."

Ramos took a step forward. "Mr. Gilman, just answer the question please," he said. "You're not a suspect. You're not in trouble. But if you keep giving us a hard time then you will be in trouble—big trouble. We don't need this kind of grief..."

"Oh," Gilman retorted. "Like I do?"

Tommy slammed his hand on the desk. The sound was so loud and sudden Ramos and Gilman both jumped. "Fuck this shit, man!" Tommy yelled. He pulled out the pair of handcuffs he kept on his belt and started walking around the desk toward Gilman. "This asshole's goin' down to the precinct," he said. "Why the hell are we bein' so nice to him? Let's charge him with something, stick his old ass in a cage with a hundred other mutts for a few hours, and then maybe let him call his lawyer."

"His boss wouldn't like that," Ramos joined in. "Then he'd really be pissed at poor Gilman here."

Gilman backed off as Tommy reached for him, hands up in a defensive gesture. "Okay, okay—alright," Gilman said.

Tommy stood right on top of Gilman, who had to turn his head to keep his nose from being buried in Tommy's chest. Tommy glared down at him.

"Okay, okay. Back off now."

Tommy pressed in even further.

Gilman pleaded. "Come on fellas, please. Okay, please?"

Tommy backed off and returned to his perch on the corner of the desk. His glare had been replaced by a condescending grin.

"Nat," he said. "It don't have to be all that, know what I'm sayin'? All we want is a couple of minutes of your time son, ain't nothin' major."

"So Mr. Gilman," Ramos began. "Do you remember seeing anyone, anyone at all, hanging around the area before or maybe even after you came upon the victim?"

"No," Gilman sighed. "I didn't even see the usual homeless assholes that hang around here when I came in this morning. It was cold last night. They sleep down in the subway when it gets cold."

"So you didn't see anyone?"

"I already said I didn't."

"How did that kid and his killer get in here?"

"I-I don't know," Gilman stammered. "Maybe somebody forgot to lock up last night."

"Who's supposed to lock up?"

"Uh, different guys..."

"We'd like their names please, Mr. Gilman," Ramos said.

Gilman looked back and forth from one detective to the other.

The telephone rang, one of its lights blinked yellow. Tommy picked up the receiver and dropped it back into its cradle. Gilman looked down at the phone, then at Tommy.

"Look, I don't know how they got in here," Gilman said. Gilman waved his hand in the general direction of the dead body. "When the weather was warmer, these kids were in here all the time," he said.

"What kids?" Tommy asked.

"You know, these goddamn spic kids, uh—no offense officer," Gilman said to Ramos.

Ramos shrugged. "Almost none taken," he said.

"Anyway," Gilman continued. "These teenagers, mostly Spanish kids, used to come in here all the time in the summer. All hours. They'd give hose jobs to any sonofabitch with a buck. Half the time the other guys would be on their knees doing the kids." Gilman shut his eyes and shook his head, as if trying to clear away a mental picture he wanted no part of. "Sometimes..." he said, "...I'd even find some guy with his pants down around his ankles while some punk kid was boning him in the ass!"

"You've seen a lot for a guy who doesn't know anything about a murder that happened in his own backyard," Tommy pointed out.

"Hey, some things you can't help but see," Gilman retorted.

"Did you notice if any of the men involved were 'regulars', you know, repeat customers?"

"Shit no," Gilman answered emphatically. "I didn't look *that* close."

"So these customers, were they also Hispanic?" Ramos asked.

"Naw," Gilman answered. "That's the part that really turned my stomach. Most of the guys were regular lookin' guys, you know, American."

"American?"

"Yeah, you know, uh...white, wearin' suits, carryin' briefcases..."

"Yeah, they were 'regular' alright," Tommy injected.

Gilman ignored him. "I'm always chasing those little bastards outta here. Well, not so much now that the weather's cooled off, but they still come around. Sometimes they leave, you know, condoms all over the place. Hey, that's really disgusting."

Ramos pulled out his notepad and jotted down some notes. Gilman watched him suspiciously.

"Hey, what are you doin'?" Gilman asked.

Ramos answered without looking up. "You know how it is Mr. Gilman, once a person reaches a certain age, he doesn't remember things like he used to." The pen stopped and Ramos looked up without moving his head. "So I can understand if maybe you have a little trouble remembering stuff too, like, uh—like what time you found the victim, whether or not the gate was locked when you got here..."

"I found the kid when I first come to the site, about five this morning," Gilman volunteered.

"Was it closer to five or five thirty?" Tommy asked.

"I told you *5:00 a.m.*"

"Then what happened Mr. Gilman?"

Gilman then recounted the story pretty much as the young cop had earlier related it to Ramos.

"So why did you check the kid for an ID?" Ramos asked when Gilman was done.

"Well, I wanted to help the kid—thought maybe I could call his parents or something."

"The Good Samaritan, huh?" Ramos asked dryly.

"Yeah," Gilman answered.

"Nat," Tommy interrupted. "Didn't you notice something strange about that kid? Like maybe that he was *dead*?"

"So what am I, a doctor?"

A note of irritation crept into Ramos' voice. "Mr. Gilman," he began. "Why didn't you just call the police right away?"

Gilman paused for a moment before he answered. "Look, I did call the cops, but first I thought that maybe I oughta just check the kid out..."

"So, what are you, a doctor?" Tommy interrupted. Ramos shot him a glance. "Mr. Gilman," Ramos said. "Why did you return to the location of the body forty-five minutes after first finding it?"

"Huh?" Sweat gleamed again on Gilman's forehead and upper lip.

Ramos continued. "You stated earlier to an officer that after trying to find some sort of identification on the youth in question, you went to your trailer to call nine one one."

"Yeah, that's right."

"What time did you place that call?"

"I don't know, ten after, maybe a quarter after..."

"You always show up for work that early, Nat?" Tommy asked.

"I get paid by the hour," Gilman replied. "I always show up early and leave late."

"How long did your call to nine one one take?" Ramos asked.

"Two or three minutes, three minutes max."

"Three minutes?" Tommy said. "What, they put you on hold?"

"Okay, two minutes, probably more like two..."

"Hey, don't change your story 'cause of me," Tommy said.

"So why did you go back to the body?" Ramos inquired again.

Gilman hesitated. "I don't know, curiosity I guess..."

"Curious about what?"

Frustrated, Gilman's voice became a whine. "I don't know, look—am I under suspicion or something? 'Cause if I am, I wanna call a lawyer."

The phone rang, two lights blinked in unison on the console. Gilman lunged for the receiver like a drowning man grabbing for a life preserver.

"Look, I got work to do," he said. He pushed one of the blinking lights and started talking with the person on the other end.

Ramos and Tommy looked at each other. Ramos shut his notepad and returned it and the pen to his coat pocket.

"Alright Nat," Tommy said. "Thanks for the cooperation."

"We'll be in touch," Ramos added as he opened the door.

Gilman looked up from the phone just long enough to give them the finger.

Once outside, Ramos sucked in a lungful of air and let it out in a noisy whoosh. Even though the interior of the trailer was cool, the air in there felt dirty. Ramos was glad to get out.

"Yo son, that mutt's hiding something," Tommy said once they'd gotten some distance between themselves and the trailer. "He knows more than he's sayin'."

"That's a given," Ramos agreed. "A couple of times back there I thought he was gonna break and say something incriminating."

"Yeah, me too."

"He's not the killer though, Tommy," Ramos said. "I just don't get that from him." Ramos raised his hand to cut off Cucitti's protest. "Oh, he's involved in something alright," Ramos continued. "That's for damn sure, but he's not the killer—I'm sure of it. If we dragged him to the stationhouse now, he'd start cryin' for his lawyer and we'd probably wind up having to let him go and maybe losing him. If we did charge him with something, what would it be? Obstruction? Jaywalking? Being an asshole?

Whatever—a lawyer would get him out just as quick. Nah, this guy knows something. I don't what it is, but when I find out, I want to be able to grab this guy by his nuts and swing him around 'til he sings me the song I wanna hear. He's gonna slip up. He ain't too bright."

As they passed the area of the murder, Ramos noticed that the body still lay on the ground.

That's gonna change soon, Ramos thought. *Once the ME confirms that the same guy who killed those two others killed this kid too, this is gonna become a high-profile case. The media will get a hold of it and turn it into a circus, the mayor will get pissed because he'll probably look bad; he'll call the commissioner on the carpet, all of a sudden the brass will get real interested in getting this case solved—and then, dead kids won't have to lay in the dirt as long. At least, not for a while anyway.*

Ramos reached his car and pressed a button on his key ring, deactivating the alarm.

"Tommy, do me a favor," Ramos said as he stepped into his car. "Stick around and watch Gilman. Don't let 'im see you. If by the end of the day nothing's happened, then meet me at the office and we'll arrange for some surveillance to watch him from then on."

"You read my mind," Cucitti said, leaning in through the car window. "I'll fix it with the precinct," he added. He straightened and stepped back from the car, a sudden breeze tousled his hair and he pulled his coat collar up. Ramos nodded, glanced once more in the direction of the body, and drove away.

CHAPTER 5

TOMMY CUCITTI WATCHED Ramos' car until it disappeared in traffic and then turned back toward the construction site. He strolled back, hands in his pants pockets, and schmoozed with the few cops who remained at the location. Not too long afterward, he saw that the body of the murdered teen was finally being removed, and he quickly strode over to talk to the EMTs.

"Yo fellas, what's up?" He asked off-handedly.

"My lunch if we don't get this fuckin' DOA into the wagon soon," a technician answered. His partner laughed and Tommy joined in.

"So where's homeboy going?" Tommy asked once the laughter had subsided. He pointed at the vinyl bag that was being zippered around the corpse.

"You know the drill officer," the same technician replied. "They kill 'em, we chill 'em. This kid's taking a trip to the city morgue."

"Yeah, uh-huh," Tommy mumbled. *It was sad,* Tommy thought. *In death, even the toughest street kids lost the hard edges of their features and looked only like the children they really were.* Tommy wondered if this kid's parents worried about him, or if they would even care he was dead.

The EMTs loaded the body into the wagon and drove away,

bouncing along the deeply pitted landscape. Tommy squatted down at the stained area where the body had lain, much as Ramos had done earlier, and visually went over the ground inch by inch. There was nothing new to see. He stood up, brushed off his jeans, and cast a peripheral glance at Gilman's trailer. A shadow at one of the windows moved. Gilman was watching him. Good.

Tommy walked back the way he'd come, keeping the trailer and its shadowy figure in the window at the edge of his vision. He wanted Gilman to see him leave. He left the site and walked around to one of the "peepholes" he'd noticed earlier. This one was a little lower than most of the others, probably meant to accommodate curious youngsters. A small dumpster on wheels, strategically placed, became a barrier to the casual eye. Tommy dumped the contents of a city-owned garbage receptacle at the curb and used the bright orange steel mesh container to sit on. The view was perfect. He could see Gilman's trailer from his seat on the garbage can. As he settled down, another cold breeze ruffled his hair and Tommy wished he'd remembered to bring a hat. *His stretch-knit "Hilfiger" hoodie would have been the best thing to wear on a day like this,* he thought. Soon, one of the officers Tommy had spoken to earlier came by with the coffee he'd requested. Tommy thanked him and, as the officer walked away, sighed and resigned himself to the most boring part of any cop's job—the wait.

# # #

Gilman stood at one of the trailer's windows, his breath fogging the glass. After a few moments, he let the corner of the dirty towel that served as a curtain drop back into place. He crept from window to window, even peering through the wire-reinforced glass of the trailer door. *Finally,* Gilman thought, *looks like all the cops are gone.* He leaned back against a wall and sighed. The phone rang and he ignored it until it stopped suddenly in mid-ring. Gilman sighed deeply and walked over to his desk. He opened one of the drawers, pulled out an almost empty bottle of whiskey and killed it in one swallow. He wiped his mouth with the back of his hand and tossed the bottle into the trashcan. Gilman rested his head in the crook of his elbow and listened to the sounds of the city as they seeped through the walls and into the trailer. He shook his head, each movement eliciting the word "shit" from his lips.

"Shit, shit, shit, shit, shit, SHIT!" Gilman kicked the trashcan as hard as he could, its contents quickly becoming part of the trailer's general untidiness.

Gilman got up and walked over to the file cabinets. After several tugs, one of the drawers slid open with a rusty squeal. Gilman reached in and pulled out a flat bottle wrapped in a wrinkled paper bag. He unscrewed the thin metal cap and took a long swallow of the bottle's contents. When he'd finished, he took the bottle from his mouth and wiped his mouth with a corner of the paper bag. His face was a bright crimson, and he smacked his lips loudly as he replaced the bottle's cap. He started to return the bottle to its hiding place in the recesses of the filing cabinet, but reconsidered it and stuffed the bottle, bag and all, into one of his pant's back pockets. He slammed the filing cabinet drawer shut, sending it rocking on the trailer's uneven flooring.

"Fuckin' cops," Gilman muttered as he returned to his desk. "I should call somebody," he said aloud. "I should fuckin' call somebody and let 'em know that these fuckin' cops think they can go around and threaten decent people!" Gilman looked around the trailer, trying to will sympathy from the four dead walls. "I'm gonna call the fuckin' commissioner..." The telephone rang again and Gilman ignored it like before. He walked over to the window and carefully peeked outside. He saw no one other than his men working on the site. No cops. Good.

A knock on the door startled him and he accidentally pulled the cover from the window. The dirty towel hung from his hand as he stared at the door. Another knock startled him almost as much as the first had. Hastily, he tried to hang the towel back in its place while he kept his eyes on the trailer door. Another knock and he found his voice.

"Y-yeah, who is it?"

The door opened and Jimson, the huge black man drove the dump truck lumbered into the trailer. His height forced him to stoop forward slightly so that his dreadlocks hung in the air in front of him while he spoke.

"Gilman," he said with a slight Caribbean accent. "We just got a new load of sand, you know."

"Yeah, and...?" Gilman growled.

Jimson rolled his eyes. "And, the place we planned to dump it is the same place where that boy got killed. We're not sure where we should be dumping it now."

"You're bothering me for this?" Gilman asked. "The fuckin' cops are gone, everybody's gone—shit, even the dead kid's gone. Dump the goddamn sand where we were first gonna."

"There's blood there, you know."

"So what? What, you and your boys afraid of a little blood? Just go do your fuckin' job and dump the sand where I told you."

Gilman recoiled slightly as Jimson took a step toward him.

"First thing, Mr. Gilman," Jimson said. "There are no *boys* working here, only men. And secondly, there are very few things any of us are afraid of. I was asking only because we weren't sure if the police prefer if that place remain undisturbed."

"Okay," Gilman acknowledged. "The cops didn't tell me nuthin' about that spot, so please just go dump the sand. Huh? Okay?"

"Very well Gilman, I'll be telling the *MEN*." As Jimson left, he muttered a few colorful epithets just loud enough for Gilman to hear.

"Goddamn monkey," Gilman said after the door had closed. He reached into his back pocket and took a swig from his bottle. Gilman held his arm up and looked at his watch. It was getting close to lunch time. He wasn't hungry, but there was a liquor store a couple of blocks away...

Suddenly, Gilman was struck by an idea. He reached deep into the back of the middle drawer of his desk, pulled out the wallet secreted there; the one he'd taken from the dead teenager, and ran from the trailer. After a few yards, he was already winded and slowed his pace to a quick walk until he reached his destination: the murder scene. He got there just as Jimson was backing the dump truck into position. Gilman went to the area where the dead boy had lain and Jimson stopped the truck cold with a whoosh of the air brakes. Jimson leaned out of the window to look back at Gilman.

"What you doing back there man? What if I didn't see you? I could have run your silly ass over."

"Forget that bullshit, Jimson," Gilman yelled back. "I'm here doing my job, just make sure you do yours, dammit."

Jimson cut loose with some more expletives and yanked the truck back into reverse. Gilman jumped, the truck's back-up warning beep loud in his ears. One of Jimson's men appeared, waving his arms to guide him toward the proper dump area.

"Hey you, YOU!" Gilman yelled at the man. "Get to the front, I'll take care of it back here. Get to the front."

The man looked puzzled and yelled something to Jimson who hollered something back. Gilman couldn't make out any of their words above the roar of the truck's engine and the constant beeping of the back-up warning. The other man looked at Gilman, shrugged, and moved to the front of the vehicle. Gilman stood slightly off to the side and waved the truck back with one hand. His other hand was hidden behind his back. When the truck was properly positioned, Gilman raised his hand for the truck to stop. Then he signaled Jimson to dump the sand. Jimson yelled back at him, but Gilman ignored him. He knew he was dangerously close to where several tons of sand was going to be dumped, but he had to remain partially hidden if he was going to do what he was going to do and not be seen.

Jimson waved dismissively from the truck and pulled the gears that would dump the sand. The tailgate disengaged as the truck bed slowly rose into the air, then with a loud shushing sound, the sand came down.

Gilman stepped back as the sand cascaded to the ground. He took a quick look around and noticing no one looking, he threw the dead boy's wallet onto the ground ahead of the growing pool of sand. The sand swallowed up the wallet in an instant and Gilman turned to walk away. The sand had other ideas, however. It rose over Gilman's shoes, causing him to stumble. The sand filled his shoes and the tattered cuffs of his pants. Gilman tried to jump away and run, but the sand grabbed at his feet and grains of it stung his eyes. It slowed him down and dragged at him like a living thing. He pushed it away with his hands and still it came. Gilman gasped with fear, there was too much sand; it was everywhere. The onrushing sand immediately obliterated every step he took. It was up to his knees now and he could barely move, he was exhausted. He tried to flee, but the sand just kept coming. Suddenly he felt himself being jerked out of the sand, away from a patch of ground that almost became the scene of two deaths. He was dropped roughly onto the ground just out of the sand's reach.

Gilman sat there and spat sand from his mouth, reaching for the bottle in his back pocket. When he looked up he saw Jimson scowling down at him.

"Thanks Jimson, I..."

"Ah, forget it man," Jimson said. "Besides, I woulda left your ass in there if it were up to me, you miserable old fool. You should thank he over there, he was the one who insisted I pull you from the sand." Jimson was pointing over his shoulder with a jutting thumb.

Gilman leaned over to get a look at his benefactor and groaned when he saw who it was.

Tommy Cucitti walked up to him and made a shooting motion at him with his thumb and forefinger. "Busted," he said with a smile.

CHAPTER 6

RAMOS COULDN'T FIND a parking space in front of the building, as usual, so he parked a block away on 118th Street. He pulled into the curb, stuck his police parking permit in the windshield, and stepped out into the autumn air. Ramos took in a lung full of air through his nose and let it exit his mouth in a long, noisy sigh. He enjoyed the brisk fall weather. He was equally fond of spring, but winter and summer? He disliked the extremes in weather, either overly hot or extremely cold. He felt the same way about a lot of things. Ramos liked it when people and things in general operated on an even keel. He didn't like surprises.

Ramos looked up at the imposing structure at 120 East 119th Street that housed the detectives of Manhattan North Homicide. He could see where someone finally tried to wash the graffiti off the front wall, but all they'd succeeded in doing was to lighten it up a bit and smear it around. Now it really stood out because, even with the smear, that was the cleanest part of the building's entire granite and brick façade.

Ramos trudged up the concrete steps. It was between tour changes; so the stairs and the area in front of the building were relatively deserted. Then he stepped through the heavy wooden doors and was engulfed in the usual sea of pandemonium.

Several dazed looking people shared the wooden bench

across from the sergeant's desk with a sleeping homeless woman. The face of one of the men on the bench was covered with dried blood, as were his hands. A uniformed officer used his nightstick to nudge a sleeping woman awake and told her that she couldn't sleep there. She yawned, nodded, and started rummaging through one of the several plastic bags gathered at her feet. As Ramos passed the officer, he asked him if he knew what had happened to the man with the blood on his face.

"Yeah," the officer answered once he noticed the gold shield dangling from Ramos' breast pocket. "We figure it's a bias crime. Some kids in the park beat him up while they yelled racial, uh racial..."

"Epithets?" Ramos offered.

"Yeah," the officer brightened. "They was yelling epithets and stuff about 'go back to Iraq' and 'fuck Bin Laden', that kind of thing." The officer leaned toward Ramos and whispered conspiratorially. "The funny thing is the guy ain't even an Arab, he's an Israeli tourist! A Jewish guy! Ain't that something? He don't even speak English so he didn't even understand what they were callin' him 'til some other Jewish guy told him. Ain't that something?"

Ramos shook his head and agreed.

"Yeah," the cop said as Ramos walked away. "Let 'em put *that* in their melting pot and cook it."

Ramos shook his head again and continued on his way. A female officer was having a loud argument with a female prostitute, two other officers were roughly "escorting" a struggling prisoner to the holding cell (or "The Cage" as they called it), a woman with vacant eyes slowly pushed a stroller with a screaming baby in it back and forth while someone from Children's Protective Services spoke to her in hushed tones. A bored looking police officer stood close by.

The desk sergeant looked up in time to see Ramos sliding past.

"Hey Eddie," the sergeant yelled out. "Lieutenant Mullen wants to talk to you this morning, 'sez right after his meeting."

Ramos held up his fingers in the "okay" sign and kept going.

At the stairs leading to the next floor, a young paralegal was trying to coax a brief-laden luggage carrier up the stairs.

"Here, let me help, " Ramos offered. He lifted the bottom with one hand while the paralegal used both hands to pull the handle. Ramos grunted. It was heavier than he thought. He held onto the handrail with his other hand and together, they bumped the luggage carrier up the steps one step at a time.

At the top of the stairs, the paralegal thanked Ramos and then stopped to speak with a well-dressed African American man in the corridor. Ramos recognized the man as Manhattan District Attorney Kahlil Williams. Ramos acknowledged him with a head nod, which was not returned. The DA stared at him with eyes as hard and dark as flint until Ramos turned, pushed the door, and entered the detectives' squad room.

Most of the men and women in the crowded, airless room stopped what they were doing long enough to look up. There were a few shouted greetings over the usual din of conversation, ringing or burbling telephones, the humming and beeping of the fax and copy machines, the clack-clack of typewriter keys and the lesser click-click of computer keyboards. An occasional laugh, cough or expletive also added to the office harmonics. The usual smells of coffee, eggs, bacon and doughnuts intermingled with a scent new to the squad room since the arrival of the female detectives...air freshener. Ramos passed the coffee maker; a hand-written sign warned coffee club members that their monies were due. Another sign, torn, stained and yellowed with age admonished detectives to: Please Clean Up After Yourselves.

Ramos took in the everyday mess of spilled sugar and non-dairy creamer, used stirrers, torn open pouches of *Sweet'N Low*, discarded tea bags, and tiny puddles of spilled coffee, milk, and cream. One of the larger puddles threatened to drip to the floor. Ramos took a paper towel and dropped it on the puddle, watching as the dark stain spread through the coarse brown paper. He picked his head up and looked toward the lieutenant's office. The door was closed, that meant the meeting must still be going on. Ramos went to his desk, removed his badge from his coat's breast pocket and dropped it on the desk where it landed with a heavy thunk. He remembered briefly back to when he was first handed his shield at the academy. It seemed disproportionately heavy for its size—and as if reading his mind, the instructor let him know in no uncertain terms that a police officer's shield always carries the added weight of responsibility. Ramos never forgot that.

Ramos slid his gun from its holster, stuck it in the upper right hand drawer of his desk, and then shut the drawer. He hooked his coat onto the nearby coat rack which then developed a precarious lean. Ramos watched it for a second or two, hands outstretched to catch or balance it. When it seemed safe to do so he left it alone and sat down. He reached over and turned on his tiny personal coffee maker, which he'd set up the night before. Soon he was rewarded with the aroma of his favorite coffee, a strong espresso ground with bits of coconut that he always bought from a shop at the South Street Seaport downtown. After filling his mug and taking a few tentative sips, Ramos sighed contentedly and pushed the button on his answering machine. There was a sort of grinding, whirring sound as the worn teeth on the player sought purchase on the equally worn tape. Ramos gave the machine a couple of taps while he absentmindedly patted his shirt pocket. Then he remembered he'd given up smoking almost three months ago. *Funny he should be looking for smokes now,* Ramos thought. The thought of cigarettes hadn't bothered him for awhile. The same thing happened at the construction site where the dead kid was. Ramos mentally kicked himself. Maybe this thing was bothering him more than he thought...or maybe, just maybe, he needed a cigarette. And with that, Ramos pushed the thought out of his mind for the time being.

The garbled noise from his machine that passed for messages consisted of the usual stuff, informants wanting to sell bits and pieces of information, the payroll department letting him know that he'd forgotten something minor on his timesheet, the lieutenant telling him to report to his office that morning after his meeting. Ramos glanced in the direction of the lieutenant's office again and saw that the door was still closed. The last message was from his wife, Linda. She was letting him know that she'd be staying late at church again tonight and that their youngest daughter, Kimberly (sixteen years old now) would be with her.

Ramos listened to that message again. Linda had been

spending a lot of time at this new church lately. Ever since she left the Catholic Church they'd worshipped in since they were married, the same church in fact that they were married in, she just bounced around from church to church looking for what she called a "new church home." Ramos admitted to himself that he had little idea what she was talking about. He'd asked her what was wrong with the "church home" they'd shared for the last twenty-odd years, the same church he'd attended as a child. But then Linda started talking about churches that cared more about doctrine and tradition than they did *The Word,* and how she wanted to attend a teaching ministry so that she could learn more about *The Word.* He'd even gone to a couple of those churches with her, but he always wound up feeling weird or uncomfortable.

Sometimes he found himself wondering if what went on at some of those other churches was all an act—people shouting, crying, *speaking in tongues*—then there was the thing where the congregants would swoon and drop to the floor when the priest, or reverend, pastor, whatever, touched them. To Ramos, it almost seemed more like some sort of mass hypnosis, or voodoo or something rather than a *real* church. He felt a lot more at home in his regular church, listening to old Father Salvatelli's soft, soothing voice conduct Mass the same way he had since Ramos was a kid. So far as he knew his wife had visited Baptist, Methodist, Episcopal, Apostolic, Pentecostal, and Seventh-day Adventist churches. She'd even sat in on a couple of Jehovah's Witnesses meetings. Until recently, it seemed she'd been unable to find what it was that she was looking for—a "place to feed my spirit" she would say. Well, she seemed to have found what she was looking for in a tiny hole-in-the-wall storefront church near their Brooklyn neighborhood. Ramos tapped his chin with his forefinger as he tried to remember the name of the little church. It was something like, *The Biblical Stairs to Our Heavenly God Teaching and Television Ministry (non-denominational).* Ramos was sure about the non-denominational part; the rest was a little fuzzy. He sighed. Oh well, it was probably just a phase or something.

The tape ended and Ramos looked up from his coffee. The lieutenant's door was finally open. He stood in the doorway shaking hands and talking with several men in suits. They didn't look like cops, so Ramos guessed them to be feds or politicians. In Ramos' mind, they were one and the same thing anyway. Ramos got up and arched his back as he stretched. *Looks like I was right,* he thought. *This case is heating up.*

CHAPTER 7

TOMMY CUCITTI TOUCHED the screen of his Smartphone and thumbed the automatic dialer button for nine one one.

"Police operator eight-six-five, what is the emergency?"

"This is Detective Thomas Cucitti," Tommy identified himself to the operator on the other end. "I got a ten eighty-five 'officer holding' at the corner of fifty-three and Lex."

"Do you need an ambulance at the location?" the operator asked.

"Nah," Tommy replied. "Just send me an RMP for transportation of the perp. I'm holding him right outside the construction site. Send a CSU back here too, there's some evidence that needs recovering."

"Yes sir," the operator said.

"Oh," Tommy continued before breaking off the connection. "And tell 'em to bring a shovel."

Tommy Cucitti rocked back and forth on his heels, quite pleased with himself. He'd expected to be stuck watching Gilman a lot longer, but here it was barely lunchtime and the guy screwed up right away. Tommy looked at Gilman. His head was bowed, his jowls hanging and quivering as he muttered to himself. He looked up and caught Tommy looking at him. His eyes were watery and bloodshot. When he spoke his breath reeked of liquor.

"Lousy cop," he said. "Lousy cop. Lousy day. Lousy fuckin' life."

"Ah, shaddup," Tommy said looking up the street for a sign of the patrol car he'd requested. "You're breakin' my heart Nat."

Gilman shook his head, setting his jowls to quivering anew. "Look," he said. "I didn't kill no fuckin' body. I was just tryin' to make a little money on the side, that's all. I didn't kill nobody."

"Hey Nat," Tommy said. "Did I read you your rights, son?"

"Yeah."

"And you understood them, right?"

"Yeah."

"Okay, I just wanted to make sure before I told you to shut up again."

When the patrol car arrived, Tommy assigned one of the officers to safeguard the sand-covered area until the Crime Scene Unit arrived. Then he ushered Gilman into the back of the patrol car and sat next to him. As the car pulled away, Gilman squirmed in his seat.

"Hey," Gilman said, addressing Tommy. "Can you loosen these handcuffs?"

Tommy ignored him.

"Hey, these cuffs are hurting my wrists, you can loosen them I said."

Tommy looked down at Gilman. "They're *supposed* to hurt."

At the Seventeenth Precinct, Tommy pushed and pulled Gilman into one of the interrogation rooms (now called 'conference' rooms by some of the newer officers), and left him there. He walked back to the sergeant's desk where a pretty African American PAA (Police Administrative Aide) was manning the telephones.

"Hi," Tommy said engagingly. He drummed on his gold badge with his fingers. "Can I use the phone for a minute?"

The PAA shrugged and went back to the call she had on another phone. Tommy picked up the receiver, careful to punch a button on the phone that wasn't already lit, and dialed Ramos' number. After several rings, Ramos' answering machine came on and made some sort of unintelligible noise that passed for a message.

"Yo Eddie, this is Tommy," Cucitti said. "I got that little shit Gilman at the one-seven. I busted him trying to lose something at this morning's murder scene. CSU's there by now and I'm going to talk to Gilman 'til he cries for his lawyer. I'll call you back later and give you the four-one-one." Tommy hung up the phone, smiled at the PAA, and went back into the room where he'd ensconced Nathaniel Gilman.

Tommy Cucitti entered the room where Gilman sat glumly on one of the hard wooden chairs. Tommy took one of the other chairs, spun it around and straddled it. He sat there with his arms crossed along the back of the chair and eyed Gilman curiously. Then he jumped up, startling Gilman. He reached into his pocket and pulled out his jumble of keys. After a quick search, he found the one he was looking for and removed the handcuffs from Gilman's wrists.

"Sorry about that," Tommy said easily. "I forgot you had those things on."

Gilman just looked at him while he rubbed the bruises on his wrists. "G-got any water," he croaked.

"Sure man," Tommy said. He opened the door and propped it open with his foot. There was a water fountain right next to the door and less than a minute later Tommy returned to Gilman with a paper cup filled with cool water. Gilman held the cup with trembling, liver-spotted hands and drank it down in one gulp. Tommy reached for the cup but Gilman balled it up and dropped it to the floor. Tommy let his arm drop and shrugged. He kicked the crumpled up paper cup under Gilman's chair and walked back to where he'd been sitting earlier.

"So Nat," Tommy began. "You mentioned that you had nothin' to do with the killing at the construction site, right?"

Gilman just stared darkly at Cucitti.

"Yo Nat, I'm talkin' to you son," Tommy said. "In fact, I'm just repeating what you told me earlier. You said you didn't kill that kid, right?"

Gilman nodded.

"Well, check this out, my partner and I, well, we believe you. We don't think you had anything to do with the actual killing either."

"I didn't."

Tommy settled into his chair. “So tell me what *did* happen,” he said.

“I don’t wanna talk to *you*, I wanna talk to my lawyer.”

Tommy ignored him. “You said you were just trying to make some ducats on the side, right Nat? What did you mean?”

“I wanna talk to my lawyer.”

Tommy shook his head. “Nat, Nat, Nat,” Tommy continued. “Listen, I understand having to make some extra bread on the side. Cops don’t make a lot of money either. Lots of cops have to work part-time jobs...”

“I said I wanna talk to my lawyer.”

Tommy sighed and stood up. “Okay Nat,” he said. Tommy walked over to the door and opened it. “Come on man,” he said, motioning Gilman to precede him into the hallway. “Go call your lawyer.”

Gilman didn’t move.

“Well man, come on! You want to get the lawyer involved, the DA involved, the judges involved...It’s like I told you earlier Nat, it could be either you and me—or you and the *world*, son.” Tommy looked at Gilman who stayed in his seat and avoided Tommy’s gaze.

Finally, Gilman waved his hand at Tommy and the open door. “Okay, okay,” he said. Let’s talk.”

Tommy shut the door triumphantly. “Now you’re talking Nat!” he said. Tommy retook his seat across from Gilman. “Now let’s just talk, man-to-man, and we’ll be able to work something out here.”

Gilman stared at Tommy. Then he sighed and started talking.

“Look, first off stop calling me son,” he said. “I’m old enough to be *your* father, and next I wanna know if I can, *we* can make some kind of deal here?”

“What, between you and me Nat? Of course man, deadass!”

Gilman stared and then shook his head. “Okay,” he said. “Look, I didn’t kill nobody.”

“Yeah, alright man. We went over that part. Tell me the part where you just wanted to make some money,” Tommy insisted.

“Yeah, right.” Gilman wiped at his face, then pinched the bridge of his nose between thumb and forefinger. “Okay, okay,” he said again. “Are we gonna work out some kind of a deal here?”

Gilman asked. "'Cause I don't wanna really say nuthin' unless we got a deal..."

Of course we're dealing, Nat," Tommy said. "You and me, we know you didn't really do anything too bad. Lawyers though, well lawyers would probably try to stick you with a murder charge. *Murder*, Nat! Make you cop a fucked-up plea! Our deal is that you talk to me and you don't go to prison for murder."

"Murder? I told you I didn't..."

"Aw shit, Nat," Tommy said suddenly. "This shit is taking too fuckin' long, yo. Just tell me the truth; tell me what happened to that kid or whatever your role was in all this. If you didn't kill the kid then you ain't got nothin' to worry about. Me and my partner are homicide detectives; we just wanna catch the motherfucker who killed that kid, alright?"

Gilman nodded his head. "Uh-huh, okay," he said. "But, uh-h..."

"But what, Nat?"

"I was wondering if I could get something in writing you know, 'cause..."

Tommy jumped up from his chair, knocking it over, his arms thrown into the air in exasperation. "Oh shit! I don't fuckin' believe this shit!" Tommy yelled. "I'm trying to hook you up, trying to look out for you, and you still want to fuck with me. Is that it, Nat? Is that it? You fuckin' with me? 'Cause if you fuckin' with me, the deal's off. Off! You can take your chances with the court system, the lawyers, the media...and I bet your bosses would love that shit too. You can forget about ever going back to work there man..."

Gilman looked cowed, but he didn't say anything. Sweat dripped from the end of his nose onto the wooden table he sat behind. Disgusted, Tommy retrieved some paper towels and slid them over to him. Gilman took several in one handful and crumpled them up in one hand. After a few moments, he used them to sop up the perspiration on his face. Tommy glared at him, hands on his hips, but Gilman refused to look at him. Instead, he stared remorsefully at the beads of his sweat as they soaked into the thirsty wood of the table.

Tommy dropped his arms to his sides. "Okay," he said. "You win. I'll give you something in writing." He righted his chair and pushed it up to the table, then he reached over and grabbed a fresh sheet of paper towel. He took a pen from his shirt pocket and started writing on the rough, brown paper. He spoke aloud as he wrote. “I, Detective Thomas Cucitti, do hereby state that in return for the full cooperation of Mr. Nathaniel Gilman, no charges will be brought against him regarding this case.”

Tommy then dated and signed it with a flourish. He showed it to Gilman, who read it and nodded slowly. He reached out for the paper and Tommy pulled it away.

“Uh-uh, Nat,” Tommy said. “I did what you said, now you talk to me.” Tommy placed the paper on the table between them. Gilman reached out to touch the paper, hesitated, and brought his trembling hand back to his lap. “You wrote it on a piece of paper towel,” he said. “That’s not official.”

Tommy rolled his eyes. “Anything a cop signs becomes an official document and can be introduced as prima facie evidence in a court of law, he said.

Gilman looked back and forth between the paper towel and Tommy’s face. Then, finally convinced, he nodded and licked his lips. “Okay,” he said. “This is what was going on...When we first started working on that project on Fifty-Third and Lex, I noticed that there was a lot of those boy prosties hanging around. Heck, one of ‘em even offered to give me a blow job for ten bucks once...”

“And did he?”

Gilman looked aghast. “Shit no,” he said. “I told him. I’m all man dammit! Told him I ain’t into none of that stuff.”

“Okay, okay. Go on.”

“Uh-huh. So anyway they was always tryin’ to break into the construction site and the cops weren’t really doin’ nuthin’ about it, even though I raised a ruckus plenty of times. So, I finally catch one of them prosties pissing against the fence. I had a crowbar with me and I was gonna whack him good with it...”

“You always happen to have a crowbar with you Nat?”

“Huh? Uh, no, no. I was just lucky I had it then, you see. So anyways, I was about to whack him good when the kid sees me. Boy, I tell you, he was so scared I thought he was gonna shit his pants.” Gilman was becoming more animated now and was gesturing as if he were still wielding the crowbar.

"So then the kid offers me some money if I was to just let him go, you know, leave him alone," Gilman continues. "So what can I say? I tells the kid sure, if he's got enough money to keep me from whacking him. Well the goddamn kid pulls a wad of bills outta his pocket big enough to choke a horse. He peels off a couple of twenties and I'm happy. I'm not greedy, see? Or else I woulda took the whole thing...but I'm a fair man." Gilman stopped talking and looked at Tommy as if for some type of acknowledgement, but Tommy kept quiet and Gilman eventually continued his story.

"So," he said. "I told the kid to beat it, but then the kid wants to talk to me. I was gonna whack him one, just to get him away from me, but then what he was sayin' started to make sense. You see, it seems that him and his fellow prosties was lookin' for a place to conduct their business so that it was away from the public view. So the kid suggests to me that I leave the gate to the construction site unlocked so he and any of his pals that use the site would give me a cut of their money." Gilman widened his bloodshot eyes for emphasis, coughed, and asked Tommy for more water. Tommy complied then sat down for the rest of Gilman's story.

Gilman downed the water in one gulp, wiped his mouth with the back of his hand and continued. "So at first, I wasn't too sure and thought about going for none of it. But the kid kept buggin' me and it kept making more and more sense after awhile. Not to mention that I could use the money seein' as I have a couple of vices of my own."

"What about security?" Tommy asked.

"Huh?"

"Don't these sites usually have a security guard posted at night?"

Gilman waved his hand, "Nah, that was just a 'no-show' type of job. We didn't think we would need security right in the middle of Manhattan, and with the precinct so close by..."

"Okay, keep going," Tommy said, cutting him off.

Gilman blinked, then continued where he'd left off. "So, uh, me and the kid made a deal, but I told him there was no way I could leave the site open all night..."

"So what did you do?"

"I, uh, gave him a key."

Tommy looked incredulous. "You gave him a key to the construction site?"

Gilman nodded, then shrugged. "Look, I told the kid that he could let his friends in, or he could come in himself to do their business, but when they left, the gate had to be locked. I told him that if anything wound up missing, I'd know whose ass to kick."

"So," Tommy said, "these kids would bring their customers to the construction site all night long, avoiding the cops and busybodies on the street. Then the kid with the key would lock up and they'd all go home happy."

"Yeah, and don't forget that they would leave me a little something too."

"Oh yeah," Tommy said. "How can I forget that? How much did they usually leave you?"

"You mean like, every night?"

"Yeah, every night."

"Well," Gilman answered, scratching absentmindedly at his chin. "Most nights I'd say there would be maybe a hundred dollars there waiting for me."

"Hmmm, not bad, a hundred bucks a night."

"Yeah," Gilman agreed. "It was pretty good, while it lasted."

"Yeah," Tommy said. "I hear that."

Gilman waited a moment, then asked, "Should I keep going?"

Tommy nodded.

Gilman took a deep breath and continued. "Yeah, so things worked out pretty good, I didn't have no real trouble from those kids. I just hated when they would leave all those goddamn condoms all over the place. That's one of the reasons I'd always make sure I got to work before anybody else. I had to make sure the gate was like it was supposed to be and clean up after those bastards too."

"Still, you made a hundred bucks a night...tax free."

"Yeah," Gilman said. "I know those little assholes probably coulda upped some more cash, but I didn't want to take a chance on them maybe gettin' mad and vandalizin' the place."

Tommy shook his head.

Gilman sighed. "When I come into work this mornin', I notice right away the gate ain't locked. Now I'm pissed, see. I figure either one of them kids was still there with some fag, or the kid with the key forgot to lock the goddamn gate. You know, them spic kids ain't too goddamn responsible..."

"You gave them the key to your workplace though."

"I gave *one* of them the key," Gilman pointed out defensively. "Anyway, I go into the site and I don't see nobody right away, and the longer I look the more pissed I get. Then, I see the kid lyin' by the far end of the fence. At first I thought the little shit was sleepin' off a bender, so I kicked the bastard as hard as I could. When he didn't wake up, I took a closer look and that's when I saw he was dead."

"Dead?"

"What, are you kiddin'? Fuckin' kid was deader than a cheap whore's cunt on a Saturday night."

Tommy shook his head again.

"So I got worried, you know? First I thought the guy who done it might still be around, so I ran to my trailer so I can call the cops. Then I remembered that this kid probably still had the key to the construction site on him, so I went back to take it off him. It took some doin', but I found it."

"So the dead kid was the same one you made this deal with, right?"

"Yeah," Gilman continued. "So I got the key and while I was lookin' for it, I found the kid's wallet too. So I start lookin' through it, thinkin' maybe I should call his parents or whatever, when I remember that I ain't been paid and this was probably the last time these kid prosties were gonna be usin' the site, so..."

"So..." Tommy encouraged.

"So, I took the kid's wallet."

"Is that what I saw you toss into that sand pile back at the site?"

"Yeah, yeah," Gilman admitted. "That was the kid's wallet. I was only gonna take what was owed me, you know? But, then I figured, hey the kid's dead—what does he need with any dough? So I just sort of took all of it."

"And how much was 'all of it'?"

"A little over three hundred."

Tommy raised an eyebrow.

"Yeah," Gilman said. "Those punks do some business there I guess."

"Yeah, I guess," Tommy agreed.

Gilman's face blushed and he reached into his pant pocket. Tommy eyed him warily.

"I, uh, I took this off the kid too," Gilman said, holding up a shiny object and letting it dangle from his fingers.

Tommy carefully took it from him and examined it. It was a thick silver-colored chain and hanging from it was a large Star of David.

"Yeah," Gilman said, laughing uneasily. "I was wondering what a spic kid was doin' with one of those too. Probably stole it off some Jew."

Tommy closed his fist around the chain and medallion. "And that's when you finally called the cops, right?" he asked.

"Uh, yeah. I guess so," Gilman said.

Tommy nodded. "Nat," he said. "You know if you're lying to me that makes our deal null and void, right? I mean, if I find out you're lyin', there's no deal. You understand that?" Tommy studied Gilman as he nodded his assent. Satisfied, Tommy got up from his chair with a grunt. Before he headed toward the door he grabbed the sheet of paper towel on which he'd written his agreement with Gilman.

"Hey..." Gilman started to protest.

"Calm down Nat," Tommy said, waving Gilman back into his seat. "Calm down. I got our deal right here. I just have to go get it notarized."

"Can I hold it, please?" Gilman implored.

Tommy walked back to where Gilman was sitting and patted him on the head. "Nat, Nat, Nat," he said. "You gotta be more trusting, yo. Remember, I'm lookin' out for you. I'm the *PO-lice*!" Tommy turned, walked out of the stuffy room and into the corridor. Once out of the room, he had a uniformed officer stand guard at the door. He tore the paper towel with his signature on it into tiny pieces, walked into the nearby restroom and flushed them away. Next, he arranged for precinct detectives to get a formal confession from Gilman, including audio and videotape. Tommy handed one of the detectives a blank paper towel.

"Just wave this thing around and remind him that me and him have a deal. Tell him that what you're doing is just making it more official," he said.

"Sure," one of the detectives, a big, brawny Irishman said. "What do you want me to do with this when I'm done?" he asked, indicating the paper towel.

"When you're done getting what we need from this asshole," Tommy told him. "You can rip it up and feed it to him."

CHAPTER 8

RAMOS WALKED AROUND from behind his desk as soon as the last of the men in the suits had gone. The lieutenant spotted him, motioned for him to follow, and reentered his office. Ramos followed and shut the door behind him. While the lieutenant seated himself behind his desk, Ramos took a quick scan of his surroundings. The lieutenant's office hadn't changed much since the last time he was here. The rough brick walls had recently been painted over with several layers of the same sickly shade of green used to cover the walls of most government-owned buildings in New York City, but the same yellowed venetian blinds still barely hid the same soot-begrimed window behind them. A credit union calendar decorated one of the walls. A personal coffee maker sat on a small sideboard near the lieutenant's desk, while a sleek new computer hummed nearby. Ramos knew precious little about computers, like how they work or how to use them. He usually relied on Tommy's computer skills or those of the younger detectives whenever he needed something from one of the computers. Ramos preferred using his trusty typewriter to do paperwork, and felt that the department wasted its money and his time when they sent him to those mandatory computer classes a year ago.

On the wall behind and just over the lieutenant's head was a wide, flat, glass covered showcase holding a collection of emblems and embroidered patches from police departments all over the country. Glowering down at him from above the showcase was a large framed photograph of the current mayor; a former federal prosecutor.

"Eddie," the lieutenant said. "Have a seat."

Ramos sat down.

The lieutenant picked up a folder from among several piles of folders and papers on his desk, looked through it briefly, and placed it back in the pile. "Eddie," he said again, "clue me in on what you found over on Fifty-Third Street."

Ramos recounted the morning's events while the lieutenant listened intently, fingers laced under his chin. When he was done, Ramos couldn't help but notice again how much the lieutenant resembled ex-talk show host Phil Donohue.

"So it looks like the work of maybe one guy, huh?" the lieutenant asked.

"So far, yeah," Ramos answered. "I'm just waiting for a call from forensics..."

"You call them," the lieutenant interrupted. He stood up and sat on the edge of his desk. "We have to confirm this ASAP," he said. "Those gentlemen who were in here earlier are from the mayor's office, and you know that long before they decided to stop in here; they already had their say with the commissioner. It seems the mayor's got a whiff of this and he doesn't like the way it's starting to smell."

Ramos almost smiled, the lieutenant always did have a flair for the dramatic.

"You know the mayor's up for reelection. Needless to say, being reelected is a top priority for the mayor and he doesn't want some psycho going around killing voters' kids and messing things up for him. To make matters worse it looks like these kids might be gay or something, and you know how he was raked over the coals by the gay community and the media a couple of years ago because of how long it took to catch the, uh, 'Gay Bar Robber'—remember that?"

How could Ramos forget? It was a couple of guys in baseball caps and phony moustaches who took turns holding up bars that catered to gay men. Sometimes the customers were just robbed, a couple of times a customer was pistol-whipped. At that time everyone just assumed it was only one guy committing all the robberies and everyone agreed that he had to be stopped soon. Each succeeding robbery was becoming more violent, and everyone agreed that it would only be a matter of time before the 'Gay Bar Robber' graduated to *murder*.

They operated with seeming impunity for the better part of a year, slipping past police stakeouts, sometimes hitting the same bar twice in a week. Outraged gay activists picketed in front of city hall almost every day. Some were even arrested on disorderly conduct charges for demonstrating in front of the mayor's residence at Gracie Mansion. Newspaper columnists and television news reporters questioned whether the mayor felt the city's gay community deserved any protection at all. The police commissioner felt the heat from the mayor and, as they say, the shit rolled downhill. The higher-ups in the department found themselves being shuffled around; moved out of choice jobs they'd held for almost a decade. The brass suddenly found themselves called on the carpet and for the first time in recent memory they were being held personally accountable for the actions or inaction of the cops under their command. Chiefs were forced into retirement, captains and lieutenants were fired or demoted. The entire department was in turmoil. There was a wild hair up the mayor's ass called "public opinion," *and he was pissed*!

The consequences of this massive shake-up even affected the average cop on the street who may have suddenly found him or herself assigned to a different tour, at a different precinct, with different days off, regardless of seniority. The powerful police union cried foul and hinted at a work slow-down, but the hint was as far as they dared to go. Ramos stared at the dour image of the mayor looking down at him from above the lieutenant's head. 'Until they were caught, it was a huge mess that left the mayor's legacy tainted and a bad taste in the city's collective mouth,' he recalled ruefully. 'And now it's happening again.'

CHAPTER 9

THE LIEUTENANT STEPPED back behind his desk and sat down. The squeaking sound made by the wheels on the lieutenant's chair brought Ramos back to the present.

"The mayor's office wants this thing taken care of yesterday," Lieutenant Patrick Mullen told Ramos. "He can't afford any more negative publicity. Personally, I think he's doing a magnificent job, but I'm not the only guy voting, am I?"

"So this case is political now?" Ramos asked.

Mullen looked at him as if he'd sprouted wings from his head. "All cases are political, Eddie," he said, "don't fool yourself into thinking otherwise. It all depends on who makes the noise."

Ramos nodded, this last part he knew to be true. The lieutenant took off his glasses and wiped them with a soft pink cloth that he produced from his shirt pocket. He put them back on and then continued.

"I want you and Tommy to concentrate solely on these latest killings. The mayor's people are already talking about forming a task force that would include the Feds. Personally, I don't like the 'Fucking Bureau of Incompetents' sticking its nose in NYPD business, but if the mayor's office is already talking about it then it's safe to say it's practically a done deal."

"But why a task force, looey?" Ramos asked, using the familiar term in referring to the lieutenant. "Whenever that happens, there's so many cops and Feds running around we wind up tripping over each other, nothing gets done."

"That's bullshit and you know it, Eddie," Lieutenant Mullen said with a wave of his hand. "The part about everybody tripping over each other is true, but the part about nothing getting done is just bullshit."

Ramos opened his mouth and then shut it. He considered reminding the lieutenant that in the case of the 'Son of Sam' serial killings, a huge task force made up of several agencies, including the FBI, participated in the largest manhunt in the history of the city and turned up zilch. The killer was finally caught only after a sharp-eyed cop who was *not* part of the task force issued him a parking ticket. And the 'Beltway Sniper' out in DC and Maryland? A huge task force made up of 10,000 members of law enforcement couldn't find those guys...it turned out a truck driver was the one who spotted them and *he* called the cops.

Lieutenant Mullen gave Ramos a sidelong glance and then continued. "So you and Tommy put your other cases on the back burner for now. I want you to concentrate solely on this, and if and when the task force is formed, you two are going to coordinate the NYPD end of things."

Inwardly Ramos felt a jolt of excitement. He had guessed that he and Cucitti would at least be part of any task force investigating these murders, but as coordinators they would actually be heading the team of NYPD detectives investigating the case.

"When do you think we'll know for sure about a task force?" Ramos asked.

"Like I said," Mullen replied. "It's practically a done deal. I'm just waiting to hear from the chief of detectives. Once he calls, then you'll coordinate things with the Feds."

Ramos nodded.

The lieutenant looked at Ramos over the top of his glasses. "Uh, Eddie," he said. "You know this is going to generate a lot of heat and media attention. In fact, the mayor has already planned a press conference for this afternoon and I don't doubt that the killings and the formation of the task force are going to be the main topics of conversation. I want you and Tommy to be on the ball when it comes to the press and the TV cameras. It's best to stay under the radar, but if it turns out you have to say something, give them some information but don't give away the hen house."

Ramos nodded again. The lieutenant stood up again and hitched his pants up on his lanky frame. He separated the blinds in front of his window, looked out at the city for a moment, and then sat on the edge of his desk before addressing Ramos again.

"Before you talk to the press, be sure to clear everything through the mayor's office first," he said. "If you're questioned by the press and you don't have any cleared material to feed them, just give them a 'no comment' or tell them that you can't divulge information concerning an active investigation."

Ramos nodded. "So everything's got to be okayed by the mayor's office," he said. "Where's the commissioner while all this is going on."

Lieutenant Mullen rolled his blue eyes. "The mayor's office will okay any and everything that's going out to the public from this squad room concerning these killings, Eddie," he said. "The commissioner is in this up to his eyeballs. He'll be at the press conference too, later."

Yeah, Ramos thought. *He'll be at his favorite spot. Just within kissing distance of the mayor's ass.*

"There's a reason I'm telling you this, Eddie," the lieutenant said. "I knew Tommy's father when we were both cops over at the seven-five in East New York, and I even met Tommy's grandfather once or twice before he retired from the force. Tommy has history in the NYPD and that's the only reason he's still on the force with some of the crazy shit he's pulled over the years. He's your partner and I want you to keep an eye on him and make sure he tows the line on this one. If he fucks up while pulling some of his John Wayne shit on this case, the mayor's going to have his balls for dinner. Am I clear?"

"Crystal," Ramos answered. An image of Tommy Cucitti in his jeans, a baseball cap on backwards, talking hip-hop to a TV camera crew materialized in Ramos' mind and he grimaced inwardly.

"You've more-or-less been a calming influence on him Eddie, and he's done some really fine work partnered with you. Just keep him on an even keel and remind him to keep that smart mouth of his shut around the reporters."

"Sure thing, loo," Ramos assured the lieutenant.

"Okay Eddie," Lieutenant Mullen said as he returned to his chair and sat down. He took a sip of coffee, smacked his lips, and leaned back in his chair. "Now, how are the wife and kids?" he asked.

# # #

Tommy Cucitti absentmindedly fingered the heavy chain with its Star of David medallion that Gilman had removed from the body at the construction site. He took another bite of his salad, chewed thoughtfully awhile, then broke off a piece of the roll that came with his salad and popped that into his mouth too. Tommy was seated at a tiny table in Au Bon Pain, a place that specialized in bread and salads. Tommy really enjoyed their salads, and today he'd chosen the Caesar salad. He sat facing the large picture window at the front of the restaurant as the throngs of New York City humanity moved to and fro. Tommy watched them with the sort of detached interest peculiar to cops who can "see and not see" at the same time. He took a sip of his iced tea, whipped out his cell phone, and dialed Ramos' desk. He got the answering machine again. Tommy left a message and then dialed the detectives at the precinct in which Nathaniel Gilman was presently residing. The telephone was picked up on the third ring.

"One seven, detectives," the voice on the other end said. "Seanley speaking."

"Yo, Seanley," Tommy said cheerfully. "What's up? This is Tommy Cucitti, remember me? I brought in that guy, Nat Gilman, earlier today."

There was a pause, then, "Right. Yeah, what's going on?"

"Well, I wanted to thank you guys for taking care of Nat for me, and I want to know what you've heard from the CSU that went back to the construction site."

"Yeah, they called a little while ago and faxed over some of the info..."

"That's butter, son," Tommy said. "I wasn't sure where I was gonna be so I gave them your phone and fax numbers..."

"Yeah, that's fine," Seanley said. "So you wanna know what the CSU guys found, right?"

"That's right," Tommy answered.

"Okay, on their fax they say that what they found was a black leather wallet. It had no money in it, no credit cards. There was a nickel's worth of pot folded in some paper stuck in one of the pockets, and some ID"

"What was the ID?" Tommy asked.

"Uh, the ID consisted of information found on the little card that came with the wallet, a clinic medical card, school ID, and a social security card."

Tommy pulled out his pad and pen and wrote all of this down.

"Okay, great," he said. "Did they give you the kid's name and address from the ID information?"

"Sure," Seanley replied. "It's right here. The name on the ID is Abraham Delgado..." He gave Tommy an address in the Inwood/Washington Heights section of the city, not too far from Manhattan North Homicide headquarters. After Tommy finished scribbling all of this down, he put his pad and pen away, thanked Seanley, and pressed the off button on his cell phone. He wolfed down the rest of his lunch, grabbed his coat from the chair across from his, and ran out into the street.

CHAPTER 10

RAMOS RETURNED TO his desk and sorted through the stack of folders filed in the bottom right drawer. He pulled out a red folder and placed it on top of his desk. This folder contained information regarding several ongoing homicide investigations that Ramos and Cucitti had either been actively working on, or older cases that remained unsolved, but that they couldn't or wouldn't let go of. One or two of the most recent or most memorable ones would no doubt be parceled out to other detectives while he and Tommy were to concentrate their efforts on finding the killer or killers who had so far murdered at least three male Hispanic teens.

Suddenly, a strange, yet not unfamiliar feeling came over Ramos as he thought about the victims in this latest rash of killings...all male Hispanic teens. It was as if a dark cloud had hovered into the room and enveloped him in an icy fog. The sounds of the busy office became muted. It seemed that the usually bright fluorescent lights had somehow dimmed. Sweat beaded Ramos' brow even as a cold chill sent goose bumps tickling up his spine. There was a smell too. What was that smell? Like something burning...plastic maybe? Yes, that was it, burning plastic...

A name fell from Ramos' lips. A name he hadn't spoken in many years, one which stemmed from his childhood.

"Jay."

"Eddie!" Mike McCaughy, whose legendary patience had finally run out, startled Ramos back into the present. Ramos looked up at him uncomprehendingly for a moment before the light of recognition dawned in his eyes. He turned back to the folder in his hands, put it down gently, and wiped his damp face with a paper napkin. He noticed that his hand was trembling slightly.

"Hey Eddie," Mike said, concerned. "Are you okay, buddy?"

Ramos nodded. He'd rarely ever felt such a huge surge of raw emotion, especially over a childhood memory. *A childhood friend. Jay*, he thought again. He hadn't thought of Jay in a long time and Ramos knew in his gut what had resurrected the ghost of his childhood best friend. Someone was killing male Hispanic teens and obviously fulfilling some sort of sexual agenda in the process.

Ramos looked up. The last few years on the job had found that whenever he'd catch a case with similar victims, the long ago memories of Jay would come back to haunt him. At home he would sleep on the couch in the living room, reluctant to talk to or even touch anyone—he shied away from his family. Dinnertime with his family, usually a gregarious, boisterous affair would deteriorate into little more than monosyllabic exercises in decorum. Yes. Thank you. Please. These words became the extent of his vocabulary. During this time, some inner part of him felt that his wife, Linda, understood. Indeed, she never pressed him for information about any of the cases and even made sure that his bed on the couch was ready for him whenever he got home. He felt that the kids, feeling hurt and ignored now, would someday come to understand. He tried hard to keep his job separate from his family—but how do you do that when you're a cop?

After all the death and misery he'd dealt with through the years, he'd been surprised at just how much Jay's murder still affected him.

"Eddie, you and Tommy catch the 'Boy-Killer' case?" It was more of a statement than a question.

"Boy-Killer?" Ramos asked with a raised eyebrow. Ramos hadn't heard the case referred to by any name yet. "Is that what we're calling it?"

Mike shrugged. "I don't know for sure if anybody is calling anything, *anything*," Mike answered. "That's just what I heard mentioned."

Ramos nodded. "Well, it doesn't matter. Once the media gets a hold of it, they'll probably call it something else."

Mike nodded and walked away while Ramos poured himself another cup of coffee and sipped at the scalding liquid, holding the steaming cup with the tips of his thick fingers.

"Jay," he said again, and then pushed the thought out of his mind. He picked up the phone and called ballistics. They still hadn't finished with their tests of the slug found at the scene of the latest killing; however, they promised to fax Ramos the information as soon as it was ready.

Ramos called several of his street contacts and made it clear to them that he was interested in any information that may link these murders to a killer. Those contacts he couldn't reach by phone, he planned to visit and give them the same mission. He knew he'd be paying for this information out of his own pocket, but that's the way things worked anyway. Nowadays for the most part it was "pay for play." You gave the mutts money, and they would turn in their boyfriends, girlfriends, wives, husbands, kids...you name it.

The telephone on his desk jangled and Ramos picked it up on the first ring. It was Tommy calling.

"Yo, son," Tommy said. "I been callin' all day, where you been?"

"Meeting with the lieutenant," Ramos answered, and he gave Tommy the rundown of the meeting.

"Task force, huh," Tommy said, sounding thoughtful. "Coordinating the NYPD end, huh? That means more resources, more manpower...Damn! So when do we go on TV?" he asked excitedly.

"We?" Ramos countered. "*We* don't go on TV, or talk to the papers, if we can help it," he said. We're gonna leave that to the mayor's public information office and the other suits...you should know better, Tommy."

"Nothin' wrong with a little air time..." Tommy began.

"Don't start any of your shit, Tommy," Ramos interrupted.

"Just wanna keep the public informed, yo," Tommy

explained. "Just tryin' to be a servant of the people, know what I'm sayin'?"

Ramos rolled his eyes. "Listen Tommy," he said. "The way we're going to serve the people is by stopping the psycho who is killing these kids."

Tommy then filled Ramos in on the results of his surveillance. He finished by giving Ramos the address found in the dead boy's wallet.

"I'll meet you there, Tommy," Ramos said, already rising from his chair and reaching for his coat.

"Yeah," Tommy said enthusiastically. "I thought you'd say that."

They both hung up.

# # #

The address Tommy gave Ramos belonged to a five-floor walk-up on the corner of Sherman and Tenth Avenues, practically in the shadow of the elevated number One train. Ramos parked his car and briefly looked around. He could hear children squealing in delight as they played in a nearby schoolyard. A teacher or coach blew a whistle and the squeals turned into whoops of joy and encouragement.

An elderly couple walked past in no particular hurry, headed toward the small but bustling shopping area nearby on Broadway.

Ramos took in a breath of the crisp fall air and exhaled almost reluctantly, then he walked to where Tommy waited for him in front of the building.

Together they walked up to the front door, which was actually a locked, intricately patterned wrought iron gate. To the right of the gate was a big, stainless steel call box studded with buttons. Directly above each button was an apartment number and the corresponding name or names of the tenants. Ramos started looking for the victim's name on the call box, but Tommy interrupted him.

"Uh, it took you so long to get here I took it upon myself to look up the name," Tommy said.

"Great," Ramos said sarcastically.

“Yeah, I knew you’d appreciate it, son,” Tommy said, giving no sign that he’d noticed the sarcasm. “And you’re really gonna like this part,” he added.

“Yeah?”

“Yeah,” Tommy said. “The Delgado apartment is on the top floor.”

Ramos looked up at the building; it seemed a lot taller now. “Figures,” he said, and then he pressed the button under the name Delgado.

CHAPTER 11

"SI?" THE VOICE that came out of the call box speaker sounded distorted and tinny. "Yes?" It asked again, only in English this time.

"Hello," Ramos answered. "Mr. Delgado?"

"Yes?"

"Mr. Delgado," Ramos continued. "This is the police, sir. May we come upstairs and speak with you?"

The box was silent now. Ramos and Cucitti waited several seconds, and then Ramos leaned over and punched the button again.

"It's about Abraham," Ramos said.

There was a loud buzzing sound and the unmistakable click of an electronic latch coming undone. Ramos and Tommy pushed their way into the lobby.

The lobby was typical of the buildings in this neighborhood. Most were built just after World War II, and were designed to hold the burgeoning families of servicemen and women who had returned from the war. The floors were made of small colorful tiles set in an intricate pattern, while the steps of the two wide stairs that led from the lobby were made of thick white marble. The walls, painted a thick royal blue, contrasted almost painfully with the teal color that covered the heavy gauge steel doors of the first floor apartments. Hung high above the lobby floor, a small chandelier cast its elegant light along the walls and stairways. Other lights shone from sconces built into the walls.

"Nice place, huh?" Tommy commented.

"Yeah," Ramos agreed. "Nice."

They ascended the stairs in single file with Tommy in the lead. As they walked up, their shoes made scuffing sounds that seemed unusually loud in the quiet stairwell. At the foot of the stairs leading to the fifth floor, Ramos stopped to take a breather. They could hear music coming from one of the apartments on this floor; apparently someone had a radio tuned to a Spanish music station. Tommy looked down the hallway and noticed that the walls had been painted the same shade of royal blue as the walls on all the other floors, but the doors were a bright pumpkin orange color.

Ramos put his hand on Tommy's shoulder and gave him a squeeze. "Let's go," he said. Tommy nodded and followed. This time Ramos took the lead going up the stairs.

The walls on the fifth floor were again the same color as the others. But also as on the other floors, the doors had been painted a different color. In this case the doors had been painted a more appealing light blue.

"Sure took you a while to catch your breath after climbing those stairs, *old-timer*," Tommy remarked once they'd made it to the top of the steps.

Ramos grunted. What he had been doing was not just catching his breath, but steeling himself for what was likely to come next. He and Tommy were about to tell someone who probably had feelings for the deceased that he was dead. Not only that, they were also going to have to tell them how he died. People react differently to news of that type. Ramos had seen the full range of emotions, from people who acted as if they couldn't care less, to individuals who practically gouged their own eyes out after hearing the news that a loved one had died.

Ramos and Tommy followed the door numbers until they came to the one that had been written on the dead boy's identification. Ramos and Tommy both took a deep breath and let it out. Ramos looked at Tommy who nodded, and then he rang the bell on the door. The bell was one of those old-fashioned types where you had to really apply pressure to the button on the door to make it chime and then it would chime again as you released it. Ramos and Cucitti both noticed when a tiny circle of light shined through the aperture of the peephole, signaling that someone on the other side of the door had pulled the cover open. The tiny light disappeared as that same someone peered out through the peephole at the two detectives standing in the hallway.

"Let me see your badges." It was a man's voice, thickened with a slight Spanish accent. Ramos couldn't tell if it was the same voice that had spoken to them through the call box on the front of the building. Tommy was reminded of the part of the classic movie, *Treasure of the Sierra Madre* when the Mexican bandits tried to trick Humphrey Bogart into thinking they were *Federales* so that they could steal his gold. When Bogey asked to see their badges, the leader of the banditos replied, "Badges? Badges? We don't need no stinking badges!" Tommy almost had to suppress a nervous giggle.

Tommy saw that Ramos was holding his badge and ID out so that the man behind the door could examine it through the peephole and he did likewise. After a moment, they could hear as the cover was dropped back over the peephole and then as the door was being unlocked and opened. The man who opened the door appeared to be about forty, tall, with an olive complexion, dark wavy hair combed straight back and a carefully cropped moustache. He had a deep cleft in his chin and large brown eyes that seemed to blaze from under thick brows. He gestured for the two detectives to enter and after they did, he closed and locked the door behind them. They stood in a tiny foyer, its beige colored walls decorated with little ceramic seraphim and cherubim that seemed to caper about in half nude bliss. The man squeezed past them, motioning for them to follow, and led them into a small living room.

The living room was barely larger than the foyer, yet the apartment's occupants had been able to fit a sofa, two matching embroidered chairs, a coffee table, several lamps and a television into the space. The effect was more cozy than claustrophobic, and the mirrored panels on the wall above the sofa helped make the room seem slightly larger than it was.

Seated on the chair to their left was an attractive woman who may or may not have been the same age as the man who had opened the door for them. She wore a simple flowered dress and what Ramos' wife would call 'sensible shoes'. A hair brace that matched her dress held back tresses of light brown that, while not as wavy as the hair of the man who'd let them in, was still wavy enough to shade her ears in long, casual loops. The woman didn't look at them and instead seemed to be busy trying to pluck something from the arm of her chair. The two detectives were made to share the vinyl-covered sofa while the man sat in the other chair.

"My name is Henri Delgado," the man who'd let them in said in his accented voice. He pronounced his first name On-ree, like the French do. He motioned toward the woman, "And that is my wife, Esther Delgado," he said. "We are Abraham's parents."

Before either of the detectives could introduce themselves, the woman spoke up; whatever she'd been plucking away at forgotten.

"Is Abraham okay? Is my baby okay?

Ramos and Cucitti turned toward Mrs. Delgado, and Ramos was the first to place her accent—it was Yiddish.

Now that they had opportunity to see Mrs. Delgado more clearly, they could see that she was a genuinely beautiful woman. Her eyes were the same shade of brown as her hair, with the same glints of gold shining there. Her face, devoid of make-up, was gently chiseled in the way of many Eastern European women and held an aristocratic, almost defiant, manner. Ramos guessed that maybe her husband had asked her not to say anything, but being a mother, she wanted to know above all if her baby was okay.

"Esther, please..." Henri started.

"No Henri," she said softly. "First I must know that Abie is fine." She pronounced 'Abie' so that it rhymed with baby.

Ramos looked into her eyes. He could see strength there, of that he was sure, but in the tiny lines at their corners and in the ones that ran from the corners of her mouth, he saw that there was worry there too.

Ramos turned toward the father, Henri. "Maybe we can talk alone first..." he started to say.

"No," Mrs. Delgado said. "There will not be division in our home. If your visit concerns Abraham, we are both Abraham's parents and you will address us both."

"Alright," he said. "Sorry about that."

Esther Delgado nodded. Her eyes never left the two detectives.

Ramos pulled out his notepad and pen, flipped it open and sat there with the pen poised to write. "Mr. and Mrs. Delgado," he said. "Do you know where Abraham was last night...who he may have been with?"

Mrs. Delgado said nothing, but her husband shifted in his chair. His elbows rested on his knees while his large hands dangled between them.

"Abraham liked to go out to parties and dances," Henri finally said with a sigh. "We know that he's too young to stay out so late, and that maybe from time to time he has gone to clubs where people are drinking, but he's such a good boy that we felt we shouldn't perhaps keep him from his little pleasure."

"And that 'pleasure' was...? Ramos probed.

"Dancing," Henri said simply. "Abraham was a very gifted dancer and an excellent student at school..."

"My Abie never brought home less than all A's on his report card," Mrs. Delgado added from across the room.

"That's right, that's right," the father agreed. He stood up and went over to a little series of shelves in one of the corners of the room and came back with a folded sheet of thin, white cardboard. He handed this to Ramos who took it and noticed the fancy coat-of-arms symbol on the front. Ramos recognized it as the logo of a private school that he passed from time to time on his way to and from work. It was a report card. When Ramos looked inside he saw that Abraham had indeed gotten all A's.

Mr. Delgado stood in front of Ramos and Tommy with a smile on his face that was equal parts pride and hope. Ramos handed the report card back to him.

"Very nice, Mr. Delgado," Ramos said. "Do you have any recent photographs of Abraham that I could see?"

"Sure, yes," Mr. Delgado said, and he jogged from the living room. He was back in a few moments with several school photographs. “See, this one here?” He said to Ramos, pointing at one of the photos. “This is the most recent one.”

Ramos and Tommy Cucitti both examined the photographs. The pictures were of a smiling adolescent, handsome and innocent looking. In one photo he wore a graduation cap and gown, and he held what Ramos supposed was a prop diploma. In the other photos, he was dressed in a school uniform. Ramos looked at Tommy who gave a little nod and handed the photos back to him. Ramos took another look at the school uniform photos before he handed them back to Mr. Delgado. It was the same boy alright.

Henri looked down at the report card and photographs in his hand, back at the detectives, and then at his wife. He dropped them carefully onto the coffee table with the air of a man who’d dealt his best hand and had gotten trumped anyway. “Abraham is a good boy,” he said returning to his seat. “If he’s in any trouble, I am sure it was probably some older boy...”

“Or a girl,” Mrs. Delgado interjected.

“That’s right! That’s right, or a girl who has caused it,” Mr. Delgado finished. “These girls nowadays are very fresh, they were always calling him. Abraham never disrespected me or his mother. He is a good boy—not like these girls...”

“My Abie is a good boy,” the mother echoed.

“No doubt,” Tommy said softly. “But we have some...”

“Yes, that’s right, there is no doubt,” Mrs. Delgado said.

Tommy sighed. “Do you know where he went last night and whether or not he met anybody—like maybe one of those girls you mentioned?”

Mr. Delgado shook his head. “No, no. Abraham did as usual. He came home from school, finished his homework, and then went out.”

“Didn’t you worry about him being out all night?” Tommy’s question came out harsh, and the father’s face registered first surprise, and then indignation. Henri Delgado rose from his chair and paced around the tiny room, but before he could say anything his wife answered Tommy’s question.

“Of course we worry,” she said emphatically, her dainty hands clasped to her bosom. “Abie is our only child and the doctors have told us that we can never have another. Whenever

Abie leaves our sight we worry about him. My God, I am his mother." A single tear coursed a path down her flawless cheek. "Abie and Henri are the only family I have...Her voice broke as she made her last statement, but her proud bearing did not diminish.

She seemed, thought Ramos, *like a woman who had been through some tough times. Such tough times, in fact, that she'd grown a steel rod for a spine and she was determined not to have anyone bend it for her. Not the cops. Not anybody.*

"Abraham is a special boy, a special son," Esther Delgado continued. "The only legacy of our love, and our hopes and dreams. Yes, yes of course we worry about Abie—but we love him too. He has never disappointed us. He has never hurt us. Even though we never seem to have the money to buy him those little things that the young people seem to treasure so, we give him the one thing we can...his freedom. Yet every time he leaves our home, his father and I fall to our knees and pray that the Lord guide him back to us safely." She stood up then, and the detectives were a little surprised to see how petite she was. "If anyone is wrong here, then of course it is we, his parents who are to blame. We were too weak and too enthralled with our son to deny him his pleasure of dance and laughter..." She stopped and smoothed down the front of her dress. "So punish us if you will, but please tell me where my son is and if he is okay."

Ramos looked down at his shoes. His face felt hot with shame. He'd wanted to get some information before he told these people that their son was dead, and now the path that the conversation had taken was going to make the telling all the more difficult. The dead boy was their only son, a straight-A student who was doted on by his loving parents. That the parents had no idea of their son's extracurricular activities was obvious. Now their shock, their grief, their pain will be doubled. *Not only was their son dead,* thought Ramos, *but the kid probably died with the taste of cock in his mouth.*

Ramos stood up, snapped his notepad shut and, along with the pen, stuck it into a coat pocket. After a moment, Tommy also stood and carefully positioned himself near Mrs. Delgado. Ramos looked up into Mr. Delgado's deep-set eyes, took a deep breath and let it out slowly.

"Mr. and Mrs. Delgado," he began. "Please accept my condolences..." Ramos heard a gasp come from the mother's direction, but he refused to turn in her direction and forced himself to concentrate on the father's eyes. Eyes that widened at his words, but never wavered. "Early this morning, about 5:00 a.m., a boy fitting your son's description and carrying a wallet with his identification in it was found dead at a construction site on the corner of Fifty-Third Street and Lexington Avenue. He had been shot. I'm sorry."

Now Ramos broke eye contact with the father and glanced toward Tommy and Mrs. Delgado. Both parents stood frozen. Like the statues of persons captured and sculpted at exactly the moment their hearts were broken. Pain and disbelief etched in their faces, their mouths open in shock or dismay.

"Abraham? Abie, dead?" Mr. Delgado's voice. Soft and mellifluous. Incredulous and fearful. Then a howl rose from behind Ramos that raised the hair on the back of his neck. It was a sound so mournful, so filled with torture, that it would wind its way into Ramos' nightmares for years to come. He turned again in time to see Tommy try to console Mrs. Delgado. He spoke to her in soothing tones and tried to put his arm around her shoulders, but she shrugged him off shaking her head like an injured animal. Then she raised her tear-streaked face toward an invisible God and a long, wailing cry issued from her delicate throat. That ululating cry ended in a scream as she grabbed at her hair, then at her eyes. Tommy tried to hold her but she fought him and he fell, sprawled over the coffee table, spilling photographs of a smiling boy, and a report card filled with As.

Henri Delgado pushed past Ramos and took hold of his wife in his long, sinewy arms. He pinned her arms to her sides as she fought him too, punching, kicking, and biting...still, he held her close. She screamed again and again, rocking her head back and forth, unable to move her arms. Her hair brace shook loose and fell to the floor, where it bounced once before disappearing under the couch. Tommy got up with a little help from Ramos, and together they stood there feeling awkward and intrusive.

"Uh, would you like us to call a relative, or someone else close Mr. Delgado?" Tommy asked softly. "There should probably be someone..."

Henri Delgado turned his face toward the two detectives and they could see that his face was wet with tears as well. He pointed at a tiny end table with his chin. "There," he said, his voice wavering. "There in the drawer is a phone book. Please call my sister and ask her to come. Uh, her name...her name..." Mr. Delgado's face seemed to cave in on itself as he was overcome. He buried his face in his wife's hair and Ramos and Tommy could see his long body heave with sobs.

"Check the drawer," Ramos whispered to Cucitti. Tommy nodded, went to the table and returned a moment later with a colorful, clothbound personal phone book.

"Mr. Delgado," Ramos said. "What's your sister's name in the phone book? Mr. Delgado?"

Henri Delgado looked up, slightly more composed. "M-my sister's name is Yvette Moreno," he said. A huge sob shook his body and he covered his eyes with his hand. Tommy looked through the phone book as Ramos approached the lamenting couple.

"Mr. Delgado," Ramos said softly, but firmly. "I need to talk with you please. Mr. Delgado, it's important."

Henri Delgado looked down at Ramos with red, shiny eyes. He looked at his wife who now cried silently in his arms. Tenderly, he kissed the back of her neck and then her hair as he let her go. She didn't seem to have the strength to stand so he lowered her into the chair she'd occupied only a few minutes ago. Mrs. Delgado hugged her elbows and rocked back and forth in the chair. She was saying something over and over, but Ramos couldn't make out any of the words. Tears continued to course down her cheeks.

Mr. Delgado knelt in front of her and took her hands in his. He kissed them and then pressed them onto his own tear-stained face.

Ramos bent so that he could speak into the stricken man's ear. "Mr. Delgado," he said. "Please sir, may I speak with you? This way?"

Ramos gently took him under the arm and helped him to his feet. Slowly, his wife's hands fell from his and onto her lap. Mr. Delgado rose and followed Ramos to the other end of the room like a man in a daze.

"I got the number," Tommy whispered to Ramos as they neared him. "I called the sister and she said she was coming right over."

Ramos nodded, and patted Tommy's shoulder. "Mr. Delgado," he said in a low voice. "They're going to need you to go down to the morgue and identify your son's body."

At the mention of his son, a low moan escaped Henri Delgado's lips and his knees started to give way. Ramos grabbed him and shored him up.

"No, no!" Ramos whispered firmly. "Henri, you have to be strong for your wife. Henri!"

Delgado looked at Ramos through eyes swollen from crying and nodded his head.

"Okay man? Okay?" Ramos asked.

Again, Henri Delgado nodded and forced himself to stand more rigidly.

"Okay. Okay. Good man," Ramos said. "My partner, Tommy, already got in contact with your sister and she's on her way. Is there anybody on your wife's side of the family we should call?"

Delgado shook his head and wiped his face with the back of his hand. Ramos looked around for a box of tissue but didn't see any. Delgado straightened himself up a little more and smoothed back his hair with one hand. He pinched the bridge of his nose hard with the thumb and forefinger of the same hand and then shook his head again.

When he spoke, his voice was almost normal. "Uh, my wife... my wife..." Although his voice sounded almost normal, Ramos could see and hear that he still struggled to compose himself. "My wife," he finally managed, "is Orthodox. Jewish."

Ramos nodded, the accent.

"Her family is very religious, her father is a Rabbi," Henri Delgado continued.

Henri Delgado reached into his pants back pocket and pulled out a clean, white handkerchief. He dabbed at his eyes a moment, then turned and blew his nose loudly. "Excuse me," he said. "Every good day, every happy occasion, every single day of our lives together have been marred by the knowledge that my beloved Esther can never share our love and lives with her family and so never truly be happy. And now you tell me that our only son is dead." Delgado looked over at his wife and she looked at him through sad, red eyes. He seemed to gather new strength from her, and Ramos could see his shoulders straighten.

"Very well officer," Henri Delgado said. "I am ready to accompany you to the morgue."

CHAPTER 12

BOTH OF THE Delgados went to the morgue and identified the dead boy as their son, Abraham. Ramos and Tommy comforted them as much as they could, but had to leave when Tommy received a call from Lieutenant Mullen summoning them to headquarters. Despite his protests, Ramos pressed cab fare into Henri Delgado's hand and then he and Tommy Cucitti left the remnants of the Delgado family to deal with their grief.

Ramos drove in silence as Cucitti stared out the passenger side window.

"Want me to come back and talk to them later? You know, get their statements?" Tommy asked.

Ramos shrugged. "We'll work it out when we get to that point," he said. "For now, we'll just let them mourn. They deserve at least that."

Tommy nodded in silent agreement.

At Manhattan North Homicide headquarters, the lieutenant called them both into his office to debrief them on the rest of the day's events. Then he updated them on the progress of the proposed task force.

When they returned to their desks, Ramos offered a cup of his coffee to Tommy, who declined. Ramos poured himself another cup, sipped, and reached for cigarettes that weren't there. Tommy meanwhile helped himself to a cup of coffee from the squad's communal coffeepot. The phone on Ramos' desk rang. It was an old-fashioned jarring ring, the kind that told you something important was happening on the other end.

The squad room had only recently shed most of the old-fashioned heavy-duty phones, in basic black of course, that had been department standard for over fifty years. Budget restraints had not allowed all of the telephones to be replaced at once and Ramos opted to still have one of these old workhorses on his desk. The receiver alone weighed more than most of the new phones that had since been installed throughout the department.

"It's Johannesen from Ballistics," Ramos informed Cucitti after putting the phone to his ear. Tommy leaned forward. After several "uh-huhs" and "okays," Ramos hung up the telephone. "Johannesen says he got a match on the bullet from the latest victim and the one from the first," Ramos said. "The bullet from the second killing was too damaged for a match-up, though Johannesen says that he'd swear the calibers are identical."

"The caliber being?" Tommy asked.

"That's the funny thing Tommy," Ramos said. "Johannesen says he'd never seen a bullet like this, he's still trying to track it down."

Cucitti nodded, confident in Johannesen's ability to solve the bullet mystery.

Ramos and Tommy spent the rest of the morning and part of the afternoon consolidating the information from what was once three separate cases of homicide into one coherent file. They worked up profile comparisons on the victims in order to list their commonalities—what was it that attracted the killer to them specifically?

Each of the victims was male, between the ages of sixteen and nineteen years old, and each was Hispanic. All were roughly the same height and weight, with dark hair and eyes. There was almost no facial hair, and all were dressed in the current Hip-Hop/Rap fashion (this last fact was confirmed by Tommy). The first two victims were originally from the Dominican Republic, having immigrated to the States within the last seven years. All of the boys lived with their parents, the two were dropouts, and all had been arrested or had received summonses for minor offenses such as urinating in public, loitering, fare-evasion, etc.

Nothing earth-shattering. Abraham Delgado, the latest victim, was the only one so far who was born in the same city he died in—New York.

Ramos scrutinized the list in front of him. All three victims had traces of semen in their mouths (they were still awaiting confirmation from the lab on whether samples of the semen collected were viable enough to get a DNA trace on. Ramos and Tommy didn't hold out much hope). Another aspect to consider was how the semen got there in the first place. Had each of the victims voluntarily performed oral sex on someone; the killer most likely, before being killed? The parents of the victims all vehemently denied that their sons could have been homosexual. So, could they have been forced to perform fellatio on their killer before he murdered them?

Ramos shuffled some of the papers around until he found what he was looking for. All of the victims had been summonsed numerous times for loitering at odd hours of the night. Loitering. Ramos scratched his chin. Often, street cops who didn't want to bother making prostitution arrests issued loitering summonses as a way of hassling hookers without all the paperwork of an arrest. Loitering was often street cop lingo for prostitution. Ramos reshuffled the papers and put them back into their original order. He opened his desk's top drawer and took out a mint, which he popped into his mouth. *These boys were hookers,* Ramos thought with conviction. *They were selling themselves for drug money, or whatever, and now one of their customers had turned on them. Boy prostitutes were referred to as chickens. The men who paid for their services were called Chickenhawks.* He was about to tell Tommy of his conclusions when the telephone rang.

They found another body.

CHAPTER 13

THEY DROVE THROUGH the Midtown tunnel into Long Island City, Queens, while Tommy peppered Ramos with questions.

"So, what makes em' think this murder is related to our other three?"

"Dead youth, male Hispanic, shot in the mouth," Ramos replied.

They drove on in silence as Ramos turned south on Vernon Boulevard and Sixty-First Street, going wide to avoid knocking over a work crew's fluorescent orange cones. This part of Queens was a brick-heavy, smog-stained mix of industry and residence. Warehouses shared crowded and oil-blackened sidewalks with one- and two-family homes. The last flies of the bygone summer beat the vestiges of their lives out against the smudged windows of the occasional pizzeria or Chinese takeout, and the dried husks of their fallen comrades on the sills were mute testimony to the futility of their efforts.

Ramos parked at the entrance of the Twenty-First Street subway station. Two large banks anchored opposite corners here and Ramos could see where they'd apparently renovated certain parts of the immediate area. Security cameras and high intensity lamps were discreetly placed in strategic locations around the banks. Two of the lamps and a camera pointed directly at the subway entrance. Ramos pointed the camera out to Tommy.

"Find out which bank owns that camera and see if we can get a tape—see if they have em' going back a couple of weeks," he said.

Tommy nodded and moved off as Ramos descended the subway's concrete steps. He noticed that they also appeared newly redone. A detective with the NYPD's Transit Bureau stood on the mezzanine level talking into a telephone attached to the token booth. The detective glanced at the gold shield on Ramos' coat, hung up the phone, and stuck his hand out. Ramos took it.

"Darrell McCall," the detective introduced himself amiably.

"Eddie Ramos."

Their hands separated. Detective McCall nodded toward the turnstiles and led the way as Ramos fell into step.

The agent in the booth buzzed them through one of the turnstiles and they walked down a flight of steel and cement stairs to the dreary platform. The vertical iron beams that supported the ceiling had all been painted violet and seemed garishly out of place.

Detective McCall led Ramos to the south-end of the northbound side of the platform where a controlled sense of disorder signaled a typical crime scene. A young uniformed police officer lifted the yellow barrier tape when the detectives stooped to go under it and Ramos nodded his thanks; following McCall to the very end of the platform where the catwalk began.

The catwalk was a narrow wood and iron walkway that led into the tunnel. It had once been painted bright yellow, but years of grime and steel dust made the yellow color all but invisible. McCall snapped on a pair of latex gloves, pushed open the waist-high swing gate that guarded the beginning of the catwalk, and held it open for Ramos. Ramos went through with an appreciative grunt, he hated having to touch that filthy gate.

Almost immediately beyond the gate (a dirty white sign warned that "No Unauthorized Personnel" was allowed past this point) another uniformed cop was stationed in order to guard what appeared to be a large irregular patch of black against the lesser black of the catwalk and tunnel wall.

Detective McCall flicked on a flashlight and pointed its light at the darker areas.

"This is where the victim was killed," McCall noted matter-of-factly. "CSU figures that those black patches on the floor and wall are blood, but we'll have to wait for the lab results to make it official."

Ramos nodded.

McCall pointed the beam a little further along the catwalk. Ramos noticed that the interminable dust and dirt had been recently disturbed here, and so more of the catwalk's yellow paint was visible.

"The perp dragged the victim deeper into the tunnel, scraping away some of the dust. We were hoping that we'd be able to get some decent footprints at least, you know; because of the dust, but that didn't happen."

"Why not?" Ramos asked.

"Unfortunately the Transit employees who found the body, a crew of track workers specifically, stomped all over the place here..."

Ramos nodded in understanding and followed closely as Detective McCall led him deeper into the tunnel.

They walked on for approximately another twenty feet, stepping aside twice to let an officer going in the opposite direction get by. Ramos winced each time his coat brushed against the tunnel wall. They reached the end of the catwalk and gingerly stepped down four rusting waffle iron stairs to the actual roadbed. Ten or so yards ahead of them Ramos saw an area awash in the blindingly bright light of several large halogen lamps. As they neared the light's glow, Ramos could smell diesel fuel and hear the whirring chug of a generator. He eyed the nearby third-rail suspiciously. Detective McCall noticed his discomfort.

"Power's off," he said, placing one foot on the rail. "These things usually carry 600 volts of electricity in 'em, but we had 'em shut off so we could work in safety—so don't worry man, you won't see any trains coming through here anytime soon." McCall took his foot off the rail and led Ramos to a door-sized depression in the tunnel wall. "Man, I know there's got to be some pissed off commuters on this line right now," McCall chuckled.

Ramos smiled.

"The ME already gave us the go ahead with this body, but we got a call from the DA's office saying you guys from Manhattan North were on your way and that we should let it lay a little longer 'til you got a look at it."

Ramos didn't sense any resentment on the detective's part and he was grateful. Too often, when he or any of his colleagues from Manhattan North Homicide were called in to investigate a homicide, the officers and detectives from the local precinct felt they were being deprived of the opportunity to investigate a high profile case. They groused about the brass not trusting in the abilities of the precinct detectives to handle an investigation and they accused Manhattan North Homicide of grandstanding. Ramos, Tommy Cucitti, and the other detectives of Manhattan North had for the most part gotten used to it.

Ramos looked at the ruined remains of what had once been a living adolescent male. The victim's head was thrown back, mouth wide open and encrusted with dried blood. Blood and dirt made it impossible to tell what the original color of his shirt had been, but Ramos saw that he was wearing a pair of oversized military-style "camouflage" pants and once-white sneakers that may have been new. The victim was also wearing enough gold jewelry around his neck and on his fingers to pay off the debts of a small country.

That certainly rules out a robbery motive, Ramos thought.

The body was wedged into the door-shaped depression detective McCall had led Ramos to. A closer inspection revealed that the body appeared to be partially mummified, and portions of the lips, eyelids, and earlobes were missing.

"Yeah, he's dried out alright," Detective McCall confirmed when Ramos inquired about the corpse's condition. "We're lucky that the weather's been so cool lately, without much rain, or else this puppy would have sprouted mushrooms by now. As far as the missing bits and pieces..." McCall gave an emphatic shrug. "Rats," he said.

As McCall led Ramos back out of the tunnel, they came to the area guarded by the solitary uniformed officer, the place where the murder was thought to have actually occurred before the perpetrator moved the body. McCall stopped so abruptly that Ramos collided into him.

"Oh," McCall said nonchalantly as he pointed the beam of his flashlight at the wall near the uniformed cop's head. "I figured I'd save the best for last..."

Ramos stared at the spot on the wall that McCall had spotlighted—a palm print! There it was, clear as day. Ramos fought the urge to pump a fist into the air and instead let his breath hiss through his clenched teeth. He approached the wall carefully, getting as close as possible. He held his breath, then exhaled slowly, afraid he might disturb even a single mote of dust. He stared at what was clearly the relatively recent imprint of a human hand in the decades-old dirt and grime of the tunnel wall. He wanted to remember it, memorize it, and sear it into his brain.

"He must have lost his balance or something and used the wall to steady himself," McCall conjectured. "I guess he figured nobody would see it in the dark, or maybe he was in a hurry. We've already taken palm-print samples from all the workers who'd been down here recently," McCall continued, drawing up next to Ramos and the print. "But I doubt if any of them will match up with this bad boy here." McCall indicated the print with a quick shake of his light.

Ramos looked at him. "How do you figure?" He asked.

"Because," McCall replied, holding up his hands. "Everyone else down here wears gloves."

CHAPTER 14

By the time Ramos exited the subway station, Tommy was leaning on the car waiting for him. Ramos could hear the vestiges of a rap beat fade away as Cucitti quickly lowered the volume on the car stereo.

"How come you didn't come down?" Ramos asked as he took up the spot next to Tommy. He reached into his breast pocket and rummaged around with his thick fingers. "Damn," he muttered when he remembered he'd given up smoking.

"I figured you had that covered, know what I'm sayin'? Besides, I'm just now getting back myself," Tommy answered.

Ramos took a deep breath. "It looks like our guy's work alright," he said.

"So this makes number four, huh?"

"Well, this kid makes it four numerically speaking," Ramos confirmed. "We'll have to wait until it's confirmed by the ME, but I think this kid was actually the first—*numero uno*."

Tommy nodded. "So you figure this is where the killer lost his cherry, huh?" He said. "This is where he went from ordinary, everyday asshole to murderer. I wonder what set him off?"

"Don't know," Ramos answered. "But it looks like that body's been down there a long time. Not just that, but the perp took a big chance on getting caught, being hit by a train, even getting electrocuted by the goddamn third rail. He dragged the body around in a dark tunnel and tried to hide it."

"Definitely a different scenario from the other killings where he just left the bodies where they fell," Tommy murmured.

"For all we know there may be other bodies," Ramos continued. "But I honestly believe this one is the first. This is where it all started."

CHAPTER 15

RAMOS TURNED TOWARD Tommy. "So what did the banks have to say?"

"Both banks have all of their cameras around here on a continuous twelve-hour digital loop," Tommy answered. "The banks don't hold onto the images. Every twelve hours the images are dumped into a central security file in a server at the bank's headquarters. Nobody looks at or accesses them unless they're requested by law enforcement or one of the bank's officers. Basically they just sit there forever unless somebody says something."

"Damn," Ramos muttered. "Then what good is it having these cameras all over the god dammed place?"

"I asked them the same thing," Cucitti said. "One of the managers told me they were having trouble with some of the local lowlifes harassing and mugging their night workers. A female employee at one of the banks working the 4:00 p.m. to midnight shift was robbed, beaten, and almost raped at the entrance to the subway here." Tommy motioned toward the subway entrance from which Ramos had just emerged.

"Why am I not fuckin' surprised," Ramos growled, taking a quick survey of the rundown neighborhood beyond the oasis created by the two banks.

Tommy nodded. "Anyway," he continued. "The banks got together and had a couple of sit-downs with some of the big heads from the Transit Authority. They worked out a deal where the banks provide security and cleaning services at this particular subway entrance if Transit agrees to keep the booth open longer to accommodate the bank's night shift employees."

"Does the security arrangement include any square-badges, or just the cameras and lights?" Ramos asked.

"At night each bank has one guard who watches the monitors from inside the bank. During the day, nobody bothers."

"Some security," Ramos observed dryly.

"Yeah well, they say they haven't had a problem since all the lights and stuff been installed," Tommy said.

"We gotta talk to the guards who were on duty around the time this kid got himself killed," Ramos said.

"Way ahead of you my brother," Tommy drawled, pulling a small tattered notepad from his pocket. "I have their names and addresses right here. It wasn't hard since the banks say these are the only guards they've had working the night shift since the program began."

Ramos nodded. "Let's go," he said, climbing into the driver's seat.

The home of the first security guard they visited, Malik Moore, was a one-bedroom apartment in a building complex in Rochdale, Queens. The complex consisted of a neatly kept group of apartment buildings sprawled over several acres of manicured grounds. Fall blooms like Asters and Mums bordered the paths that meandered between the tall buildings. Several "community" gardens boasted soon to be harvested crops of squash, pumpkins, beans, and "late" melons.

Mr. Moore was a twenty-four-year-old African American male recently certified by the state as a security guard (or as the cops sometimes referred to them, a "square-badge").

Mr. Moore had nothing new to add to the investigation.

The next stop was a tidy semi-detached house in Richmond Hill. Wrapped in light blue vinyl siding, *ugly color for a house,* thought Cucitti, topped by a slate gray roof. Black wrought iron bars covered all of the first floor windows and the front door.

The security guard who lived here, Mr. Giasuddin Ghiraj, had nothing to offer the two detectives as well.

CHAPTER 16

THEODORE "PAKI" PAKIDORAPOPULOS showed up for work the next day as usual. He was a columnist for a popular New York City based magazine. His columns, witty, thought-provoking, insightful, and often controversial, were based on his personal experiences and opinions. The son of hard-working Greek immigrants, his parents were skeptical at first of his decision to become a writer, but eventually accepted his writing as being a "real" job and even looked forward to reading his published articles and essays. His mother dutifully cut out each one and lovingly pasted them into a huge scrapbook dedicated to the accomplishments of her only child. An essay he'd sold to a Greek daily was framed and hung proudly over the television set in the living room where everyone would see it.

Paki entered his office, closed the door, and hung his overcoat on the brass coat rack in the corner. His assistant, who wasn't at her desk outside his office when he first came in, soon appeared at the door carrying several manila envelopes and a sheaf of papers. As she struggled with the doorknob, Paki waved to get her attention. When she looked up, he lifted his coffee mug and pointed to it. She looked at the mug, then at him, and rolled her eyes. She turned around, dumped the envelopes and papers onto her desk and walked off.

Paki smiled as he lowered himself into his chair. He liked his job. A lot. He jiggled his computer's mouse and watched as the screensaver on the monitor melted away. He leaned forward slightly and read through the last paragraph of the column he was working on.

He'd just started typing when Lorna, his assistant, came in bearing the bundle she had earlier under one visibly strained arm. In her other hand she carried a steaming pot of coffee. Paki watched the hot, black liquid slosh around inside the glass pot as Lorna positioned it over his mug and poured the coffee. When she finished, he took a sip and smacked his lips in an exaggerated show of approval.

"Thank you Lorna," he said setting the mug down. "I needed that."

"You're welcome Mr. Pakidorapopulos," she said. "I've brought you your mail and the hard copies of that reference material you wanted..."

"Good, good," Paki nodded as he took another sip of coffee.

"There are a couple of memos that you should look at too, I put those on top," Lorna continued.

"Thanks Lorna," Paki said fingering the pile.

"I'm getting ready to type up a requisition form for office supplies," Lorna said as she walked to the door. "Anything specific that you need or want?" she asked as she paused at the door.

Paki thought a moment. "No, just the usual stuff," he said. Lorna nodded and left the office, closing the door softly behind her.

Paki took another sip of coffee and turned again to his work at the computer. He added several paragraphs of opinion to his column, then edited his work by deleting a word or sentence here, maybe adding a word or punctuation there...

Suddenly he doubled over in pain, slamming the palm of his hand on top of the desk and spilling what was left of his coffee.

A succession of cramps spasmed through his abdomen, clutching and pulling at his entrails like a madman's dull knife. Then as the pain subsided, nausea coiled in its place like black, oily smoke, its tendrils curling and twisting up to his chest and throat. A cough sought exit and when Paki opened his mouth, a gagging, retching sound escaped instead. Soon his entire body was in revolt. An incredible amount of pressure seemed to suddenly build up in his intestines and he half-staggered, half-ran into his office bathroom. He'd barely lowered himself onto the toilet and stuck his face into the sink before his body emptied itself from both ends at once.

Long after he'd been purged, he still sat there, his chin resting on the edge of the befouled sink. Sweat dripped from his face, matted his hair to his head, and slowly diluted the mess in the sink.

Paki had never felt so ill in his life...*and he knew what it was.* He'd gone to his doctor when the symptoms first manifested themselves, and like a naïve fool he believed Doctor Posposil when the old quack told him he was probably coming down with the flu.

He lifted his head and placed it in his hands, his elbows on his knees. He let out a sigh that ended in a sob. He shook his head from side to side. Drool leaked in a thin line from his mouth and spattered onto his leg.

Paki knew perfectly well what was wrong with him. He watched the news and read the papers. He even heard people talk...after all, he was an educated man. He'd dreaded it all along, really...ever since he'd first heard of it and knew it preyed upon those whose overt and secret desires mirrored his own.

The signs were all there, and what's more he knew precisely how he got it. It. Even now he was afraid to call it by name, or more accurately by the euphemistic acronym popularized by the mindless media and the equally brainless throng...four letters of the alphabet, four marks of a pencil on paper, four strikes on a keyboard...AIDS There, he'd said it. Or thought it at least. Whatever. Auto Immune Deficiency Syndrome. Ten syllables. A pronouncement of death. He almost smiled when he thought how the word used to mean "to assist, to help." Now the word that wasn't a word heralded his impending destruction—a slow, agonizing, humiliating demise. Humiliating especially because then everyone would find him out, find out what he'd been doing on all those nights he claimed to be working late. All those supposed trips out of town to do research or attend seminars. His parents would find out. His relatives. Co-workers. Friends. The children. His wife...They would all think he was some sort of sexual deviant. A queer. They wouldn't understand.

He hated that his wife couldn't possibly understand his sexual needs and that she wouldn't—couldn't. Didn't. Satisfy him.

He hated being sick.

He hated knowing there was no cure.

He hated knowing he was going to die.

Most of all he hated those little bastards who made him sick.

Paki sat up and used his hand to roughly wipe the tears from his face. He knew what he had to do.

Paki emerged from the bathroom a few minutes later, having cleaned it, and himself up as best he could. He felt weak, wrung out and feverish, symptoms no doubt of his accursed illness.

He was surprised to find he had company.

"Whoa, you look like shit," Silverman said with what sounded like genuine concern. "Are you alright?"

Paki picked his next words carefully. "I'm fine," he said. "Just a little stomach trouble. Must be something I ate."

Silverman peered at him through thick wire-rimmed glasses. Ordinarily, Paki found Silverman's owlish features and rodent-like inquisitiveness comical. Right now, however, he could have killed him.

Herman Silverman was chief editor of the magazine Paki was employed by. He also considered himself Paki's friend.

"Paki, you've been looking kind of run-down all week. Are you positive that you're okay?"

"Yes, yes—I told you that I must have gotten hold of some bad takeout or something, I'm fine."

"I don't know," Silverman said. "You're really pale and I think you're getting dark circles..." Silverman reached a finger toward one of Paki's eyes.

"Don't touch me!" Paki snarled.

Silverman drew his hand back as if it had been singed by an open flame. For a moment, Paki thought he recognized a new element enter Silverman's questioning gaze: *fear*.

"I...I'm sorry," Silverman stammered. "I was only...well, never mind. You're obviously not well and it's perfectly understandable if you're feeling grumpy or out of sorts right now."

"My sister hasn't been feeling at all well herself lately," Silverman continued. "There's this really awful flu bug going around. She's been laid up flat on her back for close to a week already. They say it could even bring on pneumonia. You know Paki that could be what you..."

"The flu?"

"Well, yes I..."

"I'm all right," Paki said evenly. "I'll be all right too, you'll see."

Silverman nodded, speechless. For the first time since he'd met Theodore Pakidorapopulos, he felt an inexplicable yet tangible fear of the man.

"Yes, of course," he said. "Of course you're going to be all right."

Paki nodded and coughed some more. He pulled out a handkerchief, then wiped his mouth and blew his nose before putting it away again. Silverman moved to Paki's desk and fingered the hard copy of Paki's latest work. He felt better now with a little extra distance between himself and his favorite columnist.

Silverman looked up and wrinkled his nose, he'd just become aware of a faint odor seeping into the room from Paki's direction, probably from the lavatory right behind him. It was a smell that reminded Silverman of his visits with his mother in the nursing home. It was a smell he subconsciously associated with frantic, midnight runs to hospital emergency rooms, and strangely it was a smell that reminded him of the darkest corners of the subway. The smell, Silverman recognized, was a combination of shit, vomit, and disinfectant. Suddenly Silverman wanted desperately to leave. He took the papers he was looking through and edged toward the door. Paki's eyes never left him.

"Uh, Paki," he began, waving the papers in the air. "I've got your column right here and it's great as usual."

Paki nodded.

"P-Paki," he said, annoyed and chagrinned by the unexpected stammer. "Y-you don't look good at all, you're sick." Silverman tried to smile reassuringly but the result was more of a grimace. "You probably do have some sort of bug and, while I laud your loyalty and dedication, it's probably not a good idea to go around infecting everyone else." Silverman tried to add a humorous lilt to the last three words, but his voice cracked instead. "You, uh, know the people around here," he said with a nervous chuckle. "Any excuse to get out of work..."

Silverman kept talking, but Paki had ceased hearing. *Infecting everyone else*, he thought. *Infecting everyone else.* Paki mouthed the words, but could not bring himself to say them aloud.

Ever since he'd "rediscovered" his penchant for having sex with young men and boys (he'd been involved in several same-sex dalliances during his teens and early years in college, but had dismissed them later as the result of raging hormones, normal teen sexual experimentation, and a scarcity of girls who "put out"), he'd feared contracting some so-called social disease. So he'd been cautious at first, using condoms during his trysts and practicing safe sex. As the months went by, however, he became less diligent. The occasions became more numerous when he would simply forego the prevailing common sense thinking of the times and enjoy sex without the minimal constraints and relative safety of a latex sheath. He also found that the danger aspect of having unprotected sex often heightened his arousal to the point where after finishing with his paid-for partner, he would go home and have mind-blowing sex with his wife. Paki had been aware of the risks, but a part of him refused to actually consider himself vulnerable.

Infect everyone else. That's what Silverman had said. Paki's gut clenched in apprehension. He thought of his beautiful wife Katherine, of all the times they'd made love...she blissfully unaware of his other appetites. He thought of his two children, Michael and Melissa. How often had they shared food or drink? How many times had he kissed their cuts or scrapes to make them feel "all better?" Paki's mind reeled with all of the images that bombarded him now, hundreds of occasions when he, as a loving husband and father, could have passed on a deadly disease to his family. Paki shuddered. He was a loving husband and father alright. A loving husband and father with a secret that may have doomed them all.

CHAPTER 17

"PAKI? PAKI?"

Silverman's voice calling his name brought Paki back from his dark reverie.

"Oh good," Silverman said when he saw that he'd gotten Paki's attention. "I thought we lost you." Nervous laughter. Paki's expression did not change.

"So, ah, Paki," Silverman continued. "I'm speaking to you as your friend, not just your editor. I want you to take the next couple of days off...to recuperate. You know, get some much needed rest, drink plenty of fluids, and eat alot of chicken soup." He held up Paki's papers again. "You go ahead and get better Paki," he said. "We'll run this column in the next edition."

Silverman turned and opened the office door, the lively sounds of the exterior office helped to further dissipate some of the uneasiness he'd been feeling. He turned back toward Paki, who still hadn't moved from where he stood, and felt a faint tingling at the base of his spine. Silverman gave a slight shudder. He recognized the feeling as one his mother had once described as having someone walk across your grave.

"If you feel you need more time," he said. "You can use some of your vacation time now and we'll just rerun some of your earlier columns." Blinking, Silverman stood at the door and waited for an answer.

Paki cleared his throat, "Yes," he said, then cleared it yet again. "I think I'll take your advice and go home. I'll probably need a few days to recover."

Silverman waved a hand in front of his face as if trying to ward off an offensive smell. "Sure my friend, sure," he said. "Listen, take as long as you need..." He now wagged a finger at Paki. "...But not as long as you'd like!" Silverman laughed and then left the office.

Paki watched Silverman weave his way past desks and cubicles until he was out of sight, then collapsed. He fell straight down and landed in a sitting position like a marionette with its strings cut. Laboriously, he pulled his knees up and hunched forward so that he could rest his forearms on them.

He felt cold and a shiver shook him, yet sweat poured from his face and soaked through his shirt. If Silverman had lingered a moment longer, he would have witnessed Paki's rubber-limbed drop to the office floor. Paki felt weak, totally drained, and he doubted if he could have stood much longer. He sat on the floor and slowly gained enough strength to turn his face toward the door. There were no curious onlookers, no office gossips staring at him.

Paki sighed. He was lucky no one had seen him fall. There may be too many questions that he didn't want to answer.

Eventually, Paki found the strength to half-scoot, half-drag himself to a more secluded spot behind the file cabinets. He sat there hugging his knees and willed himself to gain strength. Slowly, he did get stronger and finally he was able to stand by grabbing hold of a corner of his desk and pulling himself up. He wobbled there for a moment, his eyes closed, while he let a sudden feeling of vertigo leach from him. When he felt steadier, he sighed, looked up and saw Lorna, his secretary, standing there.

CHAPTER 18

THE FACTORY WAS on fire. Kids from all over the neighborhood were converging on the congested grid of beige factory buildings that dominated this section of East New York, Brooklyn. On a corner where Dewitt and Van Sinderen Avenues met and separated like the lazy waters of a river delta, stood an older building constructed of red brick and dirty white masonry.

The factories in this increasingly industrialized part of Brooklyn had been a part of these children's lives as long as they could remember. Their fathers worked long, hard hours there, and for a growing number of the children, their mothers had to find work in the factories as well in order to make ends meet.

Most of the factories produced auto parts, nuts and bolts, nails and screws, or electrical supplies. One or two assembled and shipped furniture and cabinets made of cheap pressed-wood board covered with Formica veneer. One of the buildings, recognizable chiefly by its unmistakable aroma of vinegar and herbs, was called the pickle factory by neighborhood residents. During the hottest days of the summer, the Hasidim who owned the place would have large barrels filled with pickles wheeled outside and they'd let the neighborhood children stick their grimy hands into the barrel's cool briny liquid and eat their fill.

Today, however, the Hasidim; conspicuous in their long black coats and wide-brimmed hats, stood and watched along with everyone else as the factory across the street went up in flames.

The police, silhouetted by a backdrop of fire and smoke, made sure everyone stayed across the street and away from the firefighter's tangled hoses and frenetic activity.

Even from across the street, ten-year-old Eddie Ramos could feel the heat of the flames on his face. He looked around at the gathered crowd hoping to spot his best friend, "Jay" Pedrosa, but there was no sign of him. Jay had been Eddie's best friend ever since they sat next to each other in the first grade. Jay's first name was actually Julio, but when they were nine years old he'd confided to Eddie that he hated that name. When prodded by Eddie as to why, Jay had shrugged and answered that it was his father's name. When Eddie asked why that would bother him, Jay had simply shrugged again.

Jay had visited Eddie's home many times through the years, and Eddie's mother had commented often about the change in the usually quiet and shy boy's demeanor whenever he visited. When in the Ramos home, Jay seemed to brighten up and chatter a mile a minute. In contrast, Eddie had only been to Jay's home maybe four or five times, and even then it seemed to Eddie that the invitations had been grudgingly offered. Jay had even admitted that the invitations had actually come from his father rather than from him. Eddie shook his head when Jay told him this, sometimes he just didn't get his friend, whose brooding seemed so out of place in one so young.

On one of those rare visits to Jay's home, Eddie couldn't help but notice that the apartment Jay shared with his father could have used some straightening up. Jay's mother had left them years before and it seemed that the Pedrosa men were lousy housekeepers. Apparently the Pedrosa men were also quite the drinkers. Jay's father thought nothing wrong with letting Jay drink beer, even at the tender age of ten, and Eddie found this tremendously cool. He told Jay on several occasions that he wished his parents were cool and let *him* drink beer.

Even though Eddie found the idea of drinking beer cool, on those occasions when he may have worked up enough nerve to take a few sips of the beer proffered up by Jay or his dad, he was always too afraid of his parents somehow finding out. As a consequence, he never finished off an entire can or bottle of the forbidden liquid. Jay would usually polish off two or three while Eddie still slurped noisily at his one. Eddie didn't even really like the way beer tasted but drinking it made him feel so cool and grown-up. Jay's father, Mr. Pedrosa, was the one who handed him his first beer ever. When Eddie had looked at Jay for affirmation, Jay had merely shrugged his familiar shrug and finished his own beer in an impressive series of breathless gulps. Jay's dad urged Eddie to do the same, but Eddie's conscience wouldn't let him get past a few tentative swallows.

That day Eddie thought Jay's dad was really cool and friendly, not at all like his own father. Subsequent visits to the apartment, however, proved Jay's dad to often be as moody as Jay himself. The last couple of visits to Jay's apartment, Mr. Pedrosa was grouchy and complained about Eddie, "drinking up my beer like it was free." He accused Eddie of not contributing, of not giving up his fair share. Embarrassed, Eddie admitted that he didn't have any money.

"It doesn't have to be money," Jay's father said quickly. He repeated it several times, saying it louder each time while Jay hustled Eddie toward the door. In the hallway, Eddie apologized.

"What for," Jay asked.

Eddie looked down at his feet. "For not paying for the beer I drank and stuff..."

Jay shrugged. "Don't worry about it man," he said. "My father's drunk. You don't gotta pay for shit, man."

Eddie nodded. They stopped at the red fire door that opened onto the stairs to the lobby. Eddie and Jay usually took the stairs to and from Jay's apartment to avoid bullies, adults, and the nearly overpowering stench of urine in the elevator. Eddie pushed open the heavy steel door and a draft that smelled faintly of stale beer, cigarette smoke and the ever-present urine, ruffled his hair.

"What did your father mean Jay?" he asked.

"About what?"

"What did your father mean when he said I didn't have to give him any money?"

Jay looked at Eddie for what seemed like a long time before he answered. "Who knows? Who cares, man?" He finally said, just as Eddie was about to ask again. "I told you the fuckin' guy's drunk."

Eddie nodded and after giving his friend a playful shove, he bounded down the stairs and out of the building.

That was a year earlier and now, standing on a corner of the glorified alleyway known as Van Sinderen Avenue, the acrid smell of smoke in his nostrils, Eddie Ramos realized that was the last time he'd ever been to Jay's apartment home. Eddie scanned the crowd again but he still couldn't spot Jay. The fire was out now and the weary firefighters trudged in and out of the demolished front doors of the ruined factory. Several reentered the building carrying large shovels and at the sight of this, Eddie could feel the excitement level of the other children around him rise like an incoming tide. Soot-blackened water streamed from the open doorways into the paper-strewn gutter. Some of the smaller children tried to splash in the dirty spume, but were shooed back by firefighters, the police, or other adults in the crowd.

Then a collective cheer broke out from the children in the crowd when the event that the kids had been hoping for ever since they'd heard of the fire finally happened and the first shovelful of toys were dumped into the street. They surged forward and dove into the largely melted mass of little green soldiers, water pistols, and toy cars. They squealed in delight as the firefighters continued to shovel out more and more toys. Most had been melted into barely distinguishable lumps, but the occasional shriek of discovery told others that there were indeed salvageable toys to be found and had.

Eddie found himself caught up in the fervor and laughed out loud when he found a green plastic soldier that had not been exposed to enough heat to melt it completely. Instead, its stance and features had been warped so now the tiny figure appeared contorted in fear or pain.

Eddie took a quick look around at the crowd. *Jay would love this*, Eddie thought as he ran his thumb over the soldier's helmet. It would crack him up.

An acquaintance from school rushed by and Eddie called out and asked him if he'd seen Jay. The kid, Eddie thought his name might have been Louis or Louie, answered in the negative.

"I saw some cop cars over in front of his building though," Louis or Louie said.

Eddie tried to question him further, but by then the kid named Louis or Louie had leapt into a crowd of bigger kids jostling for still useable water pistols.

Eddie was sure the cop cars had nothing to do with Jay, but he still felt uneasy enough to take off in the direction of Jay's apartment building at a jog.

He's probably being nosy and looking at whatever the cops are doing in front of his building, Eddie said to himself. He pulled the little plastic figure of the soldier from his pocket and gripped it tight, like a good luck charm.

As he rounded a corner he saw that there were indeed several police cars in front of the building where Jay and his father lived...five of them. And an ambulance. Without his even realizing it, Eddie's jog became a flat-out run.

At the same time that he reached the cordon of black-and-whites, Eddie saw four brawny police officers leaving the building with a violently struggling man in tow. Eddie could tell almost immediately that the man the cops were dragging to a nearby police car was Mr. Pedrosa: Jay's father.

One of the police officers noticed Eddie standing near the car gawking and yelled at him to get away, but Eddie could only stand and stare. The cop yelled again, and that's when Jay's father saw him.

When Mr. Pedrosa saw Eddie, he stopped struggling and smiled. The smile made Eddie shudder, it was like a rabid animal baring its teeth.

"Well, well," Jay's father said aloud to no one in particular. "It's that little punk shit friend of Jay's who drinks up all my beer."

Eddie never felt so frightened in his young life. Pedrosa's eyes were bloodshot and wild, and even though cops surrounded him, his demeanor was dangerous and threatening. Still Eddie felt compelled to edge closer, until an officer's gesture stopped him.

"Is...is Jay okay Mr. Pedrosa?" Eddie asked.

Pedrosa's eyes bored into him with a mixture of malevolence and disdain. "Is Jay okay Mr. Pedrosa?" Jay's father repeated in a falsetto voice. "No, the little motherfucker's not okay. I killed that useless bastard last night!"

One of the cops asked the others if they too had heard what amounted to be Pedrosa's confession in the murder of his son. They all nodded in unison, and the first cop motioned for them to listen further.

Eddie was dumbstruck. His best friend Jay killed by his own father? It didn't make sense!

"M...Mr. P...Pedrosa," he said when he could finally speak. "M-maybe you're just drunk again. Y...you don't know what you're saying..."

Pedrosa laughed and one of the cops shook him hard to stop him.

"I'm not that drunk you punk-assed little shit!" he yelled. "I killed the bastard 'cause he tried to be man enough to stand up to me. Me! Shit, ever since his mother left he's been my pussy, man. That's it, nothing but pussy, whenever I wanted it, and now he wanted to tell me no. No!"

Eddie felt his heart thumping loudly in his chest, his head felt as if it were being squeezed in a giant vise. Tears brimmed in his eyes.

"Look at that," Pedrosa sneered. "Now the little faggot's going to cry."

One of the cops hit Pedrosa between the shoulder blades hard enough to cause him to stumble forward. Before he was yanked back, he managed to whisper almost in Eddie's ear.

"That's right Eddie-baby," he said. "Almost every day Jay either sucked my dick or I fucked him in his tight little ass, and the wild part is that *you were next...*"

The cop who pulled him back slapped Jay's father in the mouth. Hard.

"Toss 'em in my car boys," the cop said. "And there's no need to be gentle about it."

The other officers hustled Mr. Pedrosa into the police car, letting him hit his head on the way in. The cop who had been doing all the talking eyed Eddie curiously.

"Sorry about your friend kid," he said in a kindly rumble. He looked at Jay's father sitting in the back of the patrol car and then turned back to Eddie. "Don't worry about that S.O.B. kid," he said pointing over his shoulder with his thumb. "He's having his ass kicked all the way to the stationhouse and then some more once we get there. He ain't gonna get away with this." The cop gave Eddie's shoulder a squeeze. "What's your name kid?" he asked. "Maybe a detective would wanna come back and talk to you later, you know, about your friend..."

"Jay," Eddie sniffed as tears ran down his face.

"Yeah," said the cop. "Right, Jay."

So Eddie never gave the officer his name and address, and no one ever came to talk to him about Jay.

As the car containing a glaring Mr. Pedrosa drove off, Eddie noticed for the first time that the other police cars and the ambulance had already gone. He turned slightly and looked up at the building where Jay lived. Used to live. He saw the apartment window that Jay had often leaned out of when calling down to him in the street.

A huge sigh carried a trace of the smoldering factory back to his nostrils and he remembered the little green soldier that he still clutched in his hand. Slowly, he raised his hand and stared at the tiny figure frozen forever in its contorted expression of pain and fear. And he heard it scream. And scream. And scream.

Then Eddie Ramos, homicide detective, woke up.

CHAPTER 19

TOMMY'S CELL PHONE went off and he slid his thumb across the Smartphone's screen. It showed the number to a particular public telephone at the Port Authority bus station in Manhattan. One of the few pay phones still left in the city in fact. Tommy took the call.

"Heard you looking for chicken killer guy—I be at Port Authority usual place—bring cheese and cheddah."

Tommy grabbed his coat, paused long enough to consider letting his longtime girlfriend Daphne know he was leaving, and then he was gone. A few seconds after he'd left, slamming the door behind him, a woman's sleepy voice called out from the bedroom, "Tommy? Tommy is that you? Tommy!"

Tommy Cucitti made it into the city in record time and spotted the street person he'd dubbed Ratman years earlier at their usual place in the Port Authority Bus Terminal: the pretzel place next to the newsstand.

Tommy ordered an extra salty pretzel with mustard, paid for it, then walked next door to the newsstand and bought a men's magazine. After paying for the magazine, he rode the escalator downstairs. He didn't look behind him, he knew Ratman would be there.

At the bottom of the escalator, Tommy made a left and sat in one of the plush red chairs of an old-fashioned shoeshine stand. Without saying a word, Ratman sat in the chair next to his. Tommy handed him the pretzel and the magazine. Ratman opened the magazine to the centerfold, whistled appreciatively, then put it away and started eating his pretzel.

Tommy watched Ratman nibble at the pretzel. He'd named him Ratman the first time he arrested him for shoplifting about four years ago. Ratman didn't look like a rat per sé, or like any type of rodent for that matter. Rather, it was his mannerism and gestures that reminded Tommy of a rat. Ratman held the pretzel with the fingertips of both hands while he took tiny mincing bites. He chewed rapidly, his eyes constantly moving, as if he were afraid that someone would make off with his meal. When he was done, he licked his fingers and rolled his eyes in pleasure.

"Okay Ratty," Tommy said once Ratman was finished. "Whassup?"

Ratman spoke to Tommy between licks of his fingers and the smacking of his lips.

"Yeah, yeah *lick-lick*, how ya doin' *smack*?"

"I'm alright," Tommy replied. "But I *know* you didn't call me out of my crib in the middle of the night to ask me how I'm doin', right?"

"Heh-heh, *lick-smack*, that's right Detective Tommy," Ratman said. "I know you gonna like what I got for you this time. You gonna love it!"

"I better love it Ratty," Tommy said. "I was planning on spending the night with my shorty and a forty, not with your stinky ass."

"Nope," Ratman responded. "Keepin' it real like always Detective Tommy, I..."

Tommy Cucitti turned in his chair and looked directly at Ratman, he was tired and this was taking way too long. "Yo Ratty," he said. "I don't give a shit how real it's kept or isn't kept. I'll tell you something that's real, yo. You called me and dropped a hint that you have some information on the asshole that's goin' around killing these boy hookers—you better not be fuckin' lying to me Ratty."

Ratman looked close to aghast. "No, no Detective Tommy," he said. "It's not like that. I'm telling you man, I'm being for real."

Tommy relaxed, a little. He didn't like his informants to waste his time and Ratty knew it.

"I seen what the man look like," Ratman said. "I even seen his car, son."

Tommy smiled. He could almost imagine hearing the trumpets of the heavenly host playing in triumph, this was almost as good as it could possibly get. *This was it,* he thought. *One less looney on the streets.* Overjoyed, he pulled out his pen and pad. "Okay Ratty," he said. "You say you saw the guy's car? Did you see the number on the plate?"

Ratman looked away, now seemingly disinterested. Tommy's smile twisted into a smirk. He pulled a twenty dollar bill from his pocket and tossed it into Ratman's lap.

"There's your 'cheddah' Ratty," Tommy said. "Grade A, USDA government-approved, dead president Andy fuckin' Jackson cheddah."

Tommy sat there with his pen poised over paper, waiting for his informant to help him catch a killer. Ratman looked longingly at the money in his lap, picked it up, and examined it carefully.

"It's real, son," Tommy Cucitti said, confused by Ratman's reaction concerning the money. Usually Ratty just shoved the money into the nearest pocket. Why was he stalling now? When Ratman turned back to Tommy, Cucitti could see that there were tears in his eyes. Ratman took the twenty and carefully placed it on the open page of Tommy's notepad. Tommy's astonishment at this latest development was threaded with suspicion. Ratman never turned down money. Throughout their acquaintance, Tommy had seen Ratman hurt, hungry, sick, high, cold, drunk, sleepy and asleep, but he'd never seen him cry. Until now. True, Ratty wasn't sobbing out loud, but the tears that were gathering in his eyes like an impending storm were enough.

Tommy took the twenty-dollar bill from his pad, folded it, and stuck it into his shirt pocket. Then he closed the notepad and put it away as well, along with the pen. He looked hard at Ratty and sighed. "Okay Ratty," he said. "What's up?"

Ratman looked at Tommy, swallowed, then looked away. "Yo man," he said softly. "It ain't that I don't appreciate the 'cheddah' and all, but I need your help in a bigger way..."

Tommy shook his head. "I don't believe this shit," he said, forcing his voice to remain even. "You called me out here in the middle of the night to do you a favor? You lose your mind Ratty?"

Now it was Ratman's turn to shake his head. "No, no...uh, I mean okay, it is kind of like that," he said.

Tommy hopped out of the chair in disgust. "I don't have time to play games with you Ratty," he said. "I'm tryin' to catch a guy that's goin' around killin' kids and you wanna fuckin' play games. If I wasn't so pissed I'd kick your ass, but I'm afraid I'd kill you."

Tommy turned as if to walk away, a strategy that he'd used before with his more recalcitrant informants and, as he could have predicted, Ratman jumped from his chair and blocked Tommy's way. Tommy threw his hands up in mock surrender. "Now I know you lost your mind, son," he said.

Ratman wore an old blue bath towel draped around his neck like a scarf, his hands held tightly to the frayed ends. "No, listen to me Detective Tommy," he said, his voice more desperate than Tommy had ever heard it. "Don't leave. Don't leave. I did see the killer-guy, and his car—it's just that things are a little different right now man, I ain't tryin' to diss you or nuthin...'"

Tommy nodded. "Look Ratty," he said. "What's up? You know I want this motherfucker real, real bad and so now you figure you're gonna milk me for some more money, right? So what you want son, forty, fifty, a hundred dollars?" Although Tommy was playing angry, in reality he was more than willing to pay that and more if the information led straight to the killer. Tommy advanced on Ratman who quickly backed up a few steps.

"Maybe you know something, maybe you don't," Tommy said.

"I did see the guy I'm tellin' you," Ratman cried out.

"Give me more," Tommy prodded.

"It-it was a white guy..."

"Oh yeah, that narrows the search."

"I saw him near where that last kid was killed, by the train station on Lex..."

"You coulda got that shit from the newspapers."

Ratman looked around nervously. This was not going at all as he'd hoped. "Detective Tommy," he said. "I'm tellin' you man, I saw the guy! Another guy saw him too, a dude that was dropping some money in the night vault..."

Cucitti's heart jumped. That wasn't information that Ratman could have gotten from the papers. A local business owner did call that same night and reported a possible suspicious person near the bank where he was making his night deposit. Although it was unsure whether his experience was related to the murder that took place only two blocks away, that information was deliberately kept out of the media.

"Alright Ratty," Tommy said. "Now tell me what you know—and don't just tell me the fuckin' guy's white..."

Ratman's eyes lowered to the dirty concrete floor. "I want to tell you man," he said softly. "It's just that..."

"What Ratty? It's just what? Son, I'm just about out of that famous Detective Tommy patience that you know and love Ratty. First you call me out here in the middle of the night, then you don't want my money, and then you don't even tell me anything I can use! What the fuck's up, man?"

"This is what." Ratman sighed resignedly as he pulled the towel from around his neck. As the towel slid away, Ratman exposed a lump about the size of a baseball growing from the base of his neck, almost directly under his left ear. It seemed perfectly round, the skin shiny and taut. To Tommy Cucitti, it looked a lot like a tan colored balloon that threatened to burst at any moment.

It's a tumor, thought Tommy. *A big, ugly, death-dealing, life-defying, I'm gonna make this poor guy kick and scream in pain and then I'm gonna kill him, kind of tumor.*

Tommy looked away. "Shit Ratty, I'm sorry son."

Ratman offered a shrug in return.

"Does it hurt?" Tommy asked

"Nah, well not a lot, but it itches me like crazy." And as if to emphasize the point, Ratman scratched furiously at the cancerous growth.

Tommy felt his stomach do a flip. Even with all the things he'd seen and experienced as a cop, some things still managed to bother him. He took a deep breath and expelled it. "Alright Ratty," he said after mentally steeling himself. "You showed me your tumor and I feel bad for you, seriously—but what does that have to do with the sonofabitch that I'm tryin' to find?"

A small group on their way to a bus walked past and Ratman self-consciously draped the towel around his neck again, hiding the tumor.

"Okay," Ratman said after the group had passed. "I have a tumor..."

"Aw man," Tommy protested. "What's this, a history lesson? I guessed this part already!"

"Okay, okay," Ratman said, then he cleared his throat and continued. "I have a tumor..."

Tommy groaned. Ratman had apparently rehearsed his speech and he was only going to relate it to Tommy in its full, unedited version.

"...And the doctors say it's going to get bigger," Ratman went on. "They told me if I don't get it operated on, I'm gonna die."

"So get it operated on, son."

"That's the thing," Ratman continued. "The doctors say it's an expensive operation and they don't want to do it 'cause the city, uh, Social Services won't pay for it."

"Bullshit."

"No, seriously man. They say they won't pay for it because even if I get the operation, the doctors say there's a fifty-fifty chance I might wind up dying anyway."

"That's fucked up," Tommy said quietly and sincerely.

"F'sho detective Tommy, who you tellin'?"

There was an awkward silence during which both Tommy Cucitti and Ratman shuffled their feet and looked about them uncomfortably. Tommy was the first one to break the silence.

"Yo son, I'm sorry about what you're going through, but I'm still wondering what it all has to do with me."

"Okay, let me tell you," Ratman said, licking his lips. "If I don't get the operation, I'm gonna die for sure. If I do get the operation, I at least got a chance of being alive."

"Listen Ratty," Tommy said. "If you don't get to the goddamn point you won't have to worry about it 'cause I'm gonna kill you myself!"

"Okay Detective Tommy, now here's the deal. We known each other for a while now..."

"...And I done you a lot of favors..."

"For a price."

"Okay, yeah. For a price," Ratman conceded. "But never for no real big price."

"Yeah well, I got a feeling that's about to change."

The rest of Ratman's message came out in a rush, "The doctors said the operation cost about fifty thousand dollars and I know how bad the police want to catch the guy that's been killin' all those boy hookers, so I..."

Tommy stood there with his mouth agape. "Hold it yo, hold it," he said louder than he'd meant to. "Fifty thousand dollars? Fifty thousand dollars!" Tommy shook his head. "Sorry man, but there is just no fuckin' way the department's gonna voucher out fifty grand and they don't even know what they're getting—shit, I don't think they would give it up even if they *knew* what they were getting."

"But you guys want to catch..."

"Hell yeah, but not for no fifty thousand dollars!" Tommy's eyes flicked to the towel around Ratman's neck and back to the homeless man's eyes. Those eyes pleaded with him now. Tommy sighed, "You know what they'd tell me Ratty? They'd tell me to go fuck myself because we'll catch the bastard anyway. Sooner or later, he'll mess up or someone else will give him up for a whole lot less money."

Ratman refused to give in. "Maybe there's a reward..."

"Sure there's a fuckin' reward," Tommy said. "But it ain't no fifty-grand, you can forget that shit."

Ratman paced back and forth in a near panic. His head turned from side to side while he talked to himself, his eyes and mind searching desperately for *something* that would save his life.

Tommy raised his hands, palms out, and shrugged his shoulders. "Look Ratty," he said. "Just tell me what you know about this guy and when I go back to work in the morning I'll make some calls about your, uh, condition."

Ratman stopped his pacing. "No, no. I can't do that man, this is my only card—it's all I got. I tell you what you wanna know and you forget about me. Shit man, that probably what you want. I give you the information, you get to be the hero, and I get to be dead." Ratman resumed his pacing.

"Yo," Tommy said. "I wouldn't let you go like that, man."

"Yeah right, but what you tellin' me though?"

"If I could get you fifty-grand, I would. Look, I'll call Social Services tomorrow, or some other places..."

"I already told you the city ain't about payin' for it man."

"Okay, but maybe if I explain the circumstances and tell them who I am..."

"Who you are? Ain't nobody give a shit who you are. It ain't like you Donald Trump, motherfucker! You just a cop!"

Ratman and Tommy glared at each other. If not for the stakes involved, Tommy would have left by now, but he needed to know what Ratty knew—or at least what he said he knew.

Suddenly Ratman's glare softened and his features opened up as if he'd just been graced with a divine vision. He clapped his hands and pointed at Tommy with both index fingers. "Yo man, I got it! I know what we can do!" he said.

"Alright," Tommy said, tired and impatient. "So give it up yo, so we can move on."

"Okay, okay. You gonna like this one, man," Ratman exclaimed gleefully.

"Yeah," Tommy retorted. "You said that earlier and so far I'm not liking any of this shit."

"Yeah, yeah, but you gonna like this one." Ratman licked his lips and wiped his sweaty palms on his pants. "You a cop. You work for the Po-lice department!"

"Tell me something I don't know Ratty, before I arrest you just on G.P."

"Uh-huh," Ratman continued unfazed. "You got insurance—*medical benefits*. You can..."

Tommy shook his head. "That's N.G. homeboy, no good," he said. "For my insurance to cover you, you have to be family... *close* family. Sorry man, but that ain't happening."

Ratman's face fell. "But you..."

"Yeah, but me," Tommy interrupted. "Look Ratty, there's no way you can get that operation on my insurance—it's impossible. Even if I was to lie, which I'm not totally against, and tried to get you on my insurance at this late date, there would be too many questions. Shit, we'd both wind up sharing the same cell at Rikers for insurance fraud or some dumb shit."

"You could say that I'm your son or..."

Tommy snorted derisively. "Yeah, and when did I make you, when I was three?"

Ratman stared down at his feet, dejected. Defeated.

Tommy sighed. "Yo man," he said. "No doubt, you've been dealt from the bottom of the deck yo, but I'm tryin' to tell you the best and only thing I can do for you."

Ratman looked up. "Yo, Detective Tommy," he said softly. "Maybe you can lend me..."

Tommy shook his head. "Nah, sorry son. I don't even have fifty thousand *cents* in the bank, much less fifty fuckin' thousand dollars." *Not that I would lend it to you even if I had it,* Tommy thought before suffering a mild pang of guilt.

"There's gotta be..."

"There is a way," Tommy assured him. "Tell me what you know about the guy that's been going around killing these teenagers, and I'll go back to my office and make calls all over the place for you. Both my partner and I will make all kinds of calls until we hook you up with something. Somehow. Somewhere."

"Okay, okay," Ratty said nodding. "You guys make those calls and hook me up with the money or the operation, *then* I'll give you the information."

Ratman started to walk away, but this time Tommy blocked *his* path.

"No way," Tommy growled. "We're not playing it like that."

Ratman, head down, tried to walk around him. Again, Tommy blocked his path.

Ratman leapt back, his eyes wild. "No, no," he said, spittle flying from his mouth. "I told you this is all I got to trade for my life, man. I'm not gonna give you what you want now and trust you to make no goddamn calls for me later! I ain't no 'ho, motherfucker. I'm a man, just like you a man, and I wanna live just like you wanna live!"

Ratman yanked the towel from around his neck. "Find somebody that can get this shit off me," he said indicating the growth on his neck. "And I'll tell you what you want to know!" He draped the towel around his neck again and walked to the UP escalator.

Tommy followed close behind. As they stepped onto the escalator, Tommy leaned in close to Ratman and whispered in his ear. "You know I can't just let you leave, Ratty." Tommy emphasized his point by pulling out his handcuffs and opening them in a single motion.

The familiar ratcheting sound of the cuffs being opened echoed in Ratman's head with a terrifying sense of finality. 'This was it. Jail. Death. Potter's Field. And no one would remember a man named Juan Gutierrez, who became homeless later in his life, and who later still became known as Ratman.' He shivered.

Tommy gently took hold of Ratman's arm as he prepared to close one of the cuffs onto his wrist. Tommy didn't want to do this, but he couldn't let Ratty walk away with what he said he knew. It could very well be Ratman's information that will lead him and Eddie to the killer.

Suddenly stars exploded in Tommy's eyes and his head was snapped back by a quick thrust of Ratman's elbow. Tommy could feel himself losing his balance, and he tried to reach out and grab hold of something, anything, to keep from falling. The handcuffs clattered onto the escalator's metal steps as he clawed for the moving rubber handrail. Then Ratman was there, slapping his hand away. Tommy windmilled his arms in a desperate attempt to keep his feet under himself, but Ratman, all knees, feet and hands, pushed and kicked at him. Finally, inevitably, Tommy Cucitti fell.

CHAPTER 20

PAKI DROVE SLOWLY past the sign identifying the Cross Bronx Expressway, swung a lazy right, and entered the perpetual twilight under the tracks of an elevated train. He maneuvered through a complicated intersection and cruised past the Queensbound Q44 bus stop.

After almost an hour of driving through the Tremont section of the Bronx, the only young men who approached his car had only offered to sell him drugs or bootleg cigarettes. Although Paki did smoke or use cocaine on occasion, this night he was after a different form of diversion.

Night had completely fallen now, and the shadows deepened into inky pools of indigo and black. The *bodegas* on the corners created scattered oases of light that lured youths like moths to flame until every storefront boasted its own boisterous crowd of raucous teens. Older men, their own youth lost and wasted, deferred to the younger, stronger men and hung in the peripheries, their longing for the light eclipsed by their greater longing for the cheap, burning liquid hidden in the creased brown paper bags they held in callused hands.

Paki found himself going past the New York Botanical Garden and he slowed his vehicle even further. He was able to see the tops of the trees over the high wall that separated the garden from the surrounding neighborhood. Despite the season and the cold night air, many of the trees still sported their robust greenery, their leaves illuminated by the orange glow of tall lamps. An autumn breeze set the leaves in motion and together they made a sound that reminded Paki of a lover's sigh, and the rustle of bat's wings.

As Paki made a left at the corner, a boy stood at the curb and beckoned to him with a fierce stare. Paki smiled and pulled over. This area was a lonely overgrown patch of land between the botanical garden and a local subway station. If it weren't that the young man had been standing at the edge of the curb, almost on the corner, he would have been invisible.

Paki watched amused as the boy looked into his car and sized him up.

"You a cop?" The boy asked with a quick tilt of his chin.

"Do I look like a cop?" Paki retaliated in that wonderful voice of his.

The boy snorted. "I ain't got time for no games, man." He looked as if he wanted to leave, but after his quick examination of Paki and his expensive car, he was reluctant to lose what was obviously a moneyed customer.

Paki held his hands up in a gesture of surrender. "Alright cutie," he said. "I'm sorry, really, and no I'm not a cop—I'm a Wall Street broker."

"Yo man, don't call me no fuckin' cutie, alright? I ain't nobody's fuckin' cutie." The boy said in an almost successful attempt to sound menacing.

"Okay, whatever you say man," Paki said in mock submission.

The boy nodded, satisfied that he'd won this round. He scanned the interior of the car again, taking stock. "Brokers make a lot of money, right?" It was more statement than an actual question.

"*Lots of money*," Paki cooed.

The boy nodded again, and Paki thought how quaint it was that he was wearing his baseball cap with the visor facing forward.

"So what you want?" the boy asked. He couldn't have been more than fifteen, but his tender years didn't bother Paki in the slightest.

"I want to go around the world with you baby," Paki answered.

The kid narrowed his eyes at the word *baby*. “Okay,” he said, looking around the street for any sign of the police lurking about. “But that means you want to fuck me and that costs more money, like a hundred dollars.” He said the last two words quickly, afraid they’d be rejected.

“I think you’re definitely worth it,” Paki said.

The kid nodded. “Damn right,” he said. He stepped back from the car and hoisted a school knapsack over one shoulder. Paki exited from the car and made sure the door was locked. The weight of the big gun under his coat was like the reassuring presence of an old friend, and Paki smiled as the boy took his hand and led him off into the shadows.

CHAPTER 21

RAMOS LOOKED AT Tommy Cucitti over the rim of his steamy mug of coffee. Tommy wore an adhesive bandage under his right eye, and one dangled from his earlobe like a poor man's earring. There was an ugly bruise on his chin, a splint on the last two fingers of his left hand, and he limped.

"Your leg okay?" Ramos asked.

Tommy nodded. "Yeah," he said. "I just banged my shin a couple of times on the way down, but I'm alright."

Ramos nodded and took another long sip of coffee. By saying "*...on the way down*", Tommy meant the little trip he took down the escalator last night after being pushed by one of his street people.

"I still can't believe I let that chump-ass piece of shit do this to me," Tommy exclaimed.

Ramos drained his mug, wiped the inside with a paper towel, stood up and stretched. "Yeah well," he said. "Every time you feel that way take a look in the mirror, that'll convince you."

The meeting today was being held in the conference room on the first floor and was to include the probable members of the so-called "Chickenhawk" task force, both NYPD and FBI. Word was the mayor was also slated to attend.

When the two homicide detectives got there, the conference room was already crowded and buzzed with the barely contained energies of dozens of law enforcement personnel eager for the hunt. The assemblage had segregated themselves consciously or subconsciously into distinct NYPD and FBI factions.

Ramos and Tommy made their way to two empty chairs on the far aisle, boisterously greeting colleagues and associates on the way. When they sat down they both wore large grins, enjoying the camaraderie of the moment.

Someone calling the meeting to order focused the detective's attention to the podium up front. As Ramos and Cucitti straightened in their seats, they took mental note of who was seated in the folding chairs behind the podium.

Sitting ramrod straight and looking directly ahead was the chief of detectives. To his left sat the chief of patrol. In the two chairs beside them sat the heads of the Transit and Housing Bureaus. In the middle, directly behind the podium, sat the police commissioner. Next to him squatted Deputy Mayor Michael Nitchik, his round face red and sweaty with the exertion of simply breathing. To the deputy mayor's left sat the Manhattan district attorney.

Once again Ramos found himself the object of District Attorney Williams' intimidating stare. This time Ramos glared back and eventually the district attorney turned away. Tommy nudged Ramos and leaned over to whisper.

"What was that all about?" he asked.

Ramos shook his head. "I got no idea," he said. "But something's definitely up with that guy, he's been giving me the evil eye for a couple of days now. I'm bettin' he'll let me know what his problem is soon enough."

Tommy nodded.

To the district attorney's left sat the Assistant Director of the FBI's New York Bureau, followed by a man in a rumpled suit of mourning gray. At the end sat a geeky-looking young man in a plain black suit.

The man at the podium calling the meeting to order was Lieutenant Patrick Mullen. Lieutenant Mullen was in charge of Manhattan North Homicide, and was the same lieutenant that Ramos had the meeting with after returning from the crime scene at the construction site.

The lieutenant was wearing a uniform rather than his usual jacket and tie. *Maybe so he won't be mistaken for a Fed*, Ramos mused. Lieutenant Mullen was a much respected and highly decorated member of the department. He had earned that respect during his halcyon days as a young cop in the volatile New York of the 1970s. Now, thirty years later, he'd matured and moved up, almost every cop's dream. Ramos admired him, though he'd never let him know that if he could help it, and he knew that his partner felt pretty much the same way. That never stopped Tommy from getting under the looey's skin every once in a while though, just for the heck of it.

Lieutenant Mullen brought the meeting to order and introduced the chief of detectives. The chief of detectives, also in uniform, thanked the lieutenant and stepped up to the podium.

"As you all may know," he began. "This is a preliminary meeting made up of personnel from various bureaus and divisions in the NYPD and the FBI. The goals of this meeting are to review evidence, officially establish whether or not these so-called 'Chickenhawk' killings are the work of a single perpetrator, and if so, develop a profile of this individual."

The chief pulled a pair of gold wire-rimmed spectacles from his pocket and put them on. He then produced several index cards that he referred to as he spoke. "As of today, every recent parolee with a history of buying the services of male prostitutes has been rounded up and placed in 'protective custody'. The same goes for those parolees who are known to prefer the company of teenage boys. They will continue to be held and questioned until their lawyers get them back on the street, whereupon they will simply be picked up again."

There were some murmurs from the gathered cops and G-men. The chief motioned for silence. "As you may have read in the papers this morning," the chief continued. "Almost the entire graduating class of probationary officers leaving the academy this week will be assigned to nights. Their specific duty will be to patrol those areas known to be frequented by male prostitutes and their johns. Their job will be mostly to discourage the trade by their presence, and to keep their eyes and ears open. You may have also read or heard that the mayor has scheduled another press conference for this afternoon, part of what he's going to say will have to do with what goes on at this meeting."

The chief of detectives then leaned toward the police commissioner and said something that the commissioner answered with a few words and a quick nod. The chief turned his attention back to the podium and adjusted the microphone before speaking again.

"I will now turn the meeting over to the commissioner of the NYPD."

The commissioner stood and stepped up to the podium to polite and scattered applause.

"Thank you chief," the commissioner acknowledged as the chief of detectives returned to his chair. "Without further ado," he continued. "I would like to recap the specifics of the current investigation and the crimes themselves."

The commissioner then went over what the NYPD knew of the crimes and the evidence gathered at each crime scene.

Ramos and Tommy were intimately familiar with this material, since they'd gathered and compiled most of it themselves. Still they listened intently, re-weighing and re-digesting the facts as the commissioner went over them in his clipped, matter-of-fact tone.

"...The palm print found at the crime scene in the Twenty-First Street subway station tunnel remains unidentified, although sent through the NCIC (National Crime Information Center) and the FBI's Master Fingerprint Identification Center."

There were murmurs from the crowded room. Many of the investigators who knew about the palm print had hoped that it would be the piece of evidence that would have sealed the killer's fate.

"And finally," the commissioner concluded. "As of this date the CLIS (Criminalistics Laboratory Information System) has been unable to produce a match or history for the bullets recovered at the crime scenes."

This last bit of information elicited groans from the audience. Another piece of vital evidence that hadn't measured up to expectations.

The commissioner looked out at the assembled detectives and federal agents, and then leaned toward the microphone again.

"I have absolute confidence that through the combined

efforts of the NYPD and the FBI, we will bring the perpetrator or perpetrators of these crimes to justice," he said. There was more polite applause.

The police commissioner waited a heartbeat or two after the applause ended and returned to his seat. Afterward, the assembled crowd heard from the deputy mayor, the district attorney, and the FBI assistant director who introduced the next speaker as Special Agent Peter Sandusky of the FBI.

Special Agent Sandusky stepped up to the podium, adjusted and readjusted the knot in his tie, and then nervously cleared his throat.

"Good morning, uh, good morning ladies and gentlemen," he said as feedback from the microphone whined through the conference room. Sandusky hurriedly adjusted the microphone until the feedback died away.

"I'm going to make this brief," he said, and the crowd broke out into good-natured applause. Sandusky smiled and shook his head. "Anyway," he continued more confidently. "What I'm going to do this morning is try to introduce you to our killer." Sandusky quieted the following murmurs with a hand gesture and went on. "I know there are some members of our respective agencies who believe it's too early in the investigation to attribute all of the killings to just one perpetrator, but all of the classic signs are there that point to there being only one killer.

Most of the heads in the room nodded in agreement.

"Even though we couldn't match the palm print, the fact that the slugs from all three known crime scenes are giving us trouble can itself be considered a 'lead'."

"How do you figure that?" Someone in the audience called out as he raised his hand at the same time.

"Well, it's like the donut/donut-hole theory," Sandusky answered. "Sometimes the lack of simple conclusive evidence can be as telling as an abundance of the same."

"Oh yeah," another audience member called out. "Leave it to the Feds to come up with a *'no evidence can be evidence'* theory."

Sandusky smiled and shook his head as half the men and women in the room snickered.

The cop half, Ramos thought wryly as a smile played across his features.

Tommy saw the deputy mayor catch the police commissioner's eye and gesture toward Sandusky. The commissioner leapt up and made for the podium, no doubt to admonish the gathered detectives for their somewhat less than professional decorum.

Sandusky, however, covered the microphone with one hand and stopped the commissioner's advance with the other. He then whispered something to the commissioner who looked toward the deputy mayor for affirmation.

Nitchik at first just glared at the federal agent, then sighed and nodded at the commissioner who dutifully returned to his seat.

"Asshole," Tommy whispered to Ramos.

Ramos nodded in assent, having witnessed what Tommy had seen as well. The mayor's office pulled the commissioner's strings alright.

Sandusky mouthed his thanks to the deputy mayor and turned back to the podium and the microphone.

CHAPTER 22

ALEX ACOSTA LOVED his pet pit bull, "Pogo." What he didn't like was cleaning up after her.

Every morning before school, Alex's mother would hand him the Pooper Scooper, a plastic bag, and Pogo's leash. And every morning, as soon as he and Pogo had escaped his mother's scrutiny, he'd give Pogo her freedom, stick the leash into his pocket, and toss the plastic bag into the most convenient breeze.

This morning was no different. Alex waited until he turned the corner, out of sight of the apartment he lived in with his mother and sister, and unclipped the leash from Pogo's collar.

Together at first, they ran down the block toward the distant corner, the Pooper Scooper held tightly in Alex's hand. Pogo soon outpaced her young master, sat down obediently when she reached the corner, and waited for Alex to catch up. Alex wasn't too far behind and he soon reached the corner where Pogo waited for him, her tongue lolling and her compact body quivering with excitement.

Alex patted her head and gave her a good scratch behind the ears. He was proud that she'd waited for him at the corner like he'd taught her, and that she hadn't tried to cross the street on her own.

Alex looked up and down the street, checking for oncoming traffic from both directions. Traffic usually wasn't a problem this early in the morning, but he'd seen enough strays get run over here so that he wanted to make doubly sure for Pogo's sake.

Once he was sure that no cars were coming, Alex gave a short whistle and Pogo bounded into and across the wide street. She disappeared into the weeds of the vacant lot that was her favorite place to do her business. Alex liked the lot too. It gave him another excuse not to clean up after his dog, and every now and then Pogo would catch and kill a rat.

Alex took his time as he crossed the street. He hoped that Pogo would be done by the time he got there and then they could just go home and have some breakfast before he had to leave for school.

When Alex stepped onto the sidewalk and into the outer fringe of the lot, he heard Pogo barking and growling. Alex's heart sank. He was afraid Pogo may have run into one of the many strays in the area and that she may get hurt in a fight.

"Pogo! Here girl, here!" He called as he crashed through dying bramble and weeds. Pogo wasn't responding to his calls and Alex could feel himself start to panic. He could still hear Pogo, closer now as he ran and stumbled toward the back of the lot, and he imagined her surrounded by a pack of mangy, slavering strays. 'How would he be able to help her if they were surrounded by a bunch of other dogs?' Alex wasn't sure, but he vowed he'd try.

Suddenly, he tripped and fell, landing hard on his elbows and forearms. He laid there a moment with his eyes closed, catching his breath and mentally going through his damage control checklist. He felt a warm trickle on his cheek, touched it, and looked at his fingers. Blood.

"Shit!" he yelled. "Fuck!" He could never use those words anywhere near his mother, but out in the lot, at this moment of personal pain and embarrassment, he felt free to use them both—loudly and liberally.

Alex touched the wounded area on his face gingerly and came away with more blood. He looked nearby and didn't see any broken glass, so he figured that he must have cut his face on some bramble as he fell. He sat up and searched for what could have tripped him. He spotted the culprit, stretched so that he could reach it, and dragged it to him. It was a kid's knapsack.

Its weight and bulky shape suggested that it was filled with books. A quick peek inside confirmed it. The bag was filled with schoolbooks and the usual assortment of boring school supplies.

Barks and growls from nearby reminded Alex that Pogo may still be in some kind of trouble and he leapt up with the heavy knapsack dangling from the strap in his hand.

"Pogo," he called out. "Pogo!" Alex's cries were answered by several high-pitched whines from his dog. Alex followed the sound and immediately spotted Pogo sniffing something in a fragrant stand of wild garlic. Relieved and curious, he hurried over to her.

"What you got girl?" he asked. "You got a rat? You got another rat?"

Alex scratched Pogo behind her ears. Pogo whined again, snuggled his hand, and went back to what she was doing. Alex looked down and saw that Pogo was tugging on a sneaker. A sneaker that still had a foot in it. A foot, he saw, that was still attached to the lifeless body of a boy about his own age.

The knapsack dropped from Alex's hand...forgotten. As Alex ran home, he was only marginally aware of another warm trickle, this time going down his leg.

CHAPTER 23

AGENT SANDUSKY ADJUSTED the microphone again and cleared his throat.

"As I was saying," he began to say. "The failure of CLIS to immediately match up and ID those slugs could point to a perp who uses a specialty caliber or perhaps even a homemade weapon and/or ammunition. That possibility would narrow the search for the killer considerably."

There was some mumbled agreement from the gathered detectives and federal agents.

"And so," Sandusky continued. "Our introduction to the killer begins with someone who uses a weapon with a specialized caliber, perhaps forced to do so because circumstances prevent him from obtaining a weapon of a more common make or caliber. More than likely, however, our killer is a gun enthusiast—possibly a survivalist or member of a survivalist-type club or organization..."

For the next hour or so, Agent Sandusky "introduced" the killer to those present by providing a profile of serial murderers in general.

"So," Agent Sandusky said when he'd finished, ticking each point off on his fingers as he spoke. "Most serial killers are male, white, and fall somewhere between the ages of 25 to 35 years old. Most come from working-class, blue collar homes where they may have been abused as children. Most hope to achieve some sort of notoriety or status through their crimes, and most act totally, positively *sane*."

"In fact," Sandusky continued. "The killer can be downright charming—the guy next door."

Sandusky motioned to the geeky man in the black suit who hurried to set up a flip chart next to the podium. While that was going on, Sandusky leaned his elbows on the podium and looked out at the assemblage. To Ramos, it seemed almost as if Sandusky were addressing him personally.

"And most," he pressed on. "Feel no regret or guilt for their crimes. None."

The man in the black suit finished setting up the flip chart and at a signal from Sandusky, turned the first sheet over to reveal a simple line drawing of a man's head in profile. The brain was the only thing that was rendered in vivid color. Sandusky pulled a pen-like object from his breast pocket and telescoped it open. It was a pointer and he slapped its length against the drawing of the man's brain.

"No one really knows what makes a serial killer," he said. "Some scientists are suggesting that it's a genetic disorder; that there are persons born with an inbred propensity for killing *en masse*. There's another school of thought, of course, that argues that socioeconomic pressures may be the culprit. Maybe lack of a belief in a God or a higher-power that would take one to task, or maybe even too strict a religious upbringing can create a serial killer."

Agent Sandusky paused, tapped the picture on the flip chart a few times with the tip of his pointer, and then continued.

"The bottom line is that no one really knows. The reasons as to why someone starts killing are as diverse, as complicated and as numerous, as the people in this room, but there does seem to be a common thread linking most serial killers and most serial *killings*."

At this point Sandusky motioned to the man in the black suit again and he flipped the page over to reveal an identical drawing, only this time with S-E-X stenciled in large letters over the brain. He slapped his pointer against the picture as he'd done earlier.

"Sex gentlemen," he said as the cops and agents chuckled. "In most cases involving multiple killings, there is an underlying aspect, not always discernible at first, of sexuality."

"But haven't there been several cases where the killers abstained from sex before and during their killing spree and were, in fact, actually repulsed by the act of sex itself?" This question came from one of the federal agents seated on one of the increasingly uncomfortable chairs in the audience.

Sandusky nodded. "Absolutely," he said. "Those individuals for the most part believed that sex was dirty and they considered abstention from sex to be an act of purification. Again, it's the donut/donut-hole theory."

There were a few groans from the audience, but not as many as before.

"Our killer is definitely into the sexual aspect of his crimes," Sandusky said. "This is evidenced by the facts that semen has been found at each of the crime scenes, that each of the victims was a known or suspected male prostitute, and..."

Here Agent Sandusky paused for effect.

"...And the symbolic method of shooting each victim once through the mouth. Considering the nature of the business each victim was involved in, the way they died has very overt sexual connotations."

Sandusky leaned back, a smile of satisfaction on his face. An aide to the deputy mayor scribbled furiously into a steno pad.

Sandusky motioned to the black-suited man again and the page was flipped over to the next sheet. There was an illustration of a man wearing a suit on this page. The man was remarkable only in his unremarkableness. His plainness. His ordinariness. Sandusky slapped the pointer against this page as well and continued.

"So this is basically who we're looking for," he said. "The unsub or perp in this particular case is probably a male, white, thirty-one to forty years old. He's tall, over six feet and strong. He's got to be big enough to physically handle his victims, but not overly intimidating. He doesn't want to scare them away. He's probably not *old* money, but he has achieved some sort of higher social standing and acceptance. He enjoys his status on the upper rungs of his social circle and fiercely guards it and what he probably considers the trappings of high society—a high maintenance wife, kids in the best boarding or private schools, and a home in suburbia with a Mercedes and/or a 'Beamer' in the garage."

"You think this guy's married?" a voice called out.

"I think it is highly probable that the killer is married and is living what must seem to everyone around him a 'normal life'. That's why he's been so elusive. After he's committed a murder, he's able to shed his killer's persona and function as a normal person until the urge to kill comes upon him again."

Agent Sandusky removed a red marker from his pocket and drew a large red "X" across the figure on the flip chart. "All of those things I mentioned will become the instruments that will lead us to him," he said. "The pressures of holding down a job, keeping up appearances, sustaining an active social and marital life while operating in secrecy as a multiple killer will prove to be too much. He'll have to find an outlet. He may even divulge his double-identity to someone he considers a confidante. Either way, he's going to blow-up or slip-up, and we'll be at hand to catch him."

Sandusky nodded to the agent in the black suit, who then folded up the flip chart and moved it out of the way. Just then, the desk sergeant opened the conference room door, took a quick look around, and hurried over to the police commissioner. The deputy mayor took in their exchange with a look of impatience and distaste on his face.

Ramos saw the commissioner's jaw set as he nodded to something the sergeant was saying. Then the commissioner said thank you and gave the sergeant's shoulder a squeeze. The sergeant attempted a clumsy salute and hurried out the same door he'd entered through.

The commissioner got up, strode to the podium, and shouldered his way to the microphone as Agent Sandusky looked on curiously. What the commissioner said next instantly galvanized everyone in the room to action.

"There's been another killing," he announced.

CHAPTER 24

RAMOS WAS EXHAUSTED, but he wasn't about to admit it to Tommy Cucitti. They'd both spent over six hours at the latest crime scene near the Botanical Garden, and had basically come up empty. Besides, the place had been a zoo.

The media was there in full force, with news vans from every network clogging the street. Reporters representing every newspaper in town yelled incoherent questions at anyone in a uniform or wearing a badge. Cops, feds, people from the DA's and mayor's office were all over the place; grandstanding, and trampling all over the crime scene. It was a fiasco, and Ramos would have blown his stack if he weren't so busy trying to preserve the integrity of the scene as much as possible while keeping Tommy from punching out a television news crew member.

"Yo Eddie," Tommy hollered from the passenger's side. "Sorry about goin' off earlier, but those news people kept getting in my way; getting in my face...and they kept asking me the *stupidest* questions!"

Ramos nodded.

Tommy waited for more of a response, and when none came, he continued.

"I know there ain't no excuse man."

"That's right Tommy," Ramos finally said. "There's no excuse, so forget about it for now. We were both under a lot of pressure—the whole crime scene was a joke and I was only a step away from doing the same thing."

"But you didn't."

Ramos nodded again. "That's right, I didn't."

Tommy nodded and settled deeper into his seat. He was sure he felt at least as miserable as Ramos looked.

"Yo Eddie," Tommy said after several minutes of quiet. "Can you leave me back at headquarters?"

"What's up?" Ramos growled.

"Nothin' son, I'm just too wound up to go straight home. I figure I could start in on some of the paperwork, enter some stuff into the computer, make some calls..."

"You sure, Tommy?" Ramos asked. "I'm going home, so it would be no problem to drop you off at Atlantic Avenue so you can catch the LIRR."

"Yeah, yeah I'm sure," Tommy said. "If it gets too late, I can crash at Daphne's apartment." Tommy stifled a yawn.

Ramos raised an eyebrow as he maneuvered the car into a turn that would take them down Seventh Avenue.

"I thought Daphne lived with you at your place," Ramos said.

"Yeah, she does right now," Tommy explained. "But she's still paying the rent at her apartment in Bensonhurst."

"Bensonhurst?" Ramos asked. "Shit, if you're gonna ride all the way to Bensonhurst from up here, you might as well go all the way home."

Tommy nodded. "True dat," he agreed. No further rationalization was forthcoming.

Ramos pulled up to the curb in front of the imposing structure the Manhattan North Homicide Division called home and let his partner out of the car.

"Tomorrow," Ramos said before pulling away.

"Later," Tommy said. Then he climbed up the wide steps and entered the building.

CHAPTER 25

AS HE DROVE south, toward Brooklyn, Ramos pulled a mint from his pocket and popped it into his mouth. While he munched away at it, he considered what he had to look forward to once he got home. He expected that his wife Linda and Kim, their youngest daughter, would be at church again.

Ramos sighed, he really wasn't looking forward to another lonely evening and a microwaved dinner.

Ramos looked up, saw he was nearing Thirty-Fourth Street and made a left turn. He drove east, past Madison Square Garden, Macy's Department Store, and the gaudy lights of the Manhattan Mall. Soon he saw the distant lights of the Empire State Building floating in the sky like a huge, glowing party hat. He drove past the famous landmark, made a right, and parked at the bus stop in front of his favorite restaurant; The Jackson Hole.

Ramos put his police parking permit in the windshield as usual and entered the boisterous atmosphere of the country and western themed eatery.

Country music, casual conversation, and the smell of seared beef enveloped Ramos in their homey, welcoming embrace and he felt his shoulders relax. As he sidled past the huge antique cash register to his left, he caught the attention of the bartender and pointed over the heads of the crowd toward the rear of the restaurant. The bartender smiled and nodded while Ramos continued on past the bar.

Ramos squeezed around the seemingly arbitrarily placed tables and chairs as he made his way to his favorite spot, a big, round wooden table under a large, black-and-white photo of John Wayne and a vintage Coca-Cola sign stamped out of tin.

"Hey Nance," Ramos greeted as he pulled out a chair and sat down.

"Hi yourself detective," she said.

A waitress came by and placed a bottle of ice-cold *Dos Equis* beer and a glass in front of the cop. Next to those, she placed a saucer holding several wedges of lime.

"The usual?" she asked. Ramos nodded and she left, disappearing like a wraith into the crowd.

Nance took a sip of her own beer. Ramos noticed how she drummed her fingers to the beat of the music.

"You like country music?" Ramos asked.

Nance stopped drumming and rolled her eyes playfully. You always ask me that," she said. "And I always tell you that I like all kinds of music."

Ramos said the last part with her. "You're right," he added with a shake of his head. "Just trying to make conversation," he added.

Nance laughed. "You're trying alright," she said. "But you're just no damn good at it." She laughed again and Ramos felt his face redden; then he laughed too.

"You're lucky you caught me here tonight," Nance said. "Once I saw that none of the rest of the gang was going to show up, I was just going to grab something quick and go home."

The waitress reappeared with Ramos' usual and set it on the table in front of him before disappearing again. Nance looked distastefully at the huge burger, the fried egg on top still sizzling and leaking yolk. Ramos used his knife and fork to slice away an edible-sized piece, ate it, and washed it down with beer. He repeated this several times, at one point changing the procedure by pausing long enough to rub lime onto the rim of the beer glass.

"You know," Nance said as Ramos dug into the last of his burger. "I can hear your arteries hardening from here."

Ramos leaned back contentedly. "Yeah," he said. "But what a way to go." He downed the last of his beer and scanned the crumbs on his plate as if hoping that he'd somehow missed a particularly delectable morsel.

Amused, Nance watched him. She and Ramos had been coming to the Jackson Hole for years, sometimes alone, or one would find the others there and join them. As partners, friends, and associates came and went, the number of people at the table would swell or diminish. But in the end, the constant would always still be she or Ramos. Since Tommy Cucitti had become Ramos' partner, he was a frequent visitor and there'd been times when she'd shared the table, a meal, and a conversation with just Tommy.

Nance drained her glass and motioned to the waitress for another. She liked Tommy, but he was a lot like most of the other men she'd known, he did most of his talking to her breasts. Ramos on the other hand was enough of a gentleman to think he'd actually gotten away with the surreptitious glances he'd helped himself to when he thought she wouldn't notice, and besides, he always looked her right in the eye when they spoke.

The waitress returned with Nance's beer and Nance immediately took a deep swallow of the icy liquid. She licked the foam from her lips and sighed appreciatively. She caught Ramos looking at her and he quickly looked away, pretending sudden interest in the photo of John Wayne that hung over her head.

Ramos and Nance spent the next hour or so talking about their jobs, mutual acquaintances, even the mayor.

"So the mayor keeps talking about how much better off we are since EMS was merged into the fire department," Nance was saying.

"I thought you would've figured that for a good thing," Ramos said. He was nursing his second beer, having only taken a few sips of it. "Aren't all of your brothers firemen?"

"*Firefighters*," Nance corrected.

"Okay, yeah, Firefighters," Ramos said. "There's like what, ten of them?"

Nance laughed. "Yeah, right," she said. "Maybe there were times when it felt like I had ten brothers, but it's just the three of them."

"Oh yeah," Ramos nodded. "Three. That must have been tough on your boyfriends."

Nance's lip curled as she smiled. She knew Ramos was fishing for a clue about her love life, but she wasn't going to bite.

"M-m-h-m-m," was her response as she took a sip of beer.

Eventually, conversation turned to the case and Ramos told Nance as much as he could without divulging any of the information considered confidential.

"So I guess it's like we thought," Nance said. "Another nut job going around killing people. What do we do in this city, breed them?"

Ramos shrugged. "Must be the water," he said.

They continued their conversation for several more minutes, until Ramos checked his watch and announced that it was time he left.

"Want a lift anywhere?" Ramos asked after the waitress handed him his check.

"Nah," Nance replied. "My car is parked not too far from here, I'll be alright."

Ramos nodded, waved, and walked over to the antique cash register to pay his bill. Nance watched his broad back until he made his way out the front door and slowly shook her head.

CHAPTER 26

RAMOS CROSSED THE Brooklyn Bridge and made a right on Tillary Street. If he'd made a left, toward Park Avenue, he'd be headed straight home, but as was his habit, he planned to drive past Father Salvatelli's church.

Ramos slowed the car as he drove past the church and made the sign of the cross out of respect. There was a light on in the attached parsonage and Ramos parked out front. The light wasn't unusual, the Father was an avid reader and he often stayed up late with a good book.

Ramos got out of his car, walked up the worn slate steps of the parsonage, and hesitated at the front door. The detective looked up and down the night shrouded streets. There were lights on in most of the houses, brownstones for the most part. Ramos imagined families in those homes, finishing up dinner, watching T.V., or maybe just sitting around talking. Ramos rang the bell and waited patiently with his hands folded until an elderly man in a bathrobe and slippers opened the door.

Father Salvatelli was in his seventies, slightly stooped, and wore a hearing aid. Yet, his demeanor, his aura, spoke not of frailty, but of inner strength. His voice too, was strong and clear when he spoke.

"Hello Eddie," he said. "And what brings you to my door this chilly evening?"

Ramos was about to say, when the priest opened the door wider and ushered him in.

"Close the door tightly my boy," Father Salvatelli said over his shoulder as he walked to his study. "These old bones don't appreciate a draft."

Ramos closed the door and followed the priest into a shadowed room heavy with drapery and the lingering scent of cigar smoke.

Father Salvatelli moved a small pile of books from a chair, offered the chair to Ramos, and returned to his own seat awash in the soft glow of a reading lamp. On a small table next to the priest's chair, a cigar smoldered in an old glass ashtray. Thick blue-gray smoke curled from its lit end and gathered near the ceiling like a miniature storm cloud.

"Would you like something to drink?" Father Salvatelli asked.

Ramos declined.

The priest tapped the ash from the end of his cigar and then extinguished it altogether.

"Father, don't! You don't have to..." Ramos began.

The priest waved away his objections with the same gnarled hand that held the now unlit cigar.

"Nonsense," Salvatelli said. "I know that you've recently given up smoking, so I can imagine what a, uh, distraction my smoking must be to you."

Ramos looked longingly at the swirling fog of cigar smoke that still lingered near the ceiling. *The old priest was right of course*, Ramos thought, but it just smelled so good! For a brief moment, Ramos felt a flash of anger at being deprived a good secondhand smoke fix, but it only lasted a moment and Ramos settled into his chair with a sigh.

Father Salvatelli looked at Ramos knowingly and then indicated the dead cigar between his two fingers. "Ah, the vices of man," he said. "If I weren't so old, I'd probably do the smart thing and try to give up smoking these stinkers myself."

The priest carefully placed the cigar back in the ashtray, then rubbed his hands together and suddenly brought them together in a single loud clap.

"So my boy," Father Salvatelli said. "Tell me what brings you to my door at this hour."

Ramos told the priest about his wife's leaving the parish and her apparent recent success in finding a new church home.

Father Salvatelli listened patiently, interrupting only once or twice to ask a question or clarify a point.

"It worries you that your wife has chosen to leave the parish and attend a Protestant church," the priest stated.

Ramos shook his head. "*Non-denominational,*" he corrected.

Father Salvatelli's bony shoulders moved up in an almost imperceptible shrug.

Ramos' eyebrow matched the priest's shrug. He was mildly surprised to have seen Father Salvatelli use that non-committal gesture just then.

"No. No, I can't say I'm worried really," Ramos continued. "She does spend a lot of time over there, but I guess I was kinda hoping that you wouldn't be feelin' insulted or anything because she left."

"I have missed her at Mass," the priest said. "I'd meant to inquire after her..."

"Oh, well she's okay," Ramos said. "It's just this new church thing. It's probably a phase or something—she'll be comin' back here when she gets over it."

Father Salvatelli stroked his chin and nodded his head slowly up and down. "Well Eddie," he said. "Linda hasn't contacted the church concerning a wish to officially remove herself from the parish, or even the Catholic faith altogether."

Ramos pushed himself back into his chair and waved his hands in the air between the priest and himself.

"No, no, no," he said. "I'm sure she doesn't want to do that..."

"Few even bother with the formalities these days Eddie..."

"Nah, Father," Ramos said. "It's like I said, she's probably goin' through some woman or age thing, and she'll be back when she figures it out."

Father Salvatelli waved his hand in a dismissive gesture. "If you're worried about my being insulted that your wife is seeking other avenues of worship, Eddie...well, I'm not," he said. "I'd prefer to see her at Mass of course, as I have since the day I performed your marriage service more than twenty years ago..."

Ramos nodded.

"Your daughters, both of them, were baptized and confirmed at this church."

Ramos could only nod again.

Father Salvatelli sighed. Suddenly, to Ramos, the priest seemed very old and frail indeed.

"You know," the priest began. "See if your wife might be interested in one of those new *Charismatic* Catholic churches I've heard about. They're not exactly traditional."

Ramos made the sign of the cross. "Father, I'm sorry I..."

The priest waved away Ramos' apology and stood up. "There is no need for apologies my boy," he said tiredly. "You know your wife better than any other earthly being. If you say that she will return to the church, then I will accept on faith that return she will, and I will pray to that effect until it comes to pass."

Ramos nodded, stood, and again made the sign of the cross. Father Salvatelli gave him a warm pat on the back as he escorted Ramos to the front door.

Dead leaves riding a gust of cold air blew into the house when the priest opened the front door.

Ramos thanked Father Salvatelli and made to leave, but he stopped when the priest laid a hand on his arm.

"Ultimately," the old priest said as he patted Ramos on the arm. "Ultimately, we all serve the same God."

Ramos nodded, returned to his car and drove off.

CHAPTER 27

The next morning dawned cold and clear, with promises from the television weatherman of temperatures reaching the low seventies by mid-day. Paki awakened in good cheer, feeling much like his old self and feeling stronger and healthier than he had in days.

Paki arrived at his office as usual and sat in front of his computer. He snapped open his attaché case, removed a folder, and proceeded to review his notes.

Then the telephone rang. For some reason the ringing of the telephone annoyed him.

Paki let the phone ring several times before he punched the conference button.

Hello?" he barked into space. There was a moment's hesitation on the other end and then a woman's voice.

"Paki?" It was Katherine, his wife. "Paki?"

"Yes," Paki answered irritably.

"Oh, there you are," his wife said sounding relieved. "We seem to have a bad connection darling, you sound funny."

"I have you on conference, Katie."

"Oh."

There was another moment's silence before Paki's wife spoke again.

"In there anyone else there with you?" she asked.

"No Katie," Paki answered.

"Oh. Good," Katherine said. "I dislike those things, you know, it's like being on display."

Paki wiped his face with his handkerchief and stifled three sneezes in quick succession. Suddenly his eyes itched and began to water, and he used his handkerchief to cover his now runny nose. His immune system was breaking down, he could almost feel it.

"Katie!" Paki said. "What is it that you want?"

"Oh!" Katherine's exclamation sounded more like a yelp.

"I, uh, was just calling to remind you about the dinner party tonight. I know you haven't been feeling well lately, but seeing as we are the hosts you simply must make an appearance."

Paki's hand went to his forehead and he squeezed his throbbing temples between his thumb and middle finger.

Katherine was right, of course, he thought. *He and his wife were well-known throughout all of eastern Long Island for the high-class soirees they threw. Only A-list guests were ever invited, along with whoever the celebrity of the day happened to be. This particular get-together was supposed to be a fund-raiser for the Republican Party, even the mayor of New York City was expected to attend.*

"Don't worry Katie, I didn't forget," he said.

"Oh good."

"I'll probably even be the life of the party."

"I know you will dear. Well, I must be going; there are a million things I have to do before tonight."

"I know."

"Very well then. I'll see you tonight. Love you, bye."

Paki nodded and broke the connection. When he looked up, he saw through the glass of his office door that Silverman and Lorna, his secretary, were in deep conversation. At one point they both cast glances in Paki's direction and quickly turned away when they saw him watching them.

"Humph," Paki muttered to himself. "That's probably why I didn't get my coffee this morning."

Paki repacked his attaché case and started to walk around his desk to leave when he remembered what Silverman said about reprinting some of his old columns during his absence.

Paki packed most of those away in his case as well. What didn't fit, he shredded. Then he instructed his computer to format all drives.

Once he'd made it difficult for anyone to salvage any of his work, Paki left his office and walked past Silverman and his secretary while they stared at him with equal measures of curiosity and concern. Paki left the building a short time later, blinking his eyes at the brilliant fall day, and melted inconspicuously into the crowd.

CHAPTER 28

RAMOS WALKED TO the counter, poured himself a cup of coffee, and returned to his seat at the small kitchen table. His daughter Kim, in her school uniform, was busy slurping away at her breakfast cereal. His wife, Linda, had been telling him about her new church.

"It's wonderful Eddie," Linda said, twisting a loose strand of her long auburn hair in her fingers like she always did whenever she was happy or excited. "Last night all we did was praise. There wasn't any singing, no preaching...oh no, we just raised our voices in thanking the Lord for all of his precious gifts and mercies! Oh, there was such an anointing in that place last night!"

Linda looked off wistfully and took a sip of water from her glass. She'd already explained to her husband that she was fasting.

Ramos took a bite of his English muffin and nearly dropped it in surprise when his wife leapt from her chair and spun around the room in apparently uncontrollable glee, her slim arms flung wide open.

"Praise Him Eddie! Praise the Lord! Hallelujah!"

Ramos began to feel slightly alarmed. He'd never seen Linda in such a state of, what? Euphoria? She was acting intoxicated.

"Linda," Ramos began.

"That's right Eddie, praise Him. Praise Him with your mouth. Praise God, praise God, praise the Lord, Hallelujah!"

Ramos looked at his daughter, afraid that his wife's actions may have frightened her. Instead, Kim finished slurping down the last of the milk in her cereal bowl before she snatched the second half of her father's English muffin. Ramos' gaze returned to his wife who continued her praising and dancing into the dining room.

"Pop? I'm going to be late."

Ramos turned to where Kimberly was standing, next to him, backpack over one shoulder and tapping her foot impatiently while she munched on his English muffin.

"Huh? Oh yeah sure. Sorry princess." Ramos stood up, finished the rest of his coffee and placed the cup and his plate in the sink. "Is, uh, your mom alright?" He asked as father and daughter walked through the dining room toward the front of the house. Linda was now in the foyer praying fervently.

"Yeah," Kim answered totally nonplussed. "She gets like that after church. Last night she did it too, but kind of quietly. I guess this morning she figures she can yell all she wants."

Ramos nodded. He had noticed that after attending services in her new church, Linda would return home excited, exhausted, or both. Still, he didn't understand it.

"You should see her in church," Kim continued as they walked through the living room. "When the Holy Ghost gets her, she falls out and everything."

"Holy Ghost?" Ramos asked, but by now they were in the foyer and Linda grabbed his hand. She had Kim's hand too.

"Before anyone leaves this house," Linda said. "We are going to pray as a family. You start Eddie."

Ramos felt bewildered, but he automatically chose a Rosary he'd learned as a child and knew by heart.

"No!" Linda practically screamed, causing both her husband and daughter to jump. "No," Linda repeated. "Not that. I will lead us in prayer."

Linda then recited a prayer that Ramos had never heard before, interspersed with plenty of Father Gods and Hallelujahs, and a strange muttering that sounded to Ramos like so much gibberish. Kim explained later that the "gibberish" was actually her mother speaking in *tongues.*

When the prayer was over and everyone had said their Amens, Ramos sent Kim out to the car so that he could speak to his wife of over twenty years alone.

Ramos took Linda's other hand in his as well and looked deep into her hazel-colored eyes. They were still the eyes he knew so well, the eyes of his best friend and lover.

Her eyes aren't bloodshot or shiny, thought Ramos. *The pupils aren't dilated.* Ramos shook off his cop mode and squeezed Linda's hands.

"Uh, Father Salvatelli says he misses you at Mass," Ramos said softly. "Maybe you should give this new church thing a rest for awhile..."

Linda shook her head. "I'm not going back Eddie," she said. "I can't go back."

"Whaddaya mean you can't go back? I spoke to Father Salvatelli last night and he said he's not mad at you or anything..." Ramos said.

"Mad at me?" Linda asked rhetorically. Mad at me? I'm the one who is angry at him! I'm angry at *him* for presenting himself as a man of God and yet letting me and all those other people at his so-called church suffer a lack of salvation, a lack of the Word, and a lack of true worship and praise. No Eddie, I'm never going back to that institution of religious tradition and idol worship. Dogma and doctrine are more important there than..."

"Hold it, hold it," Ramos said hotly. "What are you talking about, *idol worship*? We don't worship any idols..."

"What about all the statues and icons that everyone practically bows and scrapes to? And what about the time you insisted on waving a stupid white handkerchief at another idol while we were at the parade this summer?"

"That's different," Ramos insisted. "Those aren't like, idols or anything, those are *saints.* And the one at the parade wasn't an idol either, it was a statue of the Blessed Virgin, *El Virgin Del Pozo.* I mean, come on Linda, that's God's mother."

Linda yanked her hands from his and knotted them into fists at her sides.

"*She-is-not-God's-mother,*" she said angrily. "The real Mary was just a vessel that God used in order to manifest himself in the flesh as God the Son."

"Well, isn't that what I..."

"No, it isn't," Linda continued. "And that thing at the parade wasn't Mary, it was a statue. An idol. And you were worshipping it by waving your handkerchief at it."

"Linda, honey," Ramos said soothingly. "I wasn't worshipping anything. It's tradition to wave a white handkerchief at the *Virgin Del Pozo*."

"That's right Eddie, tradition. You care more about tradition than the Word of God. Waving a stupid handkerchief at a stupid statue is not Biblical. It's not holy."

"It was not a stupid statue Linda," Ramos said firmly. Then he glanced at his watch and saw that Kim was indeed going to be late. "Look Linda, I gotta run," he said as he went to the door. "Kim's gonna be late for school and I'm gonna be late for work."

Linda nodded and Ramos could see that her face was wet with tears. He started to go to her, but instead opened the door and left.

Ramos drove in silence while Kim sat in the back seat as usual and finished up her homework. Books and papers were piled up on the seat next to her. Ramos glanced at her in the rearview mirror.

"You know," he said. "You should finish your homework the night before so you wouldn't get stuck trying to finish it the next morning."

"I don't mind working on it in the morning," Kim answered without looking up from her work. "I get so much homework that I'd be up all night if I tried to do it all at once. This way, I can get some sleep and maybe watch some T.V."

Kim looked up and offered her father a dazzling smile via the rearview mirror.

"Yeah," Ramos said. "T.V., that'll help get you a job someday."

"Oh, I don't plan on getting a job," Kim said matter-of-factly. "I figure I can live off my inheritance."

Ramos looked into his rearview mirror again and locked eyes with his daughter. Then they both burst into laughter.

They were still laughing when Ramos pulled to a stop in front of the school a few minutes later. Kim scooped her books and papers into her backpack and hopped from the car. Ramos put the car in park and exited from the car as well, walking around the front and meeting Kim on the sidewalk. Kim rolled her eyes when she saw him there.

"Pop," she said, drawing it out so that it sounded like, 'Pah-ah-ah-op.'

Ramos raised a parental eyebrow.

Kim looked around suspiciously, afraid that one of her peers might actually see her talking to her father.

"You don't have to get out of the car and watch me anymore I'm not a little kid."

Now it was Ramos' turn to roll his eyes. "Yeah, yeah. I know," he said. "You're a young woman now."

"That's right."

Ramos reached out suddenly and hugged her. "We never should have given you that Sweet Sixteen..."

"Fifteen, Pop," Kim corrected gently. "I was fifteen, remember? It was a *quinceñeara.*"

Ramos let her go and looked into her eyes. Eyes as dark and as deep as his own, but wider and more expressive, like her mother's.

"Yeah, that's right," Ramos said. "Fifteen."

"Right," Kim said slowly, nodding her head. "But I'm sixteen now."

Ramos nodded back and then scrunched up his face. "Hey," he said. "I know you're sixteen! Sheesh, make one little mistake..."

"That's okay Pop," Kim said lightly. "I forgive you." She laughed and Ramos smiled. "Well, gotta go," she said before taking a quick look around to make sure no one was watching. "*Bendición.*"

Kim gave her father a quick peck on the cheek and then skipped up the steps to her school before disappearing inside.

Dios te bendiga y te acompañe, Ramos said softly. He was glad that Kim still used the traditional form of greeting or goodbye that he'd grown up using. Ramos climbed into his car and headed for the bridge that would take him uptown.

CHAPTER 29

TOMMY WAS PISSED. Ramos could see it as soon as he entered the squad room. Tommy stalked around his desk like a panther in a cage, his fists stuffed into his pants pockets. As soon as he saw Ramos, he stomped over to meet him halfway between the door and their desks.

"Yo Eddie, we been fucked!"

Ramos looked down and slowly unbuttoned his coat while Tommy looked on impatiently.

"Eddie," Tommy persisted. "We have been screwed my brother, and they didn't even bother to buy us dinner first. It's wham, bam, thank you Detectives Ramos and Cucitti!"

Ramos stopped and didn't bother to take his coat off. He suddenly had a premonition that he wouldn't have to. He looked up and was struck by the fact that, Tommy's ranting aside, the usual sounds of the squad room were muted. It was quiet.

Whispers replaced the loud conversations and laughter, even the occasional cough seemed hushed. Most of his colleague's faces were turned in his direction, some of them turning away when he caught their eye. They all seemed to be waiting. At that moment Ramos became painfully aware of two things:

One, Tommy and he must somehow indeed have been fucked and everyone else apparently knew about it.

Two, it sure doesn't pay to show up late.

Ramos looked back at a seething Tommy Cucitti. "What's going on?" he asked.

"Yo, Eddie," Tommy said. "Check this shit out—we're not on the taskforce anymore, we've been reassigned!"

Ramos responded with a raised eyebrow and a grunt, a reaction leagues away from the one Tommy felt was warranted by the news he'd just imparted. Ramos took a quick look in the direction of the lieutenant's office. The door was closed.

"Who told you this?" Ramos asked.

"Mullen."

"The lieutenant?"

"What'd I just say?"

Ramos nodded, then turned and walked to the lieutenant's office. He entered without knocking. The lieutenant, his glasses perched on the end of his nose, didn't look up.

"Sit down," the lieutenant said.

Ramos hesitated, debating whether or not he should sit, then sat down anyway.

The lieutenant continued his paperwork while Ramos fidgeted in the chair. Finally, Ramos was unable to restrain himself any longer and blurted out," What the hell's going on, loo?"

Lieutenant Mullen looked at Ramos over the rim of his glasses. "You and Tommy aren't on the task force."

"That much I heard," Ramos growled. "The real question is, *why*?"

"You two have been reassigned to the DA's office."

Ramos' eyes widened. "The district attorney's office? How the hell..."

The lieutenant went back to his paperwork. "I don't want to hear it," he said without looking back up. "I already got an earful from your partner earlier and, if it weren't for the reassignment, he would have earned himself a couple of week's suspension to think about it."

Ramos stood up and walked to the lieutenant's desk. The lieutenant didn't acknowledge the detective until Ramos loomed over him.

"You don't wanna hear it?" Ramos asked.

Lieutenant Mullen nodded. "That's right, you..."

"Bullshit!" Ramos slammed the palm of his hand on the desk with a sound as loud as a gunshot. Almost immediately, Mullen's intercom buzzed. Without taking his eyes off of Ramos, Mullen pressed the flashing button on the intercom and lifted the receiver.

"Yeah," the lieutenant said, still looking Ramos unwaveringly in the eye. "Everything's fine. No, that's not necessary. Thank you." He hung up.

"You're on the verge of becoming insubordinate, Eddie," Mullen said quietly, his voice tinged with threat.

"Insubordinate?" Ramos asked. "You pull Tommy and me from..."

"I didn't pull anyone from anything," Mullen corrected.

Ramos drew a deep breath and then continued. "Tommy and me got reassigned," Ramos said. "From a case we'd been working from the beginning. Now, just as it's heating up, you're sayin' we're gone, poof, just like that?"

The lieutenant nodded.

"And now we're working for Williams..."

"The DA," the lieutenant corrected.

"The DA," Ramos repeated. He looked up at the mayor's portrait. The thin line that passed for the mayor's mouth seemed more resolute than Ramos remembered, or maybe that was just a reflection of Ramos' own growing frustration.

"So," he said after a moment. "Who did we piss off?"

Lieutenant Mullen allowed himself a slight smile. "Actually, no one," he said. "You and Tommy have been moving by the book on this one."

"Then why the reassignment?" Ramos asked.

The lieutenant looked hard at Ramos for a moment, sighed, then stood up and sat on the edge of his desk. "Eddie," he said. "We both know that the reassignment stinks, and it couldn't come at a worse time, but..."

"But..." Ramos urged.

"But," Mullen continued. "A couple of days ago when you were in my office we briefly discussed how politics affect a case...

"And this is politics?"

The lieutenant nodded, then returned to his chair and sat down. "You and Tommy take whatever you need to get settled at the DA's office, but leave everything you've got on this 'Chickenhawk' case here. Mike McCaughy's taking the lead as NYPD Coordinator now."

Lieutenant Mullen turned his eyes back to his paperwork. "I don't exactly know what's going on here myself Eddie," he said. "But I do know you shouldn't do anything at this point to rock the boat, and that goes double for Tommy. Hopefully this is just temporary and you guys will be back here breaking my balls again in no time."

"Loo," Ramos said. "The bottom line is that me and Tommy ain't interested in playing private eye or glorified security guard for that asshole, Williams..."

"The bottom line," Mullen interrupted. "Is that you're a cop and you go where you're sent."

"This is bullshit."

"You're dismissed Eddie."

"This is fucked up, lieutenant."

"You are dismissed!"

Ramos stood and left the lieutenant's office, Tommy joined him at their desks.

"So?" Tommy asked.

"So," Ramos said. "We pack up our stuff and move in with the DA."

Tommy looked aghast. "The DA? What the fuck are you talking about?"

"That's where we've been reassigned."

"What, just like that?"

Ramos was packing several files into a large, brown accordion-file envelope. "Yeah," he said. "Just like that."

"I don't believe this shit," Tommy said.

"Believe it man, we're outta here."

"Fuck!"

Tommy Cucitti went around to his desk and started tossing things into a garbage bag.

Ramos unplugged his coffeepot and made ready to take it with him. He changed his mind, however, and just stuck it into one of the desk drawers.

"Yo, son, I don't believe none of this shit," Tommy grumbled as he swept everything from the top of his desk into the garbage bag. "In fact," he said addressing Ramos. "The way you walked into the lieutenant's office, I thought you were gonna straighten this mess out."

"Yeah well," Ramos said. "See what you get for thinkin'?"

Ramos tucked the thick envelope under his arm and headed for the door where he was met by Detective McCaughy.

"So why you jumping ship, Eddie?" he asked.

"It's not voluntary," Ramos said.

"That's not what we heard," McCaughy said, signifying the rest of the room with a tilt of his head. "The word is that you couldn't handle the heat that this case is generating."

"You should know better than to listen to gossip, Mike."

"Sometimes gossip is based on truth," McCaughy said.

"Sometimes," Ramos agreed darkly. "Not this time though." He shouldered his way past McCaughy and through the door.

Tommy Cucitti finished filling his bag and hoisted it over his shoulder before heading for the door. Halfway there, the over laden bag burst open and spilled its contents onto the floor with a loud crash and clatter. The lieutenant stuck his head out of his office to investigate the noise and was greeted by the sight of Detective Tommy Cucitti standing amid a heap of papers and office supplies.

Tommy looked up from the mess he'd created and saw Mullen watching him.

"Tell you what," Tommy yelled. "You can keep all your shit!"

Tommy stomped and kicked at the stuff near his feet, sending papers flying, and pens, pencils, and stapler parts skidding across the room. The lieutenant shook his head, went back into his office, and closed the door.

Tommy, his tantrum spent, took one last look around the room and left, still clutching the remnants of the empty garbage bag.

CHAPTER 30

THE NEWSPAPERS, REPRESENTING every major New York daily, as well as their foreign-language or ethnically slanted counterparts, hit the highly polished tabletop with a heavy thud. All of the papers, with the exception of the Times, headlined the recent killings and the police department's apparent inability to catch the killer. The Times ran the story on page three, deferring its cover to Donald Trump and his latest billion dollar real estate deal.

"This is unacceptable," the mayor yelled, pointing at the pile of newspapers he'd just dropped onto the table. "The largest and, supposedly, best trained police force in the country and you can't even catch one goddamn psycho!"

The men and two women seated around the table chafed under the mayor's angry tirade. They had all been summoned to the mayor's office because the so-called "Chickenhawk" was still at large and the mayor was being skewered by the media.

Seated at the table were many of the same NYPD higher-ups who had attended the preliminary Joint Task Force meeting several days before, as well as all of the precinct and bureau commanders. One of the only two women in the room was NYPD spokesperson Sharon Dancy, who held the rank of lieutenant in the Public Relations Bureau. At the head of the table were the mayor and his Deputy Mayor, Michael Nitchik. Behind them, slightly off to the side, sat the only other woman in the room, the mayor's personal aide, Carmen Llandro.

Deputy Mayor Nitchik, hands clasped together and resting on his girth, glared around the room in an attempt to emulate the mayor's angry bearing. Carmen Llandro was busy scribbling away in her ever present steno pad.

"I cannot and I will not tolerate the lack of progress in this department's efforts, or perhaps lack of effort, in finding this killer," the mayor said staring at the commissioner of the NYPD.

The police commissioner looked around the room, as if trying to glean support or strength from his troops. He found and received—none. Sweat popped out on his already shiny brow.

"Andy?" the mayor prompted.

"Uh, Mr. Mayor," the commissioner said. "To be fair, we have over two hundred detectives assigned to this investigation, every uniformed officer has been briefed and put on the alert, and as per your directive, unconditional overtime for everyone working this case has been approved."

The mayor cut him off with an impatient wave of his hand. "Tell me something I don't know," he said gruffly. "I didn't call you here so you could hand me that PR mumbo jumbo, I want to hear about results. I want you people to tell me that you're close to catching this bastard."

The men and woman seated at the table shifted around uncomfortably. The mayor's eyes darted back and forth from underneath his dark brows, challenging each individual—demanding an answer.

"You can't, can you?" he finally said.

The chief of patrol stood up, gold embroidery flashing on his epaulets matched the gold shield pinned to his white shirt.

"Meaning no disrespect, Mr. Mayor," he said. "We've got people working on this night and day—our best people! It's only a matter of time..."

"Time?" The mayor thundered. "Time?"

"You can't expect the police department to just pull the guy out of our collective asses, like it was some kind of magic trick," the chief continued. "It takes the hard work and dedication of a lot of people, and most of all it takes *time*."

The mayor glared.

"Make no mistake, we *will* stop this maniac," the chief said. "We'll either catch him or kill him. But maybe because you've never been a cop, you just don't understand what it takes to get the job done."

The mayor glared at the chief who stared back with his own steely gaze, refusing to back down. The chief of patrol was a battle-scarred veteran of the force who'd started his career as a patrolman walking a beat in Hell's Kitchen. He'd seen mayors come, and he'd seen them go...and he'd never backed down from a fight.

The commissioner looked back and forth between the two men, mortified.

"How long have you been a cop?" the mayor asked. His voice carried the same ominous threat as distant thunderheads.

The chief of patrol blinked. "Excuse me?" he asked.

"How long have you been a cop?" The mayor asked in the same dark monotone.

"Thirty-five years," the chief answered, a note of pride in his voice.

The mayor grunted. "I'll expect your letter of resignation on my desk in the morning," he said.

"What?" The chief asked, incredulous.

The assemblage echoed the chief's shock and concern. The commissioner lowered his head and slowly shook it back and forth.

The chief gathered his wits and confronted the mayor. "I'm not going to retire," he said. "No one's going to force me to retire!"

The mayor shrugged his shoulders. "You can retire and collect a pension," he said. "Or you can be fired. Your choice."

The chief could only stare, his mouth open. His face was flushed red with anger and he looked around the room for the same support his commissioner had sought only minutes before, with the same results. His colleagues all looked away and refused to meet his eyes.

"You're excused from this meeting," the mayor said pointedly.

"I don't believe this!" The chief bellowed. "You can't do this!"

"Now!"

The chief searched the room again, but found no one willing to join him in his righteous indignation. "You can't do this," the chief repeated less loudly as he gathered his papers. "You'll be getting a call from my lawyer."

The mayor waved his hand dismissively. "And you can leave those there," he said, indicating the papers that the chief had been getting together. "That's the property of the City of New York."

The chief let the papers slip from his hands and land in an untidy pile on the desk. "Fuck you," he said in a tired voice. He turned and left the room, all eyes on his broad back until the door closed behind him.

Everyone then turned their eyes back to the mayor, who was busily rolling up his sleeves. The commissioner did all he could to avoid any stray looks from the others around the table, setting his gaze on the mayor's aide who was again writing in her steno pad.

The mayor leaned forward, resting the palms of his hands on the table. "It seems to me," he said, looking around the room, "that maybe some of you have been in the same place, doing the same thing, for far too long. You've all gotten comfortable; complacent...maybe you figure that it's business as usual. Well let me tell you, it is not business as usual, people. I am the mayor of this city and I intend to still be mayor another four years from now. I will not let a bunch of lazy, lead-assed, keystone cops and some psycho screw that up for me."

The mayor looked to his left. "Carmen," he said to his aide. "Get ready to take this down." He looked at the NYPD spokesperson. "Sharon, you take notes too and start preparing yourself for a press conference, I'm going to call one immediately after this meeting."

"Yes sir, Mr. Mayor," Lieutenant Dancy said.

"Andy," the mayor said, pointing his finger at the police commissioner. "It's time to shake up your department. Again"

The commissioner wiped his face with his hand and nodded weakly.

CHAPTER 31

RAMOS AND CUCITTI cooled their heels in the cramped waiting area of the Manhattan district attorney's Harlem headquarters. At first, Ramos and Cucitti had gone to the previous DA's headquarters at One Hogan Place in Lower Manhattan. Once there, they were informed that the district attorney had relocated his main base of operations to the Harlem office at 163 West 125th Street—the State Building. Ramos and Cucitti knew the location well, since it was the closest thing to a skyscraper in all of Harlem.

Now they sat in the pastel-colored waiting area, surrounded by African and African American inspired prints on the walls, growing more impatient and determined not to let it show.

Tommy's cell phone whistled a short tune in lieu of a ring and he answered it.

"Can't your phone just ring like everyone else's?" Ramos growled.

Tommy winked and continued his conversation in earnest whispers, hunched over the electronic device for added privacy. Ramos had seen this particular posture enough times to know that Tommy was deeply involved in a conversation with his girlfriend, Daphne. Daphne was a tough, streetwise young woman in her late twenties who'd once told Ramos that she'd grown up in the Fort Greene projects in downtown Brooklyn.

Ramos was familiar with the area since it was relatively near to where he lived now with his wife and kids. When he'd first met Daphne, he'd been slightly taken aback by her peculiar makeup job, which consisted mostly of heavily applied eyeliner that continued in thick straight lines from the outside corners of her eyes like the ancient Egyptians purportedly wore theirs.

Ramos' thoughts and Tommy's conversation were cut short when the receptionist at the desk told them that the district attorney was ready to see them.

The two detectives nodded their thanks and walked past the receptionist, entering Manhattan District Attorney Kahlil Williams' inner sanctum.

The first thing Ramos noticed was the plush carpeting that muffled their footsteps and the soft jazz music which seemed to be coming from everywhere and nowhere at once.

"Take a seat, detectives."

The district attorney was seated behind a huge oak and mahogany desk adorned with brass fittings that made it look more like a giant hope chest, a single Teller's lamp illuminated the immediate area in front of the DA, the glow from its traditional green shade reflected in Williams' wire-rimmed glasses.

Ramos and Tommy sat in the two burgundy leather chairs that faced the DA and quickly scanned the rest of the softly lit room. It was decorated in tasteful and expensive furnishings with framed prints, like the ones in the waiting area, hanging from the walls. In one corner stood a robust potted palm that partially concealed a rather large African wood carving. In fact, several such statues and carvings of various sizes and shapes stood vigil in corners or on shelves. On the wall to the DA's right, black and white photographs in slim brass frames formed a vertical row emphasized by well-placed track lighting. Ramos recognized the Reverend Dr. Martin Luther King Jr. in one of the photos, Malcolm X, and Shirley Chisolm in others. The rest of the faces he didn't know.

The district attorney shifted slightly, his movement removing the glare from his glasses. He fixed the two detectives with a stare that was almost as physical as a jab.

"The mayor..." the DA began to say...is an asshole."

CHAPTER 32

THE TWO HOMICIDE detectives didn't seem outwardly shocked by the DA's comment, and that pleased him.

"For four years," the DA continued, "This city has been run like an Eastern European dictatorship by the current mayor. He has operated like a heavy-handed bully, running roughshod over the fine traditions and long-standing institutions that have made this city the great democratic metropolis it is. He has disregarded the basic rights of the people, the unions...he uses the police as his own personal security force charged, not with serving the public, but with enforcing *his* will."

Ramos shifted impatiently in his chair, this was the second time in less than a week that he'd had to sit through a speech, and he hated them with a passion.

"Uh, excuse me Mr. Williams," Ramos interrupted, raising his hand as if he were in school.

The DA stopped talking and glared darkly at the detective.

"I can't speak for my partner," Ramos continued. "But as far as I'm concerned you can save your speech for someone who actually gives a shit. All I want to know is why I'm here."

Tommy leaned back in his chair. "You *did* speak for me, partner," he said.

The DA took off his glasses and treated both detectives to a stare that was almost lethal, then let his head drop so that instead he looked at his hands folded on top of the desk. Williams surprised both detectives by laughing, and when he looked up; a smile showed off perfect white teeth.

"Okay detectives," Williams said, his smile slowly fading. "I'll skip the preliminaries and move on to the main event."

Williams stood up, straightened a picture on the wall, and leaned toward Ramos and Tommy; resting his fists on his desk. "As I'm sure you're both well aware," he began to say. "The mayor is up for reelection." The DA waited a beat and then continued. "I plan to run against him."

The district attorney tried to gauge the detective's reaction to this news, but their faces showed little emotion. Williams sighed, gave a slight shrug and continued. "Gentlemen," he said. "I plan to run against the mayor and I plan to beat him. Unfortunately, at present, I do not have the impressive campaign resources of 'Hizzoner'." Williams spat out the last word with distaste.

Tommy Cucitti rolled his eyes. "And so what does all that have to do with us?" he asked, impatience in his voice.

Williams looked from one detective to the other then returned to his seat. He steepled his hands together in front of his face and watched the cops intently over the tips of his long fingers. "I intend to beat the mayor, come election time, by having done something for the people of this city that he has not been able to do," he said.

Ramos' eyebrows shot up and he leaned forward in his chair. Now he understood where all this was going. "You want to catch—I mean, you want us to catch the Chickenhawk for you, so that you'll look good to the voters."

Williams nodded. "A bit oversimplified, but basically yes," he said.

Tommy slowly shook his head. "I don't believe this shit," he muttered.

"Believe it," the DA said, jabbing a finger in Tommy's direction for emphasis. "I don't have the mayor's money, I don't have the name recognition his incumbency provides, and I don't quite have his extensive party and celebrity contacts...but I do have *you*."

Williams reached into his desk, pulled out two thick folders, and placed them atop his desk. "You two detectives have been involved with this investigation from the beginning. You're both highly decorated officers, and you have solid reputations as fine investigators..." The DA turned his attention to Tommy, "...And I had the pleasure of working with your father on more than one occasion. If you're anything like he was, then you're a hell of a cop."

Tommy Cucitti sat there stone faced and said nothing. After a moment Williams turned away.

The district attorney fingered the folders on his desk for a moment then returned his intimidating gaze to the two detectives. "You each have a desk, telephone, etc. waiting for you in one of the offices down the hall. This building is where you'll be working from. Anything else you need, speak to Tracy; my receptionist. Make sure you keep track of any and all expenses, and turn your vouchers in to Tracy at the end of the day—every day. Overtime is to be carefully documented; this office operates on a budget." Williams stood up and leaned forward again, this time resting on his fingertips. "You will report to me and me only. You will not divulge the nature or progression of your investigation to anyone from the NYPD or the mayor's office, understood?"

The detectives nodded in unison.

"Good," the DA said, slowly regaining his seat. "Good. We all want to stop this menace that's been stalking our streets for far too long," he continued. "You catch him, stop him, you aid me in my endeavor to higher office and your futures are secure and assured." Williams' voice suddenly became edged with flint, "... You fuck me, and you will have no future in this city as a cop or otherwise—I'll see to it that you won't even be able to get a job as a security guard at a Bed-Stuy or McDonald's."

CHAPTER 33

THE TWO DETECTIVES left the DA's office feeling as if they needed showers. Bad politics were as much a cop's enemy as a thief or murderer.

The receptionist, Tracy, handed each of the men a key and pointed them down the hall. "Don't forget your overtime vouchers every Friday," she said before letting them go. "If you need petty cash, you got to see me for that too—and your *paychecks*."

Tommy Cucitti and Eddie Ramos could only nod and then walk numbly along the carpeted hallway until they found a room with a number that matched the one stamped into their shiny, new brass keys.

Tommy made to put the key in the lock, but Ramos stopped him. The door was already unlocked and slightly ajar. Bright fluorescent light burned brilliantly from behind the mini-blinds that hung from the inside of the door. The blinds covered the four small panes of glass that made up the door's top third, effectively blocking casual observation of the goings-on within.

Ramos shrugged and Tommy pushed open the door, the idea of an office with a key was new to both of them.

"Well about fuckin' time!" a voice bellowed from inside the room.

When Ramos and Tommy entered the room, Ramos took one look at the huge man sitting at a very messy desk and groaned. Tommy didn't recognize him and was sure that he'd never met the man.

"Welcome aboard boys," the man said loudly, and then he farted; just as loudly.

CHAPTER 34

DISTRICT ATTORNEY KAHLIL Williams sat behind his desk deep in thought. Had he done the right thing by having the two homicide detectives transferred to his office? Would they do their best to catch the killer or would resentment on their part cause them to deliberately mishandle the investigation? Was it wise to have told them about his political aspirations?

The district attorney absentmindedly fingered his bracelet, a masculine affair constructed of woven elephant hair decorated with cowrie shells, while he mentally ticked off answers to his own questions.

First, the two detectives were among the best the NYPD had to offer. Additionally, they'd been involved with the investigation since the very beginning. So transferring them to his office seemed strategically logical. Two, even if they resented being moved from their beloved police department to the DA's office, their goal is still the same: to catch whoever is killing boy prostitutes. Williams had no doubt that the two detectives would remain true to their cause. They were good cops and this killer had no doubt become their Holy Grail. Lastly, his own political ambitions would become public information soon anyway. By telling the detectives, he hoped to convey to them just how high the stakes were and what little tolerance he would have for bullshit.

CHAPTER 35

BOB AVNI, SPECIAL Investigator for the Manhattan DA's office, grinned at the two homicide detectives and then belched resoundingly. "Ah-h, that's better," he said afterwards. "Why fart and waste it when you can belch and taste it?" Avni patted his huge belly, totally pleased with himself.

"You haven't changed a bit," Ramos said sarcastically.

Avni shrugged, "Wish I could say the same about you Eddie," he said. "You look kinda old, kinda fat...just kinda all fucked up. The years haven't been kind."

Tommy Cucitti remained quiet during this exchange, unsure of the relationship between the two men.

Eddie Ramos tossed his overcoat onto the desk opposite the one occupied by Avni and sat down. Tommy threw his coat over Eddie's and sat on the edge of the same desk, the only other chair in the room being filled by Avni's considerable bulk.

Ramos glared at Avni, who simply chuckled good-naturedly and leaned back in his chair; its metal joints and springs squealing as if being tortured. Avni laced his sausage-sized fingers behind his head and treated each detective in turn to the amused expression on his wide face. After several moments he addressed Ramos specifically.

"You can stop it with the evil eye now Eddie," he said. "Remember I work for that goddamn nigger Williams. Compared to him you're just an amateur."

Avni was right; his glare had nothing on the D.A's. Ramos conceded and looked away with a defeated sigh. Avni chuckled again, pleased with his small victory.

"Okay," Tommy said slowly, still unsure of what exactly was going on. He turned toward Ramos, but kept his eyes on Avni. "Aren't you going to introduce us?" he asked.

Ramos gave Tommy an annoyed look and then waved his hand in Avni's direction.

"That's Robert Avni," Ramos said. "We were in the same class in the academy."

"And?" Avni urged.

"And," Ramos added reluctantly. "We both started out as housing cops, in fact we were partners."

Tommy Cucitti rubbed his chin thoughtfully. "Word?" He said. "You never told me this."

"There's nothin' to tell," Ramos said with a shrug. "I transferred out of housing as soon as I could."

"Why?"

Avni chuckled again. "I guess he felt he was slummin' hangin' out in the projects with the rest of us."

Ramos glared. "I left because I'd signed on to be a cop, not some housing authority security guard."

Now it was Avni's turn to shrug. "Call it what you want," he said. "But I made some great busts there over the years, not to mention the 'perks'."

"Perks?" Tommy asked.

"Oh yeah," Avni said. "In those days every housing cop had at least one project babe on the side."

Tommy's eyebrow went up. "Say word," he said.

"Oh yeah," Avni said nodding emphatically. "Once you find out which apartments had the unattached women in 'em, especially single moms, getting in and making friends was easy."

"You're talking a lot of shit Bobby," Ramos said.

"And the reason behind making all these 'friends'?" Tommy asked.

"Well," Avni explained. "You had a convenient place to go if you hadda take a dump or get laid."

"Of course," Tommy said dryly.

"Yeah," Avni said. "Of course." Then he shrugged expansively. "How else do you think some of them project kids get names like O'Shaughnessy, Maldarelli, or Goldstein?" Avni threw his head back and laughed heartily, taking little notice of the other two cops' stony silence.

As his laughter subsided, Avni leaned forward and wiped tears of mirth from his eyes. He looked at the two detectives and treated them to a slow, derisive wave. "Aw, youse guys are fuckin' anal," he said.

Tommy nodded slowly. "You know," he said. "I've only known you for a few minutes and I already think you're an asshole."

Ramos looked over at Tommy, "Took you that long, huh?"

Avni leaned back again, the chair protested loudly. "The two of youse can go fuck yourselves," he said. A loud ripping sound signaled yet another emission of methane from his system.

"Okay," Ramos said. "Now that everyone's acquainted and reacquainted, I wanna know how me and Tommy wound up here."

"Well," Avni began. "Originally I'd caught the same case you guys were working on, only for the DA's office."

The two detectives nodded.

"Next thing I know, just as the case heats up, Williams takes me aside and tells me he wants to be mayor..." Avni continued, eventually telling Ramos and Tommy the same story told to them by the district attorney.

"Yeah," Ramos said when Avni had finished. "That's pretty much the same scenario Williams fed us in his office earlier."

"Uh-huh," Avni said. "He wants to be the city's next black mayor so bad he can taste it."

"So where do we go from here?" Tommy asked.

Avni shrugged his massive shoulders. "Hey, Williams says that youse guys are the lead investigators in this case now."

"We don't mean to step on any toes, Bob," Ramos said sincerely.

Avni shrugged again. "The limelight ain't for me anyway," he said. "I like working incognito. As it is, good or bad, too many people are going to know your names when this is over."

Ramos and Tommy agreed.

"The DA instructed me to assist you in any way you need," Avni continued. "And to remind you, in case you forget, that you're working for *him* now."

Avni reached under the desk and produced a dog-eared bundle of dirty, coffee-stained papers and folders. "He also instructed me to turn my files over to you, but I doubt you'll come across any revelations in there." Avni tossed the bundle on the desk, where it promptly fell apart. Several folders skidded off the desk, opening as they fell and scattering their contents on the floor.

Tommy smirked while Ramos eyed Avni and the falling papers impassively.

Avni stood, the chair sighing loudly in relief, and shambled to the door. Tommy was impressed. Avni had to be at least six six or six seven and easily weighed over three hundred pounds.

"Damn son," Tommy whispered to Ramos. "And I thought you were fat!"

Ramos gave Tommy an impatient glance then turned his attention back to the departing Avni.

"By the way," Avni rumbled. "Regardless of what Williams says, find a way *not* to need me." He waited by the door as if expecting an answer from the two cops. When none came, Avni grunted, unsatisfied, and ducked under the doorway.

"Oh," he said turning suddenly and pointed a thick finger at Tommy. "I knew your old man, he was a good cop." Avni grinned and left.

After a moment, Tommy turned to Ramos, "Now that was a for real asshole, son," he said emphatically.

Ramos agreed.

Tommy Cucitti got up and retrieved the fallen papers on the floor. He straightened them up as best he could and placed them at the desk where Avni sat. One folder caught his eye and he brought this one back to Ramos.

"Check this out, yo," he said handing the folder to Ramos.

Ramos was chewing a mint and wishing for a cigarette when he took the folder from Tommy. On the front of the folder was a dirty white label on which someone had typed two names: Edwin Ramos and Thomas Cucitti.

CHAPTER 36

JUAN GUTIERREZ, ALSO commonly known on the street as Ratman, scurried along the trash-strewn streets and alleyways of East Harlem. Cautious of open spaces, he kept close to the graffiti-scarred buildings and walls.

Ratman knew that the police were looking for him, so his movements were even more furtive than usual. He dashed across 116th Street and ducked into a shadowed courtyard before being chased off by the resident crackhead.

Ratman slid into a nearby alley and quickly settled himself between two overflowing trash cans and an old mattress stained with urine. It'd been several days now since he'd pushed Officer Tommy down the escalator, and the word was that Officer Tommy's fellows in the department wanted very much to "talk" to him.

"They want what I have up here," Ratman said aloud, tapping his dirty forehead with an even dirtier finger. *I saw that dude, yeah, I saw him. I saw the killer guy and his car. Sure, sure. I got his license plate number too. Yes, yes. I really do.* This time he patted his shirt pocket and winced, but that wasn't what hurt. The tumor he still hid under a dirty blue towel had grown considerably larger over the last few days, forcing him to keep his head at an uncomfortable angle, and the itch had become a constant throbbing pain.

Ratman dug into his pants pocket and pulled out the four remaining children's aspirin from the bottle he'd shoplifted earlier in the day. He tossed them all into his mouth and chewed glumly. He knew from recent experience the pain wasn't going to go away, that in fact it was getting worse.

Ratman sighed heavily. He was cold, hungry, and tired—all things he'd been many times before. But now there was a difference. Death had never felt so close before, so—real. Ratman admitted that he was scared, more frightened in fact than he'd ever been in his life. He'd tried to work up the courage to call Officer Tommy a few times since the incident at the bus station, but he'd never been able to go through with it.

"Just wanted to say sorry," Ratman explained to the unfeeling trash cans and mattress. "Yeah, sure—say I'm sorry and give him this too."

Ratman reached into his shirt and pulled out a dirty scrap of paper. On it was written the license plate number of the killer every cop in the city was looking for. Ratman stared at the number he'd neatly written in pencil.

"Yeah, I saw him," he said softly. "I told Officer Tommy that. Yeah, I saw him. I did. I did." Ratman balled the paper up in his fist and stuck it into his pants pocket.

"Now it's too late. Officer Tommy hates me and I'm sick, man; real sick." Tears scrubbed twin lines of relatively cleaner skin from his eyes to his sunken cheeks. Pain from the tumor seemed to intensify, pulsating in time with his heartbeat.

"Shit," Ratman said dejectedly. He looked up at the ash-colored sky, "As if my life wasn't fucked up enough? Now I have to deal with This. Shit. Too!" Ratman punctuated the last three words with awkward punches to the offending growth. "It's different when I'm hungry, man," he continued. "When I'm hungry I can beg or steal something." He shuddered as an errant breeze swept the alleyway. "If it gets too cold I can go to a shelter or into the subway, but what the fuck can I do about this? What?"

Ratman lowered his chin to his chest and sobbed. There was nothing he could do now, no where he could go. Officer Tommy hated him now, but the way he saw it, Officer Tommy—the cops, were still his only hope.

Ratman wiped the tears from his face with the back of his hand. "The cops," he mumbled. "The fuckin' cops."

Fuck it, Ratman thought as he got to his feet. *I don't need Officer Tommy. I'll just talk to the regular cops. If they want to arrest me, so what, they still need to make a deal with me. I'll let them arrest me, 'cause once they see what I got...*

Ratman patted his pants pocket confidently as he walked out of the alley. He was proud of himself for reaching such a serious decision. "Once they see what I got, they gonna want to deal," Ratman said with new determination and hope. "Shit, I might even be a hero!"

With dreamy visions of award ceremonies, parades, dinners at Gracie Mansion, and a successful surgery dancing through his mind, Ratman practically skipped down the street.

Several blocks later, he still hadn't been able to find a single working public telephone with which to call the police with his good news. Many of the telephones had either been vandalized or removed by the city more than a decade earlier in a bid to thwart the notorious crack dealers from making their drug deals. But instead of anger or frustration, Ratman felt euphoric. Everything was going to be okay, he felt it in his bones—in his heart of hearts. The cops *had* to help him; that was their job—'shit, they was always helping somebody when they wasn't beating them down.'

Ratman turned a corner and, despite his current feeling of well-being, nearly ran at the sight of a patrol car parked a short distance away. Heart pounding, he flattened himself against the coarse brick of a nearby building. The cops were in a heated dispute with two other men in front of the next building, they were trying to keep the two men separated. The men proved uncooperative, however, and insisted on trying to beat each other to a brainless pulp. .

Ratman licked his lips nervously. The cops were having a hard time and he could see they were getting angrier and angrier.

I can fix this, thought Ratman as he fingered the balled up slip of paper in his pocket. *Once I give them this paper and tell them what it's about, we all gonna be heroes and then they have no choice but to pay for my surgery.*

Ratman hesitated, caution weighed him down like a lead apron. He watched the two uniformed officers finally succeed in separating the two men and then immediately thereafter have them "assume the position" and submit to a search.

Now, Ratman thought. *I should make my move now.*

The throbbing pain emanating from the tumor in his neck told him he indeed had no choice. He stepped away from the wall and started walking as quickly as he could toward the two cops.

By now the officers had handcuffed the two men and were leading them to the patrol car. Afraid he was going to miss his opportunity, Ratman called out to the officers in a bid to keep them from entering their cars and driving away. Ratty wasn't completely sure he'd have the courage to approach any other police that day, so it had to be these two. Now. Or maybe never.

"Hey!" Ratman called out from less than twenty feet away. "Wait..."

The two officers turned at the same time, still holding onto their prisoners.

"Wait!" Ratman called out again as he reached into his pants pocket for the scrap of paper. "I got something!"

The older cop, standing in front of his partner, saw Ratman's hand reach into his pocket and instinctively shoved his prisoner to the ground. "Ah shit," he said tightly. "Don't move! Don't move!" He yelled at both his prisoner and the homeless-looking man stumbling toward him with his hand in his pocket.

Ratman didn't stop. He couldn't stop. His legs, shaky with fear and hope, propelled him forward. It was as if they knew this was his last chance at staying alive.

The other cop, the younger one, was having more trouble with his prisoner. His prisoner kept up a litany of expletives and foul-mouthed threats that were punctuated by constant yanks and tugs as the prisoner sought to break away from his arrest.

"Don't move! Don't move!" The younger cop heard his partner yell. Out of the corner of his eye, he saw his partner reach for his weapon. At the same time, he saw the homeless man coming at them, reaching for something in his pocket.

Panic and fear seized his heart and clawed at his throat. In his eighteen months as a New York City police officer he'd never been shot at and had never had occasion to pull his gun from its holster. Fumbling, he switched custody of the prisoner to his left hand while going for his gun with his right. The prisoner tried to yank free again and pulled the young officer off-balance, forcing him to take his eyes from the approaching homeless man.

The young cop clutched at his prisoner blindly, turning back in time to see Ratman pull something from his pocket. *Oh my God*, he thought. *Was that a flash of silver*?

"Gun!" He yelled exactly as he'd been taught at the academy. "Gun! He repeated as he finally yanked his own weapon from its holster, pointed it at Ratman, and pulled the trigger.

The older cop heard the shouts of, "Gun!" "Gun!", and the loud reports from his partner's 9mm before rapidly squeezing off two shots of his own. He barely took notice of the younger cop's prisoner running away, hands still cuffed behind his back.

The first shot stopped Ratman cold and he fell to one knee still holding the scrap of paper in his hand. Of the ensuing fusillade, eight more bullets struck his body, knocking him onto his back. The piece of paper on which he'd written the killer's license plate number drifted away and mingled uselessly with the street litter.

Even as his young partner kept firing, emptying his weapon's entire clip, the veteran cop felt dread inflate in his belly like a balloon filling with ice water. As soon as the shooting ended, he ran recklessly to where the homeless man lay sprawled lifelessly on the cold sidewalk and searched the immediate area.

"Where's the gun?" He yelled, dread turning into horror. "Where's the fucking gun?" The cop searched the area fruitlessly while his prisoner cowered behind the patrol car and his stunned partner blinked stupidly from behind a haze of gun smoke.

"Wha?" The younger cop said uncomprehendingly, his escaped prisoner forgotten and his ears ringing from the gunshots.

"The gun," his partner yelled again, pleading this time. "Where's the gun?"

CHAPTER 37

RAMOS TRUDGED WEARILY up the stairs toward his bedroom. He looked in on his youngest daughter Kim first, paused briefly in front of her older sister's empty room, and then padded quietly into his own bedroom.

Linda was asleep in their bed, one long leg peeking out from beneath the rumpled covers. She'd complained lately that it was too warm under the covers, and Ramos had teased her that maybe she was going through "The Change." He watched her sleep now—the deep, regular rhythm of her breathing was familiar and comforting.

Ramos stood there a few moments longer, then softly closed the door and went downstairs. As usual, the couch had been made up as his bed. He'd been sleeping on the couch for almost a week, ever since he'd started having the nightmares about his childhood friend Jay. He didn't want to disturb Linda's sleep with his thrashing and loud mumbling.

"Eddie, is everything alright?"

Ramos turned around at the sound of his wife's voice. She was standing on the stairs, her robe draped over her slim shoulders.

"Yeah," Ramos said, rubbing the back of his neck. "Just cop stuff."

Linda nodded in understanding. "Well, just pray about it Eddie," she said. "Leave it in God's hands."

"Yeah, okay," Ramos said more curtly than he'd intended.

Linda nodded as Ramos pretended to busy himself with the couch cushions, then she silently walked up the stairs and into the bedroom.

"Shit," Ramos whispered harshly. He hadn't meant to be so short with his wife. Truth was, that was the way most of their conversations turned out these days. Short. Curt. Overly polite or even downright angry. Myrna, their oldest, had called from her college dorm worried, apparently after getting a heads up from her younger sister. Ramos reassured her that all was well, but now as he got ready for his shower, he was beginning to have his own doubts.

Ramos walked upstairs again, removed a fresh towel and washcloth from the antique chest that served as a linen closet, and entered the bathroom.

'What was going on? Was Linda going through some sort of mid-life crisis? Was he wrong for not supporting her'? As Ramos turned on the hot water, the steam billowing up to the ceiling, he thought about how Linda had invited him to visit her new church. Now, he made up his mind that he would.

CHAPTER 38

KATHERINE PAKIDORAPOPULOS ADMIRED herself critically in the dresser mirror while she removed her jewelry. As she reached up to undo the clasp of her necklace, she watched the slight movement of her breasts under her slip.

Not bad, she thought. *They're not pert and perky anymore of course, not after two kids, gravity, and, uh, years of male attention, but they're still definitely sexy.*

In fact, Katherine Pakidorapopulos was a stunningly beautiful woman who wasn't above spending several thousand dollars every year or so in order to remain that way. A little nip here, a little tuck there, assured her of receiving the attention she so enjoyed. That attention was one of the main reasons she insisted on throwing all those dinner parties. That and making sure she and Paki maintained their status within their social circle. Most of the snobs she invited to these gatherings practically owned the exclusive area of eastern Long Island where she and Paki now resided. Many of them were old money, while the rest consisted of a polyglot assortment of entertainers, politicians, well-known members of the medical or legal fields, and one or two of the few surviving dot.com millionaires.

Katherine pulled off her slip and admired her breasts in the mirror again. They were full and round, with a near perfect décolletage. The areoles, only slightly darker than the rest of her skin, surrounded sensitive nipples that would jut out a half-inch in cold or arousal. *Arousal.* Katherine cupped a heavy breast in each hand and gave her nipples a slight pinch. She felt a slight tremor go through her as her nipples stiffened and her skin rose in gooseflesh.

Katherine sighed. It had been awhile since she and Theo had made love—weeks in fact. She noticed he'd been sick lately, probably this nasty flu that's been going around, but dammit she had needs. Besides, it wasn't like her lusty Greek husband to turn down sex, even when he felt under the weather. Something else was going on—something more than just the flu.

Katherine saw the worried look in her eyes reflected back at her in the mirror. 'Could Theo be having an affair?'

She suspected that he'd had flings in the past—one-night stands—especially when he was away on business, but that's all she'd ever been able to prove they were suspicions. There were never any lipstick smudges on his collar, or stray hairs on his coat...just a feeling. Still, he'd always greet her after one of his trips with an extraordinary bout of lovemaking that always left her satisfied and feeling more than a little bit silly about her suspicions...at least until the next time he was away or inexplicably late.

Katherine could hear Paki downstairs saying good-bye to the last of their departing guests. This was the last party of the season before the holidays and she was almost glad. As much as she enjoyed it, the constant pressure of playing the perfect hostess was exhausting. Footsteps on the carpeted stairs signaled her husband's approach.

Katherine quickly made her way to the side of the bed closest to the bedroom door and sat down in what she hoped was a seductive, yet casual, pose.

Paki stepped into the room, barely glanced at his wife, and went into the bathroom. Katherine could hear him blowing his nose and coughing. The sounds were absolutely wretched, and Katherine was relieved when they were replaced with the sound of gargling. Paki emerged from the bathroom looking drained and wiped his mouth with the back of his hand.

"Theo, you look awful," Katherine said in concern.

Paki's face was indeed drawn and pale. He didn't look well

at all, yet Katherine had insisted that he attend this latest get-together. They had to keep up appearances; after all.

Paki didn't say anything. He turned toward the same mirror where his wife had been admiring herself moments before and unknotted his tie.

"You told me you were feeling better," Katherine said.

"I feel like shit," Paki retorted.

Katherine nodded, unsure of what to say next.

Paki pulled off his tie and dropped it onto the floor. It was soon followed by his sweat-stained shirt and his belt. Katherine bit her lip, it was so unlike her husband to be so sloppy with his clothes—he was usually so adamant about neatness.

Katherine watched as Paki's pants slid to the floor in a rumpled mass. Paki stepped out of them, leaving them where they fell, and leaned on his wife's dresser. He stared at his reflection, his mind blank and devoid of any thoughts that may have attempted to stray into his consciousness. He coughed lightly, pulled several tissues from the floral box on the dresser, and blew his nose.

Katherine watched the smooth, round muscle of her husband's buttocks clench and unclench under the thin, clingy cotton of his briefs. *It has been awhile*, Katherine thought as she felt her desire edge up a notch.

"Come to bed Theo," she said. "You'll feel better."

Paki watched her in the mirror. Katherine noticed his gaze and slowly stretched out on her side, propping her head up so that she could still see him watching her. Sure that she had his attention, she slowly removed her panties—sliding them languidly down her long legs. In the mirror, Paki's expression did not change.

"Come to bed Theo," Katherine cooed. "You'll feel better, but I can't guarantee that you'll get any rest." Katherine laughed softly at her joke and ran her fingers lightly up and down the empty space next to her on the bed.

Paki's mouth turned up in a joyless smile, "I'm sick," he said.

"You never let a little cold stop you before," his wife insisted. "Besides," she added, winking. "The best way to get rid of a cold is to share it."

Paki whirled with a growl, "A cold? A cold?"

Despite Paki's vehemence, Katherine couldn't help notice the sizable erection her husband's briefs now strained to contain.

"Can't you understand that I'm sick?" Paki continued. "And all of these parties, concerts, fund-raisers, and whatever that you insist I attend aren't helping matters. In fact, I'm sure they're worsening things by constantly bringing me into contact with people who *do* have colds and such..."

"Well there is a really dreadful flu going around..."

"The flu?" Paki barked a mirthless laugh. "I wish it were that simple! At this point I'm sure a bout of influenza would probably kill me. My immune system..."

Tsk.

Katherine Pakidorapopulos clucked her tongue impatiently. "Your immune what?" she asked. "Theo, I understand that you're not feeling well and I apologize if my little social gatherings made you feel put upon, but I was just hoping that we could have a little fun now, make love..."

Paki threw his arms up in frustration. "Haven't you been listening?" He said. "I'm very sick Kathy, and I don't want to give you..."

"Oh please," Katherine said dismissively. "That never stopped you before."

Katherine sat up, her back against the bed's headboard, and clutched a pillow to her bosom. "Is it—is it another woman, Theo?" she asked. "Is it your secretary? Is she the reason you won't make love to me?"

Paki's mouth hung open incredulously. "You stupid, overheated bitch," he hissed through clenched teeth once he was finally able to close his mouth again. "You haven't heard a goddamn thing I've said! I'm trying to protect you and all you care about is fucking..."

"Don't say *fuck*," Katherine interjected coldly, her earlier desire having since ebbed away.

"Fuck, screw, bang, plow...it's all the same and it's all you understand." Paki pulled down his underpants and revealed his swollen penis.

Katherine stared with a mixture of fascination and revulsion. It seemed larger than she remembered, *God, has it really always been that long?* the head, flat and wide, resembled the head of a venomous snake. The entire thing seemed to throb with menace, the purple veins that crisscrossed its length seemed ready to burst.

"Is this what you want Kathy?" Paki asked as he advanced upon and then climbed onto the bed.

Katherine's face reddened and she turned away. She crossed her ankles defiantly.

Paki stopped, kneeling in the swaddling bedclothes, his arms folded with his finger on his chin—as if he were thinking. When Katherine turned and looked at him, he slowly shook that finger at her as if admonishing her. Then, without warning, he struck.

CHAPTER 39

RAMOS AND TOMMY RODE the elevator up to their new office in silence. They'd both received phone calls the night before and the news hadn't been good. Juan Gutierrez, the street snitch Tommy called Ratman, had died in a hail of police bullets.

Ramos popped a mint into his mouth and stuck the plastic wrapper into his breast pocket. As he bit down on the mint he thought it was a poor goddamn substitute for a cigarette. He watched Tommy out of the corner of his eye. He knew that as angry and disappointed as he himself was over Ratman's death (Gutierrez supposedly had an important clue as to the identity of the killer), Ramos knew Tommy was worse off. Ratman had been Tommy's snitch and, shoved down an escalator or not, Tommy felt an odd obligation to be saddened by Ratty's death. On the other hand, the outrage *he* felt was over the fact that if Ratty had indeed known the identity of the killer that information had died with him.

Ramos opened the door to their office and was hit immediately, a groan from Tommy signaled his assault as well. Ramos covered his nose and mouth with a hastily retrieved handkerchief while Tommy pinched his nose and squinted around the room.

"Avni!" Tommy exclaimed nasally, his nose still firmly between thumb and forefinger.

Ramos spotted Avni too, sitting behind Tommy's desk which, it turned out, had actually once been Avni's desk.

Robert Avni acknowledged the two detectives with an exaggerated bow then, while leaning over, passed wind.

"Aw fuck!" Tommy exclaimed.

Avni shrugged his meaty shoulders and continued the process of shoving a hot dog into his mouth.

Ramos made his way to his desk and sat down, still holding the handkerchief to his face. "Goddammit Bob," he said through the thin white cotton. "Why are you in here eatin' and fartin' up the place? It stinks in here!"

"Fuck you," Avni said casually. "I don't eat no roses and I don't drink no perfume."

"Well, what the fuck do you eat, son?" Tommy retorted. "Rotten eggs with a big side order of freshly-laid shit?"

Avni looked at him and farted loudly. "That's very mature of the two of you," he said. "You're gonna go through conniptions just 'cause I happened to pass gas a couple of times?"

Tommy rolled his eyes and cursed under his breath.

"Bob, what are you doing in here?" Ramos asked.

Avni widened his eyes and gestured at the assortment of wax paper, brown paper bags, and Styrofoam plates that littered the top of the desk. "Havin' breakfast, whaddaya think?" he said.

Ramos grunted. He wished he had a cigarette...or at least a match. Tommy stepped further into the room and perched on the corner of Ramos' desk. He left the door open.

Avni rummaged through the mess on the desk, knocking over a half-filled cup of coffee, and pulled out a stained newspaper. "You seen this?" he asked, and tossed the paper onto the desk next to Tommy.

Ramos and Tommy both glanced down at the newspaper, even though they both already knew what it read.

SHOT DEAD! The headline screamed. Underneath it, in letters almost as big: *UNARMED HOMELESS MAN KILLED BY COPS*!

Ramos and Tommy both looked back up at Avni.

"We know about it," Ramos growled.

Avni nodded while he used his tongue to dislodge some food that had become stuck in his teeth. He held a Danish in his right hand, but still managed to point at Tommy with his fat middle finger. "He was one of your snitches, right?" he asked.

Tommy nodded.

Avni finished the Danish and licked the icing from his fingers. Ramos noticed that Avni's fingernails were filthy.

"He give you anything good?" Avni asked.

"Not about the Chickenhawk," Tommy answered.

Avni studied Tommy's face for awhile and, apparently satisfied, went back to his meal.

"Those two cops are fucked, you know," he said after gulping down a quart of orange juice. "Now the mayor's got the gays, the ACLU, the spics, and the homeless advocates riding his ass."

"Oh yeah," Avni continued as he wiped his hands on his shirt. "Those poor bastards are fucked—the mayor's gonna ream 'em good."

"Those 'poor guys' killed an unarmed man," Tommy said.

Avni shrugged. "Fuck 'em," he said. "More dirt gone in the wash."

Tommy started to stand but he sat back down when he felt Ramos' hand on his arm.

"He might've had some important information for us," Ramos said.

"About the Chickenhawk?" Avni asked.

Ramos nodded.

Avni shrugged again. "Well, doesn't matter now does it?" he said. "I don't really give a shit about the rookie, but the other cop's a veteran. He doesn't deserve to be caught up in all of this political bullshit."

Ramos sighed. "Look Bob," he said. "As far as the cops are concerned, I mostly agree with you..."

Tommy jumped off Ramos' desk and threw his arms up in disgust.

Ramos held his hand up, "...But a man died unnecessarily. A man who could have told us who the Chickenhawk is."

Avni waved at Ramos dismissively and belched loudly. "This came for youse guys in the interdepartmental mail," Avni said as he rummaged through his mess again. He pulled out a manila envelope and tossed it on the desk in front of Ramos.

"This is open," Ramos said examining the envelope.

"Yeah," Avni agreed. "Ain't many secrets around here."

Ramos ignored Avni and scanned through the envelope's contents. Then he handed them over to his partner. Tommy recognized the cop's name on the report right away.

"Yo, that's the rookie we talked to at the construction site," Tommy said.

Ramos nodded. "He sent us copies of his DD5's..."

"Nothing new in here," Tommy added after scanning the contents. "The same shit we already know. All adds up to nothing."

Avni stretched and ran his hand across his shiny pate several times. The dark hair at the fringes turning to gray.

"Pretty perceptive kid," Avni said admiringly. "He's gonna make a good cop."

CHAPTER 40

KATHERINE PAKIDORAPOPULOS THANKED the young waiter who'd brought the drinks over to their table and waited until he'd left before continuing her conversation.

"...As I was explaining, Mr. Hatch," she said. "I am almost sure that my husband is having an affair. I want proof either way—I mean, whether he is or isn't. I want to know."

Alonso Hatch, former cop and current private investigator, looked at the beautiful woman in the dark glasses over the rim of his beer glass. He didn't say anything, just continued to sip his beer. Eventually, the lady who'd called him that morning about a job became fidgety and decided to fill in the silence herself.

"Your, um, advertisement stated that you do this sort of thing," she said.

Hatch continued to stare while he enjoyed the expensive imported beer Katherine Pakidorapopulos paid for. Outside, happy noises came from tourists and natives who skated back and forth under the uncaring gaze of the huge, gilded statue of Prometheus that loomed over Rockefeller Center in Manhattan.

Mrs. Pakidorapopulos fidgeted some more, her eyes barely visible behind the dark lenses of her glasses. Hatch watched as she became more and more uncomfortable until, finally, she grabbed her fashionable handbag and stood up to leave. He stopped her by grabbing her wrist.

"Sit down," Hatch said. Katherine Pakidorapopulos stared at him dumbly.

"Sit down," Hatch repeated more firmly.

Katherine snatched her arm from Hatch's grip, but sat down as instructed. Hatch slowly reached out and removed the dark glasses from her face, the purplish bruise that covered her right eye clearly visible now.

"Your husband do that?" Hatch asked.

Katherine glanced around nervously, recovered her glasses, and put them back on. "Don't *ever* touch me again," she hissed.

Hatch looked at her, drained the last of his beer and sat back. "Sorry," he said, not sounding the least bit apologetic.

Katherine smoothed her skirt, opened her bag and took out some tissue. She dabbed at her eyes under the glasses, and gently readjusted them on the bridge of her nose. "Perhaps this was a mistake..." she began.

"Maybe," Hatch agreed. "But from what you told me so far, it sounds like your husband does have a little something going on the side."

"You think so?"

Hatch nodded.

"And the rape?"

Hatch sighed and rolled his eyes. "Look lady," he said. "Personally, I don't believe a man can rape his wife. I mean, once he puts a ring on a woman's finger he pretty much owns that woman's cunt—I mean, it's bought and paid for; lock, stock and barrel."

Hatch saw the look, a dark combination of disgust and disapproval, on his potential client's face and shrugged his shoulders, "But hey, that's just my opinion," he said. "The courts may say different."

Katherine Pakidorapopulos stared at the private "eye" a moment longer and sighed wearily. "Irregardless of your opinion, Mr. Hatch," she said. "My husband brutally and callously raped me. At first I wanted to, you know, be intimate, but then he forced himself upon me despite my later pleas to the contrary. He slapped me when I resisted and threatened to kill me."

"You and your old man don't screw often?"

"Not lately."

"Why didn't you just call the cops?"

Katherine glanced around them quickly and leaned forward to whisper. "We're very prominent people in our community," she said. "It wouldn't do to have the police come to our home."

"Uh-huh." Hatch had seen and heard countless variations of this same story. "So what happened after?"

Mrs. Pakidorapopulos looked around the room as if afraid she would be overheard. The act made her appear almost child-like and vulnerable. Hatch wanted to screw her right then and there.

"After he, uh, finished, he left the room through the wine cellar access hidden inside the faux closet. I haven't seen him since."

Hatch hoped he didn't look too bored. "You guys have a wine cellar in your closet?"

"No, the closet isn't really a closet at all; it simply serves as an access to the wine cellar."

"Okay, okay," Hatch said with a wave of his hand. *These folks are loaded,* he thought. *Maybe there's room here for a little extra business on the side.* While thoughts of money, hidden wine cellars, and large breasts, swirled and surged through his mind, Hatch asked, "So now you want me to follow him and maybe get photos of him boinging his secretary?"

"I believe that it may be his secretary, yes."

"So that you can have the dirt on him come divorce time?"

"So that I'll *know.*"

Hatch nodded. "You know my fee," he said.

Mrs. Pakidorapopulos opened her small, stylish handbag again, but this time she withdrew a slip of paper that Hatch immediately recognized as a check. When she slid it to him across the table, he was chagrinned to find the amount already filled in.

Hatch stuck the check into an inner pocket of his briefcase and pulled out a computerized form that had clearly been torn from a continuous sheet. He quickly tore a stubborn piece of paper from the perforated edge and snapped the briefcase shut.

Hatch scribbled something onto the sheet of paper and slid it across the table to Mrs. Pakidorapopulos. "That's your receipt," he said. “Next week we meet here again, same time. I’ll give you the photos and/or a bill, depending on how it works out.”

Katherine Pakidorapopulos daintily folded the receipt and placed it in her bag without looking at it. “And when will you start, Mr. Hatch?” she asked.

Hatch stood up. “I already have,” he said before walking out of the door.

CHAPTER 41

EDDIE RAMOS AND Tommy Cucitti stepped out into the bright fall sunshine of 125th Street. It was midday and the area bustled with activity. The usual cadre of smokers, all employed in the State Building, huddled near the doorways; bodies hunched or stiffened against the brisk air. Ramos managed to walk through a small cloud of cigarette smoke before it dissipated and inhaled deeply.

"Linda catch you doing that and she'll put you on the serious beat-down, son," Tommy said without turning.

Ramos didn't answer, imagining himself holding onto the last, lingering vestige of sweet-smelling tobacco.

At the corner of 125th Street and Lenox Avenue, a black suburban quickly pulled up in front of them, preventing them from crossing the street. One of the black tinted rear windows slid down soundlessly and revealed the bloated, pale face of Deputy Mayor Nitchik.

"G-morning boys," he wheezed.

Both detectives nodded in reply and resisted the urge to point out that it was past twelve in the afternoon.

"I would invite you in," the deputy mayor said humorlessly. "But I've just had the interior cleaned."

Tommy could hear the driver snickering behind the wheel.

Nitchik crooked a pudgy finger at the two cops, urging them

closer to the car. Ramos and Tommy ignored him and stayed where they were. The deputy mayor lowered his voice and went on as if not noticing.

"Word has gotten back to His Honor, the mayor, that you two are investigating the Chicken-killer case for Williams," he said.

"Chickenhawk," Tommy corrected.

"Wha...?" Nitchik's face slackened in confusion.

"The killer, uh, the case is called Chickenhawk." Tommy tried to explain.

Nitchik dismissed the explanation with a wave of his hand. "I don't care if McDonald's is calling it its new chicken-goddamn-sandwich," he said. "The mayor wants to remind you that he signs your goddamn paychecks, not the DA."

Both cops looked at the deputy mayor uneasily. While not literally true, they knew that what Nitchik was saying was true enough. And like most cops, they became uncomfortable when politics intruded so heavily on a case.

Nitchik smiled, satisfied that he'd struck a chord with the two men.

"Yeah, that's right," he said, sounding like a petulant child in a schoolyard. "He signs your pathetic little paychecks, and he doesn't like disloyalty."

"Dis," Tommy said. "Disloyalty."

"What?"

"Never mind," Tommy said.

Nitchik shifted his bulk in his seat, causing the big SUV to rock back and forth. Then his hand emerged from the dark recesses of the Suburban and he handed Ramos a slip of paper.

"That's the phone, uh, telephone number and e-mail for the mayor's task force that's really investigating this Chicken-guy," he said. "There's also the mayor's private e-mail you have on there. He wants daily updates on any new leads, how far you get with your investigation...Whatever you dig up, whoever you talk to—if Williams knows about it, the mayor wants to know about it. Hell, the mayor wants to know everything you and Williams talk about, whether or not it's related to the case. The mayor's got wind that the DA wants to run against him."

"So basically the mayor wants us to, uh, spy on Williams," Ramos said disgustedly.

"Hey call it what you want," Nitchik responded. "His Honor expects your first report via his private e-mail tomorrow at three o'clock sharp. Don't use the telephone numbers I gave you unless it's a goddamn emergency."

"Yo, what if I don't feel like playing *I Spy* for the mayor?" Tommy asked. "I'm a cop, all this stuff you're talking about is straight-up bullshit."

Nitchik glared at Tommy. "First of all, *yo* is for horses," he said. "And next of all, uh, second of all, nobody says no to the mayor." With that, the window scrolled up as silently as it had gone down and the Suburban lumbered away.

Ramos and Tommy looked at each other.

"*Yo is for horses,*" Tommy said before both detectives laughed out loud.

CHAPTER 42

HATCH, THE PRIVATE investigator, waited patiently in his non-descript blue sedan. He'd parked about half-a-block away from the Pakidorapopulos house, in the driveway of a family that had already gone for the day. He held a pair of binoculars in his right hand and sipped absentmindedly from the cup of coffee he held in his left. Periodically, he'd lift the binoculars to his eyes and focus on his client's impressive home. The door, a massive affair of oak and brass, had to be worth at least two or three thousand dollars. Hatch lowered his gaze and took in the huge lawn. He noticed how, even with all the trees around, few leaves marred the green expanse.

Movement at the door caught his attention and he moved the binoculars up in time to see Paki leave the house and enter his car. Hatch started his engine and discreetly followed his quarry as he pulled out of his driveway and turned onto the main road.

Paki drove to the Long Island Railroad station and eased his car into one of the empty spaces in the parking lot grid. Hatch maneuvered his own car into one of the spaces nearby.

Curiouser and curiouser, thought Hatch as he watched Paki get out of his car and walk toward the train station. *His wife told me he drives to the city and parks in a garage paid for by the company.*

Hatch got out of his car and walked over to Paki's vehicle, casually looking through the slightly tinted glass. He had no doubt he could find evidence of Paki's infidelities in the car if he were to jimmy the door open and have a closer look. Cheating spouses were notorious for leaving clues around, as if subconsciously they wanted to get caught. A distant train whistle reminded Hatch that he'd no idea when the next train to the city was due to arrive and so he hurried off to catch it and, hopefully, Paki too.

CHAPTER 43

HATCH FOLLOWED PAKI when he got off the train at Penn Station in Manhattan. Paki strolled through the busy terminal, stopping briefly to look through the window of the Warner Brothers store. Later, he stopped again when he purchased a carton of freshly made popcorn from one of the many vendors on the terminal's lower level. Hatch wrinkled up his nose at the strong smell of popcorn so early in the morning and instead bought a coffee and a buttered bagel from an almost identical vendor nearby.

Paki exited into the crowded street and turned north; walking uptown, with Hatch close behind.

Hatch observed all the people rushing around him. Other than some tourists and holiday shoppers, most everyone seemed to be on their way to work. And they were all in a hurry. This contrasted vividly with Paki's seemingly nonchalant walk up Eighth Avenue.

Weird, Hatch thought as he struggled to follow Paki through the crowd without spilling his coffee or dropping his bagel. His camera hung from a loop around his neck and was tucked under his arm. *This guy's not acting like someone going to work. Maybe he's meeting his secretary for an early morning rendezvous?* Hatch had no doubt that he would solve that mystery soon.

Several long New York City blocks later, the mystery deepened when Hatch looked up and saw that they were now passing Fortieth Street.

"Where the hell is this asshole going?" Hatch muttered to himself. His feet were starting to hurt, the coffee was no doubt cold by now, and the bagel—well, bagels are downright indestructible; so there was no complaint there. Still, he wondered where Paki was going and what he was up to.

Paki turned east on Fifty-Thrid Street, about three blocks before they would have reached Central Park. Now Hatch had an idea where they were probably headed and he was proved correct when at Sixth Avenue he saw the twin lions that guard the entrance to the main branch of the New York City Public Library.

As Paki climbed the broad marble stair, Hatch followed Paki up the stairs, positioning himself slightly off to one side while remaining behind him. Suddenly, Paki stopped and turned. Hatch froze, sure that he'd been found out. But instead, Paki sat down on one of the cold stone steps and looked past him at the throng of people on the sidewalk. Hatch quickly recovered and continued to walk up the stairs until he was above Paki. He positioned himself in what he hoped wasn't too obvious a spot and sat down, the cold marble sending a momentary shock through his spine.

Shit, Hatch thought miserably. *I could use that fuckin' coffee right about now.* He'd gotten rid of the cooled drink and the bagel several blocks ago.

Hatch spotted a discarded newspaper, retrieved it, then returned to his "spot" and placed it between himself and the cold, hard stone. *Yeah, that's better*, thought the private eye as he settled in for the duration. *The secretary should show up any minute now.*

Two hours later, Hatch was still waiting. He was cold, miserable, and his feet still ached from the long walk to the library. Paki, he noticed, showed no signs of wanting to leave anytime soon and no one had shown up to meet him.

Would Paki wait two hours or more to meet someone? Doubtful, Hatch thought. From what he'd learned about Paki—he wouldn't wait two minutes for anyone.

Hatch wondered again if he'd somehow been found out. It was unlikely, but not impossible. Paki's actions and body language so far indicated that he had no idea he was being followed.

What the fuck was he doing just sitting there? Hatch thought. Then a gut feeling coalesced into an idea. Hatch jumped up, grabbed the newspaper he'd been sitting on and, after carefully folding it, stuck it into the pocket of his overcoat. He pulled his collar up and walked down the steps past Paki, past the lions and around the corner. Once he was out of Paki's line of vision, he pulled out his cell phone. Using the information supplied by Paki's wife, he dialed Paki's office. The phone was answered on the first ring.

"Editorial," a woman's voice said.

Hatch referred to his notes to get the name right. "Uh, good morning," he said. "May I please speak to Theodore Pakidorapopulos?"

Slight hesitation. "Who's calling please?"

"Oh, I'm sorry," Hatch replied. "My name is Doctor Isaacs and I'm calling Mr. Pakidorapopulos about his test results..."

Another hesitation. "Mr. Pakidorapopulos isn't available to take your call..."

"Lorna?" Hatch broke in before she could terminate the call.

"Yes," the woman answered, slightly taken aback. "How...?"

"Theodore speaks often about you," Hatch said.

"*Me*?"

The woman sounded both incredulous and dubious. Hatch seriously doubted that any affair was going on there. "Yes, well this is rather important and this number is the only daytime phone we have on file. Would it be possible to leave a message? Like I said, this is impor..."

The woman on the other end, Lorna, exhaled impatiently. "Mr. Pakidorapopulos is on leave," she said.

"Oh," Hatch said as he tried to squeeze surprise and disappointment into the one word. *On Leave usually meant fired or laid off in the real world*, thought Hatch.

Lorna's tone softened. "He hasn't been feeling well at all lately," Lorna continued. "He's been on leave for a few days now and we haven't heard from him. Truthfully, we're a bit worried for him. Is he okay?"

Hatch thumbed the off button and hooked the phone back onto his belt. As he crossed the street, back toward the library, he thought about how most people would easily tell a doctor stuff they wouldn't dream of telling a cop.

Paki wasn't having an affair with Lorna; that much Hatch was able to learn from his brief conversation with her. A lover wouldn't have reacted the way she did upon hearing that the man she was involved with had mentioned her to someone else. Women especially liked knowing they were being thought of and being spoken positively about, even if the person doing the thinking and talking was her married boss. If they had indeed been involved, she would have responded with curiosity, surprise, or even denial. Lorna's response was that of an employee shocked to hear that her boss mentioned her to his doctor of all people. *Why?*

While he was still out of Paki's line of sight, Hatch pulled down his collar, unbuttoned his overcoat, stuck his camera under the other arm and clutched the now unfolded newspaper in his hand. It wasn't much of a disguise, but during his years on the force Hatch learned that very few people actually pay attention to the other people around them, which is why eyewitness accounts of accidents or crimes always seemed so dubious. One person would describe a six foot tall perp as being six feet three inches tall, while another would swear the same person was more like five foot ten."

Hatch came around the corner and climbed the library steps at an angle away from Paki. As soon as he was again in a position where he could watch Paki without the threat of being seen, he placed the newspaper on the stair and sat down.

Damn, he thought. *I should've gotten a cup of coffee.*

CHAPTER 44

IT SOON BECAME apparent to Hatch that Paki's daily visits to the library were part of a pattern. Over the next three days, Hatch followed Paki to Penn Station, then to the library, then for an early evening stroll through Central Park (which was crawling with cops, Hatch noticed), then it was back to Penn Station and home.

Hatch no longer found Paki's behavior unusual. Many men who'd lost their jobs found it difficult, if not impossible, to break the news to their spouse. Most of those men did what Paki was doing now: Going out every morning as if going to work, then killing eight hours before heading home as if everything was still a-okay.

If Paki were true to this form of behavior, he'd keep this up until he found another job. *Pretty hard to do if you spend all day sitting on the steps of the public library*, Hatch thought *or until the financial situation became so critical that it was no longer possible to sustain the charade*. To Hatch, Paki didn't seem the type to keep something like losing his job from his wife—but hey, here he was—probably waiting for his unemployment to run out or his severance to kick in.

Hatch hawked and spat, remembering how his own wife left him after he'd lost his job with the NYPD.

The C.O. had given him the news about being canned in the morning, right after he'd finished working the night shift.

It was all on the up and up too, his union reps were there as well as a couple of rats from Internal Affairs. The C.O. let him know right away that he was being fired and not being offered the option of resigning. Then one of the I.A.B. rats told him about how they knew he'd been shaking down small-time drug dealers—confiscating money and narcotics that never made it to an evidence locker—how they knew that he'd used some of the drugs himself and sold off the rest.

Hatch, against the advice of his union rep, asked why if they knew all this wasn't he under arrest. The other rat chimed in with the explanation Hatch half expected—it was one thing to know something, it was another to prove it. The dealers he'd robbed made unreliable witnesses, especially when testifying against a cop. Despite their best efforts, Internal Affairs did not have enough hard evidence supporting what they knew to be the truth: that he, Hatch, was a dirty cop. What they did have, however, was a scapegoat—his partner. Even though he steadfastly refused to name Hatch or anyone else as a co-conspirator, they had enough circumstantial evidence to indict him on corruption charges. Even if he were to beat the charges, they would be enough to destroy his career.

"You're a lucky son-of-a-bitch," one of the I.A.B. rats said. "Your partner is a stand-up guy. He refused to take a deal and give you up."

Now it was the C.O.'s turn again. He told Hatch that, as it was, the official reasons for his termination were consistently sloppy paperwork, poor performance, abuse of sick leave, and insubordination. Hatch smiled. All of these last charges, although absolutely true and documented, were still not enough to get him thrown off the force. The charges attributed to him by I.A.B. were also true, but apparently unprovable. Hatch actually considered fighting his dismissal. The department was currently reeling from the fallout caused by two major back-to-back scandals and, Hatch reasoned, it was very possible they didn't want the added publicity that his arrest would generate.

Hatch was about to mention that last point when one of the representatives of the police union leaned over and whispered in his ear.

"Don't be an asshole," the rep said. "Those I.A.B. bastards want you as another notch on their guns; the department just wants you to go away quietly. You insist on sticking around or making any noise, it'll only be a matter of time before I.A.B.'s parading you in front of the T.V. cameras like your partner's gonna be. Then it'll be a trip upstate, and you using plastic utensils and soap-on-a-rope."

Hatch stared hard at the union rep, "For this you cocksuckers took money out of every goddamn paycheck?" he said.

The union rep shrugged and turned away. Hatch stood, walked over to the C.O.'s desk and left his gun and shield there before signing the papers and walking out.

He'd already disposed of twelve beers before the bars at the Seaport opened and he could get at the hard liquor. *One thing the police department had taught him*, he thought sardonically, *was how to drink. By three o'clock in the afternoon he was functionally drunk, by five he was barely coherent, and at seven he felt like going home.*

Hatch couldn't remember how he got home, but he vaguely remembered the fight afterward. His wife, Janey, left him that night.

He spit again.

CHAPTER 45

IT WAS ALMOST the end of the week, the last day Hatch figured he would keep Paki under surveillance. He was so sure of Paki's M.O. by now that he'd wait until Paki was on the train, then he'd drive into the city and park near the library. Today, he'd been lucky enough to score a parking spot in close proximity to the library so he could watch Paki from the warm confines of his car.

The way Hatch figured it, once Paki was on his way home, he'd call the missus and remind her of their meeting tomorrow. He'd also remind her to bring the rest of his money. He would give her a detailed and boring summary of her husband's activities, along with some photos of him sitting on the library steps, and collect his paycheck. All in all, it had been a real easy assignment. A real "tit" job. Hatch's eyes momentarily lost their focus as he remembered his meeting with Paki's wife.

Now she has great tits, he mused. He'd already decided to watch her reaction to the news of her husband's unemployed status. He knew that a lot of these women who could afford to pay him to spy on their hubbys would feel more betrayed, more hurt and more afraid, to learn that their meal ticket was gone than to find out their husband was having an affair.

Yeah, Hatch thought. *I'll watch her eyes when I drop the news. If she looks hurt, vulnerable, then I've got a chance of getting her in the sack.* Hatch was so lost in his lustful plans that he missed Paki's exit from the library steps.

"Oh shit!" Hatch swore loudly when he noticed Paki was gone. He quickly turned his head in every direction, his eyes searching the streets and sidewalks in a near panic until he spotted Paki boarding an uptown bus.

Hatch followed the bus doggedly as it lurched its way through the early evening rush-hour traffic, stopping when it stopped and scanning the disembarking passengers for his quarry.

Paki finally got off the bus at 111th Street, oblivious to the blue sedan that parked six yards from the bus stop. He sniffed at the cold autumn air after the bus had driven off, blew his nose, and then crossed the street; heading west.

Hatch sat up slowly from where he'd crouched down behind the steering wheel. Even though the possibility was slim, he didn't want to take a chance on being recognized by Paki.

Curiouser and curiouser, Hatch thought as he watched Paki cross. *He's heading for the park.*

Hatch drove to the intersection and made a left; keeping Paki in view and followed at a discreet distance. The sun, tired of holding up the New York City sky, settled into its slumber in the west, letting go appreciative sighs of cool air that chased each other through the streets of the city and down the paths of the darkened park. Paki stopped at the park entrance and blew into his hands as if to ward off the cold brought on by one of these stray draughts. Hatch parked his car and grabbed his camera.

Something definitely is going on, Hatch thought. *Maybe Paki is having an affair after all and he's meeting her here.*

Hatch dismissed that idea almost as soon as he'd thought of it. There are a thousand more accommodating, not to mention safer, places in this city for an adulterous rendezvous. No, there was something else happening here—drugs maybe—and he was going to find out what.

Hatch waited until he saw Paki melt into the park entrance's shadows, then got out of his car and followed. Paki stayed off the leaf-strewn path and skulked through the trees, the loamy earth muffling his footsteps. Hatch did the same, remembering the large presence of law enforcement personnel that he'd seen earlier in the week.

Hatch couldn't be sure how far they'd gone, but he figured it to be at least a couple of dozen yards. He almost lost Paki in the gathering night more than once, and had to suppress a yelp when he almost tripped over a tree root.

Paki veered off to the left, toward the asphalt path and a bench that was almost invisible in the darkness under a broken lamp. Hatch followed, then hunkered down and duck-walked the last few feet into the deeper shadow of an overgrown Rhododendron. Without taking his eyes off of his quarry, Hatch reached into his coat pocket and pulled out the heavy, bulky object he carried just for this purpose. With practiced ease, he removed the regular lens from his camera and replaced it with the big "Light-Gathering" lens he'd just removed from his pocket. It settled into place with a satisfying click after a single half-turn.

Hatch hefted the camera into position, cursing softly at the added weight of the special lens. The lens, in fact, was just another item he "appropriated" from the NYPD before he'd been asked to leave. It had proven itself to be a very useful tool in the past, and as night finally closed its black shroud around them, Hatch was able to focus on Paki's nocturnal activity on the park bench. It had proved its usefulness yet again.

The space-aged camera lens, formerly the property of the NYPD, harvested whatever little light was available, even starlight, and concentrated it in a way that allowed Hatch to clearly see what would have been invisible, or very nearly so, to the naked eye.

Paki was seated sideways on the bench talking to a young man wearing a down parka and a knit cap. As Hatch watched the conversation, he wished not for the first time, that he could read lips.

Drugs, Hatch thought as he snapped a photo experimentally. "It's gotta be drugs," he whispered as he pushed the button again.

Hatch kept taking pictures of Paki's conversation with the young man on the bench, hoping to catch the actual drug deal on film. When Paki reached out, Hatch felt his stomach tighten in triumph and anticipation.

This is it, he thought. *This is it!* But instead of reaching for a plasticine bag of cocaine, heroin, or pot, Hatch was stunned when he saw Paki grab the other man's crotch.

This wasn't the first time Hatch found that a client's husband had a secret appetite for "knockwurst," and he recovered from his initial surprise quickly. He photographed Paki's brief struggle to unzip the other man's pants, and continued taking pictures as Paki performed fellatio on him. As he watched the ongoing action, Hatch felt a curious stirring in the pit of his stomach—an unwelcome combination of revulsion and arousal.

When Paki finally lifted his head, Hatch made sure he got some close-up photos of the grin on his face.

"Yeah," Hatch whispered to himself. "SOB didn't waste a drop...why can't I find a fuckin' broad who does that?"

Hatch aimed the camera at the other man's face and saw that this *man* was actually more of a boy. Hatch snapped a photo of the glassy-eyed youth's face and adjusted the camera's lens for a wide-angle shot. He took several more photos as the youth now performed the same sex act on Paki, who soon spasmed in release. Hatch actually managed to take a nicely framed shot of Paki's face contorted in ejaculatory pleasure and silently congratulated himself on a job well done as he turned the camera around and quickly scrolled through the collection of photos.

Before bringing the camera up to his face again, he peered out at the darkness. They were virtually invisible, which was why they obviously felt safe enough to indulge their appetites in public this way, especially with all the cops around. In fact, the only way Hatch knew they were still there was because he knew where they were and he could just barely make out a slight rhythmic movement coming from the bench. Apparently they were at it again.

Hatch hoisted the camera back up, steadying the lens with his left hand the same way he steadied his pool cue during a game of billiards. He sharpened the focus and still didn't quite understand what he was seeing. A close-up of the young man's face showed that he was again performing the act of fellatio, but something was clearly wrong. His eyes weren't glassy anymore, in fact they were clear and wide with fear; one of his hands clutched the bench and held it in a death grip.

Hatch slowly readjusted the lens, pulling back to a wide-angle shot. The scene still didn't make sense. It looked like Paki, a wolfish grin on his face, was forcing the other guy to perform fellatio on some sort of sex toy; a black dildo or vibrator...then he noticed Paki's grip on the object in question—the way the long, black cylindrical shape caught and reflected the meager light...it wasn't a toy at all, Hatch realized in horror, it was a gun.

CHAPTER 46

HATCH WATCHED PAKI feed the long gun barrel to the young man on the park bench. A combination of shock, realization, awe, and terror iced his spine and made the hairs on the back of his neck stand on end.

"Holy shit," Hatch whispered to himself frantically. "That's the son of a bitch that the whole city's looking for—this fuckin' guy, Pakidorapopulos, is the Chickenhawk!"

Hatch continued to stare through the camera's viewfinder, his mouth open in disbelief. Greater comprehension hit him and he shook his head vigorously to clear it. He was looking at this surreal scene through the *camera's* viewfinder! Hatch mentally kicked himself and muttered a year's worth of expletives as he once again fired off photos of the two men on the bench—only this time the stakes were higher—*much higher*, Hatch thought darkly.

The report from Paki's gun was incredibly loud and made Hatch swear and jump even though he'd been expecting it. Hatch caught the young man's death in frames—the flame from the gun's barrel visible through the victim's cheek as a bright red glow, the jerk of his head as the large caliber bullet slammed into it, and the mass of blood, hair, and gore as it exited.

With the report of the gun's blast still ringing in his ears, Hatch grabbed his gear and made ready to bolt; he knew that it would only be a matter of minutes before the place would be crawling with cops and feds. He turned toward the scene on the bench one last time and was shocked again to see Paki still there; seemingly unhurried. The ice that had gripped his spine earlier returned—it seemed to Hatch that Paki was staring right at him. *Could he possibly see him? Impossible,* Hatch reasoned. He could barely make Paki out in the dark and *he* knew exactly where to look.

Hatch turned at the distant sound of sirens wailing, a crashing sound in the underbrush indicated heavy bodies, cops, making haste toward the location of the bench where Paki had just committed his latest murder. When Hatch quickly returned his gaze to the bench, Paki was already gone.

"Shit!" Hatch swore under his breath as he started to run back the way he'd come.

Hatch prayed that the same ground cover of soft, dead leaves and pine needles that cushioned his steps earlier would hide the sound of his running footsteps now. As the crashing sounds of determined men came closer, the jingling of his equipment seemed to also increase in volume, threatening to give him away. His breath became ragged, the pounding of his own heart in his ears louder than the shot from Paki's gun. Finally, in desperation, he ran the last few yards full out, caring less about the amount of noise he made than with his immediate escape.

Hatch leapt from the park's entrance and sprinted for his vehicle, the car's keys already in his hand. He jumped into his car, hearing shouts he believed were directed at him over the roar of the engine. He pressed his foot to the gas pedal and peeled away from the sidewalk, lights off, tires screeching in protest. He almost lost control, the heavy car fishtailing as he took the corner without slowing and raced headlong away from the park.

More than ten blocks later, he pulled into a side street and stomped on the brake. The brake lights flared red for a moment as the car jolted to a halt, then extinguished as Hatch threw the gear into park. Hatch gripped the steering wheel in both hands, his knuckles white. He was shaking uncontrollably, sweat running down his face and soaking his shirt despite the cold air in the car.

After a few moments, the tremors subsided and Hatch's breathing had almost returned to normal. He loosened his death grip from the steering wheel and dropped his hands into his lap, taking deep breaths and exhaling loudly.

Although Hatch hadn't committed the murder, he knew that his presence in the park made him suspect. The cops were under an enormous amount of pressure and that pressure combined with the frustration of not being able to catch this killer may incline some to be a little quick on the trigger.

Jeez, thought Hatch, *Look what happened to that fuckin' homeless guy.*

Hatch considered his options had he stayed in the park after Paki had committed his little murder...being caught and considered a suspect in the murder was one. After seeing his photos they could imagine that he was somehow involved in some sort of sick ritual murder thing where he took pictures of the murder as an accessory. He could be questioned as to why he remained at the scene taking said photos instead of calling the cops and maybe preventing a murder. Of course there was also the small matter of his being in possession of stolen police property. All of these propositions struck Hatch as being lose-lose.

Hatch ran a hand down his face and then wiped it, glistening with his sweat, on his pants leg. Getting caught in Central Park, near the scene of a murder, was definitely not the kind of trouble he needed right now. Then he picked up the camera he'd hastily tossed onto the next seat and looked it over approvingly before carefully stowing it away.

Besides, he thought as he started up the car, turned on the lights and drove away at a much more leisurely and lawful rate of speed. *Getting busted would put a serious crimp in my plans.* Hatch grinned as he joined the light, early morning traffic.

"Yeah," he chuckled. "Me and ol' Paki-boy have plans alright—business plans."

CHAPTER 47

RAMOS LOOKED UP at a sky that resembled a bad watercolor painting. Streaks of varying shades of gray ran and bled into each other in lazy uninspired patterns. The sun was just a lighter blotch of gray behind clouds the color of dirty, January slush.

"You gave those up," Tommy said to him, motioning toward the breast pocket of Ramos' overcoat.

Ramos was absentmindedly rummaging through the pocket looking for the cigarettes that weren't there. Not anymore anyway. He sighed and stuck his hands into the coat's side pockets.

"Yo son, I told you not to put your hands in the pockets," Tommy admonished. "It ruins the cut of the garment."

Ramos rolled his eyes and looked dubiously at Tommy's modernly fashionable attire, including dark glasses with tiny oval lenses that barely covered his partner's eyes.

"So what's with the shades?" Ramos asked.

"Late night," Tommy replied, grinning wolfishly.

Ramos held up a hand, "Spare me the details," he said.

Tommy shrugged and casually leaned against a parked city ambulance. They both went back to watching the army of cops and FBI agents troop in and out of the park. Ramos and Tommy Cucitti had already examined the body and the crime scene, arranged for investigators from the district attorney's office to photograph both, and had interviewed potential witnesses.

Ramos hung his head and slowly shook it back and forth in frustration. He looked up at the literally hundreds of law enforcement personnel gathered here and knew that each one of them wanted this killer stopped. He also knew that they all wondered how this sicko murderer had been able to elude them—why he wasn't dead or in cuffs by now—and he also knew that, like himself, each and every one of the men and women here carried at least a tiny measure of guilt concerning this killer's continued freedom. What did they miss? What didn't they do? Who didn't they talk to? Deserved or not, consciously done or not, they all insisted on shouldering part of the blame themselves.

"Head up Eddie," Tommy half-whispered, breaking into Ramos' reverie. When Ramos looked up, he saw District Attorney Williams stomping in their direction.

Williams nodded to the two men and glanced around to make sure no one was within earshot.

"So detectives," Williams said conspiratorially. "What have we got?"

"We don't have nuthin'," Tommy retorted.

Williams favored Tommy with a withering glare and turned his attention toward Ramos.

"You'll have our report on your desk this afternoon," Ramos told him.

Williams shook his head. "Not good enough," he said. "This motherfucker has to belong to the DA's office. He's got the mayor and the entire police department resembling nothing more than a bunch of incompetent, impotent assholes. We get him, it's all over but the swearing in."

Tommy looked away disgustedly. He could almost imagine Williams rubbing his hands together in glee, like an old silent era movie villain.

"So nice to know you have the public's best interest at heart," Ramos growled.

Williams dismissed Ramos' comment with a wave of his perfectly manicured hand. "Please save the sarcasm for someone who honestly gives a damn," he said.

"You forget that me and Eddie are part of that so-called *entire police department* you're talking about," Tommy said.

"No," said Williams, his eyes smoldering. "You forgot that you two are working for me now, and I have to tell you that so far I'm very disappointed in your lack of results. Apparently your reputations are undeserved."

"You know what they say," Tommy said. "Don't believe the hype."

"If you're unhappy with the quality of our work you can always send us back," Ramos added.

"That's not an option!" Williams shot back. "I know you want this killer every bit as much as I do—maybe more. You find him, y'hear? You find him for me—for the DA's office—and your reputations and careers are assured. You fuck me over, purposely or not, and I will make it my life's endeavor to destroy you."

Tommy started to say something in retaliation, but was stopped short by Ramos' hand on his elbow. Then together, they turned and walked away from the DA.

"You'll have our report on your desk this afternoon," Ramos said without turning around.

"I don't want reports, I want results!" Williams shouted at their backs as they walked away. When he realized that his tirade was having no effect, Williams waved after them disgustedly and stomped his way back in the direction he'd come from.

Ramos and Tommy continued to walk away from the center of police activity in silence.

"I can't stand that idiot, Williams," Tommy finally blurted out.

"Nitchik's the idiot," Ramos said offering Tommy a mint; which he turned down. "Williams is the asshole."

Tommy stopped and held his chin between thumb and forefinger. "I thought Avni was the asshole," he said thoughtfully.

"No, no," Ramos said before tossing the recently proffered mint into his mouth and pulverizing it with a mighty crunch. "Avni is the scumbag."

"Ah, true dat," Tommy agreed. "So then who's the spineless, gutless, no-balls, back-stabbing shithead?"

"That," Ramos said peering through the reflective glass doors of one of the buildings, "Would be the police commissioner."

Tommy hawked and spit. “You telling the truth now, son,” he said. He eyed Ramos curiously. “What’s up?” he asked.

Ramos was standing with his back to the mirror-like doors. He positioned himself at a slight angle, slowly lifted his arm and brought it back down at shoulder height, his hand open. It looked like some sort of slow-motion karate chop. Ramos closed one eye and sighted along his arm, back up the street toward the spot where they’d just had their most recent run-in with District Attorney Williams. Without a word, Ramos dropped his arm and clomped back up the street with Tommy in hot pursuit.

“What’s going on?” Tommy asked.

Ramos motioned for quiet as he led Tommy back to almost the same exact place they’d been standing when Williams approached them. Cops and feds were still going in and out of the park, curious pedestrians were still being kept away from the crime scene by yellow tape and uniformed cops, and the same ambulance was still parked there.

Ramos motioned toward the ambulance’s tires. Tommy looked but didn’t see anything—at first. Then he made out a dark smudge on the asphalt, black on gray; like the sky, that disappeared under the large emergency vehicle.

Tommy jerked his head up and quickly went to the vehicle’s cab, but it was empty. When he turned around, Ramos was already motioning Nance Collins over to where they were. The E.M.S lieutenant joined them and Ramos quickly made his request. Nance turned around and spotted an EMT coming out of the park. She placed two fingers in her mouth and let loose with an ear-splitting whistle that caught everyone’s attention, including the EMT who had been exiting the park.

“Yo!” she yelled, pointing at the startled EMT, and then jerking her thumb back toward the ambulance. “Is this your bus?”

The EMT shook his head no.

Nance nodded, then pointed back past the EMT toward the park. “Get back in there, find whoever belongs to this bus and tell ‘em they gotta move it—now!”

CHAPTER 48

ONCE THE AMBULANCE had been moved, Ramos, Tommy, and Nance Collins were able to make out the skid marks on the street. They led away from the curb at a steep angle before ending abruptly about four feet away.

"Someone was in a hurry," Ramos observed.

Tommy shook his head. "How the fuck did you see that?" he asked incredulously.

"I noticed it while we were standing here earlier," Ramos replied. "It didn't click then, it didn't make sense."

"What didn't make sense?" Nance asked.

"Well, if there's a possibility that those tracks belong to the perp's car, why hasn't this entire area been preserved as a crime scene? Why isn't CSU here measuring and photographing those tracks?"

"And now they make sense?" Nance asked.

"Well, the fact that they're not being made a fuss over makes some kind of sense," Ramos said. "If you're the cop who saw the suspect make his getaway, and you didn't or couldn't stop him. Plus you got no description, no plate, no nuthin'...do *you* wanna be the cop to take that to the commish or the mayor?"

Tommy snorted, "Talk about killin' the messenger," he said.

"Damn right," Ramos agreed. "If somebody saw a vehicle leave here in a hurry last night, and I don't see how that couldn't happen with all the fuckin' cops all over the place, then he's keepin' his mouth shut 'cause he don't need the grief."

"But what if he saw something that could help catch the killer?" Nance asked.

"Nah," Tommy said. "If he saw anything he could use, he woulda made a big noise about it. Something like that can make a guy's career, make him out to be a hero. Nah, I believe it's just like Eddie said, somebody figures that the brass might think he let the big one get away and he, or *she*, is keepin' their mouth shut."

Nance looked at Ramos, "So why bother with it now?" she asked.

"Yeah," Tommy agreed. "And what was all that weird shit I saw you doing in front of that building?"

"That's what finally made it click for me," Ramos said looking up at his partner. "C'mon."

Nance stopped him. "You really think that could have been the Chickenhawk?" she asked.

Ramos shrugged. "There's always a chance," he said.

CHAPTER 49

RAMOS LED TOMMY back to the building with the mirrored doors.

"So now you gonna let me in on the secret?" Tommy asked.

"No secret," Ramos replied, opening the one of the doors for Tommy.

They entered the lobby, the door closing behind them with a pneumatic wheeze. There, built into a recess in the wall, were two Automated Teller Machines...*ATM's*.

Tommy's mouth fell open. "For real son," he said. "Now you gotta tell me how you saw these!"

Ramos shrugged. "While you were yapping, I was looking," he said.

Tommy stopped in his tracks, a combination of surprise and admiration on his face. "Oh no he didn't..." he muttered to himself before hurrying to join Ramos at the machines. They in turn were joined moments later by a middle-aged man in an inexpensive blue suit. His occupation was stitched in bright red over the breast pocket: SECURITY.

"May I help you gentlemen?" His deep voice sounded as if it had been slow simmered in the West Indies. When Ramos and Tommy turned around, he saw the NYPD shields on *their* breast pockets. "Oh," he exclaimed, then indicated the goings-on outside of the lobby doors with a quick tilt of his head. "What happened out there?" he asked.

"Ongoing police investigation," Ramos answered.

"So we're sure you'll understand if we can't talk about it," Tommy added.

"Yes, of course," the security guard answered politely.

"Do these machines have cameras in 'em?" Ramos asked.

"Yes they do," the security guard answered.

"We need the pictures," Tommy said.

The security guard considered a moment. "The machines are serviced by a private company," he said. "I'll have to get the building manager..."

"Get 'em!" Ramos and Tommy said together.

CHAPTER 50

IT TOOK THE rest of the morning, part of the afternoon, and a mound of paperwork before the two detectives were able to get the photos from the ATM's two cameras. A technician, accompanied by an armed guard and the building manager, handed an inexpensive USB drive over to the two detectives.

"These things are digital now you know," the technician remarked.

"Oh yeah?" Ramos asked disinterestedly while he rolled the small, plastic drive around in his hand.

"Yeah," the techie continued. "Regular film is a thing of the past, it's all just digital—photography, movies, you name it..."

"Yeah, I read about that," Tommy said thoughtfully.

"If film was workin' just fine before, why fix somethin' that ain't broke?" Ramos asked.

Tommy and the technician glanced at each other.

"That's just the way it is, man," the technician said. "Out with the old, in with the new."

Ramos muttered something unintelligible.

"Never mind him," Tommy said to the tech as he closed the ATM door under the watchful gaze of the armed guard. "He thinks High-Tech is the name of a Japanese restaurant."

The two detectives stepped back out into the dreary day. Cops and feds still milled about, although in much lesser numbers and with less urgency than before. Tommy pulled his coat collar up against a sudden gust that left behind it the scent of a promised rain.

Then suddenly an ominous-looking car pulled up to the curb directly in front of the detectives and blocked their path. The rear window rolled down and revealed the shiny fat face of Deputy Mayor Nitchik.

Nitchik stared straight ahead, not bothering to make eye contact with the two cops, and stuck a pudgy hand out of the window. "Give it to me," he said as he made grasping motions with his hand. The gesture reminded Tommy of a child asking for candy.

Ramos sighed and kept his hands in his pockets, "Good morning to you too," he said sarcastically.

The deputy mayor squinted angrily at him through pig-like eyes. "Don't give me any of your crap, detective," he said. "Just give me the pictures."

"What pictures?" Tommy asked innocently.

Ramos still kept his hands in his pockets.

Nitchik looked back and forth between the two detectives, the unruly, white hairs of his eyebrows knit together in consternation. "You know what pictures," he said. "You have the pictures from the ATM's in the lobby of this building, pictures that may have recorded the Chickenhawk entering or leaving the park."

The deputy mayor's attention was drawn away as the limo's driver said something that Ramos and Tommy strained to hear, but were unable to make out. Eventually, the deputy mayor nodded in understanding and returned his attention to the two detectives, "I know you have the pictures on a USB," he said. "You can play dumb all you want." "And some of us ain't playin', son," Tommy interjected.

"Precisely," the deputy mayor agreed, not knowing why. "That USB drive is supposed to be turned over to the *mayor's* task force. It could be instrumental in the capture and conviction of a, ah, a serious criminal."

"The district attorney's office is investigating these murders too," Ramos said quietly.

"Fuck the DA," Nitchik said shrilly. "He'd better come around to realizing that he belongs to the mayor as well. This is the *mayor's* city, the *mayor's* investigation, the *mayor's* pictures! You screw-ups were supposed to have been reporting Williams' activities back to the mayor's office since the beginning—you think we don't know you've been feeding us mostly bullshit? If I do not get that drive, you will be charged right here, right now, with obstruction of justice, evidence tampering, impeding an investigation...And those are just the local charges, I'm sure the feds can come up with a few of their own."

Ramos stared hard at the deputy mayor for a moment and then his shoulders slumped in defeat. He pulled his hand out of his pocket and dropped the USB drive into Nitchik's pillowy palm. Tommy hung his head and slowly shook it from side-to-side. Nitchik's hand, and the drive, disappeared into the limo's dark interior.

"You'll be lucky if charges aren't brought against you anyway," Nitchik said before turning to the driver. "Let's get out of here," he said. "I can't stand the stink."

CHAPTER 51

THAT EVENING, RAMOS trudged through the front door of his home weighed down by defeat. He hated to admit it, but he felt defeated. He felt...*old*.

He was so preoccupied with his thoughts that at first, he didn't notice the strangers in his house.

"Hello Eddie," his wife said from the living room.

Ramos could tell she was worried and she hugged herself as if trying to keep her slight frame warm.

"Yeah, hi," Ramos replied, not taking his eyes off the two men seated on his couch as he finished removing his hat and coat. The two men politely stood up, the older one buttoning up his jacket reflexively. Ramos placed them immediately—*cops*.

Ramos wondered if Nitchik had made good on his threat to bring he and Tommy up on charges. If so, then these guys would be IAB, but then why were they smiling? Not the predatory grins that cops sometimes exhibit when they've cornered their quarry...no, these smiles were genuine; warm, even welcoming. Ramos grew even more wary.

The older man stuck his hand out and approached Ramos. "Hello Detective Ramos," he said genially. "I'm Detective Harding and that's Officer Meissmer."

"Soon to be Detective Meissmer," the younger man called out amiably.

Detective Harding chuckled. "Yeah," he said. "Soon to be Detective Meissmer—the kid never lets me forget it."

The pleasantries grated on Ramos' nerves. "Yeah? Well let's see some ID gentlemen," he said, keeping his hands at his side.

When Harding saw that no hand was being proffered in return, he let his own hand drop slowly to his side and his smile lost some of its wattage. He pulled out his shield and ID and showed both to Ramos; Meissmer did the same.

"What do you want?" Ramos asked gruffly, after barely glancing at the shields and identification.

"We're from the Chaplain's office," Harding sighed, as he and Meissmer tucked their shields away.

Ramos felt like he'd been sucker-punched, the *Chaplain's* office? Flummoxed, he looked back and forth between the two men and his wife.

"The *Chaplain's* office?" he asked aloud, confusion evident on his face and in the tone of his words. "Is everything alrigh..."

"Uh, we came at your wife's request," Harding explained.

Ramos stared as understanding eluded him. He looked at his wife, "Linda, are you okay?"

Linda shrugged slightly. "Physically I'm fine Eddie," she said. "But spiritually, I'm in pain."

Ramos' confusion only increased, he glanced at the two cops and then back at his wife. "Linda, what are you talking about?" he asked, concern in his voice.

Detective Harding stepped forward. "Eddie, uh, Detective Ramos," he said softly. "Are you saved?"

"Wha...?"

"Are you saved?" Harding repeated. "Have you accepted Christ Jesus as your personal Lord and Savior?"

"What the hell are you talking about?" Ramos asked heatedly. "Linda, what the fuck is going on here?"

"Eddie," Linda admonished. "Please don't curse, especially in a loud voice—Kim is right upstairs."

Ramos briefly considered bellowing a particularly virulent stream of expletives at the top of his lungs, but realized that his young daughter didn't deserve that. Instead, in a more modulated tone he said, "Linda, what the goddamn, mother fuck are these two Jesus freaks doing here and what the hell is going on in my house?"

The other two cops blushed visibly and Ramos saw Linda shudder at his words.

Detective Ramos...," Harding began, but Ramos cut him off with a raised hand.

"Eddie," Linda said, eyes downcast. "The Word says that you're going to have to account for every idle word you speak and that by your words you will be condemned."

Ramos glanced at the two cops and realizing that he'd find no help there, looked back at his wife. She looked up at him.

"When you curse, especially in front of these men of God, you bring a curse down on your house Eddie," Linda said. "You curse all of us."

Ramos threw his hands up in disgust. "Does anybody here talk regular?" he asked.

"Detective Ramos," Meissmer piped up. "Sister Ramos, your wife, asked if we'd just stop by and minister a little to the two of you—maybe provide some counseling and see if you're prepared to turn your life over to Christ."

Ramos glared at him.

Meissmer pulled a pad out of one of his pockets and leafed through it. "Now, Sister Ramos told us that you're most comfortable attending a Catholic church. We have a list of Charismatic Catholic churches that are full of Born-Again Believers. Maybe you could just visit..."

"Get out," Ramos growled.

"But..."

"Get out," Ramos repeated.

"But if you..."

"Stan," Harding broke in. "Let's go."

Meissmer seemed about to say something more, but changed his mind and retrieved his coat from the sofa. He handed Harding his coat and the detective shrugged it on heavily.

Ramos opened the front door and held it open for them.

Harding nodded his thanks. "We apologize if we've mis-spoken or over-stepped our bounds, Brother Ramos."

"*Detective* Ramos."

"Uh, right. *Detective* Ramos. It's not our job to try to convert anyone or force anyone to come to our Lord Jesus, but as members of the Body of Christ…"

"No," Ramos interrupted. "Your job is being a cop, and right now every real cop in the city is trying to catch a killer. What have you been doin' besides preaching and handing out religious tracts?"

Harding looked coolly at Ramos and gestured for Meissmer to precede him out the door. Meissmer muttered good night as he stepped over the threshold.

"Read Colossians 1:28-29, Eddie. That may help you understand what my job really is," Harding said quietly before following Meissmer into the night.

Ramos shut the door and turned toward his wife. "What the hell was that all about?"

"Please don't curse Eddie."

"Linda," Ramos yelled. "This is my fuckin' house, I pay the fuckin' bills, and I'll fuckin' curse any fuckin' time I fuckin' feel like it!"

Linda's temper flared as well, "I knew you would act stupid about this! That you wouldn't even take the time to listen."

# # #

Kim listened to her parents argue from her perch at the top of the stairs. Although her parents had minor spats in the past, this was different. She'd never seen or heard them so angry at each other before and she bit her lip in worry. She wished her sister Myrna was home. She wished her parents weren't arguing. She wished everything was like it used to be before the Chickenhawk.

CHAPTER 52

THE NEXT MORNING Ramos settled in behind his desk and after a fruitless search through his pockets for a cigarette, considered a mint, and settled for coffee from the vendor down in the lobby instead.

He returned to his desk, stirring the hot liquid with the little wooden stirrer, and took a sip. It proved to be hot, but little else and he wished for his own personal brew.

"You know," Ramos drawled at Tommy between sips. "If the mayor's task force was able to come up with anything from that USB drive, what you're reading there becomes moot."

Tommy looked up from the report he'd been looking through. "Moot? Moot?" He laughed out loud. "What, you been sneaking looks at the dictionary again, son?"

Ramos shifted in his seat, making himself more comfortable. "Moot," he repeated. "If they were able to get anything useful out of that drive, the task force is probably knocking on the Chickenhawk's door right now."

"No doubt," Tommy agreed, still looking over the reports concerning yesterday's action at Central Park. "But if they don't get anything useful, then we're still in the game—we still have a chance."

Ramos grimaced. "Yeah," he said remembering his conversation with Nance the day before. "There's always a chance."

"That's all I'm sayin'," Tommy said. Then, "I would still like to know who gave us up to the deputy mayor when we got that drive."

Ramos shrugged. "We made a lot of calls so we could get to those photos," he said. "It could have been anybody."

Tommy nodded and then let out a low whistle, "Yo, check out who all got busted in the park last night..."

"By the task force?"

"Mostly, yeah."

"Who?"

"Well, there were a total of eleven who were arrested and charged with loitering and soliciting a prostitute. There were two cases in particular that you might be interested in—soliciting a minor for the purpose of prostitution and endangering the welfare of a child."

Ramos' attention perked up. "Tell me more," he said.

Tommy smiled," I knew you'd say that, son," he said. "All eleven were observed engaging in various illicit sexual acts for gratuity (prostitution) in a public place (Central Park North). All of the alleged prostitutes in this instance were male, with two of those being minor in age."

"You figure one of those two could be our guy?" Ramos asked.

"Shit if I know," Tommy answered as he sifted through several pages of documents before finding the one he was looking for. After a brief scan, another whistle escaped his lips and he gave Ramos a quick glance.

"They both got cut loose last night," Tommy said in a low voice.

Ramos jumped to his feet, spilling the dregs of his coffee onto the floor. "What?" He yelled, "That's bullshit!"

Tommy turned the document over, read it briefly, and then turned it over again. "Yeah, well, it's true though," he said.

Ramos stomped over to Tommy's desk, practically tore the form out of his hand and scanned through the document, turning it over and reading the back as Tommy had done.

Ramos handed the paper back to Tommy. "You still know how to work computers, right?"

"Of course."

Ramos nodded. "Good," he said. "Get on one of the computers here, work with one of the DA's people if you have to, and see if you can get any more info on those two perps."

"I'm on it," Tommy said, jumping up from his seat.

After Tommy had gone, Ramos put his glasses on and began reading through the various reports. As he read he unconsciously patted his breast pocket in search of a cigarette.

Forty minutes later, he'd finished going through the reports and Tommy was returning from his mission.

"Any luck?" Ramos asked.

"Yes and no," Tommy answered, tossing some printouts on the desk in front of Ramos before planting himself on the edge of the desk.

Ramos took off his glasses and pinched the bridge of his nose between thumb and forefinger. He'd had enough of reading, his eyes hurt. Leaving the printouts untouched, he looked up at his partner and put his glasses away. "How 'bout you just tell me what you found out," he said. "You're real good at that."

"Yeah, flattery will get you everywhere, son," Tommy said.

"You're too easy," Ramos pointed out.

"Yeah, true dat," Tommy agreed with a chuckle. "Daphne tells me that after one good compliment I'm a regular ho."

Ramos lifted his hand in a stop gesture. "Spare me the details," he said. Then turning serious, "So what did you find out?"

Tommy began with a sigh. "Those two guys got cut loose 'cause they knew people—the right people anyway. And it turns out they also had iron-clad alibis."

The first guy is Dermott McDonnell. Says here he works as a writer for a major magazine right here in the big city. He got caught with his pants down and a sixteen-year-old dick in his mouth. The kid, one Jose Santiago, has no priors and has a documented history of having learning and cognitive disabilities that leaves him with the functioning mental capacity of a six-year-old."

"Damn," Ramos said.

"Yeah, son," Tommy agreed. "Damn is right, and it only gets better. The kid says McDonnell lured him into the park, and apparently into the aforementioned compromising position, with promises of money and a puppy."

“And what was his get out of jail free card?” Ramos asked.

“He’s working as the senior campaign advisor for that extreme right wing, neo-fascist nut who is running for president.”

“Concannon?”

Tommy nodded. “The very same,” he said. “Nut or not, apparently his office made some calls on McDonnell’s behalf and that was enough to get him sprung.”

Ramos considered this a moment. “And the other guy?”

Tommy looked at his printouts. “The other guy is an even bigger fish,” he said. “His name’s Haymes Jansen, a republican senator from some shit-kickin’ state out west.”

Ramos whistled. “A senator?”

“Yeah, son,” Tommy confirmed. “He was caught hugging a tree while seventeen-year-old Herman Aponte played *hide-the-salami* in his ass.”

“And he came all the way to New York just to get reamed and creamed?”

Tommy shook his head. “Nah,” he said. “Apparently he was here attending a republican-led conference on welfare reform hosted by our very own mayor.”

“Yeah, I heard about that,” Ramos said as he searched for his non-existent pack of smokes.

“Uh-huh,” Tommy said. “And here’s the really weird part, son—Aponte says that Jansen insisted that he repeat, ‘Utah is a welfare state,’ over and over again while he was bangin’ his head into that tree.”

“Bangin’ his...? Oh, I get it,” Ramos said. “So what were their supposedly ironclad alibis?”

“They were both already in custody at the time of the killing.”

“Shit,” Ramos said in a subdued tone.

“I’m feelin’ you, son,” Tommy said. “I’m feelin’ you.”

CHAPTER 53

"WE'RE TIRED OF playing this game with you Hatch!" The burly detective slammed his hand down hard on the table that separated him from the private investigator with the unconcerned look on his face.

Ramos had been right of course. The mayor's task force, using the USB drive from one of the ATM's, had been able to make out the license plate number on Hatch's car. At 5:45 that morning, the heavily armed and armored task force converged on Hatch's cluttered apartment and took him into custody.

Now, in the bowels of the Manhattan Correctional Center; a federal detention facility within a stone's throw of police headquarters, he was being questioned by alternate tag teams of New York City cops and agents of the FBI.

"You're garbage Hatch, you know that? Garbage!" The big cop continued to rant at him. "You think we're gonna take it easy on you just 'cause you used to be a cop? Well, that stuff don't mean nuthin' no more! We know what a fuck up you were then, and we know what a fuck up you are now. You're a fuckin' scab on society Hatch, just another goddamn skel; and the only thing that might just save your skin is if you talk to us now and tell us what you were doing at the park."

Hatch leaned forward, placed his elbow on the table, and motioned for the cop to get closer. The detective complied and hungrily leaned toward the private eye in anticipation of a message spoken in confidentiality. Hatch then slowly and deliberately raised the middle finger of his hand.

The look of surprise on the big cop's face quickly turned to anger and he slapped Hatch's hand away. "You know what they do to cops, even ex-cops, in jail," he breathed menacingly.

"I certainly hope I didn't observe you assault my client."

The cop hung his head and shook it. He pushed tiredly away from the table and walked to a corner of the room like a spent fighter between rounds without bothering to acknowledge the voice of Hatch's newly arrived lawyer. The lawyer, Stewart Turtledove, tattooed the cop's retreating back with blistering looks.

"I wish I could say that I am surprised by your actions officer," Turtledove said. "But the rapid erosion of civil liberties under the current mayoralty is commonly and widely known. My client and I will brook no abuse, however, and you should prepare to find yourself facing charges of your own."

Turtledove turned toward Hatch, who wore a look of benign amusement on his face. "Do you wish to press charges against this officer?" Turtledove asked gently.

Hatch hid a smile behind his hand. "Nah," he said after a few moments. "The guy's a fuckin' ape, what do you expect?"

Turtledove nodded in understanding, then turned to the officer, whose face had visibly reddened in response to Hatch's comment.

"Has my client been charged with anything?" Turtledove asked.

"Not yet," the cop growled.

"Then charge him," Turtledove said.

"What?"

"Charge him, I said," Turtledove repeated, planting his feet as if for a fight. "Either charge my client or send him home, you cannot hold him indefinitely."

"Your *client*," the cop spat out the word client as if it were a particularly bitter morsel. "Was at the scene of a murder."

"Is he being charged with this alleged murder?"

"Not yet," the cop countered.

"Choose your words carefully officer," Turtledove said, wagging a disapproving finger at the scowling detective. "*'Not yet'* implies intent and that in turn implies knowledge—does or does not the NYPD have knowledge of my client committing a crime?"

"He was *there*," the cop said.

The door to the tiny, austere room opened and admitted a tall, African American woman dressed in a navy blue pantsuit.

"I'm Agent Madsen with the Federal Bureau of Investigation," she said flashing her shield and ID

The expressions on the faces of Hatch and Turtledove didn't change. Disappointed that her announcement had no visible effect, Madsen folded her shield and identification away and continued in her clipped, business-like manner.

"Your client, Mr. Hatch, has been positively identified as being present in the immediate area of a homicide—at the same time that the homicide took place. At the very least, your client is being held as a material witness."

"Witness? Witness? Witness to what?" Turtledove asked as he turned toward Hatch. "Did you witness anything?"

Hatch shook his head. "Nope," he said.

Turtledove turned back to Agent Madsen. "Who was it that *'positively identified'* my client as allegedly being at the scene of this alleged crime?"

Agent Madsen cleared her throat and looked uncomfortable. The big cop from earlier stepped forward from his place in the corner.

"We have a picture of his car, big as day, right there at the park!" the cop said triumphantly.

Turtledove's eyebrow went up. "A photograph? Of his car?" He asked incredulously. "You people have the temerity, the gall, to bring my client to this barbaric facility—humiliating him before his neighbors and submitting him to this illegal questioning—because you have a photograph of his *CAR*?"

Agent Madsen rolled her eyes while the big cop stood there slack-jawed.

"Someone matching your client's description was seen running to, entering, and driving away in the car in question," Madsen said in an attempt to salvage this quickly unraveling interrogation. "He refused to stop when ordered to do so by a pursuing officer."

"And this officer positively identifies my client as being the person who drove away in the car?"

"He matches the description," Madsen reiterated.

"As does half the male population of this city," Turtledove countered. "That is a subject to be argued in court, if it ever comes to that. Apparently all you have is a photo of what you say is my client's automobile and a dubious report by an obviously incompetent police officer stating that someone who may or may not resemble my client may have driven his car away from the scene. That's barely circumstantial and you know it. If you people had anything concrete, my client would have already been charged by now—and absent those charges, we are leaving."

Turtledove signaled to Hatch, and together they headed toward the door.

"You, you can't just leave, this investigation isn't over," the big cop said loudly.

"It is for my client," Turtledove said.

Hatch made a point of deliberately pushing past the big cop who had threatened him with jail. "Assholes," he said as he left the room.

CHAPTER 54

RAMOS AND TOMMY shared a rare lunchtime booth at Jimmy's Uptown Café—130th Street and Lenox Avenue.

Soft jazz bubbled from speakers hidden in the textured acoustic ceiling, taking turns with the occasional *salsa* or *merengue* number. The air was redolent with the aromas of Latin and Neo-American cuisine.

"Gimme a steak and fries," Ramos instructed the young waiter. "You got Corona beer?"

The waiter nodded yes.

"Lemme have one of those too," Ramos finished.

The waiter, pimpled and wearing his hair in a style that reminded Ramos of a nest of short, fuzzy worms, continued nodding and turned toward Tommy.

"I'll take the tamarind-lobster salad and a Perrier," Tommy said.

Tommy noticed Ramos watching him. "What?" he asked.

"Tamarind-lobster salad?" Ramos asked dryly. "That's like ordering one of them pretty drinks with the umbrella in it."

Tommy looked confused for a moment and then laughed. "What, I can't have a salad without you going all Archie Bunker on me, son?" He asked. "Shit, I could hear your arteries hardening way over here just while you were ordering."

Both men laughed.

"Is that it?" The waiter asked, slightly annoyed.

"Yeah, that's it," Ramos said. Then, looking over at his partner, "Tommy?"

"Yeah, I'm straight," Tommy acknowledged.

As the waiter started to walk away, Ramos stopped him with a light touch on his sleeve. "Oh, uh, I want that steak real well-done, okay? I mean burn it," he said.

The waiter nodded and moved off.

After they'd both eaten, Ramos relaxed and settled back into the green faux ostrich leather upholstery with another Corona while Tommy still sipped from his original glass of sparkling water.

"Yo, I can't get over the feeling that we missed something," Tommy said.

"No shit, Sherlock," Ramos growled.

"No, I mean yeah," Tommy continued. "Some of the stuff Bob was saying earlier, before you walked in the room, was starting to click."

"I thought we agreed earlier that we'd already gone through whatever stale ideas Bob had come up with."

"Well, yeah," Tommy agreed reluctantly. "But what Bob was saying is that the answer we're looking for about this guy's identity, is probably right in front of us, but it's a subtle kind of thing. It's like we're tryin' to kill a mosquito with a sledgehammer, that's why we keep missing it."

Ramos considered this a moment. "You mean like this guy being just an ordinary, everyday Joe?"

"Yes and no," Tommy answered, downing the last of his Perrier. "This guy may not be out and out crazy, but he can't be living in a vacuum either. He probably does have a family, a wife and kids, maybe goes to church, works, takes vacations..."

"We went over this, Tommy," Ramos growled. "The Fed profiler said as much..."

"Yeah, yeah," Tommy said. "Maybe we need to look at what we got again."

Ramos sighed, "Tommy, we've been over those reports a hundred times."

"If I told you once, Eddie, I told you a *million* times," Tommy interrupted. "Don't exaggerate."

The two detectives laughed.

"You know," Ramos said thoughtfully once their laughter had subsided. "As much as I hate to admit it, maybe Bob does have something after all—you too. This guy's way under the radar, even our snitches keep coming up blank."

"Keep talking son," Tommy said, an image of Ratman flashing through his mind. He called the waiter over and paid the check.

Ramos nodded his thanks. "First we'll find out if the task force was able to get anything useful outta that drive and, if so, what they did about it..."

'Cause if the task force already has our guy," Tommy said. "Then this whole thing is moot."

Ramos laughed. "Exactly," he said. "But if it turns out that the task force and the pictures scored a zero, then we're back in the game."

CHAPTER 55

HATCH SMILED. IT hadn't been easy, but he'd finally ditched the small army of cops and G-men who had been following him ever since he walked out of the M.C.C. in the company of his lawyer a couple of days ago.

Now, bundled up in a big wool coat, a paper cup of coffee in his hand, he sat on the steps of the Manhattan Public Library. He shifted, more or less comfortably, on the small cushion he'd brought along with him.

He took a sip of the coffee and savored the liquid's heat as it almost, but not quite, burned its way down his throat. Hatch's eyes wandered up to the cloudless sky of brilliant blue and then back down to the steam that billowed and swirled from the depths of his cup. The day had shone up as clear and bright as any he'd ever known, and breathing its air reminded Hatch of biting into a cool, sweet apple.

Hatch chuckled humorlessly and gulped down the rest of his rapidly cooling coffee. He crumpled up the empty paper cup and let it drop onto the wide step. A stiff breeze rocked the paper ball back and forth before finally sending it rolling and bouncing down the library's stone stair. As he watched the remains of his coffee cup make its escape, the object of his vigil came into view.

Theodore Pakidorapopulos walked up the stairs, turned, and sat at his accustomed place with nary a glance at the private detective. Hatch waited, he was a patient man. Being a cop had taught him that.

After several minutes, Hatch "crab-walked" his way into position behind him, dragging his cushion as he went. Once comfortably in place, he placed his hand on the butt of his gun and, leaning forward, whispered four words into Paki's ear...

"Don't turn around, asshole."

Except for the sudden intake of air and the sudden stiffening of his shoulders, Hatch wouldn't have been able to tell whether or not Paki had heard him. Good. He nodded to himself, satisfied. Paki started to slowly raise his hands in surrender and Hatch poked him hard in the back of his neck with his finger.

Paki flinched. "Officer, I..."

"I told you not to move!' Hatch warned.

Paki slowly tilted his head to the side. "Are you the police?" he asked. The question didn't surprise Hatch, but the note of—what was it, relief?—in Paki's voice almost did.

Hatch poked him in the back with his finger. "I've got a gun pointed at you, pretty boy," he said. "And since I'm *not* a cop, you're in a helluva lot more trouble than you thought."

Paki nodded his head.

"Ah, so we understand each other," Hatch said.

"Not really," Paki stated. "What's this all about? What do you want, is this a robbery?"

"I saw you kill that guy in Central Park," Hatch said. "I know you're the Chickenhawk."

Hatch poked Paki in the back with his finger again when Paki started to fidget.

"Relax, asshole," Hatch warned. "You try anything stupid and I'll do you like you did that guy in the park, and I don't mean the fun stuff. Hey, I'd probably get a medal."

Paki stopped moving.

"You learn fast, cocksucker," Hatch said. "Now here's the deal..."

Hatch described how Paki's wife was sure that he was having an affair and how she hired him to follow him around. He told him how he witnessed the murder in the park, took photos of the actual murder in fact, and how he came to be waiting for Paki to show up here on the library steps.

Paki sighed. "What now," he asked. "Are you going to turn me in for the reward? Report back to my wife? Sell your story to the tabloids or maybe just kill me outright?"

Hatch shook his head. "Nah, I'm looking to conduct a little business with you," Hatch said sincerely.

"Blackmail then," Paki said, and stifled a sneeze.

Hatch placed the tip of his index finger on the side of his nose. "Er-r-r!" he said in imitation of a game show buzzer. "You hit the nail right on the head with that one."

"How much?" Paki asked.

"I'm not greedy," Hatch said. "Much. I'm thinking twice the amount of the reward that's sitting on your head right now."

"And that is?"

"What, you don't read the papers?" Hatch asked. "It's up to twenty-five grand."

"Fifty thousand dollars?"

"That's what twice twenty-five grand comes out to, isn't it?"

"I guess..."

Hatch poked Paki in the back again—hard. "Don't guess a goddamn thing," he said. "I want fifty thousand dollars, and not a penny less, by tomorrow."

"I can't get fifty thousand dollars together by tomorrow..." Paki began to say.

"You can and you will, pretty boy," Hatch said. "Fifty grand. Tomorrow. Right here. And your secret is safe with me...for the time being anyhow."

"How am I supposed to...?"

"That's your problem," Hatch said as he made to leave. Then, as an afterthought, "Your wife has a great pair of knobs on 'er," he said. "Why you would rather mess around with a bunch of guys instead of banging *her* 24/7 is beyond me."

"I would imagine there are a lot of things that are beyond you," Paki said.

Hatch grinned. "Yeah, keep being a wiseass," he said. "It just cost you another ten grand."

Paki shrugged, but by then Hatch was already gone.

CHAPTER 56

HATCH WAS PICKED up again, but this time it was by a pair of detectives who claimed they were actually working for the district attorney.

"This is getting monotonous," Hatch complained.

Ramos and Tommy Cucitti both shrugged.

"My heart bleeds," Ramos said.

Hatch didn't say anything else and turned away.

They were all in a drab and dingy replica of the interrogation room from the Manhattan Correctional Center. This room, however, was located in the detention area of One Hogan Place, District Attorney Williams' offices in Lower Manhattan.

"What were you doing in the park?" Ramos asked.

Hatch ignored him.

"We know about the pictures, son," Tommy drawled.

Hatch's heart jumped. 'The pictures...'

"The pictures from the ATM's camera prove you were there," Tommy finished.

Hatch's emotions crashed like a wave hitting a Rockaways jetty. They weren't talking about his photos of Paki, they were just talking about the photos of his car that some ATM took. They were mining the same ground that the other cops had earlier, and, Hatch promised himself, with the same results.

Tommy tried. "Yo, on the real," Tommy said. "The cops have your ride in impound, they have those pictures, and now we have you. It's only a matter of time before you wind up deep in the shit—charged, booked, indicted, fucked. The DA is willing to offer up a deal. Don't be stupid."

That got Hatch's attention. Not what Tommy said, but the way he'd said it.

"I know you," Hatch said, the fog lifting from his memory. "Or maybe I should say I know of you. You're that dick from Manhattan North Homicide who goes around talking like he's a rapper wannabe."

Tommy leaned forward, resting his fists on the desk in front of Alonso Hatch.

"Yeah, in fact, I knew your father," Hatch said. "He was a goo..."

Tommy sailed over the desk, knocking Hatch and the chair he sat in over backwards. The two men struggled on the floor, leaving a surprised and dumbfounded Ramos standing with his mouth agape.

"What the fuck...?" Ramos exhaled as the initial shock left him. He ran around the desk and narrowly averted being hit several times by the wildly flailing fists before he was able to separate the two combatants.

"What the—hell—is his—problem?" A disheveled and winded Hatch gasped. "Fuckin'—guy's—crazy."

Ramos, his hands still up and keeping both men at bay, looked over at his partner. He could see that Tommy was livid.

"Go take a break," Ramos said.

"I'm alright," Tommy said.

"You need to take a walk," Ramos said.

"I'm alright, man," Tommy insisted.

"No you're not," Ramos countered.

This wasn't the first time Tommy had blown up with a suspect. He had a longstanding reputation as a hothead, but he'd kept himself pretty much under control lately...until now.

"Go splash some water on your face," Ramos said, his own anger starting to mount at his partner's violent indiscretion. Something like this can blow the whole case, and besides, he promised Mullen that he'd keep a lid on Tommy.

"Go," Ramos repeated. "We'll still be here when you get back."

Tommy started to protest, then instead turned on his heel and left the room with his argument unsaid.

Ramos turned toward Hatch and started reciting the Miranda warning.

"What the hell is that for?" Hatch growled as he slicked his hair back into place and adjusted his clothes.

Ramos ignored him and completed his recitation.

"Do you understand your rights as I explained them to you?" he asked.

"I'm an ex-cop," Hatch told him. "Of course I know the goddamn Miranda..."

Ramos nodded, cutting Hatch off. "Good, glad to hear it," he said.

"What, that I know the Miranda or that I'm an ex-cop?" Hatch sneered.

Ramos smiled. "You're being charged with assaulting a police officer, resisting arrest, and interfering with the administrative..."

"What? That's bullshit! Your partner attacked me, he hit me first!" As soon as the words left his mouth, Hatch knew from experience that they'd be futile. How many times had he heard them from prisoners he had roughed up?

"That's not the way I saw it," Ramos said confirming Hatch's misgivings.

"Fuck!" Hatch exclaimed a moment before Tommy reentered the room nursing a split lip.

Ramos nodded, "Better now?" he asked.

Tommy nodded in return. "Sorry I riffed, son," he said.

"That's understandable," Ramos said. "Seein' as how you were attacked by the suspect."

Tommy's eyes widened in understanding and he immediately followed Ramos' lead.

"Yeah, unfortunately he had to be restrained," Tommy said.

"You guys are full of shit," Hatch muttered. "Where's my lawyer?"

Ramos and Tommy both shrugged.

Hatch righted his chair and sat down again. Ramos and Tommy automatically resumed their positions across the desk from the private eye. Hatch eyed Tommy warily.

“Frank,” Hatch said suddenly.

Ramos could see Tommy tense and placed a hand on his shoulder.

“Frank,” Hatch repeated with more conviction. “Your father’s name was Frank.”

Ramos watched for Tommy’s reaction. Tommy only nodded.

“Yeah, I remember,” Hatch said. “Your father was a good cop.”

Tommy glared at Hatch, then spoke. “My father was a good cop,” he said. “Right up until the day he got railroaded by Internal Affairs ‘cause he wouldn’t give up the names of a couple of crooked cops.”

“Your father wasn’t a part of that stuff...” Hatch began.

“I know that!” Tommy snapped. “Maybe if he had been it wouldn’t have hurt him so much.”

Tommy continued. “My father was a good cop right up to the day they took away his shield and his gun. He was a good cop right up to the day he blew his brains out because being a good cop was all he’d ever known. All he ever wanted to be. He was a good cop right up to the day he left his goddamn kid behind because he couldn’t stand the thought that his kid wouldn’t see him as a *good* cop anymore!”

The room rang with the young detective’s words.

Ramos had heard the story before, of course, even before Tommy became his partner. But he’d never heard the real reason why Tommy’s father ate his gun. Like most cops he assumed it was a way out of the hole he was in...rather a bullet in the brain than having to endure an endless series of humiliating hearings, trials, maybe even prison.

At that moment the door to the room opened and in walked Hatch’s lawyer.

“What is going on here?” Turtledove demanded.

The three other men in the room looked at him and then at each other.

“Nothin’,” Hatch finally said with a sigh. “Not a goddamn thing.”

CHAPTER 57

PAKI QUIETLY SHUT the door behind himself, taking a moment to glance at the clock on the mantle in his living room. The clock, designed to closely resemble an old-fashioned wind-up, actually ran on batteries. The ornate hands on the faux Mother of Pearl face indicated that it was past midnight. Paki smiled. That clock reminded him that he too wasn't what he seemed.

Paki took a deep breath that he then exhaled with a small cough. Phlegm still rattled in his lungs and he still suffered from a low fever, but he felt better than he had in days, much better in fact. His muscles still ached and he felt wrung out, but the constant headache and congestion were all but gone. *Maybe*, he thought, *just maybe he'd beaten this thing—developed some sort of immunity*.

Paki nodded to himself, hadn't he heard about something like that? About people with some sort of special gene or whatever that makes them carriers? Out of all of the newspaper and magazine articles he'd read, sometimes in a state of near panic, hadn't he seen something about people who have the disease, don't suffer from the symptoms themselves, but have the ability to infect others? Paki was sure of it. He was a carrier then. He possessed the special gene necessary to make him so, and didn't that make sense?

He'd gotten a little sick from it, maybe that was his body's way of developing the immunity—you know, creating antibodies or whatever.

Paki nodded again. Of course he had the special gene. Of course...

Suddenly beads of perspiration formed on his forehead and upper lip. He was a carrier, but he could infect *others*.

Paki bounded up the stairs as quietly as he could, almost tripping on the top step, and entered his son's bedroom. Nine-year-old Michael slept beneath one of the handmade quilts his mother had bought at some fundraiser or other. His dark hair was tousled, and in the wan glow of the SpongeBob SquarePants nightlight, Paki could see that his son's face was shiny with perspiration.

Paki gingerly placed the back of his hand on his son's face, as his own mother had done him when he was a child, and quickly pulled it away. Michael's face was hot with fever. Paki yanked the quilt from him and could feel the heat his son's small body gave off in waves—like a tiny furnace.

The quilt slipped from Paki's fingers, dropping slow motion onto the foot of the bed and the floor. He sat on the edge of the bed and looked at his son through eyes blurred with tears.

"My baby," he said. "My baby..."

Michael's eyes fluttered open at his father's voice, his brow furrowing as he tried to focus on his father's face in the room's dim light.

"Daddy? Daddy, I don't feel so good," Michael said.

Paki stifled a sob and roughly wiped the tears from his face with his hand.

"I-I know Mikey," he said. "I know."

"Mommy told you?" Michael asked.

"No Son, no. Mommy didn't tell me anything," Paki said through gritted teeth. He remembered his earlier conversation with the blackmailing private detective hired by his wife.

Michael moaned and Paki's attention returned immediately to his only son.

"My tummy and my head hurt," Michael said.

Paki scooped his son up and held him tightly against his chest. He felt the terrible heat of his son's fever radiate against him and he held him closer still—willing the sickness to leave his son's body and reenter his own. He ignored the tears that fell from his eyes now, tears as hot as the little boy he clutched to his breast. He sobbed into his son's hair, his tears mingling with the sweat there.

"Daddy it's okay," Michael said, his voice muffled by his father's embrace. "I'll get better."

Paki's sobs increased in intensity at the innocence of his son's words, and so it was with infinite difficulty that he was finally able to nod his head and agree.

"Yes Mikey," he said shakily. "You will get better."

He placed his son back on the bed and smoothed his hair.

"Daddy will make it better baby," he said, his voice catching. "I'm not going to let you hurt anymore. I'm not going to let anyone hurt you ever again."

Paki slid the pillow from under his son's head.

"Why are you taking my pillow Daddy?" Michael asked sleepily.

"Shh," Paki shushed him quietly and smoothed his son's hair again. "I'm just going to move your pillow for a minute so I can make you feel better. Don't move for Daddy, okay?"

Michael sighed, already almost asleep again. Okay Daddy," he said as he drifted off.

"I love you baby," Paki said kissing his son's fevered face before gently placing the pillow over his head. Michael muttered something unintelligible in his sleepy child's voice.

Paki bent and picked up the fancy quilt, still hot and wet with his son's fever. He stood and, for the first time in a very long time, said a prayer to the God he only marginally ever thought about or even believed in. He pulled his gun from its hiding place on his belt and wrapped the quilt around it, his hand disappearing inside the quilt as well.

He thumbed back the gun's hammer, the sound he usually relished lost within the folds of the quilt. He slowly pushed the barrel of the gun into the pillow until it met with the resistance of his sleeping son's skull. Tears fell anew, for himself this time as well as for the little boy he and his wife had named after heaven's Archangel. The tears fell for his little girl, Sasha, and even for his traitorous bitch of a wife. He'd have to save them all from the undignified and lingering death that until so very recently had been his alone. He cried because of all the things he'd done in his life, the children were his finest accomplishment—perfect and beautiful in every way...and he cried because out of all the things he'd done in his life, he knew that what he would do tonight would surely condemn him to the deepest pits of hell.

Paki pulled the trigger.

CHAPTER 58

TWO DAYS LATER Paki was seated at his usual place on the library steps. He was alone, as the days had grown increasingly colder and his usual cadre of neighbors had chosen the warmer climes of their offices and cafeterias in which to enjoy their repasts.

It wasn't long after the noon hour when Paki felt the familiar and annoying pressure of Hatch's finger in his back.

"You weren't here yesterday," Paki said.

Hatch snorted, "That's because I was in custody for most of yesterday. They think I'm you."

Paki, genuinely surprised, barked a laugh and slapped his knees with his hands.

Hatch smiled despite himself. "Yeah," he said. "Glad you're amused. Hatch's eyes scanned the neighborhood while he spoke to Paki. It took even the impressive Mr. Turtledove more than a day to get him out on bail, and it was several hours more before he could lose the cops on his tail. Right now he was hotter than a monkey shittin' on a hot plate. He poked Paki in the back with his finger.

"You got the money, pretty boy?" he asked.

Paki sighed and nodded his head. "Yes, I have the money."

Hatch gave him a quick look over. "Where?" he asked. "Don't tell me you're carrying sixty grand around in your pockets."

"I thought it was fifty thousand..."

“Uh-uh,” Hatch said shaking his head. “I fined you another ten grand for coming off wise. I hope you didn’t think I was kidding.”

“No, I wouldn’t think that. I’d just forgotten,” Paki said.

“Yeah, it’s an age thing,” Hatch said. “Sometimes I forget where I left my keys, or the remote, and I go nuts.”

Paki nodded. “I...”

Hatch poked him. “Okay, enough small talk. Where’s my money?”

“Home,” Paki said.

“What?”

“Home,” Paki repeated.

Hatch’s hand left the handle of his gun long enough to slap Paki on the back of his head.

“What are you, stupid?” Hatch asked. “Or maybe you think I’m the stupid one.”

“No, no—nothing like that,” Paki protested. “I couldn’t leave the house with that much money. A good portion of it is in small bills.”

“And you couldn’t just put it in a briefcase or toss it in a sack?”

Paki shook his head. “It would have been too obvious. My wife would have noticed something.”

“Suspicious lady,” Hatch said.

“She hired you, didn’t she?”

Hatch considered this. “I think you’re trying to fuck me,” Hatch said.

“No,” Paki said. “Listen, listen...”

Despite the chilly weather, Paki could feel the prickle of sweat popping out all over his body.

“Listen to what?” Hatch asked shortly. “I’ve had enough of this bullshit to last a couple of lifetimes.”

Paki licked his lips nervously. “Look, maybe you want to believe me, maybe you don’t,” Paki said. “The truth is that there’s fifty thousand dollars in cash waiting for you back at my house. I don’t want my wife to know anything about this. I just couldn’t take a chance on her seeing me leave the house with this money.”

“The reward money’s looking better and better,” Hatch said, unmoved by Paki’s explanation. “Reward money in the hand’s worth fifty grand in the bush."

"Look," Paki said, his voice almost pleading. "The goddamn money is there I tell you—every cent of it. It's stuffed in a pillowcase in my bedroom..."

"It's in your bedroom and you're not afraid your old lady's going to find it?"

Paki shook his head in tiny increments. "My wife is not a domestic," Paki said. "The only time she touches a pillowcase is when she lays her head down at night to go to sleep, that's it! That's the biggest reason why I couldn't be seen leaving the house carrying the money—I don't even take out the garbage."

Hatch nodded. Okay, this was making just a little more sense. Maybe this guy really couldn't get the money out of the house. Rich people are weird that way.

Paki said softly, "It's there. It's all *there*."

Hatch made up his mind. "Okay," he said. "So the money's at your place. How do I get a hold of it?"

Paki shrugged. "That's the easy part," he said. "Come home with me, maybe on the pretense of collecting your pay from my wife."

"That ain't no pretense," Hatch said. "She does owe me money."

"Very good then," said Paki. "We'll find you a large bag that you can carry into the house. You leave the bag in the hallway or foyer, and once my wife is distracted by your payment demands, I'll slip the pillowcase with the money into the bag and you walk out with it. Simple."

"Yeah simple," Hatch repeated.

"Yes, like I said," Paki agreed.

Hatch tapped Paki on the side of his head. "No, simple this isn't," he said. "It's too complicated. You were just supposed to bring me the money—wham, bam, thank you Theodore. I don't like complications."

"I understand," Paki said. "I dislike unnecessary complication myself, but in this case it has to be this way in order to reduce suspicion."

"Uh-huh," Hatch said, not sounding convinced. "And you don't think it'll look suspicious when you and me walk into your house together? You, the subject, and me, the detective who was supposed to be shadowing you?"

Paki considered this. "Let me handle her..."

"Handle her? You asshole, she has you so whipped you can't even leave the house carrying a fuckin' pillowcase!" Hatch said.

"I'll just explain..." Paki began.

Hatch shook his head. "Nah, don't explain anything. I'll tell her that you finally noticed me following you and confronted me, and insisted that I come back home with you just so I can confirm to her in your presence that you're clean—not having an affair, anyway. Then I'll ask for my money and when her back is turned, you put the cash in the bag."

After a moment, Paki nodded. "That's very good," he said.

"What do you expect," Hatch explained. "I'm an ex-cop."

The two men sat there, each lost in his own thoughts. Then Hatch leaned closer to Paki.

"Don't move pretty boy," Hatch said. He reached under Paki's coat, his hand covered by a handkerchief, and removed Paki's gun from his belt. Paki didn't move or object. Hatch took a quick glance at the gun before returning it to its owner.

"Hard to believe that thing's real," Hatch said. "It looks like a toy or some crazy movie prop."

"Oh, it's real," Paki said.

"I know it's real, dipwad," Hatch said. "I saw it in action, remember?"

"How could I possibly forget?" Paki said sarcastically.

"I would take it from you, but with all the heat that's on me right now, being caught with the murder weapon is the last thing I need," Hatch said.

"That reminds me," Paki said. "When do I get the incriminating photographs?"

"You don't," Hatch said. "They're my insurance."

CHAPTER 59

TOMMY CUCITTI AND Robert Avni both raised their heads in anticipation. Ramos wondered briefly if he looked as tired as they did and he immediately knew the answer was yes. He and Tommy had been poring over the Chickenhawk and Alfonso Hatch files all night. Avni, citing boredom, grudgingly joined them about four hours ago. Now Ramos looked at the bleary-eyed faces peering back at him and hoped they weren't all just grasping at straws—again.

"You know," Avni said after several moments had passed. "The fuckin' suspense is killing me—not to mention that I'm starving to death."

"Yeah, well, quit trying to cheer me up," Ramos said getting up and walking around his desk. He carried two sheets of paper over to the desk currently being shared by Tommy and Avni. Avni snatched the papers out of Ramos' hand before Tommy even had a chance to get a glance at them.

"You're a real prick," Ramos said.

"Yeah, well this prick's the best damn investigator in this room, so you should be nice to me," Avni said.

"So what's the 411 on those papers?" Tommy asked, ignoring Avni.

"One's a list of the slugs collected at the crime scenes..." Ramos began.

"The other one has the results of the ballistics tests done by the Feds, who by the way, also have possession of the only casing found at a crime scene," Avni finished.

"And?" Tommy inquired.

"And it's all the same shit," Ramos said. "The results on the slug are inconclusive and all the Feds were able to get from the brass is that it belongs to a 357Mag, but other tests also proved inconclusive leading the Feds to believe that it may not be factory made."

"Gun nut, probably," Avni said.

"What about the task force?" Tommy asked.

"We got this *from* the task force," Ramos said.

"Feds ain't worth shit either," Avni interjected.

Ramos nodded. "It wouldn't be the first time the Feds dropped the ball on what should be a local case anyway."

They all nodded in agreement.

"So, what did we miss?" Tommy asked in exasperation. He looked at the orderly piles of paper arrayed on the desk. The police reports, legal documents and other papers were carefully arranged by date, importance, and type of form.

"I can't think of anything we might have missed," Ramos said.

"It's all nothin' but a bunch of dead ends," Avni added.

"Maybe," Ramos acknowledged. "But I don't think so. There's got to be something here that adds up to who the killer is."

"Well, we ain't found nothin' on Hatch that could make him the Chickenhawk, son," Tommy said, evoking an exasperated look from Avni.

"Can you tell this guy to at least *sound* like a cop?" Avni complained, pointing a sausage-sized thumb in Tommy's direction.

"Tell 'em yourself," Ramos replied.

"Hatch has shaky-to-rock solid alibis for the dates and times of at least three of the murders. He doesn't match any of the descriptions we got from anyone. A couple of folks said the 'Hawk has, like, a singer's voice or whatever, and Hatch definitely don't sound like no singer...unless we're talkin' about the sewing machine," Tommy said.

Ramos nodded. "Yeah, my gut tells me Hatch ain't the killer, but he's definitely hiding something."

"Shit, son," Tommy said. "What *your* gut should be telling you is that you need more vegetables!"

Avni and Tommy both guffawed at Ramos' expense. Ramos glared.

"What the hell are you laughing at?" Ramos asked, pointing at the immense form of Bob Avni.

Avni and Tommy looked at each other and laughed again.

"You guys must really be tired," Ramos grumbled. "You're both gettin' punchy."

The telephone on the desk rang and Avni punched up the speaker so everyone in the room could hear.

"The task force has gotten a warrant to search Hatch's apartment," Williams' voice said through the speaker. "Get over there, now!"

CHAPTER 60

RAMOS AND TOMMY arrived at Hatch's apartment while the search was in full swing. After showing their shields to the cop at the door, they were allowed to enter the already crowded apartment. Avni, a telephone already to his ear, cited physical weakness and a possible low sugar count as the reasons for his choosing to stay behind and ordering takeout.

Hatch and his attorney, the apparently ubiquitous Mr. Turtledove, stood fuming in the middle of the small living room as the cops from the task force unceremoniously tore the place apart.

Hatch spotted the two detectives enter his apartment and, after snatching a form from the hand of his lawyer, stomped over to where they were standing.

"This is bullshit!" Hatch yelled waving the copy of the warrant under Ramos' nose. "That bogus arrest led to this, this..." Hatch motioned around his wrecked apartment with both arms, "...Bullshit!"

Hatch stomped back to where his lawyer stood in the center of the room. The tinkling sound of breaking glassware coming from the kitchen sent them both hurrying to that part of the private detective's living space.

Ramos grinned at Tommy. "Maybe there is some justice after all," he said as he popped a mint into his mouth.

"So what are we supposed to do here, son?" Tommy asked. "This place is filled with mad cops."

"Yeah, well I'm getting pissed too," Ramos grunted. "There are way too many people in here, somebody's gonna mess up something important."

"Nah, son," Tommy broke in. "Not mad like angry, mad meaning like, *a lot*..."

Ramos looked at his partner dubiously. "*Mad* means a lot?" he asked.

"Yeah," Tommy answered looking around the room.

Ramos started to say something, but a look and a nod from Tommy brought his attention to a door just off the kitchen that appeared to be guarded by what was obviously a federal agent. The two detectives sauntered over.

"What's up?" Ramos asked, using his chin to point at the closed door behind the agent.

"Off limits," the agent answered curtly."Even to the DA?" Tommy asked.

"Even to the Pope unless I hear otherwise," the agent sneered.

"What's the problem here, detectives?" A familiar voice asked from behind them.

Ramos and Tommy turned around, mildly surprised at the presence of their former lieutenant, Patrick Mullen, at the suspect's apartment.

"Hey loo, how're you doing?" Ramos said by way of greeting. Tommy simply nodded.

The lieutenant kept his hands at his sides and nodded in return. "I should be asking you that," he said. Then, motioning across the room with a quick nod of his head, "Let's go."

Tommy planted his feet. "Go where?"

Ramos looked at Tommy, then the lieutenant, and then back at Tommy. "Come on," Ramos said.

"What for?" Tommy asked. "Last time I followed you I wound up working for the DA"

Ramos ignored him and followed the lieutenant, after a moment Tommy joined them.

"You won't be able to get past that Fed," Mullen said. "Hatch's lawyer pointed out that the original warrant didn't specifically state that the task force could go through or confiscate Hatch's computer files. The judge refused to amend the warrant over the phone so the Feds went to get it done in person. The guy at the door's keeping everyone out, including the cops, until those guys get back with the amended warrant."

"This case was ours," Ramos growled. "Those files belong to the NYPD, not the Feds."

"Technically they still belong to Hatch," Mullen corrected. "But I agree with you. Once the Feds get their hands on those files we'll be left out of the loop, the way they operate, we may never even see them until the trial."

"How long ago did they leave?" Ramos asked.

"About twenty," Mullen answered. "I figure they should be back in about ten. And," Lieutenant Mullen added while he stared straight at Tommy Cucitti, "there's a fire escape out back."

Tommy started for the door, but was held back by Ramos' tight grip on his arm.

"Whoa, whoa, whoa! Where the hell do you think you're going?" Ramos asked.

"There's a chance that if Hatch is the 'Hawk, he might've saved information about his crimes in his computer. If Hatch ain't the killer, then there's a chance that the 'Hawk might be one of Hatch's clients and that means an even better chance there's information on that computer's hard drive we can use to find him," Tommy said breathlessly.

I think what you're asking Tommy to do is unfair," Ramos said turning to the lieutenant.

"I didn't ask anyone to do anything," the lieutenant retorted. "I thought we agreed that this case should belong to the NYPD; that's us!"

"No, that's *you*," Ramos said. "We're working for the goddamn DA, remember? Now you're asking Tommy to risk his job? Prison? You're the one who told me to keep him out of trouble! Yeah, this case should be ours, but..."

"Yo," Tommy broke in, taking Ramos' hand from his arm. "I'm a grown-assed man, and nobody can make me do what I don't want to do."

"Tommy..." Ramos started.

"Look son," Tommy said. "I got less than ten minutes to, to...I don't know what, but I have to go. I'm out."

Tommy ran from the apartment, his departure followed by the curious stares of the cops and G-men still looking for incriminating evidence against private eye Alfonso Hatch. After a glance at his former lieutenant, Ramos returned to the door guarded by the Federal agent and casually leaned on a nearby wall chewing on a mint. Lieutenant Mullen watched him a moment, nodded, and then melted into the crowd of cops.

CHAPTER 61

TOMMY CUCITTI DASHED around the corner, toward the rear of the old, brick apartment building. Looming above the trash-strewn alley like the product of a huge erector set was an equally old, iron fire escape. Tommy looked up and guessed which one of the numerous grimy windows belonged to the guarded room in Hatch's apartment. He also saw that the fire escape ladder that would lead to the street was pulled up and out of reach.

Tommy took a glance at his watch, according to Mullen's time estimate, he had about five minutes before the Feds returned with their warrant for Hatch's computer files. Tommy ripped off his coat, started to throw it into a corner of the alley, thought better of it, and carefully folded it before placing it atop a pile of cardboard boxes. He looked around and saw the end of a dumpster poking into the alley from the street. Tommy raced to the dumpster, wrestled it into the alley, and pushed it as quick as he could under the ladder of the fire escape. He slammed the twin covers of the dumpster into place with a loud crash and climbed up. Balanced on top of the dumpster, he reached the ladder easily and pulled it down, avoiding the pieces of the thick black paint that chipped off and fell toward him, revealing years of rust. He climbed up toward Hatch's window, the ancient fire escape squealing and swaying with his effort. Paint chips rained down into the alley with a rain-like patter.

Tommy peered into the window that led to Hatch's apartment and was greeted by the sight of a computer sitting on a small desk in the room. He looked at the thin sliver of light that came through the bottom of the door directly opposite the window and could see the shadows of many feet going back and forth. Tommy tried the window and cursed under his breath when he found that it was locked. Still cursing, Tommy took out his folding knife and flicked it open. He wedged the knife blade into the tiny space where the upper and lower windows met and twisted. The two windows separated just enough to allow Tommy to turn the tip of the curved blade up into the brass colored latch that held the windows shut. With a few deft taps of the knife blade, the latch turned and Tommy Cucitti was able to open the window and quietly crawl inside.

As soon as he was in the room, Tommy checked his watch—three minutes to go. Maybe. He went to the computer and sat down in the chair. Tommy hesitated, realizing that he'd left his gloves in his coat, but then proceeded anyway. He saw that the computer was already on and so gave the mouse a quick shake. The computer's desktop immediately brightened into view, exposing a very seductive photo of Pamela Anderson. Tommy hit the space bar and was disappointed when a field requesting the password appeared on the screen. The detective tried several combinations of Hatch's name, the address of the building, and even the word *chickenhawk*, but came up empty. Finally, he lifted up the computer's keyboard and looked underneath, the password was taped to the bottom. Tommy smiled, good thing the average computer user was notorious for forgetting passwords. He typed the letters, G-R-E-A-T T-I-T-S, into the empty field and hit the enter key. He was rewarded with immediate access into Hatch's system and wasted no time opening his documents file. He checked his watch, one minute to go, he didn't have time to go through the files here, he'd have to copy them. Tommy rifled through the desk drawers and found a box of blank CD's. He inserted one into the computer and proceeded to copy the files onto the disc. Less than a minute later, Tommy had copied as many of the Word and Excel documents as he could find, now he was out of time. He stuck the disc into his shirt pocket with one hand while he shut the computer down with the other.

He froze, there was a commotion at the door. He heard people arguing and he could make out his partner's voice as the loudest among them. It was time to get the hell out.

Tommy got up, pulled a handkerchief from his back pocket and wiped down everything he'd touched. Still holding the handkerchief, he replaced the chair and wiped off the windowsill. He cursed under his breath when he saw how much cleaner the sill was now than the rest of the apartment. Hoping no one would notice, Tommy swung one leg out the window and then the other, and he'd just finished closing the window when the door to the room opened.

Tommy flattened himself against the cold brick wall beside the window. He could hear voices raised in disagreement, but he couldn't make out the words. He considered a hasty retreat down the fire escape but put that notion aside with the memory of how much noise the creaky metal contraption made on his up.

Tommy sighed, he didn't realize he'd broken into a sweat until the cool fall air hit him and he broke out in goose bumps. It looked like he was going to have to wait it out.

CHAPTER 62

RAMOS LEANED AGAINST the wall and tried to look as casual as possible. He popped another mint into his mouth and watched the proceedings with only mild interest. Cops wearing latex gloves pulled out drawers, collected papers, turned over chairs and checked underneath. The agents of the FBI, Ramos noticed, looked behind paintings, confiscated utility and telephone bills, and even checked inside lamp shades. Ramos shook his head, what he was really interested in was inside that room with the Fed guarding the door. He assumed that most, if not all, of the other officers in the apartment also wanted to get their hands on whatever was in there. Ramos didn't know much about computers, but he knew about human nature. People generally feel safe in whatever private, little sanctuaries they create for themselves. Ramos couldn't count the times he found voluminous notes containing incriminating information carefully filed away or stored out in the open in living rooms, bedrooms, home offices...

Hatch, sans his mouthpiece, walked over to where Ramos stood and studied the detective at length.

"Where's your crazy partner?" Hatch asked.

Ramos' belly tightened. 'Was it possible that Hatch knew something?' He hoped his surprise at Hatch's question hadn't given anything away.

"He's around," Ramos answered.

Hatch glanced at the guard on the door to his home office, and nodded. "Yeah, I didn't know he was gonna go nuts the other day when I mentioned his dad. None of us wanted what happened then."

Ramos nonchalantly looked around the room. "We all got our demons," he finally said. "It ain't me you gotta talk to about it. In fact, why the fuck *are* you talking to me?" Ramos growled. "You're a suspect."

"I'm an ex-cop," Hatch said. "Is this all the respect I get from you guys after all my years as a member of the Force?"

Ramos just glared at him.

Two men in suits, suddenly bustled into the apartment, and Ramos knew he and Tommy were out of time. These two men, their demeanors detached; yet focused and businesslike, had to be the agents who went out to get their warrant amended to include Hatch's so-called 'electronic' information.

Ramos stepped away from the wall and moved to intercept them, slow them down, and give Tommy more time.

Hatch and Turtledove beat him to it.

"I will take a look at those documents now if you will," Turtledove said, holding his hand out.

The agent holding the warrant held it out and continued toward the room, Turtledove stepped in his way.

"No, I'm afraid not," Turtledove said. "You will not enter that room until and unless I am first satisfied that these papers are in order."

"Tell you what," the agent responded. "That's all well and good, and while you're doing that; making sure all the *I*'s are dotted and all the *T*'s are crossed, we'll be in that room unscrewing the hard drives out of those computers."

The agent tried to push his way past the stubborn attorney, but Turtledove refused to budge. When the agent tried to get a little rougher, Hatch joined in and a tussle ensued.

"You would do well to keep your hands to yourself, you bullying Nazis," Turtledove fairly screamed. "I am an officer of the court!"

When the other men in the room heard and saw what was going on, they rushed to join in; their pent up frustration and anger now had found a new focus and the tussle now threatened to become a melee.

Lieutenant Mullen watched the goings on with distaste, and after a few moments signaled Ramos to step in.

"Hey! Hey, cut it out you guys, slow it down! Slow it down!" Ramos bellowed at the top of his lungs as he moved into the center of the pack of men and women and started shoving them away from each other. Mullen had entered the fray as well and was doing plenty of pushing and shoving of his own.

As the mob of cops and agents were pushed and pulled away from the private detective and his lawyer, some of them raised their voices in protest or uttered threats, but no one refused to cooperate.

"That was dumb, people," Ramos yelled out for Tommy's sake as well as for those assembled in the room around him. "We're all under a lot of pressure here, but there's no excuse for this shit!"

Mullen looked angrily around the room, hands on his hips, "Are you trying to jeopardize this case, get fired, or both? I can't believe this!"

Turtledove, his hair mussed, glared about the room while waving the warrant in his clenched fist. "There will be charges filed, gentlemen," he yelled hoarsely. The lawyer then cleared his throat and attempted to smooth his hair. "I will not allow myself, nor my client, to be accosted by a bunch of pseudo-hominids who believe they are capable of operating above the law. There will be consequences and they will be dire!"

The congregation of cops and G-men in the room stopped for a moment, then turned away from the attorney and his threats. The agent who'd brought the warrant back, glared at Turtledove, then straightened his jacket and tie before approaching the door to Hatch's computer room.

Ramos blocked his path.

The agent barely glanced at Ramos, "Scuse me guy," he said.

"Sure," Ramos replied, not moving.

Now the agent looked up at him.

"I just want to remind you that whatever you take out of there isn't sole property of the FBI," Ramos said, just a little loudly.

The agent looked at Ramos wearily, then turned to the rest of the room, "Doesn't anything easy ever happen here?" He asked before turning his attention back to the former homicide detective.

Ramos shrugged, "Just tryin' to make sure we're all on the same page," he said.

"If I had my way, you'd all be sharing the same *cell*!" Turtledove spat from behind them.

"Shut up!" The agent responded. Then to Ramos, "C'mon, you're in the way."

"Look *Mulder*, just as long as you understand," Ramos began.

"Just as long as you understand that right now you're real close to obstructing justice," The agent broke in. He looked at Ramos, then at the closed door over the detective's shoulder. A hint of realization broke over his face and he pushed Ramos out of the way.

"Get out of my way, asswipe," the agent said as he reached for the doorknob.

Ramos tried to get in the way when the lieutenant spoke up.

"Eddie!" Lieutenant Mullen called out, "Let it alone."

"Loo..." Ramos began.

"Let it alone," Mullen repeated with a soft shake of his head.

"I'd listen to him if I were you," the agent said threateningly.

After a heartbeat's time, Ramos acquiesced and stepped out of the way.

When the door was finally opened, half the people in the other room tried to rush in at the same time.

Ramos squeezed his way in and looked around nervously. The two FBI agents looked around the room as if searching for suspects, even looking under the desk and inside a small closet.

Not finding anyone, the agents turned their attention to dismantling the computer while the cops went through the desk's drawers and the small bookcase.

Ramos' gaze went to the closed window that everyone else had virtually ignored. The thickly painted wooden windowsill in front of it was practically dust-free, while the corners were caked with dust, cobwebs, and the chitinous shells of long-dead insects. The detective stepped over to the window and sat on the ledge, making sure to polish the wood with the ample seat of his pants. The agent he'd called Mulder looked up at him suspiciously, then went back to what he was doing. Ramos breathed a sigh of relief. From the next room Lieutenant Mullen gave him a slight nod and walked away.

CHAPTER 63

THAT NIGHT PAKI drove up the driveway to the front door of his home, the car's tires crunching on the gravel and the barrel of Hatch's gun in his ribs. Then, for some time after Paki put the car into Park and had shut off the engine, both men sat in the dark and listened to the ticking sound of the engine cooling.

"Okay, you know the drill," Hatch said, jabbing Paki with the gun.

Paki nodded. Hatch had insisted on going over his so-called drill over and over again—in great detail, so Paki felt confident that he indeed knew it quite well.

At Hatch's signal, both men unlocked and opened their door at the same time. Then they slowly got out of the car with Hatch pointing his gun at Paki over the car roof.

"Nice, you did good pretty boy," Hatch said. "Now let's walk to the front door nice and easy—you first."

Paki complied wordlessly. Hatch followed closely, carrying the large brown paper shopping bag they'd literally picked up at Macy's Department Store. When they reached the front door, Hatch ordered Paki to stop. Paki looked at him curiously.

Hatch placed the bag on the ground and reached under his coat, showing off the butt of Paki's gun.

"I wiped my prints off this thing in the car," Hatch said as he let his coat close over the gun handle again. "You can have your toy back as soon as I get the money. I don't wanna take any chances on getting caught with it. My luck's been lousy that way lately and that crazy gun of yours would be all the cops would need to put me on death row—I'd rather let you have that pleasure."

Paki nodded.

"Open the door," Hatch growled, motioning with his own gun.

Paki did as he was told and both men stepped into the house. Hatch blinked, it looked like every light on the first floor was on, bathing everything in a harsh glow.

"You must have a hell of a light bill," Hatch said.

Paki ignored him.

"C'mon," Hatch said, motioning with his gun again.

The two men lock-stepped into the living room while Hatch tried to take in every nook and cranny at once.

"Where's the family?" Hatch asked, tucking his gun into the holster on his belt.

"Upstairs," Paki answered.

"What's upstairs?"

"The bedrooms."

"No kidding Sherlock," Hatch said. "That's it? Bedrooms?"

"That's it," Paki said.

Hatch nodded, letting go of the gun's handle long enough to wipe his face. He was surprised to find that he was sweating, despite the chilly air in the house. And it really was chilly.

"What's the matter?" Hatch asked. "Didn't pay your heating bill?"

"My wife prefers it somewhat cool," Paki said.

"Yeah, lovely," Hatch said. "Cool is one thing, but it's freezing in here. Hey, maybe she's going through menopause, you know, hot flashes?"

"Wait here," Paki said. "I'll go upstairs and get the money.

"No you won't, pretty boy," Hatch said. "We're sticking with the original plan. Call your ole' lady down here, and while she's cutting me a check for what she owes me, you go get the money *you* owe me."

Paki shrugged and called out for his wife. Both men watched the landing at the top of the stairs expectantly. When no one appeared, Paki shrugged again.

"Maybe they're napping," Paki offered.

"Yeah, and maybe on one's home and you knew it," Hatch said drawing his gun.

Paki shook his head. "No, they're here," he said. "I know they're here." He called out to his family again with the same results.

"I've had enough of this bullshit," Hatch said poking the barrel of his gun into Paki's back. "We're going upstairs and you're going to give me the money, I don't give a rat's furry ass what your wife thinks about it."

Hatch shoved Paki toward and up the stairs, the handles of the shopping bag still clutched in his left hand. At the top of the stairs, Hatch grabbed Paki's coat with the same hand that held the gun, bringing him to a stop. Hatch looked at the doors that led to the different bedrooms. They were all closed and they all looked alike.

"Which door, pretty boy?" Hatch asked.

Paki pointed to the furthest of the two doors on the right, prompting Hatch to push and prod him in that direction. When they reached the door, Hatch stopped Paki again and reholstered his gun.

"She better be here," Hatch breathed into Paki's ear. "More importantly, that money better be here."

Paki nodded and at Hatch's signal, opened the bedroom door and stepped inside. Hatch was right behind him.

"Honey, we have company," Paki said in his smooth voice, before stepping aside.

Paki's move gave Hatch an unobstructed view of the bedroom's brightly lit interior, especially the huge king size bed that dominated the room.

Three figures lay reposed on the bed. They lay atop the otherwise neatly made covers and may have been asleep except for the grimace of pain and fear on the woman's face—and the rust colored stains on the pillows.

A sudden movement to his right told Hatch that his moment's hesitation at the grisly sight of a slaughtered family may have been a moment too long.

Hatch reached for his gun, at the same time pivoting to his left in an attempt to increase the distance between Paki and his weird looking gun. But Paki was taller, had longer arms, and had Hatch's moment of hesitation to use to his advantage. Paki's hand closed around the butt of his gun as Hatch's own gun practically leapt into his hand. A loud explosion tore through the cold, still air and brought an abrupt halt to the struggles of both men. They stared into each other's eyes, each knowing the outcome of their brief battle, until Paki leaned forward and kissed Hatch roughly on the mouth.

Paki pushed Hatch away and leveled his gun at the detective's head. Hatch looked blankly into the gun's barrel and then down at the blood spreading across the front of his pants and running down his pants leg. When he looked back up, he saw Paki thumb back the hammer on his ridiculous looking gun and start to squeeze the trigger. Hatch tried to raise his own gun, but it fell from his hand and onto the carpeted floor with a soft thump. Hatch's eye went back to the infinitesimal black aperture of Paki's weapon.

Hatch saw the flash just before a feeling, like chewing on aluminum foil, filled his head and pushed it outward. The force of the bullet snapped Hatch's head back like a boxer's well placed uppercut. The private detective staggered and actually took a step forward, surprising Paki, but then toppled over—his shattered head making the same soft sound on the carpet that his gun had made earlier.

Paki stood over Hatch's body and prod at it with the toe of his shoe.

"How's that feel, not-so-pretty boy?" he said.

CHAPTER 64

TOMMY FINISHED SCRIBBLING into his pad and hung up the phone, the two other cops in the room watched him expectantly.

"Avni come through with anything from the gun club people?" Ramos asked.

Tommy nodded in assent. Earlier, Avni had gone to visit some of the gun clubs and shooting ranges that encourage members to make their own ammunition.

The two former homicide detectives stood in the NYPD's ballistics lab, located in the labyrinthine basement of One Police Plaza in Lower Manhattan. The other cop in the room was NYPD lab rat Augie Johannsen.

August "Augie" Johannsen was an old-time cop. Like Ramos and Avni, he was a throwback to a bygone era when bending the rules was *Standard Operating Procedure* and breaking them often made your career. In those days, cops were expected to stand by cops— no matter what. Augie Johannsen's curly red hair had gone gray early, matching the color of his eyes. He wore a lab coat with the department's patch sewn onto the right shoulder and his name embroidered over the left breast pocket, white sneakers covered his feet.

Johannsen had been recruited into the NYPD's Forensics Division almost immediately after graduating from the academy.

His twin degrees in engineering and forensic science made it more than clear that he'd be best suited in the department's underground lab than patrolling the streets.

"So what's up?" Ramos asked Tommy as his partner joined him and Johannsen.

"Bob was able to get the names of 1,131 shooters in the tristate area who are known to make their own ammo," Tommy said after a brief scan of his notes.

Ramos nodded, "I guess that tub of lard is good for something after all."

"Yeah, but that's only good if the guy we're lookin' for even belongs to one of those clubs, yo," Tommy lamented.

"It's someplace to start again," Ramos said. "At least we got another direction to look at."

Tommy nodded, not totally convinced. "So what's the four-one-one on the feds info?" he asked Johannsen.

Johannsen held up the folder containing the FBI's ballistics report. "In their report," Johannsen began. "The Bureau describes the only casing found at a crime scene as being a .357 Magnum case. Further tests have proven inconclusive, or so they say, but then they also go on to state that it could have been modified so as to allow it to fire a round from a .256 Winchester Magnum rifle. The report also states that this type of ammunition could also have been fired from a .25 rifle, hence; inconclusive."

"Can you tell us something conclusive?" Ramos asked.

Johannsen rolled up the report into a tube and held it to his ear. He closed his eyes and nodded as if he were agreeing to something he could actually hear through the rolled up file. After a few seconds he stopped and looked at the two detectives.

"This report is bullshit," he said, holding the report up. "It's useless. The person doing the measuring may be a scientist, but he or she has no true gun knowledge and apparently has no idea what an actual .357 should look like."

True, the case is a modified .357 Magnum, but it's been necked down to a .257; and not in a factory. If it had been factory-made, it probably would have had the designation '.256Win' engraved onto the casing. The majority of homemade brass of this type would have been engraved with .357Mag, like this one obviously is. All this modification, the slugs themselves also being homemade, and the feds owning the only actual casing recovered are what made the ID tough to determine. Sorry it took so long."

"That's okay, thanks. I think we're finally on to something," Ramos said. "It's got to be a gun nut, like we thought."

"Actually, I think it was Bob who said it was a gun nut, son," Tommy corrected.

Ramos shot his partner a look.

"Actually it doesn't have to be a 'gun nut' as you say," Johannsen said. "It could just be someone with the knowledge and ability to make his own ammunition, it really isn't that hard to do, or maybe the shooter had the ammo specially made."

"Either way it narrows things down," Ramos said.

"That it does," Johannsen agreed.

Ramos turned to Tommy, "Then it shouldn't be too hard findin' out what kind of gun this guy's using and then track him down from there," he said.

"Oh, I can tell you exactly what type of weapon that case came from," Johannsen said. "This weapon definitely isn't a rifle, and although they're similar in some ways, it isn't the better known Blackhawk revolver."

There was a slight pause which the two detectives knew Johannsen was using to build excitement prior to his announcement. Tommy could almost hear the drumroll in the background.

"The gun you're looking for..." Johannsen finally continued after his dramatic pause. "...is actually a Ruger Hawkeye, model RH-28. It's a single-shot pistol that, although it may physically resemble the Blackhawk, has had its cylinder replaced with a rotating breech block which turns to the side and extracts the fired round from the barrel, allowing another round to be inserted."

Ramos and Tommy stared at Johannsen dumbfounded.

Johannsen shrugged. "It's my job," he said. "The technician at the FBI, whoever he or she may be, flubbed this one up completely. Anyone with a desk ruler, the appropriate reference materials and the actual brass casing should have reached the same conclusion I did.

"Yeah, well we're just glad you're on our side," Ramos said.

"Well, here's another tidbit that may interest you," Johannsen said. "The gun you're looking for is rather rare, only a little over 3,000 of them were manufactured back in the early sixties."

Ramos and Tommy looked at each other.

"Yo Augie, your skills are off the hook, son," Tommy said.

Johannsen chuckled. "Thanks, I think," he said. "Now go out there and nail this bastard."

CHAPTER 65

ROBERT AVNI LUMBERED into the office later that afternoon, his arms laden down with Chinese takeout.

"Whoa, just in time," Tommy said. "We're starvin' over here, son."

Avni dumped his load onto the other desk and sat down with a groan. "Yeah well, I guess youse will just starve then 'cause this is my lunch," he said.

Tommy's eyebrows shot up. "You lie," he said, staring at the three plastic shopping bags packed with paper and Styrofoam containers.

"Hah!" Ramos said. "When it comes to food, that's the only thing Bob's honest about."

Avni stuck up his middle finger, the nail black with dirt as usual. "Screw youse," he said, digging into the bags.

Ramos shook his head. "That shit's gonna kill you," he said.

"Look who's talkin'," Avni said after gulping down half a quart of wonton soup. "It won't kill me no faster than that greasy Puerto Rican crap you go home to every night."

Ramos stood up, his hands balled up into fists. "Yeah, well I..."

"Alright fellas, chill, chill," Tommy interrupted.

Ramos and Avni backed off grudgingly.

"So exactly what were you able to get at the gun club?" Ramos asked.

Avni used his chin to point at a disorderly pile of stained papers that he'd brought in with his food. "Augie was right," he said between bites of an eggroll. "That's a short list of the assholes that like to spend their time making their own ammunition. It ain't a complete list 'cause not all the ranges decided to cooperate...not yet anyhow."

"Nah, son, it's all good," Tommy said. "From what you told me over the phone, that's over a thousand names we got to work with, it might be enough."

Avni shrugged yet again. "Might be, kid," he said.

"Did you notice if Hatch's name was on any of the lists?" Tommy asked.

Avni shook his head. "Nope."

Ramos gestured at the computer surrounded by faxes and Post-it notes on the other desk. "He's not on any of our lists either," he said.

"And none of the files I got from his computer even mentions any of the murders," Tommy added. "And just 'cause Hatch isn't on any of the lists doesn't mean he's not the Chickenhawk."

"Ah so, asshopper," Avni said in a mock Chinese accent. Then he belched again, a sound that could have doubled as a fog horn.

Ramos gave Avni a dirty look. "Now it's time for us to see what we come up with," he said.

Ramos gathered up most of the pile of papers on the desk while Tommy returned to his seat in front of the computer monitor. Avni wiped his hands on his pants and lifted one end of the long sheet of continuous computer paper that he'd also brought back from the gun club.

For the next hour or so, Avni, Ramos and Tommy Cucitti pored over and compared the names on their respective lists

"Olson, Ronald," Avni called out in a bored voice.

"No match," Ramos responded.

"Nah, here neither," Tommy said.

"Owens, Felix."

"No match."

"No."

Avni sighed, took off his glasses, and rubbed his eyes with the heel of his palm. "This is bullshit," he said.

"Quitting already?" Ramos asked.

"Fuck you," Avni replied. "The only thing quitting around here is your goddammed deodorant."

A snicker escaped Tommy, and Ramos shot him a scathing look.

Tommy shrugged sheepishly. "Sorry son, but that shit was funny," he said.

Ramos ignored him and turned his attention back to Avni. "Well?" he prodded.

"Hey, just takin' a break here," Avni said as he stretched. "All this reading is startin' to wear me down. I'm tired."

"That ain't no surprise after all that shit you just ate," Tommy jibed.

"Bite it for me kid," Avni retorted. "I mean, really, take a big chunk."

Avni picked up the folded computer paper and read off the next name. "Packl...Paki...Paki...ah shit, fuckin' foreigner...Paki-dora-populos, Theodoro."

"Hold up, hold up!" Tommy called out. "I think we got something."

"Here too," Ramos said in a hushed voice.

All three men looked around at each other, excitement quickened their pulses.

After an interminably long silence, Ramos was the first to speak. "I got a guy with a name like that, only his first name's Joseph," he said. "Bob, spell that last name for me."

"Oh, I'm fuckin' *Bob* now?" Avni raised his hand to check Ramos' oncoming bluster and continued. "Alright, alright, here's the spelling," he said.

After Avni spelled out the letters of the name in question, Ramos let out a low whistle.

"That's it," Ramos said. "It says here that my guy is a gun collector and makes his own ammo."

"Had to be a gun nut, like I said," Avni added. "My guy's a member of a ritzy indoor/outdoor gun range out on Long Island. Think your guy's name could be an alias?

"Not on an NYPD issued gun permit," Ramos answered.

"Could they be the same guy?"

"Doubt it," Ramos answered. "Says here my guy's in his

sixties, the Chickenhawk's been described as being younger."

"Okay, now check this out," Tommy said. "My Paki—whatever is a female; Katherine. Seems she hired Hatch to spy on her husband 'cause she thinks he's cheating on her. Husband's name is *Theodoro.*"

"Bingo," Avni said.

Avni and Ramos both got up and brought their papers to where Tommy sat. Everyone compared the other's information to their own.

"Good thing you got that address on Theodore," Avni said. "My list has him with a PO Box in Manhattan."

"I knew Hatch's fingerprints were in this somehow," Ramos said. "But I couldn't see him as the killer and I was right."

"Maybe he was blackmailing the guy?" Avni asked.

"Wouldn't be no surprise," Tommy said. Then, still looking at the computer screen, "Son-n-n..."

"What's up?" Ramos asked.

Tommy looked up from the computer. "In Hatch's personal profile of this guy Theodoro, it says that he sings on the church choir."

Ramos banged his fist on the desk. "Get Williams on the horn, Tommy," he said. "We're gonna need a warrant."

CHAPTER 66

A LITTLE OVER two hours later, almost thirty men and women, including District Attorney Williams, were assembled in the Harlem building's underground garage.

Ramos looked around at the group of law enforcement officers that he was expected to lead on the assault on the Chickenhawk's home. They were all professionals and they were all hungry to be the one who nailed the latest crazed killer to terrorize their city.

"Ramos!"

Ramos groaned inwardly and turned in Williams' direction. The district attorney motioned for Ramos to join him. Ramos scanned the crowd for his partner but couldn't spot him in the throng and finally walked over to where Williams stood adjusting his flak jacket. All around them were the staccato sounds of Velcro being fastened and/or unfastened as people put on or adjusted their body armor.

"Your briefing and P.O.A. (Plan of Action) earlier was very thorough and on point," Williams said. "Good work."

Ramos nodded, popped a mint into his mouth and crunched it loudly.

"I don't give compliments lightly—or frequently," Williams added.

"I don't give a shit for compliments," Ramos said. "I just

wanna get this bastard and then me and Tommy want back in the NYPD."

Williams stared at Ramos and then nodded slowly.

Ramos turned away and spotted his partner talking to members of "Charlie" squad. Earlier, during the briefing, he'd broken up the twenty-eight investigators into four groups that he designated squads—Adam, Boy, Charlie, and David. The senior person in each group was made squad leader. Everyone was assigned a task; everyone knew what he or she had to do.

Ramos looked hard at the normally combative Manhattan district attorney. He knew what was happening here, the cop's equivalent of opening night jitters. They were going after the city's most notorious killer and there was the chance that everything would go off smooth as silk and so the DA's office would wind up covered in accolades and glory. There was also the chance that everything would go to hell and a cop would get hurt or killed. If that happened, the probability was that the DA's office would wind up covered in something a great deal more vile than accolades or glory.

"Yo, everybody's ready," Tommy said as he joined them.

"Bob?" Ramos asked.

"He's driving 'Boy' squad—says he's too big a target to be doin' anything else," Tommy informed him.

Ramos nodded, "What about the Task Force?"

"We'll notify them of our action once we're at the halfway point to the suspect's location," Williams interjected.

Ramos and Tommy Cucitti looked at the DA.

"That's gonna bring us heat from the mayor and the feds," Ramos said.

"Fuck 'em," Williams retorted. "This is our show. I don't want them showing up until it's all over, we can't afford to let them steal our thunder."

"You mean *your* thunder," Tommy corrected him.

Williams glared at Tommy as he continued, "The judge holding the warrant is a friend of mine and he lives out on the island, we'll stop at his place just long enough to grab the warrant and go."

Ramos nodded, crushed another mint in his teeth and wished fervently for a cigarette. "You riding with Adam Squad?"

Ramos asked Williams. "Might be a good idea, that way you can direct the driver to the judge's house, the drivers already have Pakidorapopulos' address."

Williams nodded. "Good idea," he said.

"We ready to roll?" Ramos asked Tommy.

"As ready as we'll ever be, son," Tommy replied.

Ramos smiled grimly. "Saddle up then," he said.

Tommy spun and, using his lips and tongue, emitted a high-pitched whistle that immediately ceased all conversation and caught everyone's attention. He made a circling motion over his head with his index finger and everyone separated into their respective squads and climbed into their designated vehicles.

Ramos and Tommy made to join their squads when Williams stopped Ramos.

"Good luck," Williams said.

"Yeah," Ramos said. "You too."

CHAPTER 67

THE CONVOY OF four large, black vehicles kept close to the speed limit while they were in the city in a bid to avoid attention. Once they hit Long Island and the highway, however, their speedometers didn't register below 80 miles per hour. Tommy dropped a CD into the player in his vehicle. Soon the poignant strains of 50 Cent's song, *I'm supposed to die tonight* filled the car.

Ramos rode in the last vehicle. It was the only van and was the one designated for David Squad. Ramos had chosen it because it had actually been equipped as a Communications van and it contained an actual telephone instead of one of the lightweight cell-type phones everyone was using. He picked up the telephone now and dialed up Adam Squad in the lead Suburban.

"Adam," came the crisp voice on the other end after only one ring.

"Lemme talk to Williams," said Ramos.

"Williams."

"We closing in on the judge's place?"

"Another twenty minutes or so."

"And...?"

"And then once we leave, warrant in hand, he'll notify the Suffolk County PD that we're on our way and make sure they know they're just riding shotgun on this—backing us up."

"They're not gonna like that."

"Tough. I keep telling you this is our show."

"You're playing this real close to the vest, Williams," Ramos said. "I hope it doesn't blow up in our faces."

"Too late to worry about that. Now hang up, I'm going to call the Task Force and let them in on what's going on."

Ramos shook his head. "I'm glad I'm just a fuckin' cop," he said and hung up the phone.

The convoy of vehicles, three huge Suburbans with the van bringing up the rear, pulled up to the judge's Long Island home a little over twenty minutes later. After a brief conversation between Williams and the judge, the warrant exchanged hands and they were on the move again. Ramos and the others never left their seats.

As they neared the address of Theodoro Pakidorapopulos, Ramos called each squad in turn and instructed them to perform a final weapons check. When he put the phone down it rang and he picked it back up.

"David Squad, Ramos."

"This is Deputy Mayor Nitchik."

Shit, Ramos thought as his stomach tightened up into a knot.

"You must have a death wish for your career, Ramos," the wheezy voice on the other end said.

"I don't..."

"Yes you do! You were supposed to inform the mayor's office of the goings-on with this DA Williams and his Chicken-Killer investigation..."

"Chickenhawk."

"Whatever! All I know is that the mayor's pissed and he's looking for rolling heads."

"What?"

"The mayor is looking for heads to roll over this. You were supposed to let me know what was going on over there and now I find out that you're all the way the hell out on Long Island."

"Your beef is with the DA," Ramos said.

"It was the goddamn DA who gave me this number," Nitchik countered.

"I just follow orders," said Ramos.

"That's right," Nitchik practically screamed on the other

end. "Your orders were to give me information!"

"My orders, Mr. Deputy Mayor, were to stop this sonofabitch, and that's what I'm on my way to do," Ramos said before slamming the phone down.

Suddenly there was the unmistakable sound of tires on gravel and when Ramos looked out through the heavily tinted window, he saw that they were there.

CHAPTER 68

THE FOUR VEHICLES pulled into the driveway, maneuvering around the eight Suffolk County PD vehicles already there or parked on the lawn.

Everyone piled out as soon as the cars came to a halt and took their positions around the house. Ramos walked over to the lead vehicle where Williams was having a discussion with three men, two of them in Suffolk County PD uniforms. Ramos could tell by the fancy braid that the uniformed men were brass.

"I don't like this," the third man, dressed in a plain black suit, said. "I'm the DA for this county and if this man is the killer, he's in our backyard and we should have the lead on this."

"Sorry," Williams said, not sounding sorry at all. "This man may live under your jurisdiction, but he committed his crimes in mine. I have an arrest warrant from a judge here that makes it quite clear who has jurisdictional authority in this matter."

The Long Island DA snatched the warrant from Williams' hand and, along with the two uniformed officers, started reading it.

"No one answers the phone in the house," Tommy said.

"Well if he's home, he sure as hell knows *we're* here," Ramos said.

Williams walked up to them, his face as grim as always. "Everything's settled," he said. "Start the operation."

Ramos took another quick look at the assembled troops and signaled for the squad leaders to join him. Tommy rounded up the Suffolk County cops and brought them over as well.

Ramos nodded. "Good, thanks. Now I need you guys to form a second row behind my perimeter," Ramos said pointing to half of the Suffolk County cops. "Don't let anybody coming from that house get past you." Now he turned to the rest of the Suffolk County officers, "You guys evacuate everyone from these other homes here. We don't want any nosy neighbors catching a stray bullet. Push 'em back to that street lamp over there and keep 'em there. Any reporters show up, they get to keep the neighbors company."

Ramos turned his attention back to Tommy and Adam Squad. "Let's go," he said.

Ramos went up to the front door of the big house, followed closely by his partner and the seven armed investigators from Adam Squad. He watched silently as the cops evacuated the homes he'd indicated earlier. Once he saw that everyone had been herded to a more or less safe distance, he gave Tommy a nod.

"Everybody in position?" Tommy asked over his radio. All of the squads responded in the affirmative. "It's all good, son," Tommy told Ramos.

Ramos, his .38 revolver in his left hand, gave Tommy a thumbs up. At this pre-designated signal, Tommy depressed the button on the radio again and called out one word, "Go!" he said.

CHAPTER 69

RAMOS, TOMMY, AND the fourteen heavily armed investigators of Adam and Boy squads burst into the house. Boy Squad, who'd been positioned at the back door, met up with all of the others in the middle of the living room. Then, with almost military precision, the cops searched every room and closet on the ground floor. They found no one.

"Yo Eddie, why are all the windows open and the lights on," Tommy asked once the ground floor had been given the all clear.

"No idea," Ramos answered, looking up the wide staircase which lead to the second floor.

"I smell gas," one of the Adam Squad investigators whispered.

Everyone stopped and began sniffing at the cold air. The sight would have been comical if not for the inherent danger the odor represented.

"I don't smell nothin'," Ramos said after a few loud sniffs. The others agreed. Tommy got on the radio and asked the cops still on the first floor to have the stove checked. A few moments later the result was negative, everything on the first floor, including the stove and oven, were five-by-five.

"I still smell something," the investigator who'd originally mentioned the gas smell insisted.

"Okay," Ramos said. "Everybody keep your eyes, ears, and *noses* open." After a few nervous snickers, everyone got back down to the serious business at hand.

The cops fanned out, with Ramos and Tommy choosing the door at the far end of the corridor. Ramos and Tommy heard the doors of the other rooms being slammed open, and were about to open the door in front of them when one of the other investigators called out, "There's blood here!"

Everyone ran to the room in question and cautiously stepped inside, mindful of the fact that this was a crime scene.

"Shit," someone said.

Ramos nodded. There was indeed blood here. Someone had stripped the bed, exposing a large burgundy and black stain in the mattress. That stain, along with the bloodied sheets that lay wadded up on the floor, established the bed as a possible murder scene.

"It's a kid's bed," Ramos growled as fleeting images of a boyhood friend flashed through his mind.

"I smell gas again," the same investigator who'd mentioned it before said. "Only it's stronger this time."

Now several of the other officers agreed, and Ramos and Tommy could smell it now as well.

"That's not gas..." someone started to say.

"Aw fuck!" Ramos exclaimed. He spun toward the open doorway in time to see a tall figure strike a large wooden match. Ramos lunged through the doorway, clawing at the man's hands just as he dropped the match onto the gasoline-soaked carpet.

Ramos crashed into Paki, knocking him into the opposite wall as the carpeting beneath and behind him exploded into flame with a whoosh. Ramos felt the heat immediately, and then the pain on his back, arms and legs, as his clothes caught fire. He looked for Paki through the growing flames and smoke, and saw him duck into one of the rooms. He could hear the shouts of his men in the room behind him, but he couldn't make out what they were saying over the screams—his screams.

A dark figure leapt into his line of vision, through the wall of flames, and started tugging at his clothes.

"Come on Eddie, you gotta get this shit off!" Tommy yelled. And with Tommy's help, he succeeded in getting out of his burning flak jacket.

"There," Ramos coughed, pointing to the room Paki had escaped into. "He went in there." Tommy nodded and together they crawled on their hands and knees to the still open doorway.

Ramos and Tommy were now on either side of the door. He held up his hand so Tommy could see it and silently counted off three seconds with his fingers. At three, they leapt into the room.

Ramos moved to his left, his gun drawn, Tommy went to the right, his 9mm. in his hand. As in the rest of the house, all of the lights were on and it only took a second for the detectives to spot the three bodies on the bed, and the one on the floor.

Ramos pointed his gun at the one on the floor. "Check out the folks on the bed," he said.

Tommy went over and, with barely a glance at the bodies, checked their pulses. He kept looking around the smoky room until a loud bang made him jump and turn his weapon in his partner's direction.

"Close the door," Ramos said. "Buy us some time."

"Son, you scared the shit out of me," Tommy said, scanning the large room again.

"Sorry," Ramos said. "Checking the guy on the floor now." Ramos bent and placed two fingers on the man's neck. Nothing.

"He's bought it too," Ramos told Tommy.

"Theodoro?"

"Hatch," Ramos replied. "They might have had a falling out or something."

While they were talking, both men had made their way to the closet. The mirrored double doors were closed and both men leveled their guns at their reflections.

Tommy opened his mouth to speak but wound up coughing instead. The smoke was rapidly getting worse and, Chickenhawk or no, they knew they had to bail soon.

Tommy got over his coughing jag and wiped at his mouth with the back of his hand. "Okay asshole," he yelled. "Come out real slow and real nice or you're gonna wind up real dead."

Something crashed to the floor in the hallway and there was the sound of more glass breaking. Through the open window came the wail of sirens—whether it was from the approaching Task Force or the fire department, Ramos couldn't tell. He would have bet on both.

"Come on motherfucker!" Tommy screamed, his eyes tearing from the smoke. "Come the fuck out!"

There was another crash in the hall outside the door, a big one that made Ramos tear his watery gaze from the closet just as the bedroom door exploded into the room.

CHAPTER 70

RAMOS WAS BACK. Back at Manhattan North Homicide, back behind his desk with the clunky old telephone and his favorite coconut flavored coffee. It felt so good to be back, Ramos didn't even mind the rickety coat rack. He smiled, took a deep breath, and there, in an old-fashioned glass ashtray, was a cigarette. The end was lit and an inviting curl of bluish-gray smoke unwound its way to the ceiling.

Ramos couldn't believe his luck. So it was okay to smoke again? And not just smoke, but apparently it was okay to smoke in the building again—just like old times!

Ramos gingerly lifted the cigarette from the ashtray, tapped the accumulation of ash from the end of it, and lifted the cigarette reverently to his lips.

The detective then put the cigarette in his mouth and took a long, luxurious drag.

He couldn't breathe.

He started gagging and coughing, he couldn't get any air into his lungs and he panicked. The office, his desk, everything, faded into gray. Desperately, he reached out, clawing for purchase like a drowning man. Someone or something pushed his hands away, he could hear voices—and he opened his eyes.

Ramos woke up in the back of an ambulance. An EMT placing an oxygen mask over his face was the one who was pushing his hands away. Ramos noticed that his hands were bandaged before letting them drop back onto the gurney.

"Lemme check your IV," the technician said as he fussed over the needle and tube taped to Ramos' arm.

"Tommy—my partner," Ramos rasped before his parched throat wouldn't let him say anymore.

The EMT looked at him, "Your partner, the other cop, he's worse off than you are," he said.

Ramos groaned. "How..."

"He's not DOA," the EMT hurriedly offered. "He's got a concussion, two broken wrists, and first and second degree burns. There might be some internal injuries or other stuff, but they'll find that out at the hospital."

"What happened?"

"The explosion blew your partner right out the window," the tech said after a moment's hesitation. "Lucky for him he landed on the lawn and there was an ambulance crew nearby. He's hurt, but he'll be alright."

Ramos nodded weakly, "Thanks," he said.

"No prob," the tech said, checking his watch. "We'll be there soon—they'll probably wind up medi-vaccing you to the city anyway."

"The guy we were after, the killer...?"

The EMT shrugged. "I don't know anything about that."

Ramos nodded again and let his head drop back onto the gurney's thin mattress. Through bleary eyes he watched as the technician said something more to him, but it sounded as if he were a million miles away.

Ramos was still trying to figure out what the tech was saying when he slipped back into the sweet ether of unconsciousness.

CHAPTER 71

IT SEEMED LIKE forever since Ramos had been to Jackson Hole. Most of the waitresses were different, but thankfully the food and the company were still top notch.

"So detective, I went to see Tommy at the hospital today and they told me they'd already kicked him out," Nance said.

"You should have called beforehand," Lieutenant Mullen suggested after swallowing his beer. "That's what I did."

Nance rolled her eyes. "Who invited this guy?" She asked, jabbing her fork in the lieutenant's general direction.

Everyone at the table laughed except Patrick Mullen who seemed genuinely surprised by Nance's question.

"The mayor's screaming for their heads, you know," Mullen said softly. "He's even talking criminal charges."

"Criminal charges?" Nance exclaimed loudly. "You're shittin' me."

"No, I'm not," Mullen said evenly. "He'd like to bring criminal charges against Eddie and Tommy, but only if he can be sure of making them stick."

"Yeah, yeah," Ramos said, waving his hand dismissively. "That's not to mention the departmental charges that the commissioner's bringing against Tommy and me, the complaints and possible charges from the Suffolk County PD, and the same from their fire department."

"Ew-w-w," Nance said. "But what about the DA? I thought

you were working for him?"

"As soon as the shit hit the fan in Long Island, the DA started his damage control and distanced himself from what happened."

"As did the mayor and the police commissioner," Mullen interjected.

"That's right," Ramos agreed. "They all needed scapegoats, and me and Tommy were frontline and center."

"I'm sorry about the way this all went down," Mullen offered.

Ramos shrugged. "You did what you had to do, that's just the way the job is. Me and Tommy ain't the first cops to get caught in the shit."

Everyone at the table agreed.

"For the good of the service," Mullen said sarcastically.

"For the good of the service!" The other two called out simultaneously, raising their glasses.

They all touched glasses over the center of the table and laughed.

"So, was Hatch the main guy; you think?" Nance asked once the laughter had subsided into awkward silence.

"No, well not really anyway," Mullen explained. "Even though we don't know the full extent of Hatch's involvement in the murders, his presence at the house points to at least some knowledge or culpability."

"You know, we had that sonofabitch," Ramos growled. "Hatch's car was at the scene of one of the murders, he was picked up for questioning by the Task Force, me and Tommy picked him up, his apartment got tossed...nuthin'."

"Yeah, Hatch knew something but he wasn't the killer," Mullen continued. "Hatch's gun was recovered at the Pakidorapopulos house and it doesn't match the caliber of the weapon the Chickenhawk was using."

Ramos smirked. "I told Tommy that my gut was telling me those same exact things," he said.

"And your gut was telling you right," Mullen said. "Theodoro Pakidorapopulos, *Paki* to his friends, hasn't surfaced anywhere, dead or alive. The gun hasn't come up either. Dimes to duckets, when we find one we'll find the other."

"Well, isn't the gun registered in the father's name? Joseph, uh, Joseph...whatever?" asked Nance.

"A gun of the same caliber is registered in the father's name," Ramos said. "Joseph Pakidorapopulos says he bought that gun years ago for hunting and never used it. Finally, he gave it to his son as a keepsake 'cause he found out how rare it was."

"Bet he regrets that move," Mullen said.

Everyone else at the table nodded or voiced their agreement.

"Well, who knows really," Ramos said, standing and stretching. "That gun, a different gun, a knife...whatever it was that set him off, he would have found some way to do his killing."

"It's horrible how that poor family was killed," Nance said. "They should take this Theodoro guy and they should hang him by his balls over a pit of starving Rottweilers."

Ramos tossed some money on the table. "Settle up for me guys," he said. "I'm tired, I hurt, and I'm going home."

Nance stood up too. "You're not driving home after all that beer you drank," she insisted. "Gimme your car keys."

Ramos, from prior experience, knew better than to argue and handed Nance his keys. The first few times she'd insisted on taking his car keys after he'd had a few drinks, he'd gotten royally pissed. As time went on and their friendship deepened, however, (not to mention a few lectures from Tommy of all people), Ramos grew to appreciate her concern.

Nance tossed the keys to Mullen, who looked at her quizzically after he'd caught them.

"You've been nursing that same beer all night," Nance said. "Make sure you get home safe."

Mullen nodded. "I'll bring Eddie his car in the morning," he said. "You know, the devil takes care of his own," Mullen said. "You watch, we'll find this guy, but we'll probably trip over him on a humble."

All Ramos could do was nod wearily.

"Come on detective," Nance said, as she wrapped a powerful arm around his waist.

Ramos was about to protest when he noticed, as they made their circuitous route around the closely packed tables, that he felt a lot more woozy than he thought he would.

"Oops, sorry," Nance apologized to a young couple when they bumped into their table.

"I'm the one who is sorry, Nance," Ramos said once they were outside. "I guess I had a few more beers that I should have."

"Actually, you had a lot more beers than you should have," Nance pointed out. She pulled her own car keys from her pocket and Ramos heard the familiar double-tone of the car alarm being deactivated. A few minutes later, they were on their way to Brooklyn—the borough they both called home.

Even though he felt somewhat invigorated by the cold night air once they had left the restaurant, Ramos wasn't aware that they'd arrived at his home until Nance woke him up.

"Rise and shine detective," Nance said. "You're home and I have to get to mine."

Ramos woke up groggily, and a little embarrassed at having fallen so deeply asleep.

"Did I...?"

"Snore and/or drool? Yeah, you did both," Nance said. "Good thing I have vinyl upholstery."

Ramos felt himself blush; embarrassed.

"Just kiddin', detective. Now you better get inside before Linda thinks we're doin' it and comes out here and kicks both our asses."

Ramos laughed, "I can believe it," he said.

Ramos twisted in his seat and fumbled with the door and the catch on his seatbelt at the same time, his thick fingers seemingly not up to the task of opening either. After several moments of growing frustration, Ramos heard Nance give an exaggerated sigh of impatience.

"Why are the big ones always so helpless?" Nance asked as she leaned over him to unlock and open the door on his side.

Ramos was chuckling self-consciously when his eyes fell to Nance's cleavage. He was surprised when he felt an erection swell to attention. As often as he'd seen her cleavage, and as often as he'd commented on or heard comments about the generous swell of her breasts, his body had never reacted with such immediate and almost painful longing.

"Now let's get you undone and you're out." Nance said as she leaned back and reached for the buckle on Ramos' seat belt. That's when she saw the unmistakable bulge that strained against the confines of his trousers. Nance glanced up into

Ramos' face and their eyes locked. Ramos' face grew hot, and he felt at once both mortified and relieved.

Nance looked back down at the front of his pants again. "Well, you really *are* one of the big ones," she said through her trademark crooked grin. Then, with a single, deft move, she undid the buckle on his seatbelt and he was free.

"G'night detective," she said with a laugh while she pushed him gently from the car.

Ramos climbed out of the car somewhat unsteadily and closed the door. He was aware of Nance watching him as he walked up the front steps of his house, and he felt oddly self-conscious.

At his front door, he got his keys out, turned, and waved at Nance in her car. She tapped lightly on the horn before pulling away and disappearing around the corner.

Ramos turned back to his front door, suddenly feeling childish because of his wave, unlocked the door and went inside.

The house was dark and quiet inside, just as he expected it would be. It was the perfect insulation from the outside world that it had always been.

Ramos pulled his coat off and rolled his shoulders. He'd gotten home later than he'd planned and slightly drunker than he'd planned, but at least he was home. After visiting Tommy at his apartment, he'd gone to the Jackson Hole hoping to find comfort and distraction in its familiar environs—but Tommy's absence had been glaring, and after a while he found that he just couldn't talk about the Chickenhawk case anymore. The way that investigation had soured and then had just gone downhill from there.

Ramos hung up his coat and went through his nightly ritual. Kim was asleep, her T.V. on, and her covers in disarray. Ramos straightened out her covers and pulled them up to her chin, taking the time to pick up and replace the stuffed animals she'd kicked off the bed in her sleep. Ramos was about to shut the television off when he noticed the old Bugs Bunny cartoon that was playing. He watched as a small, brown bird explained his obsession to a much larger bird—a rooster.

"I'm a chickenhawk," the little brown bird said. "And I'm looking for a chicken."

Ramos shut it off.

A short time later, after taking a hot shower and brushing his teeth, the detective made his way to his bed on the couch. He'd just settled in when he heard the light pad of footsteps on the stairs.

Linda sat down softly on the edge of the couch. Even in the room's darkness, Ramos could see her looking at him intently. He pulled back the covers and she slid in next to him, snuggling close and placing her perennially cold feet against him for warmth.

Ramos put his arm around her and gently twirled a lock of her hair around his finger. She touched his face and he turned toward her. Their lips met and they kissed, lightly at first, and then more deeply. Their tongues touched and explored, their kisses becoming more urgent and intense. Ramos' hand moved to her breast, gently kneading the delicate mound of flesh under her nightgown. Linda sighed and maneuvered her arm so that she could more easily reach his lower body. She made contact with her goal and wrapped her slim fingers around the rapidly thickening shaft of her husband's penis.

Now it was the detective's turn to sigh as, for the second time that day, he was possessed of a throbbing erection. Actually, his wife was in possession of it and soon her gentle squeezes and rubbing had Ramos' arousal stretched to almost painful proportions.

Linda Ramos repositioned herself so that she ended up atop her burly husband, careful not to move around too much on the overburdened couch lest she take an embarrassing tumble to the floor. They both laughed quietly and a little self-consciously while she accomplished this, and then she helped Ramos wriggle out of his pajama bottoms.

Ramos kicked the bottoms from one leg and left them still wrapped around the ankle of his other leg. Linda leaned her weight onto his chest with one hand while she reached behind her with the other. Her hand searched fruitlessly for a moment until Ramos placed her hand on the meaty shaft of his erection. Together, they guided his penis toward the silky warmth of her sex.

They both gasped as the broad head of his manhood initially met with resistance before slowly being nudged past the petite aperture of her vagina.

Linda placed both of her hands on Ramos' shoulders as she slowly wriggled and lowered herself onto him by degrees. Ramos, his hand still partially gripping the base of his penis, pushed himself into her. As Linda's muscles relaxed and the sweet liqueur of her passion welled forth, Ramos felt himself slide deeply inside her, a feeling that was as familiar and comforting as it was erotic. The hand that he'd been using to hold himself went to the graceful curve of her hip, while the other hand gripped the back of the couch and helped keep them from falling off.

Although their position was awkward, they'd done this before and Ramos was able to plunge into her again and again. The force of his drives almost propelled her onto the floor more than once and they were both soon covered in sweat. Their love-making was silent except for the occasional grunt and the rhythmic slap of flesh against flesh.

Low murmurs coming from his wife made Ramos increase the intensity of his thrusts, the pressure building slowly in his testicles threatened to send him into orgasmic overload.

Through the twin fogs of love and lust, as part of Ramos hoped he would last long enough to bring his wife to satisfaction, odd scraps of his wife's murmurings were able to reach him. Almost against his will, those scraps evolved into words, the words developed a distinct rhythm, and that rhythm gelled into the unmistakable cadence of a universal expression...

Linda was praying.

CHAPTER 72

THERE WAS NO mistaking it, Ramos could clearly make out his wife's hushed words.

"...And likewise the wife to her husband. The wife's body does not belong to her alone, but also to her husband...Do not deprive each other...Devote yourselves to prayer..."

Ramos' erection withered and drooped like a marathoner in one hundred-degree heat. Her ride interrupted, Linda quit her gyrations, opened her eyes, and looked down at the expression of shock and revulsion on her husband's face.

"What's wrong?" she asked.

"Get up, get off me," Ramos growled as he fought the urge to just dump her onto the floor. Puzzled, Linda complied. Settling back on the couch and modestly covering her breasts with the blanket.

"What happened?" Linda asked. "Did you finish?"

Ramos jumped from his bed on the couch as if a poisonous snake had revealed itself under the covers. He pulled up his pajama bottoms and paced back and forth in front of his wife before turning toward her.

"What the fuck were you doing?" he whispered harshly.

Linda's mouth went slack for a moment, then tightened into a resolute line. "I thought we were making love," she said.

"Yeah, so did I," Ramos said, his voice rising. "But that was before you lost your mind and decided to go to church instead."

"What are you talking about Eddie?" Linda asked. "What's wrong with you?"

"Me? What's wrong with me?" Ramos asked incredulously. "You were praying!"

"So what?" Linda shot back. "There is absolutely nothing wrong with prayer—you should try it sometime."

"No, no, no," Ramos insisted. "You were prayin' while we were"—Ramos lowered his voice again—"While we were fuckin'," he said.

Linda rolled her eyes. "I was praying while we *made love*," she corrected.

"I don't care what you call it, that's some sick shit," Ramos said.

"Why?" Linda stood up, one fist clenched at her side, the other still clutching the blanket to her breast. Ramos had often found her habit of covering up, even if they'd just had sex, curious and endearing. But now he wondered if it hadn't been a sign of something darker all along.

"We were making love," Linda repeated. "Love is God and God is love. I was praying that with the union of our bodies, there would also come a spiritual union. Second Corinthians 6:14 says, 'Do not be yoked together with unbelievers...'"

"Bullshit!" Ramos said. "I don't care what anything says, you can't pray when you're having sex—it's like, like blasphemy!"

"Blasphemy? You don't know what you're talking about Eddie. God gave us these bodies so we can enjoy each other and be pleasing to one another in His sight," Linda said as she dropped the blanket at last. "What, you don't think God sees us when we're in our private places doing things in the dark? God has seen us every time we've been together Eddie."

Ramos groaned. "It's still not right Linda," he said. "And the way you just explained it made it even creepier."

"It wouldn't bother you unless you thought being with me was something dirty," Linda accused.

"No, it's not that," Ramos said. "It's just, just—aw, fuck it."

Ramos went to the closet, pulled out a pair of old workpants and pulled them on over his pajama bottoms. He slipped his bare feet into a beat up pair of Rockports and, out of habit, strapped on his .38.

"Eddie, where are you going?" Linda asked as she put on her nightgown.

Ramos didn't answer. He put on his overcoat, pushed a hat onto his head and grabbed the doorknob.

"Eddie, you need salvation," Linda called out. "Please Eddie, please. I love you and Jesus loves you."

Ramos opened the door and braced himself against the blast of cold air that met him. "I just need some air," he said without turning, and then went through the doorway and slammed the door shut behind him. It was snowing slightly and icy flakes as brittle as glass crunched under his feet as he walked down the front steps of his house. When he got to the bottom, he briefly scanned both sides of the street for his car before remembering that Nance had driven him home. He heard the door open behind him and turned, seeing Linda's face and bare right arm braving the elements through the partially opened door.

"If you leave Eddie, then keep going," Linda screeched. "This house is dedicated to the Lord and there's no room for the unsaved, unsanctified followers of religious dogma. You need Jesus, Eddie, you need Jesus!" Linda slammed the door shut.

Ramos took a step back toward the house when he glimpsed Kim's worried face in one of the upstairs windows. Suddenly feeling ashamed, he turned and walked briskly to the end of the street. Once he'd made it around the corner he just kept walking, head down against the stinging fusillade of wind-driven ice crystals.

A patrol car slowly rolled by, a young cop riding shotgun sized him up, then the car gained speed and was gone.

Ramos looked after the car, wishing he'd asked one of the officers inside for a cigarette...or a ride somewhere. He thought about calling Tommy, but he knew that his partner would probably be asleep and the poor guy needed the rest. Ramos mulled over his options, dismissing ideas for who to call and where to spend the night as quickly as they came to him. He knew that he should go home, he'd never walked out on his family before and the pull of home and responsibility tugged at him mightily, but this most recent episode with his wife left him feeling particularly repulsed and angry.

How can she do that? Ramos thought. *How can she pray while we're screwin'? That's disgusting, I don't care how religious she thinks she is, there're just some things you don't do. It's common sense...*

Across the street, the lights of a lonely subway station entrance cast its wan glow on the area immediately around it. A homeless man in his cardboard tent was situated on the grating nearby, finding comfort in the drafts of warm air that rose from the station below.

The sight of the subway entrance, leading to the C train, helped Ramos make up his mind. He would take a C train into the city, switch to an E train at Forty-Second Street, and take that to Jamaica Center—the last stop. After that, a short bus ride would deliver him to his mother's house in Queens. Although he didn't need to, Ramos checked his key ring and found the key to his mother's Springfield Gardens home.

"This is embarrassing," Ramos muttered. "Here I am a grown man in my fifties, and I wind up havin' to stay at my mommy's."

CHAPTER 73

THE RIDE INTO the city was reasonably comfortable and uneventful. Ramos had been able to get a seat and the car was heated.

The E train at Forty-Second Street was a slightly different matter. Before the train had even rolled to a stop, Ramos could see there were no seats to be had. As he boarded, he hoped the situation would change as people got off—he sure didn't feel like standing all the way to Queens.

The train instead became even more crowded when more passengers boarded at Lexington Avenue, and Ramos had to endure being jostled by the mass of people surging onto the train from the platform. The number of people taking the subway at night never failed to impress, and sometimes annoy, the detective. Ramos glanced at the faces of the people who shared the subway car with him, most belonged to the hard-working men and women who kept the city going—factory workers, nurses, secretaries...one woman wore the uniform of a subway employee, while a group of three men talking and laughing together wore the dust-covered boots and hard hats of construction workers. A few of the passengers were undoubtedly students, weighed down by their oversized and overstuffed backpacks.

He contemplated getting off at the next stop and returning home, he was sure he and Linda could talk this thing through.

But Ramos stayed on the train. *Maybe we could both use a night to cool off,* he thought.

As the train pulled away from the Jamaica/Van Wyck station, most of the passengers who planned to get off at the last stop began their usual migration toward the front of the train. Being in the first car when the train reached Jamaica Center would leave them nearest to the escalator leading to the street. Ramos followed them.

Ramos and the other passengers crowded into the first car of the train just as the doors closed and it slowly rolled into the tunnel. The warmth of the train's heaters, combined with the dozens of bodies pressed together in the car, soon made it uncomfortable. Ramos, sweating under his hat and coat, looked around the car for a more comfortable place to stand and spotted a slightly less congested area near the front of the car. Ramos slowly made his way through the mass of commuters until he found the reason for the relatively less significant crowding at this end of the car. The overly ripe odor that emanated from the homeless man curled into a tight ball in one of the corner seats was enough to dissuade anyone from venturing too close.

Almost anyone, Ramos thought wryly as an elderly man in a rumpled security guard uniform squeezed himself into the seat beside the homeless person. *Poor old guy,* Ramos thought. *He was probably on his feet all da...*

The homeless man turned in his seat and glared at the interloper who'd intruded on his sleeping space. The old man ignored him and looked straight ahead—Ramos stared at the homeless man. Then the homeless man, perhaps feeling the weight of Ramos' stare, turned his dirty, unshaven face up and met the detective's eyes full on.

Recognition sparked between them in white hot flashes of memory—a face illumined by the flare of a match, a hallway in flames, a desperate lunge, an explosion.

Cop and killer recognized each other simultaneously, and both went for their weapon.

Ramos had his gun out first, the long barrel of Paki's weapon making it difficult to pull it out while sitting down. Ramos held his gun tightly at his side, the eye of the short barrel pointed at

Paki. Ramos' shield was clenched tightly in his left fist and he slowly brought it up over his head.

"Police," Ramos said evenly, loud enough for Paki to hear. "Don't fuckin' move."

Most of the passengers crowded around them paid them no notice, one or two looked at Ramos curiously. Paki finally succeeded in freeing his gun and he held it with its cartoonish barrel pointed toward the ceiling.

"Police!" Ramos boomed. "Drop it! Drop it!"

Some of the people in the crowd stirred uneasily, while others in the rear of the car craned their necks for a better glimpse of what was going on.

Paki smiled and lowered his gun's barrel until it was level with the old security guard's head.

"Shit," Ramos exclaimed. "Don't do it! Put it down!"

Now, like a sluggish animal finally coming to its senses, the crowd began to shift and take notice of what was going on—but it was too late.

"Police!" Ramos yelled again. "Police! Everybody down!"

The old security guard looked up at Ramos, and then turned toward Paki just as the gunman pulled the trigger.

The blast was deafening. Ramos was sure he yelled, but he couldn't hear himself.

The back of the security guard's head disappeared, most of its contents spewing out onto the nearest shocked passengers. The ensuing pandemonium was almost instantaneous. Screaming and clawing, the crowd surged away from Paki and toward Ramos, who fought a losing battle against the human tide in an effort to reach the killer.

"Get down, get down!" Ramos yelled, holding his gun and badge aloft. The crowd ignored him as they stampeded mindlessly in an attempt to get away.

Even through the ringing in his ears, Ramos could hear Paki's insane laughter. He tried to push past the desperately fleeing patrons, but he couldn't budge past them. He couldn't fire his gun for fear of hitting someone in the mob that surrounded him on all sides. Paki had no such reservations. Ramos caught a glimpse of him loading another round into his gun's chamber and thumbing back the hammer.

"Stop!" Ramos yelled, trying to bring his own gun to bear. "Everybody get down goddamnit!"

Paki pointed his gun at the detective, then seemingly changed his mind and shot a young woman.

"No," Ramos screamed. "No!"

The multitude swarmed back and forth, panicked screams mixing with grunts and curses as everyone searched for an escape route that wasn't there. Another shot and someone shrieked horribly before going down, blood spurting from a ravaged throat.

Ramos lowered his gun and took aim through an opening in the crowd, only to almost have the gun knocked from his hand by the mob. A youth appeared at his right, his eyes wild with fear.

"Shoot him man! Shoot that mother..."The next bullet caught him in the face with a sound like a tenderizing mallet slapping against a slab of bloody meat.

As he fell, the wounded youth reached out and grabbed Ramos' coat, pulling him off balance and dragging him down onto the bloody floor.

Someone succeeded in opening the door that lead into the previous car and fights broke out as the crowd tried to escape through the narrow opening. There was another shot and someone in the throng behind him yelled in pain.

On his hands and knees now, Ramos looked up and saw an opening among the flailing arms and kicking legs. He lifted his gun and fired off two shots in Paki's direction. A loud exclamation told Ramos that at least one of his shots had hit home. He struggled to his feet in the midst of the thinning crowd and was stunned when he came face to face with the coldhearted killer. Paki smiled a demented grin, mucus running from his nose and into his mouth, his gun pointed squarely at the detective when someone pulled the train's emergency brake.

Ramos and an equally surprised and unprepared Paki hurtled through space. Ramos banged his hip painfully on the armrest of a corner seat and fell to the floor, while Paki crashed into and bounced off the train's forward door, landing sprawled out on his back next to the detective.

Ramos' badge fell from his hand and clattered away as each

man tried to point his weapon at the other. The stainless steel door of the train operator's cab, the same one Paki had crashed into, opened and the train operator, wearing a cumbersome set of hearing protectors, stuck his head out into the car.

"Who pulled the brake?" He demanded before standing there mouth agape in surprise at the scene of carnage that lay before him.

Ramos grabbed Paki's wrist and held it in a death grip, while Paki struggled to bring his gun to bear on the homicide detective. A quick sidelong glance brought the train operator, and his unfortunate location of being in the line of fire, to Paki's attention. Paki squeezed the trigger and the Train Operator was slammed back into his cab by the force of the bullet.

"Fuck!" Ramos spat.

The two men rolled around on the gore-covered floor in a life and death struggle. Paki wrestled his way atop the detective and in one terrifying move, brought his gun up to Ramos' eyes. Instinctively, Ramos' hands shot up and grabbed Paki's wrists in a bid to keep Paki's gun away. Ramos' own gun, still in his right hand, pointed uselessly in the wrong direction as Ramos fought to push Paki's weapon from his face.

Paki leaned into the back of his gun, driving the outlandish barrel closer and closer to Ramos' face. The detective's eyes widened in fear as he became aware of Paki's intention. Ramos redoubled his efforts, his arms straining, but the gun's eye moved inexorably closer and closer to his mouth. Ramos jerked his head from side to side, but the still hot gun barrel found its target and pushed against his tightly pressed lips.

Paki pushed again and Ramos tasted blood. The detective tried to gain control of his own gun, but Paki drove on leaning all of his weight into the next push. Ramos felt the brilliant pain of the gun's steel as it broke past his front teeth, and he opened his mouth in a muffled scream. A lone tear of pain and frustration wrung itself from his eye as the cop felt the strength in his arms start to recede, yet he kept his hold on the killer. He shut his eyes against the inevitable and heard Paki's yowl of triumph. A part of Ramos' brain refused to acknowledge the horror of what was happening and insisted on asking over and over, 'So this is it? So this is it?'

Paki cocked the hammer back and pulled the trigger. The big gun's hammer slammed home with the finality of Death's gavel.

And nothing happened.

Ramos opened his eyes in time to see the perplexed look on Paki's face. Paki saw him and the killer's features contorted into one of rage. He roared and lifted his arm to bludgeon the detective with his suddenly traitorous weapon.

Ramos spun his gun around in his hand like an old-time gunslinger, stuck it in Paki's ribs, and pulled the trigger.

The first shot stopped Paki in mid-swing, his face registering surprise and then anger as he tried to bring the gun down on the detective's head. Ramos pulled the trigger again and again until his gun was empty.

Paki rolled off the cop and onto the floor of the train. A moment later Ramos was astonished to see him stagger to his feet.

Ramos struggled to his own feet, blood leaked from his mouth and down his chin. Paki saw him stand, reached into his pocket and pulled out a handful of ammunition. He stumbled backwards, trying to load his gun with shaking fingers, and dropped most of the bullets on the floor. Still, he was able to get at least one in the strange gun's cylinder.

Ramos spat blood and bits of teeth onto the train floor and limped toward the deranged killer. Then just as Paki raised his gun, Ramos balled up his fist and hit him in the ribs. In the same exact place where he'd just shot him. Paki's eyes rolled back in pain and his mouth opened soundlessly. The big gun dropped from his hand with a thud. Ramos hit him again and Paki fell back against the wall. Paki tried to straighten up and Ramos hit him one last time, a haymaker to the chin that would leave Ramos' hand bruised for weeks. Paki spun, crashed into the train doors, and crumpled to the floor. Ramos made to kick the prone body, saw the faces peering at him from the other car, and retrieved his badge instead.

"It's okay," he mumbled as he retrieved and held his shield up to the spectators. "I'm a cop."

EPILOGUE

SEVERAL WEEKS LATER, the lurid stories about Paki's life and death had finally begun to recede from the media and the majority of the public's attention and conversation had finally moved on to the next latest thing.

Ramos, Tommy, Daphne and Nance were relaxing at their usual haunt, the Jackson Hole, when their conversation nevertheless drifted back to the topic that it, perhaps unfortunately, always seemed to drift its way back to.

"So how'd the hearing go today, son?" Tommy asked.

"Not so bad," Ramos replied around a bite of his Texas burger. "So far I've been demoted, suspended without pay for forty days, and I gotta ride a desk for at least another six months before the department will even consider givin' me back my gun and shield. The union says it coulda gone worse for me if it weren't for the fact that I stopped the Chickenhawk *and* the mayor got reelected."

"That's not too bad," Tommy agreed as Daphne wiped some ketchup from the corner of his mouth. Tommy looked at her and rolled his eyes. "Look where my mother got reincarnated," he said, eliciting a laugh from the assemblage.

"Oh yeah," Daphne countered. "Well if I'm your mother, you know what that makes you—right?" This time the close little group guffawed while Tommy blushed a bright crimson.

They continued chatting good-naturedly, laughter

occasionally punctuating their bright conversation. Eventually the talk again turned, as it all too often did, back to Paki and his murderous rampage.

"I still don't believe it, yo," Tommy said, shaking his head. "I got blown out a window and that bastard escaped without a scratch.

"Yeah, we didn't have a clue about the secret entrance to his wine cellar in that bogus closet." Ramos said.

"Or that the wine cellar had another opening that led to the garage," Tommy finished.

"I guess catching AIDS the way he did really pushed him over the edge," Daphne said as she stuck her fork into a slice of carrot cake. "Knowing that you're going to die like that, that can make anybody go nuts."

The conversation quieted and Daphne looked around uneasily.

"What? What'd I say?" she asked.

"Oh, I guess you don't know," Nance said softly. "When they did the autopsy, it turned out that he didn't have the AIDS virus after all. He wasn't positive for the HIV antibodies or anything."

Daphne's eyes grew wide. "You're kidding," she said. "But in all the papers they said that the cops found a lot of stuff about AIDS and dying on the guy's computer!"

"Yeah, well, apparently that's what he thought," Nance said. "They interviewed his family doctor and he said all the guy had was a bad case of that flu that was going around. In fact, he had diagnosed the whole family as having come down with the same bug."

"Right about the time Paki killed them," Ramos interjected.

Everyone became quiet for a moment and let the weight of the situation and circumstances that drove a man to first kill street kids, then his own family, and finally innocent strangers in a subway car, settle into their minds.

"Hey everybody, am I late?" Detective McCall said as he strolled up to their table and pulled out a chair.

Daphne looked down guiltily at the remains of her carrot cake.

"Nah, not at all," Ramos said patting his belly. "You're right on time."

THE END

ACKNOWLEDGMENTS

I WOULD LIKE to acknowledge the following whose efforts, help, information, and/or participation, whether knowingly or otherwise, contributed in the creation of this novel.

My great friends at Operations Training: Leila Boddie, Peggy Redd, Pamela Parker, Karen Jeffrey, Wendell Scott, Solun Wong, and Derrick McCall. My other great friends at NYC Transit: Peter Aviles and Clifford Benton, who kept pushing me to finish! A.J. Magwood and Joan Napoleon, two very gifted and talented ladies. Tarsha Lawson; always supportive and beautiful.

The NYPD: for hiring me way back when and then years later letting me hang out in the 17th precinct annex, and answering so many of my questions.

MTA NYC Transit: for hiring me years later and giving me a front row seat to the greatest show in the world!

To the real-life Ratman who did indeed succumb to a tumor very similar to the one described in the novel.

To all of my friends, strangers and relatives, including you Lorrie Robinson, who put up with my constant yakking about the novel and who may have even read through excerpts, drafts, etc.

If I forgot anyone, please forgive me. Thanks!

CPSIA information can be obtained
at www.ICGtesting.com
Printed in the USA
BVOW06s0223291216
472148BV00001B/75/P